Sugar Land

Sugar Land

~~IIII~~ ~~IIII~~ ~~IIII~~

tammy LyNNE stoNer

~~tammy lynne stoner~~

🐓 Red Hen Press | *Pasadena, CA*

Book design by Hannah Moye

Library of Congress Cataloging-in-Publication Data
Names: Stoner, Tammy Lynne, 1968– author.
Title: Sugar Land / Tammy Lynne Stoner.
Description: First edition. | Pasadena, CA : Red Hen Press, [2018]
Identifiers: LCCN 2018025572 (print) | LCCN 2018026726 (ebook) | ISBN 9781597096263 (1-59709-626-1) | ISBN 9781597096270
Classification: LCC PS3619.T6859 (ebook) | LCC PS3619.T6859 S84 2018 (print) | DDC 813/.6—dc23
LC record available at https://lccn.loc.gov/2018025572

The National Endowment for the Arts, the Los Angeles County Arts Commission, the Ahmanson Foundation, the Dwight Stuart Youth Fund, the Max Factor Family Foundation, the Pasadena Tournament of Roses Foundation, the Pasadena Arts & Culture Commission and the City of Pasadena Cultural Affairs Division, the City of Los Angeles Department of Cultural Affairs, the Audrey & Sydney Irmas Charitable Foundation, the Kinder Morgan Foundation, the Allergan Foundation, the Riordan Foundation, and the Amazon Literary Partnership partially support Red Hen Press.

First Edition
Published by Red Hen Press
www.redhen.org

To Karena,

who I've loved since the day we met—
when we were existential teenagers.

All of this is because of—and for   you.

CONTENTS

BOOK ONE

BOOK TWO

BOOK THREE

Sugar Land

BOOK ONE

miss dara

THE LONG SHADOW OF HEAVEN

My first workday at the Imperial State Prison Farm for men was February 8, 1923. I wore a dress that made me look like a curvy brown sack and I couldn't stop burping up the oatmeal I'd had for breakfast. The kind folks at the prison helped me find a place to live, which I called my "shanty." It came with minimal furnishings: a mostly green love seat as comfortable as burlap, a single bed that poked a little, and what they called "a bistro table with two sitting chairs"—leaving me wondering what other kind of chairs there were. They also paid the first month's rent.

The penitentiary was an easy ten-minute walk away, up a street with clean, new telephone poles running down the center. Folks called the area "Guardtown" to separate it from the real town of Sugar Land. Most of the houses in Guardtown had trees out front, and the street even had streetlights—though I did miss the windmills of my hometown, Midland, Texas.

As I walked down those clean, paved streets that came straight from under a child's Christmas train set, my nerves jumped more than a grasshopper on a griddle. On my training day, I'd had a tour of the prison and met the Warden—a big-chested man with precisely trimmed sideburns—and a spattering of random folks unhitching horses outside, but that was *it* by way of preparation.

Truth be told, I hadn't thought much about possible dangers of prison life until I got closer to the white walls of the penitentiary. They looked like the walls of heaven—if heaven were an institution to house murderers and thieves, which it may be since we are all murderers and thieves in our own way.

A horribly freckled guard with a sweat-stained, tan shirt walked me past the meager wooden gate—the only fencing of any sort around the prison. That might seem strange to folks these days, but back then there were very few places to run, so there was no real need for a fence. Still, convicts did run, and when they did, the guards released the dogs and hunted them down on horseback—catching or shooting most of the escapees who didn't drown in the Brazos.

We walked through the gate, across a wide patch of dry grass, and into the kitchen building, which—as the guard explained—connected the three main "tanks," or dormitories, of the prison—one for whites, one for blacks, and one for Mexicans.

"Stay here. I'll get Beauregard."

I stood with my back against the raw wood, which let off a hot, musty smell. Cigarette smoke thicker than swamp fog hung in the air. I tried to look at ease.

A few minutes later, a man with a waxed mustache, who was both broad-shouldered *and* skinny, sauntered up as if he was going to ask me to dance. His white kitchen shirt had no name on it.

"I'm Beauregard," he said, holding out his hand to me after he wiped the sweat off on his pants. "I lead the kitchen staff and whatnot. Follow me." He grunted to the freckled guard, who didn't care much about us. "Don't worry, we're allowed to smile inside the kitchen proper, even though it is quite literally frowned upon out here."

Beauregard had a charming look to him, like a man who could skip over every puddle during a rainstorm. Maybe it was that mustache of his, all curled and comical and confident. And he smelled nice, which was something in that place.

The hallway we walked down was just big enough for two adults to walk side by side. At the end sat another beat-up door. When Beauregard opened it, I felt like we had entered a secret chapter of *Alice in Wonderland*.

A dinged-up nickel counter with absolutely nothing on it stretched the length of the long wall opposite the stove. Giant, oversized pots sat on the floor. Utensils were hooked to the wall with chains, as if otherwise they might spring to life and start tap dancing. Seemed bleach was the cleaning method, as evidenced from the overwhelming stench in the air.

Beauregard said, "I hope you enjoy the smell of Old Dutch."

I smiled, noticing that he slicked his hair similar to the way Rhodie—the girl I'd left behind in Midland—did.

"You were scheduled an hour early so I can take you on a brief tour and get you punched in before we begin prep. Today's inmates will be in to help get the line up and then the head cook will come in. You'll meet him later." He leaned in, even though there wasn't anyone there that I could see. "Careful of the head cook. Something in his eye gives me goosebumps." Beauregard lifted his wiry forearm and ran a hand over it as if he was getting goosebumps just talking about it. "Chicken flesh," he said.

I nodded and looked behind him at that long, hot room that didn't have one soft object in it.

x x x

Everything went well with me and Beauregard. It felt good and right to be in that antiseptic kitchen, where there would be little to remind me of Rhodie.

Beauregard stationed me as one of the two people who worked in the area protected by bars. The only person standing without bars between him and the inmates was the last person, who handed out the food trays.

I buffed the steel of the line for a good hour, as instructed, until the food pots came out. No matter what food they brought over, it all managed to smell like old motor oil.

Beauregard and a prisoner wheeled the last pot over to me, at the end of the line. They lifted it into the hole I'd prepared. Beauregard's face got red and his hands shook from the weight.

He said, "You're scooping. One blob of gravy on each tray in the upper left corner." He nodded his head at the prisoner who was lifting an equally heavy pot into the hole next to mine. "Follow Edgar, who lives and works here. He'll be giving them a biscuit right before you." Edgar grunted as he wiggled his pot into place.

A few whistles tooted and then, after two loud clicks, a pair of guards with enormous key rings opened the doors to the cafeteria. The guards wore their own clothes, but you could tell who they were by their cowboy hats and the leather straps fastened with buttoned loops to their belts. Some also carried "the bat"—a leather whip two feet long, four inches wide, and a quarter-inch thick. These were the field guards, and the bat was used to beat inmates in the fields who weren't "compliant."

The fields were the worst of it at Imperial State Prison Farm. Inmates—mostly Negroes—worked sixteen hours a day out there. For lunch they ate stale or rotten bread, molasses, beans, and rice. If they caught a squirrel, they were allowed to eat it. When they had to relieve themselves, they did so in trenches lined with lime along the back of the barracks.

"Trustys"—prisoners who the guards trusted—watched over the others, so no one kept regimented order. Sometimes they whipped other convicts as a form of retribution for previous offenses against them. At night, the colored men slept in hot, humid, lice-infested bunks with empty bellies, wearing the same clothes they'd been wearing for days on end.

White lights clicked on and the convicts entered. My stomach flipped a few times, me being worried about being just two feet from rows of violent criminals, bars or not.

A guard yelled, "File in!"

Two quiet lines of white prisoners, most wearing faded gray-striped uniforms, walked in. I was taken aback by how muscular they were, even the skinny ones. On the outside, most of the folks I knew had muscles here and there, but they were usually hidden beneath a healthy layer of fried chicken chub.

Some of the inmates eyed me up through the bars, me being new and female, but no one said anything.

As advised in training, I wore a shirt under my kitchen coat, since there might come a time when I'd need to remove my uniform top due to the edge catching fire or some other kitchen accident that they called "kitchendentals." I was glad that shirt was there now to catch my sweat since handling that hot, foul gravy under the intensity of a room of convicts was harder than it looked.

Ten minutes in, the Warden—whose wife, Beauregard had told me, won the Sugar Land Family Barbecue Cook-Off two years running—cut in between two inmates in the food line and walked up to me. The prisoners stepped back. They were slight steps, but I could tell they were respectful of the Warden, with his perfectly squared-off auburn hair and wet cigar stump in his teeth.

"Welcome to our humble penitentiary," he said to me.

I nodded.

"I've stopped by here to give you the *three tips* that are key to kitchen work."

The line waited as the Warden raised one finger. "*One,* never add too much sugar to the food; it riles them up. *Two,* never smile back at these boys in the cafeteria line. And *three,* never serve meat that's still bleeding because it turns them into animals. Keep to that and you'll do all right." Without waiting for a response, he lowered his hand, turned, and headed back through the crowd of gray-striped clothes—a general in charge of a brigade of dead men.

After the Warden left, the guards whistled and the white prisoners filed back out. A minute later, they opened a door on the other side of the dining hall and the colored prisoners came in. Leading the pack was a tall man with a jack-o'-lantern smile on his blacker-than-black face. *Damn* that man was black—black as a crow's beak, especially with those wet, white eyes staring out at you.

I couldn't help but look.

Meanwhile, the head cook, wearing a white uniform stained by gravy and with "Head Cook" sewn on the breast pocket, walked down behind the line. His scalp was red under his blond hair, seemingly from some strange, internal anger. His hands were also red, under a lawn of blond hair.

He noticed me looking at the colored inmate. Without introducing himself, he leaned over my shoulder, near my right ear. "You like that one?" he asked me. "That's Huddie. Been here five years. Came in for some violence perpetrated after he'd been living under the fake name of 'Walter Boyd'—the *same* Walter Boyd who had escaped the chain gang six years back. That crazy nigger. You like him? That the kind of friend you want?"

I kept slopping gravy as if this was all perfectly natural, while the inside my body went static with fear.

"You watch yourself, *girl*," he said before leaving, me wondering if he had some kind of salivary issue since every time he talked his mouth slopped with wet noise.

When Huddie got to me, I heard him humming and I averted my eyes. He clicked his tongue and waited his turn to get a tray with a biscuit and gravy, bacon, coffee, and sugar. It seemed he didn't have a care in the world, and certainly wasn't noticing me. That made me want to know this man who set himself above the walls of the prison.

A white guard crept up real close behind Huddie. "Quit humming," he said, smoke sneaking out of his nostrils. And Huddie did, for a moment—but as soon as the guard walked on, he started humming again. He was either the dumbest colored man in the history of colored men, or he knew that the key to happiness was maybe just the key of C.

"Five minutes to finish!" the walking guard yelled.

"The white folks got twenty minutes," I whispered to Beauregard as he passed by.

"Yes, ma'am, but colored folks have long since learned how to eat fast."

After everyone cleared out for the fields, I lifted my steaming tin from its hole and dropped it onto a wobbly wheeled cart. I say this casually, as if this was an easy task. In truth, lifting those hot metal pots onto the cart was as challenging as getting an elephant to stand on a teacup.

From there I wheeled the pot to the trash, where I ripped it over so I could scrape out the leftover gravy without having to hold the pot. My forearms ached and my back broke out in beads of sweat as I put my girth into it. Metal spoonfuls of wet hit the inside of the trash can with slurping and slapping noises. This food waste would all be collected up to feed the pigs out back, Beauregard had told me, the ones who would be slaughtered—their bacon staying in the prison with the rest of the meat sold to the outside.

Beauregard cleared his throat. He pulled a round wax can from his back pocket, opened it with a fast twist, and re-waxed the curls at the ends of his mustache. He propped open the kitchen doors for us to wheel through and clicked up the radio before we got to working.

"I brought this radio in a year ago," he said, "when I started working here. I told them that if they want my best work, they best let me hear my music." He tapped his black boot on the concrete floor—a man always ready to dance.

The radio was quite a fancy piece of machinery—all wooden with rounded edges and mesh in the front cut into diamond shapes.

"I sold my car to buy this radio. Now I ride my bike to work. It's more important to have music than a car—a theory that you will witness proven true every Friday afternoon when beautiful ladies in long dresses come to pick *me* up to go dancing in Houston." He twirled his mustache, wiggled his eyebrows like Chaplin, and nodded to me. "You enjoy dancing, Miss Dara?"

I nodded *yes* and smiled, a little—the way I did back then.

The prisoners working with us that day moved over to the back room with the head cook to start the food prep for sack lunches—the

"Johnnys"—for the Negroes in the sugarcane fields. What the cook lacked in height he made up for in the thickness of his arms, which he kept crossed in front of him. As the inmates filed by, he eyed them up, daring them to say something so he could use those arms.

Beauregard, happy as one of Santa's elves, slid by me. "That head cook is a mean one."

"He seems about as mean as my mama's senile chihuahua who spent her days tinkling on our herbs and chasing small children down the street."

"Ha!" He laughed like a car horn. "I'm so relieved that you *talk*! I was afraid you were mute—why else would a woman take this job? I figured you were either mute or running from some kind of trouble."

"I just like adventure."

"That right? Well, in case no one told you, this is where adventure comes to die."

Beauregard tuned his radio, something he'd do every half hour or so, and a Billy Murray song came on.

"It was on my fancy radio here that we all in the kitchen got to hear President Harding give his address. I bring not only music, Miss Dara, but news of *worldly events* on my radio."

"I appreciate that," I said.

"Good. Now, let me show you where the soaps are."

Beauregard helped me through the rest of the day, giving me order after order on where things go and why. I barely said a word, which seemed fine by him since he had quite a bit to say on nearly everything.

PRISON PEACOCKS

The next day, while we were listening to "I Ain't Nobody's Darling"—the horns in the song sounding as if they were snickering—a guard walked Huddie up to the kitchen doors and motioned that he go in first.

Huddie tipped his imaginary hat to me. "Miss."

The guard wore a close-cropped haircut under his cowboy hat and had muscles that stretched at the edges of his long-sleeved shirt. His hands were the kind that had veins of puffy ivy running all over them.

With his arms crossed, the guard watched Huddie walk over to me, open Cabinet #3, and pull out a pair of yellow rubber gloves. The music played on from the radio. I nodded to Huddie. He nodded back, smiling big at the radio. This kitchen was his escape too, it seemed.

There were eight of us working that day since one man had called out sick—eight people to cook for a prison of 950 beds. Beauregard told me that every man who calls out sick means two extra hours of work for the rest. And, as often happens in that part of Texas, we were having a hot February with temperatures in the eighties and that heavy feeling of rain—good for the sugarcane, but miserable for us and even worse for the folks in the fields. I can't express to you how grateful I was to see Huddie that day, when the ovens were still waving heat even though they'd been off for nearly an hour.

"They never let coloreds help us," Beauregard whispered to me, "but the Warden promised Huddie's daddy a while back to let him rest every now and again—no doubt with some kind of currency involved. Plus, the Warden here fancies himself a progressive." And here he looked at me. "*Obviously.*"

This was how it worked: there were usually nine or ten of us—the head cook, who dictated the menus; the cutters, who chopped and prepped all the meals of the day; and the line servers, who stirred the hot pots, served, and did most of the cleanup—though the cutters helped out by hauling pans after they'd wiped down the metal tables out front.

The cutters—like Beauregard—were a step above the line servers because they got to stay out of the steam during the cleanup and could grab a cigarette while they took their good old time wiping down the cafeteria tables. Convicts, obviously, could not be cutters.

I'd never seen anyone move a knife as fast as Beauregard, even with a cigarette in his teeth. He could make chitlins pot-ready in two minutes.

Since we were short one line server, a cutter had to line serve and the head cook had to be a cutter, when he'd rather be checking the pantry, ordering food, and scratching the inside of his ear with a pencil, which seemed to be his favorite hobby. That inconvenience made the head cook even meaner. And when the head cook was mean, everyone was afraid of dropping something because—according to Beauregard—the head cook had no qualms about hitting someone right in the kidneys if he was in a mood, like he was.

Huddie hauled a pile of heavy steel trays from the inmate drop-off area. He carried them over to the deep sink where I was scrubbing dishes in the steam, silently cursing Jackson, who had called off because he'd had a fever when no one—and I mean no one—gets a God damn fever when it's eighty degrees. *No one.*

Beauregard, his face red again from lugging trays, smiled over at me. He hauled a load by Huddie. "Glad you joined us, Huddie," he said. "That there is Miss Dara—the new girl. Well, the only girl, and she's new."

Huddie nodded. He gave me a look that said he hadn't seen a woman in a while, and he liked women. It wasn't threatening. He was just a hungry man examining a rack of ribs.

Temperatures as high as they were that day made the food cuttings stink quicker than usual. The trash was only taken out at sundown— when a guard could attend you—so all the food from breakfast and lunch sat rotting in the heat.

"Sometimes," Beauregard told me, "you can hear it buzzing if you got your ear too close to the cans."

I cringed.

"Thankfully," he said as he raised his eyebrows, "we hardly ever serve fish. Maggots *love* fish."

Beauregard walked off.

Huddie understated: "Ain't pleasant."

"Not one bit," I agreed.

Huddie had creases under his eyes, the kind you got from working outside. Little moles of sweat formed on his forehead and along those lines under his eyes. I watched one fall like a tear when he carried over his second load of trays. He didn't seem to notice.

Beauregard walked back past me and whispered, "The convicts love to work in here. They don't care how hot it is—at least it's not the fields."

The head cook strolled through and tossed his sponge in my sink. "Keep working," was all he said before going to his office now that we were better staffed.

Beauregard explained: "He has a fan."

The radio hissed and clicked, the way it did when the music was being changed to a new record—mostly ragtime, since it was Beauregard's radio and ragtime was Beauregard's choice. Without the cook there, Huddie sang along, making up his own words to an instrumental song: *"You said you'd wait for me, by the trees and the ramblin' river, but you never said for just how long."*

I wiped the side of my face with my forearm and smiled at Huddie. The guard nodded to me. "His singing bothering you?"

"No more than a four-leaf clover bothers an unlucky man," I said.

The guard looked genuinely confused by my answer, so he let Huddie keep singing.

"Few know the way I know how long these nights can be. I know you said you'd wait for me, but you never said for how long."

The music ended and another song started up. We could barely hear it, though, since I'd started using the loud water faucets at my station to clean down the trays. I sprayed and glanced over at Huddie, fascinated. Not wanting to get him in trouble, I tried to be casual in my examination. Huddie reminded me of a clown, with those yellow gloves on over his gray striped sleeves and his coal-black face. The guard noticed me looking, cleared his throat, and took a step in, letting Huddie know he had his eye on him.

"Stay to yourself, boy," he ordered, as if Huddie had done anything. "Not too close."

Huddie hauled another load over, winking at me as he walked by. "You heard him now, not too close." He lightly hopped a step away.

I smiled back. From the side, I saw the guard grit his teeth. The light from the only window in the kitchen—a dingy thing covered on the outside by spiderwebs—shone on the side of Huddie's face and made him look a little crazy, the kind of crazy I was attracted to. The kind of crazy that understood secret things about this world the rest of us walked through blindly. Wisdom rose off him like steam off a simple stew, all deep and calm and comforting without meaning to be. Without caring that it was.

"Keep decent," the guard said, as if he didn't know what else to say, as if he was new to power.

Off to the far side, the head cook worked with the blunted knives. He accounted for each one on a special sheet that had to be filled out at the end of every kitchen shift—every piece of metal had to be accounted for. The knives were easy, since they were all tied to the wall. The loose spoons took a bit longer to add up.

In the middle of all the silence, Beauregard burst into the kitchen, lobbing a cloth over my head and into his sink. I turned off my faucets and gave a sloppy dry to the trays. Beauregard wiped down the edges of the huge three-foot steel pot sitting on the floor that we used to make some of the soups. Another song came on.

For no reason I could see, the guard yelled out, "No more singing!"

"What kind of man are you to stop a bird from singing?" Beauregard said before he slammed through the doors like he was pitching a fit, when I knew he was just off to the toilet. He'd told me the day before that the sound of water always encouraged him.

Huddie passed me more trays and hummed quietly to the radio. He hummed and scraped and lifted while I soaped and rinsed and stacked. After a while we developed a private rhythm, with him not once looking over at the guard, even though the guard never took his mean green eyes off Huddie.

"That bother you?" I asked him when he got close enough.

"Oh, I's always been watched, Miss. My whole life I been watched."

Huddie's hands slipped and he dropped a pan into my sink. The guard jumped.

"What the hell, boy! Keep it down."

Huddie whistled low. "We down, sir, we down." He smiled at me. His teeth looked bright and slick, as he stood there in that one bar of sunlight.

I felt afraid for him, knowing about the leather straps and the way they'd put some inmates out in the sun for hours to balance on barrels or hot rocks.

The guard sucked in some air. "You smarting? That'll get you time in the Box."

"That was me—" I started, but Huddie stopped me.

"Sorry, sir," he said. "My apologies, sir."

We waited. The guard shifted on his clean boots, but didn't say anything.

"Don't you ever take the fall for someone now," Huddie whispered, "even for a man as handsome as myself."

I was embarrassed that I'd tried to take the blame, but before long Huddie was humming again. I wanted to cover his mouth or nudge him or something, but I realized he knew what he was doing. He was making a choice to be who he was, despite the consequences. Few folks are capable of that kind of bravery—definitely not me.

The gray concrete floor made my feet ache down the middle, where I wished for a stronger arch. We had to be careful when we walked across that floor carrying wet pans, since the water made the concrete slippery and the head cook still seemed mean, over there counting his spoons.

Huddie and I each took an edge of a massive stack of trays. The metal was still hot and a little wet. The stack pressed hard into the crease where my palm ended and my fingers began, and caused me to strain so much that I grunted.

In this way, we carried several stacks over to the drying counter, where we towel-dried them, along with the mountain of pots and pans. Drying each deep pot was like drying off a fire engine—you had to approach every side of the big thing as a separate, individual area to keep from getting overwhelmed.

After everything was dry, without saying a word, we placed them in the order they always went on the tall metal racks along the back wall. Huddie flipped one of the biggest pots over by its thick steel handles and landed it with a gentle clank on the top shelf. I was moving some pots around on the lower shelves underneath him so the smallest ones could fit inside the bigger ones.

Huddie looked down to me. "I just can't seem to stay on the outside of a prison these days, but why *you* here?"

"Work," I said.

"No other kind of work out there? Sure a girl like you with some schooling under you could get a bird's nest on the ground, if you wanted."

"I like this job fine."

He shook his head. "True now, why you here?"

"It's easy for me to hide in here, I think," I said, surprised by my honesty.

"Who you hiding from?"

"Everybody else, I suppose. Me, maybe." All the while I thought: *I'm hiding from being me—the girl who loves another girl.*

"Why?" he asked.

"Because I can."

"Must be nice," he said, "having a chance to hide every now and again."

Huddie walked back across the wet concrete, grabbed another big pot, and flipped it to the top rack. He acted as if he had to wipe some water from the metal bars of the shelf so he could talk closer to me.

"Seems strange, you feeling the need to be here," he whispered, "when you could be out there." He looked down at me past his armpit stains. "If I was out there, I'd have me a bottle of liquor, a guitar, and a woman—no, *two* women—right now, in the middle of the day."

"Sounds good." I smiled, adding: "For you."

"What'd you have if you outside right now?"

"I don't know," I lied.

"Maybe you gotta be out there to *learn* it, then."

"Nigga, shut the hell up!" The guard took five giant steps over and smacked Huddie on the back of the head. "You finished yet?"

"Yes sir," we both said.

The kitchen was empty now. At some point the radio had been clicked off and all the dish towels had been thrown into the laundry. The utensils were locked up. The rags had been moved under the sink. Not one thing was left out.

"Stand over there, both of you."

We stood against the now-dry edge of the nickel counter at a right angle from the pot rack. The green-eyed guard counted the pots and pans, matching them to the diagram while the two of us waited, our arms at our sides, my left forearm warming in that ray of sunlight.

"All's here!" the guard yelled and jerked his neck left for a fast crack.

The head cook emerged from his office to confirm the count. We waited until he was done. He gave a head nod, which meant all was accounted for, then sized up the guard, who had at least fifty pounds on him, but looked like he'd lose in a fight.

"For clarity's sake, this one here is on *my* team," the head cook sneered as he lit up a cigarette, "so you take mind not to line her up again with the convicts, especially niggerly ones. Understood?"

The guard's neck bloomed angry red. "Understood."

The head cook left and the guard walked to the door. It took him a minute to get it unlocked, just enough time for Huddie to turn and grin, showing me an extra bit of biscuit he'd tucked inside his cheek.

× × ×

At the end of my shift, I walked alone down the dark hallway to the kitchen time clock, which sat across from the head cook's office. His name was Billy. Billy watched me and I knew there was some evil in it, so I tried to stay in the best-lit portions of the hallway.

The door to his office opened and I heard him shuffle up behind me. He leaned over my shoulder, the way he did, and talked into my ear.

"Seems you got yourself a Negro boyfriend," he said, making those wet noises with his mouth again.

I punched my time out, willing my hand not to shake. I swallowed, then managed to say: "No, I don't."

"No? Why's that?"

"Because that's ridiculous."

"I can't hear you."

I had no choice but to turn around since there was nothing else to look at, so I did. "I said, 'Because that's ridiculous.'"

He pulled a Lucky Strike from behind his pink ear, where his blond hair was nearly white, and lit it using one hand. The spent match he'd bent out from the matchbook hung there like a tree hit by lightning. "Love can be found at work, and maybe you love the coloreds. You, a *woman* in a prison kitchen filled with hungry nigger men. I said no women should be in this kitchen." He sucked the smoke in so deep that it took a few words to start coming out again. "You feedin' them all right, but not food. You feedin' their *dreams*. You enjoy doing that to poor niggers?"

Just then I heard Beauregard's telltale whistle as he strolled toward the time-clock hallway. The head cook heard too, but he took his sweet time moving out of the way, blowing a line of tight white smoke before nodding to Beauregard and making his way back to his office.

Beauregard gave me a hard look while he searched for his time-card, though he knew where it was, of course, there only being three lined up. "Anything happening here?"

I looked down and pushed strands of flyaway brown hair behind my ear. "Gossip, I suppose."

"He doesn't seem much the type."

"Hmm." I nodded.

"You doing all right?"

"He's just peacocking."

"Well, you come get me if he starts to play *rooster*." Beauregard leaned in and curled his mustache up in that charming way he did. "Don't let my thin arms fool you, I am *all muscle*. Lean, strong muscle that strikes terror in the hearts of men. *Terror*, Miss Dara."

"I will make note."

He held out his bent arm for me. "For now, allow me to escort you down through this rank dancehall to the well-lit gardens."

"Thank you kindly, sir."

We walked arm in arm out across the dry patch and through the sickly-looking front gate. All the while, I could feel the head cook staring at me from that dirty kitchen window.

BUTTERFLIES & BULLFROGS

This is how it goes in life: sometimes you're born with a cleft palate or rickets, like my bow-legged granddaddy, or a touch short on brains, like my Great Aunt Cal who everyone called "Stool."

Me? I'm a double hitter. In addition to being what folks call "large-boned," I came into this world with homosexual tendencies—though back then I thought of it only as my strange, strong affections for some female friends, having no such notion of "homosexual tendencies" as a thing, at least not in my hometown of Midland, Texas.

Notions of this nature found footing in me eight months before I ran away to work in the Imperial State Prison Farm kitchen, when I got a job at the egg store in Midland, Texas.

The egg store was all wood. Wood floors, wood ceiling beams, wood shelves—that rugged, knotty, reddish wood. The simple kind of wood they used to bury folks in before the floods, when rotting coffins popped from the ground like splinters and dead bodies dropped out in maggoty heaps.

The egg store smelled of wood, too, which I liked. That and just the tiniest hint of smoke from Bibby's metal pork smoker two streets over. I swear he ran that thing day and night, crazy redneck. And that's where I fell in love for the first time, there in the egg store that smelled of wood and smoked pig fat.

When she came into the store, her brother—this short little thing with ears like filthy cauliflower—called her Rhodie. She had light brown hair slicked off in a part on the left. Her glasses were round wire and she carried an archery bow, but no arrows. Her tangerine skirt came down to her knees and she wore a matching jacket with a white V-neck shirt underneath. The scarf around her neck had painted butterflies on it.

"Six eggs, please," she said, "and some beef jerky for my brother."

I reached into a nearby crate filled with eggs nested in straw, while squinting at her scarf. "Those butterflies?"

"These are my *interview* butterflies," she said. "I just came from the University of Texas for a college interview. I shoot bow and arrow pretty well, so my mother had me carry my bow in for the interview. My mother's *very* keen on me going to college." She leaned in a little and tipped her head sideways to get closer. "I felt ridiculous, though, seeing as how I have a bow but no arrows."

I held in my ample stomach and counted out six clean eggs, all brown, then put them into a bag with a flat of jerky three times the size of a slice of bacon.

She looked around. "You sell anything other than eggs and jerky?"

"We do pies every now and again, and at Christmastime we sell Mrs. Jameson's fruitcakes. I help her do all the cooking. The secret is letting them ripen for six months in pitch black."

"Not much of a secret if you're telling it," she said.

My face flushed and I lowered my head to concentrate on wrapping up her bag. Rhodie, meanwhile, examined a pile of books I'd stacked up between the tins of jerky on the shelf behind my stool: Joseph Conrad, E.M. Forster, Zona Gale.

"Wow," she said. "You going to college, too?"

"No, no," I smiled, looking down at my fat feet in my strappy sandals, feeling the dampness in my armpits running down the sides of my cotton shirt. I hoped my hair wasn't too greasy.

"With reading like that, you could surely be a college girl yourself."

"I've never known a girl to go to college before."

Rhodie smiled. "Well, now you do. Since we can vote, we need to be educated. Oh gosh, I sound like my mother."

Rhodie's brother hollered from outside, where it was much brighter. "Let's get goin'!"

She whipped her head toward the door. "I got you jerky, so simmer down!"

"It's November," I said. "They make you interview for school so far in advance?"

"I'm fixin' to go in January. I took a few months off after high school to move here. We come from Pecos. My brother'll be going to Midland High next year."

"I just graduated from there."

"Yeah?"

"Rhodie!" he screamed. "We got to go get the *wasp house* down."

She jerked her slicked-over hair toward her brother and sighed. "Well, I got to go but I'm sure I'll be in for more eggs, hopefully with me not looking so silly."

"I don't think you look silly," I said, coughing to cover my blushing.

Rhodie shrugged and left. As I watched her step out into the sunshine, I felt this warm spot in the center of my chest loosen up and wave out, like the long tail of a red kite.

× × ×

Rhodie came in the next day, telling me that her family knew fresh eggs and *these* were fresh eggs. She said she was likely to be in every day—and she was. That's how we got to talking. We'd conversate about what I was reading or the places she wanted to visit someday— top of her list was California, where she'd heard that dolphins would swim right by you.

"You can pet them like a cat—only wet, of course."

All the while I sat there, falling in love against my will and eating beef jerky even though it hurt my jaw.

One day, I watched Rhodie walk up the dirt path to the store. I remember it so clearly. She had on a yellow and light blue striped dress with long sleeves. Halfway up, between two scraggly rosemary bushes, she stopped dead in her tracks and closed her eyes. A second later she opened them and, with a huge smile, nodded out to something in the dry, grassy area on the side of the egg store.

When she came in, I asked what she was doing and she said that a little deer had stopped to eat at the edge of the path.

"I didn't want to startle her so I stood real still until she was finished. When I opened my eyes, she was looking at me—maybe thanking me for not interrupting her supper—then she hopped off as quiet as a breeze."

"You sound like a poet," I said.

"Baby deer can make anyone sound like a poet." She shrugged. "You done?"

"Just need to close up."

"Want to go for a walk with me down Old Spider Road?"

"Oh, I don't know," I said. Rumor was that a killer lived in a shack down Old Spider Road with the bodies of the children he'd caught coming onto his land.

"You scared?"

"You not scared?" I asked, locking up the money box.

"I'm excited! Those emotions are similar, but they're not the same." She leaned toward me, over the counter. "Maybe you're just excited but you can't tell the difference."

"All I know is that I can't run too fast."

"You won't need to run. Nothing to run from. Let's go!"

"Oh, all right," I said.

I just wanted to be with Rhodie, and if that meant walking down Old Spider Road, well, then I guess that was where I'd be going. Hopefully I'd make it back. Word had it that two boys rode their bikes down there last summer and were never seen again.

Old Spider Road was mostly a heavily trodden dirt path between some ratty trees, on land nobody seemed to own. You could only access it by following two connected walking paths, the first of which started not too far from the back of the egg store, right next to the Watsons' yellow windmill.

Rhodie stood outside the door while I took my time covering the eggs up. She tapped her foot. "My goodness you *are* slow! Fright freeze your fingers?"

"No . . ."

"I'm going to wait at the trailhead. You come on now."

I joined her a few minutes later, just on the edge of the meadow before it became the woods. The path was so thin you had to walk single file, which was lucky for me since Rhodie couldn't see my jittery, scared eyes. As we walked on, the trees got thicker and thicker. If you wore camouflage—which no doubt the killer did—you could easily hide behind *any* of those trees.

Thinking talking might calm my nerves, I asked her, "You're new here, so how do you know about Old Spider Road?"

"My brother. As our mother says, my brother can find trouble on a cloud of sleeping angels."

We hiked up and over several large boulders to the second path. The sun started setting and my stomach ached with nervousness. If we got chased, I couldn't run well and I *definitely* couldn't run well over boulders.

Finally, we turned on to Old Spider Road, which was wide enough for us to walk side-by-side. I put my feet down, one in front of the other, on a dried bike track, hoping it wasn't the tread from one of the dead boys' bikes.

Five quiet minutes later, we spotted the murderer's house: an old cement building without much of a roof—some living watercolor painting, all milky whites against the green and brown trees.

Rhodie whispered, "Come on."

"I don't know."

"Come on!"

I took in a breath for courage. Even though I was terrified, I walked over to the cabin through the tall, browning grass and trees. It looked like something blown out in a war. It had no door, just a concrete opening where a door had been. We stepped inside, over layers of old, moldy newspapers covering the cement floor—some dating back to 1900—and empty brown bottles of moonshine.

She asked, "Where do you think he relieved himself? I didn't see an outhouse. Ew, I don't think we should sit down in here."

"I don't think he'd pee where he slept."

Her eyes got wide. "Maybe he slept outside, on the mound where he buried all those dead bodies! Maybe this here is his bathroom."

"Your mind goes wild sometimes."

"That's why my mother says I'm so suited for college."

The mention of her leaving caused my heart to curl up into a baby's fist, all tight and pained. On that deep, primal level, I knew I loved her even then—but of course I didn't say anything. If I'd had my choice, I would've only felt for her the feelings of a friend. There was something in the joy I got just making her laugh that might have been enough. Maybe.

A gunshot flared from the denser trees farther down Old Spider Road. The sound nearly loosened my bladder, to be sure.

Rhodie jumped up. "Shit! What is that?"

"A *gun*—the killer's got a gun. Dammit, I told you I can't run fast!"

"I can!" she shouted, a thrilled terror in her voice. "Come on!"

Rhodie yanked me by the side of my shirt, which was damp with fear, and we ran. We ran so fast and hard I saw white flickers in the corners of my eyes and thought I was going to faint.

"Footsteps!" she yelled, and sure enough I heard them too—footsteps trampling through the dry grasses behind us, gaining ground.

Powered by fright, I passed Rhodie, my arms and legs finding some energy I never knew I had. She followed me, the edges of her dress flapping up. I skipped down around the boulders, my legs getting shredded by twigs, and off to a small side path I knew about from years and years ago—a shortcut to the creek. From the creek we could walk the long way back home, and make it in time for supper—if we didn't get killed first.

Behind me Rhodie screamed, "Oh my God! Oh my God!"

I focused only on the green trees ahead—the ones near the creek. Once we got there, I knew we'd be safe.

"I can't run anymore!" she panted.

For a second I thought of leaving her there, but I didn't. I stopped and we stood together, just outside the woods in the dimming light. My eyes ached from straining into the distance to see if the killer was still following us. I listened; no more footsteps—nothing but crickets and a slight trickle of water from behind us.

"He's gone," she said between heavy breaths.

"You excited *now?*" I asked her.

She laughed and slapped my arm. "I hear water. There a creek nearby?"

"Right behind us," I said. "We can hide down in the grasses if we need to."

She looked all around. "I don't think we need to."

"Shhh!" I focused on calming my breathing. "OK, it sounds all quiet now."

"Maybe we were imagining it."

"No. I heard steps."

"Me too," she said, stopping for air. She moved a little closer and scanned the distant trees. "We'd see him now, though, coming across the meadow. He's got nowhere to hide."

I nodded my agreement. "Let's go sit by the creek. I need to rest."

Rhodie smiled, always up for an adventure. "You ever hunt bullfrogs?"

"We almost *died* and you're bringing up frogs!"

"I think we've earned ourselves a nice meal. And to show my apologies for such a silly notion as Old Spider Road, I will make it for us. I already got the razor blades."

"What now?" I asked, my legs still shaking a little.

Rhodie leaned on me, then lifted her shoe. Underneath, on the sole, she had taped down a razor blade. "One on each shoe," she explained. "Two of them, in case we got caught by the murderer."

I rolled my eyes. "Of course."

"I come prepared."

"Prepared to take me into the lair of a murderer!"

"Or, it seems," she said, taking in a slow breath, "to catch us some bullfrogs."

I didn't care that Mama and Daddy might worry—or worse, get angry—that I'd be missing supper. "Well, all right," I said, "but we better catch quite a few. Seems almost getting *killed* can raise a girl's appetite."

Following Rhodie's directions, we walked around the creek's edge until we found the perfect hunting sticks. We cut notches in them and sat down. She took out the razor blades.

"Slip your blade into the notch, and then we'll tie them in place with some of that vine there."

I did as instructed, rolling my spear over in my hands.

"The idea," she told me in the new moonlight, "is to stab the bullfrogs through the heart with the razor so they don't suffer. You got to be quick and steady."

"OK."

"The males have yellow throats, which makes them easier to see."

Rhodie hunkered down a bit along the edge of the creek and listened. When she didn't hear anything she continued: "We're doing our *civic duty* by killing these bullfrogs. They don't really belong here. They were brought in by somebody a long time ago and now they are ruining the creeks for other creatures since most animals aren't accustomed to eating bullfrogs."

"Except us."

She smiled, her face tan and her hair nearly blond, despite the oils she used to slick it over. "Yes, except us."

She gestured that I follow her closer in to the water's edge. The breeze felt good there, all cooled by the water.

"They're really *awful* creatures. They eat all kinds of things—like crawdads and ducklings. Some even eat *baby birds.*"

"Lord," I said.

"It's true." She leaned in and scanned the water, her knee resting in some mud. "Remember, hit just below the yellow throat."

I whispered, "How did you get so smart?"

She put her finger to her lips and nodded her head to the right, where a croaking noise started up. "*Shh.*"

We caught six over the next half hour—her killing five and me one. I sat back and watched, amazed that this college girl could kill, butcher, and cook up a nice set of frog legs over a fire she'd built with little more than a clump of dry kindling and a match she'd put in her bra to set fire to the killer's shack if the razor blades didn't work.

"Didn't work?" I asked.

"Basically, if I couldn't kill the killer."

"I think you could have."

She looked over at me. "I don't know—*you* were the one who ran us out of there."

"I ran on fear alone."

"I think you have hidden strengths."

We ate the frog legs right off the cooking stone she'd used—after rubbing dandelion leaves on it so the legs wouldn't stick—and drank some discarded liquor I'd found under a bush near where the creek narrowed. There were always half-drunk bottles lying around from kids who stole them and had to abandon them to run home.

While we ate, Rhodie didn't say much.

Finally I asked her, "You OK?"

"I'm leaving for college in three weeks, Dara. Exactly three weeks."

I knew it was serious because she hardly ever said my name while we were talking.

"I know."

The creek trickled by, and the trees made this kind of rattling noise above us when the wind passed through the leaves. It was as if the whole world was shushing us. Still Rhodie continued: "You're the best friend I've ever had. Makes me wish I hadn't let my mother push me into going away to school. Maybe I could put it off for a year."

"You can't do that. Everything's lined up. Plus, they already turned your bedroom into a sewing space!"

Her eyes looked greener than usual in the moonlight.

"I love you," I blurted out, the words leaving me before I had time to consider them. I wanted to add "like a sister" but thought on it too long. I was stuck there and feeling sick about it. *Dammit!* I yelled in my mind. What did I do?

Rhodie stayed quiet and I wanted so badly to take those words back, but I knew that if I did I would be a coward, so I let them just hang there as my guts churned.

After a minute, I took in a big breath and looked back at her. A flush had come onto her cheeks.

"I'm sorry," I said. "Let's just pretend I didn't say anything."

She looked away from me and shook her head *no.*

Half-digested bullfrog rose up in the back of my throat. I smiled as best as I could against the pounding in my ears and the feeling of panic. "My daddy told me that in every friendship there's one moment when we get to turn back time. I want to use my moment now."

Rhodie still didn't say anything. I set my hand on the dry ground near my hip and moved to get up. She turned back to me. The grin on her face was as big as any Best Pie winner's. She pulled on my arm, hard. "No, no! *I love you too,* Dara."

"You love me the way I love you?"

She nodded her head *yes* half a dozen times, and my chest felt like it cracked open to let out this ocean I'd housed inside myself.

"Like a man might love you," she clarified.

"Me too," I said.

"Come to school and we can be university girls together!" She leaned close to me, her bright eyes looking like she might cry. "Be with me."

"Well, maybe you *could* stay here another year? Stay here and kill bullfrogs with me every day. Do our *civic duty.* Do you really have to leave?"

"Do you really have to stay?"

When she said this, the world shifted back a bit, back to the way I knew things were: I could never be with her. Even while the love I had for her and the amazement at the love she had for me made me full enough to burst, I knew I could never be with her. It just wasn't done. Ever.

"You know I can't go," I said to her, anxiety already gripping me at the thought of someone finding out.

"You *can't*—or won't?"

I looked down, destroyed. "I'm sorry."

Then she did it—my beautiful Rhodie tipped my face up and kissed me. Her lips were as soft as a ripe peach.

The kiss startled me, but I recovered quickly. I put my hand on the itchy ground behind her, where our bullfrog spears were, and fell into that kiss, forgetting all about the world. It started so slowly, like dipping your foot in cold water, but it got crazy fast, with her pushing against me and me lying back on the grass with her above me. I felt as if we were floating, and linked together only by our lips touching.

A minute later, Rhodie rolled off me and sighed, as if she needed to recover. I know I did.

Each of us propped up on one elbow so we were face to face. The world got so quiet, and I just looked at her, amazed. *We had kissed.*

"I loved you from that first day in the egg store," I said. "I just didn't know what it was."

She smiled and leaned her forehead against mine, perfectly natural, the way she could make anything seem. "Well, seems we have three weeks to live a whole life. You ready, Miss Dara?"

"I'm ready, Miss Rhodie," I said, and I was. Although I couldn't be with her forever, I decided then and there that I would swallow my fear and pledge to be with her for those three weeks. We could keep this secret for three short weeks, and then I would go on and be who I needed to be.

I asked, "You ever felt this way for a girl before?"

"No," she said. "Honestly, I wasn't really sure I felt this way until you said you did, and then it all just clicked."

"Are you scared?"

"I probably will be later, but not now."

I nodded.

She smiled and her fingers dared to run along my forearm, making the hairs stand on end. "Why did you fall in love with me?" she asked.

"I just did," I said, thinking: *How could I not love a girl with a butterfly scarf and a bow with no arrows?*

THE WHATFOR

The next day Rhodie went shopping with her mother, so I worked the slowest day I ever worked. I read the paper twice, and on the second read I saw an ad for a cook needed at the Imperial State Prison Farm. Paying it no mind, I folded the paper and stuck it in my pocket.

The clock ticked by every minute I was away from Rhodie. It pained me, not seeing her. Finally, I closed up shop.

Sullen, I walked home on the dirt path between the cotton farms that had suffered so badly the year before. The police station, where my cousin Earl was sheriff, sat a short stretch in from the dirt road, on the mostly paved part. Life as a sheriff treated Earl pretty well. His loud-mouthed wife wore a real raccoon coat, they owned a car, and Daddy said they kept decent drink. Earl enjoyed good things. I knew he kept a plate of fancy goodies on his desk, so I decided to stop in for a treat to help improve my mood.

The sheriff's building sat covered in a thin coat of dry dust, as did most things in Midland. It'd been fifteen years since folks voted to build a firehouse, though I have no idea why it took so long since Midland always seemed like one bad candle from going up.

I opened the heavy steel door and walked in. Earl and some good-old-boy police officer I'd seen before but had never been introduced to were talking at his desk. Not wanting to interrupt, I sat down on the only chair in the entryway, behind a tall plant, and waited for them to be done.

They both wore beige cowboy hats, white shirts with black ties, and camel-colored vests. Their tin badges were pinned to their vests over their hearts. Earl had a scratch on his neck that looked fresh. A smear of blood brightened his collar.

"I got to go soon," the other officer—who I think was named Clarence—said to Earl. "My wife needs milk to make some new kind of custard."

"I'll drive you. I need milk too," Earl said. "I could use some nourishment after all that *work* we put in last night."

He nudged Clarence hard enough that Clarence had to straighten his hat. Earl, whose baby face looked like it'd never felt a razorblade, continued on. "This is the thing: if those girls—those perverts—want to congregate, they are *asking* for trouble, if you ask me. Though I do believe we performed a sort of *conversion* last night, huh? We showed them that *this* is how it's done."

Clarence examined the cream tarts resting on one of Earl's wife's china plates, looking for the right one. He smiled. "Yup. We sure did. Gave those perverts a lesson in the whatfor."

Earl hooked his thumb into his belt loop and lowered his head, the way he did. "You think it's safe for us?"

"*Safe?*" Clarence laughed and started in on a tart. "You think those girls are going to tell anyone? Who would believe them? No one. Of that I'm sure."

My legs went numb with the realization that my cousin Earl and that tall, mean-looking police officer, Clarence, were talking about violating those women—women like Rhodie and me. I wanted to throw up, my stomach rolling with fear and shame. I forced myself not to cry, and pressed the chair as far back against the wall as it would go, hoping my belly wouldn't stick out and give me away.

The chair squeaked and both men turned toward me.

Earl leaned over and squinted. "Dara, that you?"

With every bone in my body on fire, I peered around the plant and faced those men. I smoothed down the front of my blue blouse and tried to smile.

Earl said, "Didn't hear you come in. I got some business here before I drive Clarence home. I can give you a lift too, sugar."

I nodded *yes.*

Clarence chomped away while I sat there on that weak chair, sweating. He flipped his handcuffs around his thick finger.

Earl shook his head and lowered his voice. "I tell you, last night I felt the fire of a damn animal." He turned to me. "Pardon the language," he said, as if the word "damn" was much more terrible than what they were casually conversating about, maybe thinking I didn't understand.

Earl tipped his hat back a bit. "Dara," he said, "you feeling all right?"

I didn't say anything. I was afraid if I spoke that he might identify me as one of those perverts, just by the tone of my voice.

I wondered if Clarence had kids. I knew Earl did. How could these men be the men they'd been the night before and then go home and kiss their children hello?

My chest tingled with panic, knowing that I held in me the potential to raise that kind of ire in folks. Beyond that, I saw that no one would protect me if I was ever found out—not even the police. We all knew that there were different rules for the police, especially when it came to Negroes, but now I knew those different rules applied to me too.

Clarence sighed and wiped his mouth on his sleeve. "Well, we got to let them go, don't we?"

"I reckon we do," Earl said.

"Here." He turned to Earl with the plate. "Offer them a sweet."

Earl shook his head and smiled, but he didn't take the plate. Clarence opened up a file on his desk and looked over four pieces of paper, presumably papers on the women they'd arrested.

I heard the thick jail door open and looked up. The women weren't shackled, as I thought they might be. Earl easily walked them out. They kept their heads down, in single file—a line of women heading for a firing squad. Three wore dresses, which had no doubt been nice before. One even had a flower pinned to hers—though it was all torn petals now. The fourth woman wore a suit, the kind you see Hollywood types wearing, and I wondered if she was from out of town. Her suit had no doubt been what raised the flag.

The shortest one—and the prettiest one—lifted her eyes to mine. She had a slightly bruised ring around her neck as if she'd been choked. I wondered if Earl had done that to her—my own cousin. Her eyes were red and the bags under them as deep and dark as a secret.

Clarence yelled out without looking up while Earl opened the front door for them. "No charges filed! You all just find your way home—and by that I mean into the arms of the Lord. We best not ever see you four together in any way again, not in this town."

The women walked out into the bright sun and around the side of the building, still in single file. I could see them out the side window, through the chalky dust, as they continued down the road. The one with the flower turned around to the woman in the suit and made a slight—very slight—gesture with her hand, as if to say, *We are all right.* But the woman in the suit shook her head *no* and stopped right there in the middle of the road. The other three stared at her. Then, without any notice, the woman in the suit sprinted off, running so fast that you'd think someone was chasing her—and I suppose in her world, someone always was. The other three watched her run off. A minute later, without saying a word, they separated and went in three different directions.

Earl strolled over to me, carrying what was left of the tarts. "Care for some?"

I could barely hear him since my ears were pounding with a fright so intense I thought my heart might stop. I shook my head no.

He shrugged. "Suit yourself."

I knew I had to look casual. "I just don't like cream tarts."

"Since when?"

"Just since now. My stomach's upset."

"You want that ride?"

"No, no. I'll walk from here."

"Well, all right. Hello to your mama and daddy."

I nodded and thought about Mama and Daddy—just two of the townsfolk who would publicly say that they believed the police officers and not the women, but who would privately agree that the incident probably happened and those women got their comeuppance. They might think it was unnecessarily harsh, but they would agree that it was for the overall good of Midland, where the overall good was of foremost concern.

The world worked this way: women were property to be managed and kept in line as needed. It wasn't uncommon to see a woman in Sunday services with a bruised eye hiding beneath her makeup and sunglasses. Back then, there were no domestic violence shelters for women—why would there be, since beaten women brought it on themselves?

Children were even lower on the rung. The purpose of most children was to help with the work and to give assistance in their parents' twilight years. When I'd dared to consider myself higher than that, I knew the sting of Daddy's belt and the difference between getting slapped with the front of Mama's hand or the back.

So there I was, an unmarried female child and now, adding to it, a *deviant*. Even if the police didn't get involved, discovery of my affections would surely result in a brutal beating. They might even land me in a clinic where doctors would remove my baby-making parts, same as they started doing years earlier up in Portland, Oregon—or so the preacher told us. All those men arrested during the scandal, then sterilized for being with each other. Lost their jobs, got beat up—by the police *and* by the people of the town. I truly would have eaten a bullet if I'd been in their place.

That, I knew, was my future if I let things go on: beatings and shame and suicide and eternal damnation.

I stood up slowly, knowing now that me overhearing the police was a message from *above*—a warning from God not to be deviant. I came into that building right when I needed to, to hear what I needed to hear in order to take a good look at what Rhodie and I were getting ourselves into.

I walked to the door, wanting to get out of that place where all the air was being sucked out. Without looking at Clarence, I pushed the door open just as I heard him throw his police file in the trashcan and say, "No need for paperwork on something that never happened, now is there, Earl?"

× × ×

That night, away from Rhodie's magic, I nearly drowned in a panic over the realities of the world. For at least three weeks I might be in the kind of position that could cause my cousin Earl to behave the way he did.

The thought of me and Rhodie kissing—a moment that should have been the best in my life—was now shadowed by the idea that there existed many folks who not only hated us, but thought our love warranted a *hastening* in getting us to our rightful places in the fires of Hell. That people might kill us, and before that they might drag us into dark, cockroach-infested jail cells to be chained to walls and done in.

This juggle of thoughts made me nearly sick. I could see no bright spot in it, and I wished I could just go numb—that I could kill all those feelings I had for Rhodie.

Three doors down from my house, a German shepherd they called Shut Up howled and barked at nothing. The owners said they thought she could see ghosts, and possibly she could because she only howled that way at night. Usually it made me smile, but that night I imagined she might be howling at people she saw coming up to my house—people who knew my secret and wanted to haul me out and beat me after they'd exposed me to Mama and Daddy. Or maybe that dog was barking at some ghost who'd taken over my body and made me kiss Rhodie back. Something that God had sent to test me. Something wrong and wicked.

I rolled over and plugged my ears with my fingers, hoping to block out Shut Up's damn howling. Tomorrow was church, with me sitting between Mama and Daddy, as always. The thought of entering that place of worship, under the eyes of God and all the good folks in their pressed clothes, caused me to sweat with worry.

I decided I just couldn't do this. I could not love Rhodie anymore. I simply could not.

When I rolled back over I felt the newspaper in my back pocket. I pulled it out and flipped to the back page. There it was: the ad for Imperial State Prison Farm. Wetting the edges around it in a perfect square, I removed the job notification and put it under my pillow. If it was still there the next morning, I would apply. If they'd have me, I'd leave here. I would.

DEFINITIONS OF ADVENTURE

My resolve not to love Rhodie lasted all of two days. Two *miserable* days with me finally working myself into such a state that I knew I'd deny my family—my whole town —to be with her.

When Rhodie came by the egg store on Monday, her laugh made everything feel OK. We were just two people inside this bubble of love. Maybe, I thought, it could be just simple as that.

"You worried about us getting caught?" I asked.

She shrugged. "We're just close friends frittering away our summer. That's all they'll see."

I smiled, though I knew that folks look for trouble. They keep watch—and when they find it, they chew on it for weeks, savoring it.

"Now, you almost done?" she asked. "There's a bandstand going up outside the bank to celebrate its twentieth anniversary and my mother said the bank president's wife made orange slices."

I forced myself to block out any bad thoughts and focus instead on how it felt to be there, with her, two people in secret-love on our way to getting some orange slices. Simple. Besides, I reassured myself, it was only three weeks until she was off to school. I could handle living in a world of the best of emotions and the worst of emotions for three short weeks. So I smiled at Rhodie and knew I was ready while I said goodbye to God, telling Him I needed a break and that I'd be back next month.

× × ×

Two weeks later, Rhodie and I snuck away after I closed up the egg store. Holding hands, we ran down to the creek where we kissed again in the grasses. She sat with her legs crossed, across from me, spreading out a napkin to use as a picnic area and talking about building a mud hut where we could meet when she was back from college on vacation.

"I don't want to think about the future," I said.

"But I *like* the future, especially when you're in it."

"I'm just trying to stay here with you."

She pulled back. "You mean you want to go *away* from me?"

"No, no," I lied.

"Good." She leaned over and kissed me gently. "You know, with the way you read, you'd love college."

I rolled my eyes and changed the topic. "I'd rather go off to work."

"Go off? Where?"

"Maybe as a cook. I already sent off a letter telling them that I helped with the lunch cooking in high school, which I did, and saying I helped Mrs. Jameson make the pies and cakes here. The job includes your first month's rent free. Sounds perfect, especially since I really don't like eggs anymore."

"But *where?*" Rhodie asked again as she scooped out some jam with a cracker. Her hair was greased over to the side again, like some cute girl from France.

I gulped. "Imperial State Prison Farm, in the kitchen."

"Prison!" she gasped.

"It's good money."

"'Course it's good money, it's a prison!"

I tried to explain. "It's some place where I can be around people in a way that makes *sense* to me."

"What kind of sense?"

I shook my head, not knowing how to get my meaning across. "Being in prison might be a kind of freedom to me. I'll have a uniform. I'll have a specific role with a specific set of guidelines and processes.

And I'll have people around me who really aren't in a place to be judging anyone else."

"You're locking yourself up to avoid *judgment?*" She stopped. "Did I bring this on by kissing you?"

"No, no," I lied again. "It's got nothing to do with this."

Something splashed in the creek next to us. I looked around. If someone was coming, the grasses around us were tall enough to hide us if we laid down. To my relief, the splashing stopped. Probably a bullfrog.

Rhodie smiled and cracked us some more walnuts, showing she was not going to fight during our last week together before she left. "You serious?"

"No, I'm not really serious. I was just down in the mouth at the time."

"Good, because I want to see you over the summers and during Christmas."

"I want to see you too," I said, wondering what kind of fool idea it was to go work in a prison anyway.

"Prison," she laughed. "You had me."

I threw our walnut shells into the creek and rolled over. Rhodie followed suit and the two of us gazed up together through the grasses, the dry kind that separated at the top like split ends. She tipped her head toward me to avoid the sun and twirled a piece of my hair into a spiral.

"My parents are taking my brother to New Mexico to see my grandma this weekend," she said. "I said I wanted to stay here to get a head start on my reading for college. So maybe you can stay over with me? My parents would sure be grateful."

I smiled. "Well, if it will make your parents feel good about leaving you, sure."

"You are so *selfless* to do such a big favor."

She kissed me and we rolled over so I was on top of her, me conscious of not crushing her since I carried a bit more weight. Her hair smelled like cocoa butter.

"Friday?"

"Saturday."

I groaned.

"It's only *one day*."

"It's another twenty-four hours."

"See," she smiled, "you should go to college—all that math skill of yours."

"Uh huh."

We kissed again, then she nudged me off. With her serious face, she asked: "Really, now, why did you ever want to lock yourself away in some prison?"

"Adventure."

Rhodie made that puff sound with her mouth that told me I was full of it. "Adventure?" she repeated. "You know, there's plenty of adventure outside penitentiary life."

I reached up over my head, pulled a blade of grass and started chewing on it. "Like what?"

In answer, she took my free hand and put it under her striped sweater then under her bra and said, "Like this."

FROM THE TALL GRASSES

I lived life on a roller coaster, going through moments of true highs—sneaking kisses in the egg store—followed by horrible lows filled with breathless terror that my parents or the neighborhood kids or the preacher might find out about us. At night, in my dreams, a gaggle of country boys stumbled on us near the creek and threw rocks at us. The rocks cracked against our skulls. They yelled "Pervert!" and "Sickening!" and "Die!" while they kept chucking those rocks with so much force that their faces were red with it.

One of the rocks split my eyebrow and blood ran down into my eye. Another rock—so big that one of the boys had to hoist with both arms over his head—crashed into my ear and left me with a loud ringing noise. The sun shined down, bright overhead. I stumbled around, looking for Rhodie through the blood and the ringing and the sunshine. Then I saw her on the ground. They were kicking her. Rocks kept hitting me.

Off in the distance my parents came over the ridge of the meadow. Daddy stood tall and heavy in his red flannel and black cowboy hat and Mama, with her arm wrapped through his, wore her best Sunday dress—the light pink one. Her pale nail polish glistened in the sunlight. As the boys stepped closer to me, their hands filled with rocks, my parents saw what was going on, shook their heads, turned, and left. Through the blood I watched their bodies become shadows against the huge yellow sun.

Every morning after I had that dream I woke up covered in sweat, feeling around my head for blood, to be sure it wasn't real. Then I'd tell myself to calm down. We would be careful and wouldn't get caught. It would be OK.

Rhodie would be gone in less than a week and I couldn't let our last days go by in such a ridiculous state. Besides, I reminded myself in the darkness of my stuffy bedroom, you have no choice—you can't stay away from her if she's nearby. It's just too strong.

× × ×

I showed up to Rhodie's house—one of the few, I noted, without a windmill for pulling up well water—on Saturday with a huge bouquet of flowers and honeysuckle I'd stolen from various cutting gardens and fences around the neighborhood. The whole day I felt jittery and smiled so much my daddy kept calling me "cat," as in the cat who swallowed the bird, which of course only increased my nerves.

I knocked and she answered, wearing a thin blue dress and that butterfly scarf. As usual, the minute I saw her the rest didn't matter—the fear, the doubt, the nightmares.

I poked my head in. "New Mexico?"

She smiled. "Yup, they're all in New Mexico."

She clicked on the light in the hallway.

"Wow, you got switches!"

"We had kerosene back in our old place but my mother said that if we were moving here she wanted to have it *modern*, so we got a new house with all these switches. We even got heat from switches too."

"That right?"

"Next, Mother wants a toilet."

"Imagine," I said, doubting I'd ever see the day when we had an indoor toilet, especially since my mama questioned why anyone would bring filth into their home like that.

Anyway, there I was, being as modern as modern could get in the most modern house I'd ever been in with a girl on her way to *college*. I brimmed over with pride. I felt grown up and ready for all the weekend had in store. Ready and then some.

Rhodie put the flowers on the key table by the door, then slipped her hand between the buttons on my shirt and pulled me up the stairs to her bedroom. Candles were already lit and a tray of snack food sat on the floor by the bed.

"So we don't have to leave to eat," she explained.

The windows were open and a heavy heat rolled in.

"It's going to rain," I said.

"Supposed to be a thunderstorm."

"Best not answer the phone then."

"I know."

Rhodie smelled of rosemary oil, and she'd put some color on her cheeks. Imagine a girl like that making herself so pretty for a girl like me.

She stared at me. "Your eyes look like what I think ice on Neptune would look like, all blue and crystallized."

The room filled with the pressure of the incoming storm. Gray clouds moved in and the sky grew as dark as midnight.

Rhodie shut the window and turned on the fan. With the candles flickering in the grayness, it seemed as if we were in a room in the middle of nowhere, some place where no one would ever find us. We weren't on the second floor of her parents' white Colonial; we were in the attic of a castle or in an underground cave. Just us.

I kissed Rhodie and moved my hands to her waist. I could feel her ribs through her dress.

She said, "Don't tickle me now."

Outside, the clouds crashed into each other, making us jump for the first few claps of thunder. We lay down on the bed and she rolled over so I could undo the buttons up the back of her dress. I kissed a patch of freckles on the back of her knee, and she asked me if my goal for the night was to find all her ticklish spots.

"Why yes," I said, "as a matter of fact, Miss Rhodie, it is."

To my surprise—especially given my nerves beforehand—I wasn't nervous. I knew I was born to be doing what we were doing.

Rhodie rolled back over and lifted the dress above her head. I kissed her stomach, asking her if she was ticklish there.

"No," she said.

"How about here?" I asked, kissing her collarbone.

"No."

"Here?" I asked, with my hand reaching up between her legs.

"Shhh," she said.

× × ×

We spent the day and night together. It rained almost the entire time, flooding down the streets outside and causing the world to smell like grass and heat. I pushed all thoughts of the police officers and those four women and the boys with their rocks from my mind, having agreed to myself to let myself be a full-on pervert for the weekend. It was as brave as I could be then.

Rhodie's bed was an old four-corner one, with battered up poles on each edge that she'd hung scarves on. The wood was so dark it was almost black. The sheets were the same green as the curtains, which was just a coincidence, she told me, seeing that her favorite color was actually orange.

On Sunday morning she said, "I can't see you tomorrow because my parents are driving me over to my cousins' so I can say goodbye to everyone. My going off to college is more exciting news than when Jerome won the state auto show."

My guts dropped like a dead bird. "Then you're leaving."

"Yeah, then I'm leaving. I'll come by to say goodbye before I go, though."

"I love you, Rhodie."

She sniffled and sat up on the edge of the bed. "Shush."

Clasping my hand in hers, Rhodie's crying started full tilt. I reached over to my backpack on the floor and pulled out a white hand-kerchief my mama always had me carry in case I got myself muddy.

"Last time—please, Dara, *please* come with me."

I turned my head down, thinking of what going with her would mean: rejection of my family, never having children, eternal damnation.

Rhodie grabbed my handkerchief, which was really just a cut-up piece of Daddy's oil-changing T-shirt, and held it to her eyes. After a minute, the water seeped through the material she was crying so much.

More to myself than her, I whispered, "I don't think I can be that person."

I *wanted* to be that person—someone who could put love above everything else. I wanted to be brave. I wanted so much to be the girl who could go away with her. But I couldn't. I couldn't live in fear and isolation every day of my life. I couldn't tell my parents they'd never have grandchildren or walk me down the aisle. I couldn't sit out every Sunday while the rest of the town went to church and had coffee and talked about baseball. I couldn't be the girl who would never again have another friend to confide in about her life, *all* of her life.

Rhodie, who could have quite a temper on her, answered, "You could have at least tried!"

"Rhodie—"

"Never mind." She slapped the wet hankie into my hand and walked over to a piece of paper wrapped in a bright purple ribbon with those curly ends you make using the blade of the scissors. "Let's not keep at it." She handed me the scroll. "I drew this for you."

I unrolled it and held it out in front of me. It was a black-and-white picture she'd done with pen—I could tell from the way the lines crossed over and over again to make the black parts dark. The drawing was simple: a big black circle overlapping another big black circle. The oval-shaped middle, where they overlapped, was white.

She sat down and looked deep into me, recovered now from her outburst. "There, in the middle—the white part—that's our love."

She smiled and relaxed. "Us—two same circles—joining together with pure, protected love in the middle."

I nearly cried I was so happy. "I got you something too."

I pulled out her gift, which I'd wrapped in old newspaper—the clean bits—that I'd pulled up from the ground of that killer's hideout down Old Spider Road. She recognized it right off and smiled that big smile of hers.

"You sneak back down there?"

"Here you go," I said.

She unwrapped it slowly, pulling out a small picture frame filled to overflowing with wildflowers I pulled from our meadow and dried and pressed. On the back I wrote, in my neatest handwriting: *From the Tall Grasses*.

She nodded and laughed and cried, over and over.

I said, "I wrote it so no one would know."

"I know that!" She smiled and cried. "It's so pretty."

While she stared at it, almost like she was half-expecting the flowers to bloom up out of the glass, I ran my finger around the outside of the two circles she'd drawn for me. The symbol for infinity. I wondered if maybe I could do it. Maybe I could leave with her—no one would question two best friends rooming together in college.

But to live with the worry that they might find out? No, I couldn't.

Rhodie pushed my hair back. "Why do you look so sad?"

"Because it's time for me to go," I lied. "Your family's due back in an hour."

"And Daddy drives fast."

I kissed her.

Rhodie said, "You even kiss sad."

"I'm going to miss you."

Looking at her bedspread, she said, "You're not even going to *think* about coming with me, are you?"

"I love you," I said.

"Is that a *no*? Because if so, that is one messed-up reply."

"I just can't be that kind of person."

"We *can* be those people. We *are* those people!"

After weeks of hearing the same thing, I finally snapped. "Rhodie, you want to be *defiled?* You want to be shamed and maybe even *murdered?* That's our future. We are living in a little dot on the Texas map. If it weren't for Permian Oil, Midland might not even be here. This is where we are, who we are.

"Folks do whatever the hell they want to do around here," I went on. "We are like baby moles set out in the middle of a field for anyone to swoop down on. And there's no protection. People like us, girls who kiss girls, we got nothing to stop life from becoming a full-on nightmare. No family, no friends, no God, and not even the police, who are supposed to be protecting folks."

"But we'd be together," she said, oversimplifying everything in that romantic way she had.

Sighing, I rolled her picture back up, wondering how I could go from utterly happy to utterly forlorn in such a short time. Maybe that's the thing about having a strong emotion—it opens the door for all the others.

"I went down to the police station a while back and overheard my cousin Earl talking with another police officer . . ." I started.

"Yeah?" She straightened up on the bed, wearing just her white bra with the sheet wrapped around her lower body.

"They talked about how they'd taken these girls—girls like us—into the jail for the night. Four women, really. They talked about the things they did to them and how these women would never speak about it because it would be worse to be what they are than to call out such horror."

"The police did *what?*"

I looked at her, though I could tell she already knew. "They did *that.*"

"What? We need to go down and file a complaint! You can go to court—you heard them *confess.* You are a witness to—"

"Dammit, Rhodie, *no!* Think about those women—I'd be calling those women into the light."

She shook her head. "It's not right, though."

"And this is why we can never be together, not in the long term: you think you need to fight what's not right, even though it might mean hurting folks—"

"—and you just duck your fool head under!" Rhodie grew so angry that her hands shook. She stood up and threw some of my clothes around, looking for her nightgown.

"Stop!" I said, catching my underwear with my outstretched arm to prevent it from landing on the tall cactus in the corner of her room near the window—the one with the small needles.

"You want to let those women go without any help?"

"There is no help," I said. "If anything, *they* would be sentenced to jail time."

Rhodie gave up looking for her clothes and plopped back down on the bed. She grabbed my hand, half angry, half sad. "I'm just talking about me and you, two friends going away together."

I kissed her cheek. "I'm sorry."

She sighed. "I wish you thought with your heart more than your fool head."

"I do love you."

"I know that." She softened and touched my face with her warm fingertips. "I know that. Now kiss me *good*, since this is goodbye."

I leaned over and kissed her. Lost in the middle of a kiss—one that tasted like peppermint from brushing our teeth—neither of us heard the bedroom door open.

"*Rhodie Marie!*"

It was her mother, and there we were in a messy bed with our hands on each other's faces, kissing in that hungry way.

"Mama!"

Rhodie sprung up. She should have grabbed the sheet first, but she didn't, so she stood there, naked from the waist down in her white bra with her hair sticking up on one side and a kissing mark low on her neck. I stayed put and scrunched down into the sheets a bit, enough to cover my belly and my breasts.

"What in the name of all that is holy is *this?*"

"You know that Dara was coming over to—"

"I knew she was coming over. And now I see clearer *why.*"

Rhodie's mother had a little Mexican blood in her, all of which seemed to drain away, leaving her as pale as sun-bleached bone. She grabbed her stomach, where her dress was held tight by a belt, and clutched one of the posts of Rhodie's bed for support.

My body turned to ice, frozen and cold and ready to crack into pieces.

Her mother turned to the door and yelled at Rhodie's brother, "Go help your father unload the Model T! Go back out—git, now. I need some time with your sister. Go!"

While her mother's back was turned, Rhodie managed to snag her nightgown from her vanity chair and put it on. I gestured for her to get my shirt and she shook her head, not knowing where she'd just thrown it. The muscles in her face flexed and her eyes were wide.

The world slowed down. This trembling started inside me, as if panic could become a real, visible physical condition. It grabbed hold of my ribs and my throat and my hands and my legs until they all shook. The bed sheet jittered with my shaking. Fear had overtaken me.

My mind exploded: thoughts of my parents finding out, the preacher being told, my friends in high school hearing. The weight of it all made me dizzy and I gagged and coughed, trying to figure out whether I was going to vomit or stop breathing. And through it all, I shook like madness itself.

Her mother turned back to us, a bit more composed now. This was a woman who snapped chicken necks and delivered her son long after the doctor said one of them wasn't going to make it. This would not break her.

Her shiny black hair, pulled up high on top of her head, dripped a bit from the rain outside. Her pale pink cotton dress stuck to her, showing her bra and her skin through.

"We came back early," she said. "The storm."

Rhodie nodded, looking so hollow I thought she might topple over.

Her mother let go of the bedpost and took in a deep breath. "I worked my *whole life* to get you here, Rhodie. When I was your age, I couldn't go to college. I could not, but I told myself that if I ever had a daughter, *she*—she will go." Her black eyes burned into Rhodie. "Do you know how many college students are girls these days? *Eight percent*. Eight in every hundred students are female. You understand me? *You* are one of those eight. You are going. You are going to be a teacher or a nurse, or *something*! You will make it."

With a sudden shift, her mother got sad, that deep sadness, and shook her head. "A lifetime of planning this. You know what your daddy said? He said you'd be *unmarriageable* with higher schooling. That it's *unladylike* to be educated. I told him—and it took years and years of telling him over and over—I told him that that wasn't true anymore. I told him, and eventually he listened to me, and we got you into school. *We* did! We all did. And look here at what you do. *This*." She shot a sickened look my way, and I felt shame so deep that it left a hot scar inside me.

Rhodie clasped her hands in front of her yellow nightgown. The windows and curtains were closed, but we could still hear the rain coming down in streams.

"I'm sorry," she said.

"You are more than sorry. You are *disgusting*, and you have something wrong in your mind! Your whole life for *this*." She looked my way again.

I sat there, shaking like a beaten dog, trying to breathe. I didn't realize it right away, but I was crying—slow, hot, quiet tears.

Rhodie said, "Please—"

"Please *what?*" Her mother stood firm, framed by the closed bedroom door. "I can't tell your father. He would throw you out, and you would never see the inside of a college, much less the inside of our home again." She paced briefly in a short line. "But I can't send you away, not like *this*—not when I know that this is what you might be out there in the world."

Her mother had strong arms; you could see their muscle through the wet fabric. With all that strength, she slapped the post of Rhodie's bed until the whole thing wobbled. I pulled the covers up to my neck, scared she was going to beat us.

"Please," Rhodie said again.

"You are going to the preacher," her mother said. "You are going *tonight*, and you are staying there for the next few days to work through these demons. He will be sworn to silence so your father will never find out. That's his duty. I am not telling *her* father either, for fear he'll tell someone else." She clutched at her stomach again, as if the pronoun 'her' just made her nauseated. "I am not ruining this chance you have."

Rhodie nodded.

"Now *you*," she yelled at me, "take that sheet off, you *doxy*."

I didn't know what that word meant, but the meaning rang clear. With my fingers clutched around the fabric, I lowered the sheet but didn't raise my eyes.

Rhodie's mother walked over to me. Rage shook off her like steam.

"Thank you for not telling my parents—" I started.

Her open hand hit me on the side of the head—a hard, solid hit that echoed inside my skull and hurt all the way down to my collarbone. I think she meant to slap my face, but missed.

I flinched and raised the sheet back up again, stunned and terrified. My head ached, and I cried more. I was so scared I nearly threw up.

"You get yourself collected and get the hell out of here right now," she said. "If I ever see you again, I will risk the ruin of *my* name and go to your parents. This whole town will rise up in scorn against your horrid *atrocities*. Rhodie is a good girl who is going to college, and you, you are nothing but the work of temptation and sickness."

With that she turned and left, slamming the door behind her. Rhodie fell on the bed, crying and rocking her whole body while I got dressed—still shaking. I stuffed my dirty socks and underwear and her picture into my bag, tasting panic like tin in the back of my throat.

Rhodie looked up. Her face was a wreck of tear tracks. "I love you. I'll give it all up. You just say the word, Dara." She wiped her nose on her sleeve. "I will."

I nodded, so scared to go out of her room that I couldn't form any words. Silent, I left her and walked out of the house as fast as I could through the front door, which her mother had left wide open for me, even though it let the rain in.

Not knowing what to do or where to go, I ran down to the creek and sat in the slick mud on the edge. I let the cool water run over my big, sore feet. I shoved my bag under the grasses to keep it as dry as possible, and let the sound of the rain and the creek and the frogs cover my crying.

I couldn't separate out the feelings of sadness over losing my beautiful Rhodie, shame over being caught, anger about being in the situation in the first place, gripping fear over everyone finding out, worry over what the pastor might put Rhodie through, and hatred of myself. The rain trickled over my hair and down my face, giving me more cause to shake. With my head spinning, I finally just fell into my emotions and let myself go to pieces there, alone by the creek.

× × ×

I got home hours after supper, and the way I looked must have let Mama know not to dare say anything about me missing a meal. Without telling her or Daddy goodnight, I walked down the creaky hallway and went to bed, my body feeling as if I'd been in a boxing match.

While I lay there, I pulled out the picture Rhodie drew for me and looked at the two circles with the white spot in between, where they fell over each other. When I looked at the circles, they took on a new meaning. They were black, black as *secret evil*. While the love they made together might be good and light—it was love after all—the circles themselves were not. And more than that, although the circles kept the love between them safe, *they* were not safe. They were hanging out in the middle of nothing, vulnerable and somehow alone—separated from each other by this love.

"Shit, Rhodie."

I pushed the picture carefully under my mattress and leaned back against my flat pillow, worried about what the preacher was saying to Rhodie right then. How terrible it must be for her, that shame and exposure. We should've stopped.

All my anger and fear made me want to punch myself hard and deep in the stomach. I thought about Rhodie's mother, and I wished she would've hit me harder. Wished she'd caught my face with her full hand and left a big blue bruise. I wanted my body to hurt worse than my heart did just then, though I didn't know if that was possible.

THE PREACHER SAID SIT DOWN,
SO I SAT

On the fifth day after Rhodie moved to school—which was two days after she'd left the preacher's—Daddy came into my room. "Here you go. Some letter from Sugar Land—the prison there, seems. Something you need to share here?"

"I applied for a cooking job."

"You know you could learn to cook by working with Miss Kendal."

Miss Kendal and Daddy grew up together, and she ran a little breakfast place. "Daddy, I want to do this on my own."

"Not the kind of place to meet a man," he said. "Unless maybe a guard or something, I reckon."

"No matter," I said. "This is probably a rejection."

He grunted. "We leave for services here in ten. Get yourself ready now."

"Yes, sir."

I read the letter. Wonder of wonders: I got the job, though at the time I didn't think I'd take it.

Daddy, Mama, and me went to our regular Sunday worship, with me preoccupied with that letter. We walked over and sat as we always did, with me between them, looking like a perfect set of dolls propped up from tall to medium to small.

Daddy leaned over. "You get an offer?"

"I did."

"Well, now," he said, with something nearing pride. "We'll talk later."

I looked around, nervous that Rhodie or her mother had said my name to the preacher, though I knew he'd have to keep it confidential.

All through services, the church smelled the same—lemon polish and incense smoke. Folks all nodded hello the same. The candles burned the same. There was nothing different in the service either—no new people, no drama of any sort, no flarings from the pulpit, as Daddy called them, when the preacher got political about this and that. It all felt pretty ordinary.

Afterwards, though, in the entryway, it turned the opposite of ordinary—and quick. Daddy, me, and Mama walked out holding hands, as if I was the glue binding my parents together. I overheard the town's biggest gossip, Mrs. Gigi Turner, talking about Rhodie to a group of six or seven women, most with children playing around their legs.

Mrs. Gigi Turner, her bulb of brown hair streaked with yellow highlights, leaned into the group. "I heard little Miss Rhodie had to stay with the preacher for a few days, then they *sent her off.*"

One of the other women leaned in while the rest asked, "Why'd they send her away, you suppose?"

"I don't *suppose,*" Mrs. Gigi Turner said, "on account of this being the house of the Lord. But I do *wonder.*"

All those terrible women with their terrible hair, sculpted to look like solid whipped cream, nodded as if they knew my Rhodie. They wiped their lips, wet with the blood of talk about some young girl getting pregnant—a hideous sin to be sure, though a far lesser crime than bedding down with another girl.

One asked, "Where do you think she went?"

"I think," said the learned Mrs. Gigi Turner, "that she simply went *away.*"

Somewhere deep inside me must live a small pond of bravery, because at that moment I got nourishment from it. I walked beside them and I said, "Rhodie is in San Antonio, going to college."

"That's what her parents say, true."

"She is nowhere else," I said. "Nowhere."

They all turned to look me up and down, the dumpy girl still holding her mama's hand—the girl who would never marry well.

I continued, "You might not know, but only *eight percent* of females go."

Daddy and Mama stood back. I could feel Daddy's pride at seeing
me defend my friend. All of the women faced me and continued to
size me up, their eyes going narrow.

I felt a warm hand on my right wrist, and turned to see the pastor.
"Miss Dara, you speaking of Miss Rhodie?"

Mrs. Gigi Turner nodded, hands crossed in front of her like one
of those tiny-handed dinosaurs. "She is."

The pastor squared me up, toe-to-toe and shoulder-to-shoulder
and eye-to-eye. His brown eyes looked hostile. "What I suggest, Miss
Dara, is you stop throwing words into the wind and go *sit down*." His
voice rose a little, enough to send the group of women scattering and
everyone looking at us. "I suggest you sit down *right now*. And maybe you stay there until this *righteous* congregation empties out. And
while they file past, these *virtuous* people, you think about your life.
You worry about your life and not your *friend* Rhodie's."

He implied enough to cause Mama to cough and cover her mouth
before she went back in to pray. Daddy squinted, wondering if he
should defend me or walk away. His hands always hurt from working
at the lumber mill, and when he got uncomfortable he'd rub them
together, just like he did then—round and round.

All of the women who were in the circle looked over at us from
their various posts in the entry as I dropped my head and walked over
to the only bench, my back hot with their stares.

Fear came over me again, gripping with its metal fingers down the
inside of my throat. Fear and that now-familiar shame.

As the churchgoers moved past me, putting on their gloves and
hats and giving me strange looks, I sat there acting as if I was just
waiting for Mama to finish up her prayers. A minute or so later, I
yawned to show how tired I was and maybe that's why I was sitting
down. Then I rubbed my feet through my black flat shoes to let folks

know that my big feet *hurt*! Whew, I sure was glad I had this bench here.

I know it probably didn't happen this way, but I truly felt that every person leaving the service stared at me and knew my evil. The whole time, Daddy stood off in the corner by the water bowl with his big, brown-haired arms crossed in front of him, unsure what just happened.

The scene caused me to sympathize with the way an ice cube feels on a countertop in broad daylight, wanting so badly to either melt away or fall off the Earth entirely.

By sitting me there, the preacher had dished out just a small taste of the wrath of the world that controlled every inch of my life. I understood his message in my bones—and then and there I decided to take that job.

At least at Imperial State Prison Farm I'd be able to see the walls of my imprisonment.

RHODIE LETTER #1

A week later, I got a letter from the University of Texas, San Antonio.

My Dara,

All I want to do is throw college and everything else away and grab your hand and run and run until we are someplace no one will find us. I love you so much. I feel as if I'm never going to be able to get to sleep again without you here. But I'll have to. It's just what has to happen in the world. I hate the world. I hate the world almost as much as I love you.

The preacher was terrible, but I got through it. My mother didn't look at me during the whole drive here, and my father didn't ask why. It was all so terrible. But again, I got through it. Now I'm just left with these feelings of missing you.

Please write me, and tell me where to send you mail at that awful prison. My brother said it's the talk of the town—you going away.

I will love you forever.
Rhodie

I put the letter in the front of my coveralls and headed out to the egg store as everything inside me drained away. I was the *definition* of hopeless. There was no point to anything, really, because the love I felt could never find root anywhere and flower. This beautiful, living thing would wither away in the darkness inside me.

To help me keep my resolve not to go to her, I hung the picture she drew for me on the wall right beside my bed. I reminded myself that I didn't want to be that black circle with another black circle. I vowed *not* to be who I was, come hell or high water—or both.

Rhodie's letter stayed on my person at all times, even when I slept, for fear someone might find it. I must've read it twenty times a day— about the same number of times I looked over at the picture she'd drawn for me to remind myself what it told me.

I wrote Rhodie twice a day, every day. Each time I finished a letter, I burned it down by the creek. I burned those letters and cried, wanting so badly to have all the emotions I'd written in them go up in those flames too. I knew it would damn near kill her, not hearing from me, but a terrible part of me blamed her for making me be this way. Another part of me made myself believe that it was easier for her to be brave *out there*. Another part even hated her. And it's tricky when you hate what you love. It can cause you to do mean things—callous and spineless mean things, like cutting yourself off from someone who's waiting for you.

Rhodie wrote me several times a week, as any best friend might. I burned them all, too, unopened. I sat there with the sounds of the creek and the crickets—me fat and sad and empty, watching her hand-drawn hearts and bullfrogs and the words "love" crinkle away in the orange flames until the paper turned black and blew away.

OCEANS INSIDE

They say that black holes were once bright stars that collapsed and now sit there, dark as dark can be, trying to suck everything alive and bright into them. That is the best way I can describe my mood after Rhodie left. I didn't care about reading. I didn't care about making my bed. I didn't care about pie.

Every God damn thing reminded me of her: the bare trees, the sound of water running, dark clouds, light clouds, no clouds, pictures of butterflies. All of it.

I told my parents I slept so much to be rested for my new job in the kitchens of Imperial State Prison Farm, where I might have long hours, but the truth was that I didn't want to see or smell or taste anything since it would all lead back to her. I cried every day, mostly by the creek or when I was running our clothes through, telling Mama I got some washing soda in my eye.

My days went like this: I'd have a cup of coffee with Daddy before he left for work. We'd hardly talk—just clink our spoons as we added cream and sugar. After he'd go, I'd get out the dolly stick and the washboard, to scrub and beat the washing, check the mail, grab too much food for one girl, and retire to my room to eat. I only went down for dinner to appease Mama, who seemed more insightful since that Sunday worship than she let on.

At night, I'd roll around, unable to get comfortable. For hours and hours, I'd lie there, praying to Jesus to take away those dreams where people are stoning me and Rhodie to death, with the worst part—the part that hurt me so much I buckled—being when Daddy and Mama let them continue on, when they just walked away.

That's how January passed.

By February 1, I had more control of the restless dark ocean I held inside me. I said goodbye to my folks and hopped on the bus with my suitcases—the same ones Mama brought with her when she married Daddy—to start my new life, grateful to be away from those letters from Rhodie that kept coming every few days like yellow jackets attacking the same spot over and over again.

I'd asked Mama to return any letters from Rhodie, lying and saying that Rhodie would get them and route them to Sugar Land. I didn't want those letters lying around my house, for fear Daddy might not read who one was addressed to and open it up.

I could see him sitting there with a glass of 'shine, all big belly and shoulders, using his thick fingers to tear into my letter from Rhodie. In my mind I watched him lift the glass to his mouth, reading all those words of love that would fill him up with hate. I watched him throw his glass against the wall and stomp over to slap Mama a few times, saying she caused this.

Those fears and the separation from Rhodie's charms gave me space to convince myself that I had done the right thing—that maybe I'd even been the *strong one* to do what had to be done and break this mess off.

In getting on that bus, I thought I'd escaped. I'd made it. I didn't know then that the way your body and mind *wants* to love is the way it *needs* to love. Nothing can change that. Nothing—though I surely tried a thing or two over the years.

RHODIE LETTER #31

Imperial State Prison Farm was situated in the city of Sugar Land, Texas, home to Imperial Sugar. Sugar Land sat all the way down near Houston, or what we in Midland called the "armpit of Texas" on account of its humidity and its tendency to collect strange odors. The ride to Sugar Land was ten hours from Midland—the perfect distance to leave where I had come from without leaving who I was.

To my dismay, though, all that distance didn't stop the love. As some kind of compromise, I kept writing to Rhodie. It made the days less lonely, having this pretend relationship that couldn't hurt me, at least not directly.

A few months in, I wrote to her about Huddie, who'd I dared to call my friend.

Dear sweet Rhodie,

Greetings from Sugar Land! I miss you. I miss you every time I see the sun or the stars or the grass.

Other than that, things are going well here. In addition to Beauregard, who I told you about, I met the head cook—who is as frightening as Beauregard told me he was. Something evil in him. It scares me, but I try to put on a face.

I'm also working sometimes with one Huddie Ledbetter. I'm getting to know him pretty well, or as well as I can in an open kitchen with me being a white woman and him being a Negro—and him only here one or two days a month. I like Huddie. You probably would too, maybe.

I watch his eyes and can tell when he is finding something funny that he's not supposed to find funny, or when he's upset but can't really show it for fear of being placed in the Box.

Huddie's eyes have this dullness to them that I can tell he works hard to maintain. When I watch those eyes, I understand just a little of how it must have been to live a life being constantly watched, of being stopped on the street every day by people saying, "Where you going, boy?" "Look at me when I talk to you, you filthy animal," "Your father still a lazy son of a bitch?" "You still stupid?" Every single day. Can you imagine?

When we was growing up, I remember people talking to Negroes that way, right in the middle of town or in a store, even outside church—as if colored people had been put there for white people to dump all their anger onto. And I thought nothing of it.

Well, today I thought about Huddie and all those terrible questions from people, and I realized that sometimes it's the assumption of something that can create it. You hear these awful things about yourself and someday you'll more than likely become some of these things, if for no other reason than to prove you did something right. Know what I mean?

I wonder if it would have been that way for us. I wonder if us hearing over and over that we were evil, and our kind of love is bad and wrong, might have turned us bad and wrong. So maybe it was best for us not to try—to leave it as the most perfect three weeks I'll probably ever know. But I still love you and in my dreams we have one heck of a life together.

I signed the letter on the right-hand side at the bottom, and I lit up a cigarette. The way I missed her hurt, deeply. I didn't know if it would ever go away. I wondered if the happiness of it would ever outweigh the sadness.

After pulling a few inhales, I held my cigarette up in front of me and put the letter above it until the heat set it on fire. The orange-and-black flame reminded me of a flickering pirate's sail. When it got too close to my fingers, I dropped the letter into a coffee can filled with the gray ashes of all my other letters to Rhodie. Then I went to bed, secure that I'd put myself in the safest place for me to be: a men's prison.

QUICK TO FIRE

Huddie dropped a hard lima bean into one of those gigantic pots, just as I started washing it. The water jetted the thing around and around inside the steel. I looked up at him.

"City?" he asked, keeping our interactions at a minimum due to the guard.

"What now?"

"City."

"Midland."

"You have tiny dreams then."

I smiled. *Oh, I get it.* Not the city where I was *from*, the city where I wanted to go.

He looked at me and asked again: "City?"

"Atlanta," I said.

I dried the pot. He took it from me and carried it over to the shelf.

"You ever been to Atlanta?" he asked.

"No."

"I have," he said. "You oughta pick again."

I smiled. "All right then, how about New Orleans?"

"Good one." He grunted as he hoisted the pot up.

The guard overseeing us wore thick black glasses that turned his eyes into little chipmunk eyes. He glanced up with those beady eyes from the newspaper he was reading, nodding to let us know that he could see we were talking and he didn't like it. Every now and again he spit tobacco juice on the floor—me making a mental note to be careful not to slip in it.

Huddie grabbed the broom and swept up with his head down as he passed by the guard on his way back to my area. I tossed the lima bean back to him. Just when I thought it was going to hit him in the chest, he reached out and caught it.

"Music," I whispered.

He smiled. "Easy. *My* music."

"That so?"

"Oh yes, ma'am. I sing and play just about anything you can think of."

Using my shirt, I rubbed up a line of sweat up, tickling my ribs. "Yeah?"

"You mark me, Miss Dara," he said as he shuffled by me, collecting flyaway onionskins in the bristles of the broom, "you will turn on the radio one day, and I'll be singing back to you."

"I look forward to that day," I said.

He nodded, knowing I was telling the truth.

I walked into the canning closet, careful to keep my eye on the head cook's office door, in case he came out and caught us talking. It was dark in there, and I couldn't help but check over my shoulder to be sure the guard and Huddie were still in the kitchen so that the head cook wouldn't open his door and see me alone in that room. Antsy, I fumbled around for the fattest jar I'd ever seen, full of pimentos that looked like squirrel kidneys.

After lugging it out of the closet, all red in the face and grunting more like a moose than a woman, I grabbed a small piece of wood to beat around the edges of the lid until the seal popped. Midway through banging I felt a ping on the top of my head, and turned to see Huddie sneaking a smile as he brushed by.

I leaned over and retrieved the bean from the floor by the sink.

When I had it in my hand Huddie shuffled by and whispered, "Dessert?"

"Easy. Lemon meringue pie."

"Yes, ma'am!" He smiled. Clearly a shared favorite.

Without me seeing it, the head cook had snuck up behind me, slithering his way around the edge of the room.

"Am I interrupting?" he asked us.

Huddie and I both stood tall.

"No, sir," I said.

The head cook flashed his yellow teeth at me. "I been watching you two in here, getting on." He turned to Huddie. "Nigger, *you* finish up her work. Put those pimentos in that big pot until she gets back. She and I got some talking to do. Just friendly words."

Huddie nodded, but kept his eyes up on me.

"Follow me," the head cook said.

He tucked his shirt into the back of his pants as we walked along. My stomach flipped and flopped but I tried to look easy, though I knew there was no escape from whatever might be going on here.

The head cook's office was no bigger than a washroom and smelled twice as bad. He grinned and asked me to shut the door. I did.

"You think you know the *world*?"

"I'm sorry?"

He sat down behind his desk and pointed to the ground where he wanted me to stand and face him. I did. A black lamp that looked like the crooked finger of a witch sat on his green metal desk. The sight of it made me more nervous. And there was no music in his office—no sound whatsoever.

"You think you *worldly* enough to be conversating with the likes of Huddie there? You two talking about places to travel and good restaurants and whatnot?"

"I'm just doing my job."

He cleared his throat. "You doin' *somethin'*, you are."

I looked down and willed my hands not to shake.

The head cook settled back into his black chair—a man enjoying himself.

"You think you pretty smart coming into this man's world, don't you? Smart girl. Since you think you know it all," he said, "how about you tell me this . . ." He looked around the room, then leaned forward. "Tell me how I *told time* when I got lost in Sheldon Park."

"Told time? I've no idea," I answered, being only twenty years old and not really acquainted with the crude side of cruel men who are given jobs with a pinch of power and an office with no windows.

"Come here and I'll show you."

The head cook stared at me with loose, pinkish eyes that told me that he liked to drink.

I stepped forward, and he motioned that I should come around the side of the desk, to get a better look. I assumed the answer was to be found in the drawers of his desk—not the drawers he was *wearing*. But there, in all its somewhat sad, maroon-tipped wonder, was his penis. It stood as straight as it seemed capable of standing, poor thing. The light glistened off the top, where the pee-hole sat, like it was waxy or wet. I gawked, having never seen such a thing.

"When I got lost in Sheldon Park," he said, "I told time with my *sundial*."

I backed away. No thoughts came to my mind. I only wanted to move out of there as fast as I could. I walked backwards and reached out behind me to feel for the door because I didn't want to turn my back on him.

The head cook laughed and waved his penis up and down, saying, "Bye bye—for now, *woman of the world*."

I tripped over my fat feet, turned, and fumbled with the doorknob, finally stepping into the lit hallway, where the air was cooler and fresher. The loud thumping of my heartbeat made me jittery—still, I straightened my white shirt down the sides and held my head up as I walked into the kitchen and over to the sink to finish the prep for lunch. With all my strength, I held the posture of *nothing happened*.

Behind me, I heard the head cook laughing before he clicked his door shut.

Huddie was nearly finished with his sweeping. When he saw me, he dropped the broom and walked over in quick steps that sounded louder than usual without the radio on.

The guard, his black eyebrows raised in high half-moons over his black glasses, dropped his newspaper right quick and yelled, "Inmate. Stand! I said *stand*, dammit!"

Huddie raised his hands and deliberately laid them on his head, as "stand" instructed. He stood tall and still, his chest wide in his gray uniform and his breathing angry. The skin all around his eyes squeezed up, causing him to squint in the way a man does before he shoots someone.

The guard walked behind Huddie and cracked him on the back of his thighs with his big stick. Huddie didn't move.

"Just heading over to get a rag," he said.

The guard pushed his glasses up and lit a cigarette. "The hell you were."

I nodded to Huddie to let him know I was doing all right, although clearly I wasn't. *Let's just stay calm*, my eyes told him. *Relax.*

The head cook walked up behind me, sucking on his teeth as if he'd just had the best meal he'd ever eaten. He put his hand on my shoulder and I cringed. I didn't want to—I knew what might happen if I did—but I did anyway. It was a reflex.

The cook moved his hand and caressed my neck as if he owned me. Huddie raced forward so fast I barely saw him until he stood in front of me. The head cook looked right at Huddie as he slowly moved his pointer finger down the front of my white uniform shirt. Huddie, his eyes on fire, lunged forward and punched the cook on the side of his face. The hit sounded like thick branches cracking over a knee.

"I'm fine!" I yelled to Huddie while I put my hands forward to hold him back. I'd never seen anger so fast to light. "I'm fine!"

The head cook held his face and spit out: "You nigga son of a bitch!"

The guard grabbed Huddie, pulling his arms behind his back using that stick of his. Huddie, half-restrained now, kicked out at the head cook, who raised his leg to block the blow before moving behind me for cover.

The guard spit out more juice and yelled: "Calm down!"

The head cook panted through the pain. I could smell his anger in waves of musky heat. He shouted, "I want him in the God damn Box and never again in my kitchen!"

There's no tiger alive ever as focused in a fight as Huddie was right then. Despite the clear agony of having his arms twisted up in the guard's stick and the threat of confinement out in a tiny box in the middle of the hottest part of the yard, he kicked around me somehow and got the head cook hard on the knee.

The cook—the side of his flabby pink face already growing purple—leaned to one side and slapped at Huddie the way a girl swats flies. Huddie easily dodged him.

"The Box!"

The guard pulled Huddie backwards, twisting and groaning with enough force on his stick to finally cause Huddie to yield.

The cook yelled while his nose bled, "Out! Now! Take this fucking nigger out of here!"

When I looked over at Huddie, my mouth hanging open and my eyes wide, he did the most remarkable thing: he started humming. Then, still humming, he nodded and stood up as proper as a king and let the guard escort him out.

GUTS, CROTCH, FACE

After they took Huddie away, I stood there, the very definition of vulnerable. I knew there were hardly ever more than three people in the kitchen at one time, and often I was there alone while Beauregard hauled trash and the inmate staff mopped down the eating area, with the guard standing post out there

Meanwhile, the head cook had the freedom to go wherever he pleased in the food processing area, and with whomever he pleased. If I was in the kitchen alone, he could order me into the supply room or the icebox or out back near the trash bins with him any old time, and if I didn't comply, he could fire me. I nearly suffocated with my position, my cage. The thought of it caused me to have the kind of nausea that starts at your throat and continues all the way down to your knees. The kind of nausea that settles in and stays with you in its misery.

And now, Huddie was gone and would never be back. Poor Huddie who'd defended me. He hadn't just resisted a guard: he'd hit the head cook in the face then kicked him solidly on the kneecap. The guard would support the head cook's story. From what I could tell, not many guards liked the head cook, but they respected his title— and they all hated Negroes, every last one.

For the rest of the day, I did my best to stay within eyeshot of the guard on duty. My body tingled, alert to the presence of the head cook, who nodded and smiled at me every time he walked by. Once, he grabbed his crotch and rubbed himself before disappearing into the hallway. I nearly vomited.

Back in those days, there was no recourse for the kind of behavior
exhibited by the head cook and his sundial. There was no union or
group for women's rights. He was my boss, and bringing his behavior
into the light would have just proven that working women were a
distraction. I would have been let go, no doubt after being chastised
for being seductive—though I felt about as seductive as an acorn in
the mud.

At clock-out time, just when I was thinking I made it through
the day, the head cook called me into his office again. My palms went
damp. My head felt like someone had just wrapped it in cotton, all dull
and numbed out. I wished I'd gone to college with Rhodie after all.

"Close the door," he said, his face looking considerably more swollen on the one side than the other.

I closed the door, only this time I stayed right up against it, with
the doorknob pressing into my tailbone.

"What you are afraid of?" he asked, his mouth smacking with saliva.

I didn't answer, so he stood up and walked over to me.

He smiled. "If you don't come to me, I can always come to you."

He positioned himself right in front of me. With only that desk
lamp of his—no overhead light, no windows—everything got dim-
mer further away from the desk. We were in one of the darkest spots
of his office with him backlit in front of me like some evil spirit.

His breath smelled of heavy tobacco. He took off his white cap
and threw it on the ground, then reached out, put his hands on my
hips, and pulled me into him so I could feel him pressing his urgency
into my girl parts. My mind raced with a dozen different thoughts:
*Are there any sharp objects nearby? Can the guard hear us—would he
care? Will it hurt? I've never been with a man before. This just can't be
happening.*

"You are just the right height," he said into my ear, his eyes looking not at me, but at the white door behind me. "We work just right
together."

He sniffed my hair. I shut my eyes and started praying. Then I remembered something: when I was a little girl, my daddy told me that

if a bear attacks, make yourself look bigger and create lots of noise. Don't be passive, he said.

So, despite the panic that was creeping over me, I stuck out my chest and said, "Keep your penis to yourself, Billy." This was the first time I'd ever said his name.

He laughed, and I thought maybe my bluff had worked.

"Listen to you getting all powerful and familiar-like!" he said.

I relaxed and smiled—this was all a friendly misunderstanding!—until he grabbed me by the throat. My eyes flared up with fear and I held my breath.

"Don't you ever call me anything but 'head cook.'" He unbuttoned his pants and pulled out his penis again. "I will do what I want, when I want. This here is *my* kitchen. I didn't want you in my kitchen, but here you are. Now I'm thinking I'll make the best of it and do what I want with you, *woman.*"

I closed my eyes again. My mind spun around. I felt dizzy and sick.

He moved his hand fast, and he grunted as he said, "I do what I want."

I prayed that I'd vomit right there, all over him, but I didn't. It was all I could do not to fall into a panic and cry. I listened to my heart beating and looked off to the left.

A moment later, the head cook moaned and arched back slightly. He pressed hard into me two or three times and squeezed himself dry. When he finished, he said, "Wash your uniform. You're a dirty mess, nigger lover."

My legs shook. I put my hand behind me, grabbed the doorknob, and let myself out.

I don't remember walking down the short hall into the kitchen. I only remember cleaning the evidence off my uniform—the look of it on the sponge and the feel of it when I wrung out the sponge under water. I had this sensation that I couldn't get it off my hands, so I kept washing them over and over again. Still, I could feel it on me.

I smelled him, even though he wasn't around me. His smell stunk stronger than it had in real life, and it was *everywhere.* Suddenly, with the feeling of being kicked in the stomach, I leaned over the sink and threw up.

Not wanting to fill my unclean hands with water, I tipped my head sideways and let the faucet run on my face to clean off the vomit. I grabbed some water in my mouth, swished it around, and spit.

The head cook opened the door to his office again and my guts dropped. He shouted, "You can go home early today, Miss Dara. We don't need you anymore."

I don't remember clocking out or walking into the sun.

I clicked back in on the tiny sidewalk leading into my shanty. In a numb daze, I walked inside, wrapped up the trash, and fed the stray cats who stopped by for dinner. I pulled out a dozen cookies I'd made a few days before and ate every single one of them. They made me feel better, as if I was replacing the anxiety in my stomach with something solid.

That night, for the first time in memory, I locked my front door and checked every window, putting sticks up where the locks didn't work. I kept all my clothes on in case I needed to run—in case the head cook came to my house. I reassured myself with the memory of how fast I'd run down Old Spider Road with Rhodie to escape the killer chasing us. I slept with my finger on the trigger of my rifle, who I called Dead Eye. The rifle that could shoot a tin can off a fence at a hundred paces. I'd shoot him in the guts and the crotch and the face, I said to myself over and over again, like a prayer. *Guts, crotch, face.*

Then I lay there, forcing myself not to cry, until morning.

DOING WHAT YOU CAN

At every mealtime, I searched the cafeteria for Huddie. Folks say that after three days in the Box you start seeing things. If you are in for more than five days, they say a part of you dies in there—you leave some piece of your mind or your soul behind. It'd been eight days.

Sometimes, I'd look out when I was working, and I'd see the silhouettes of inmates who'd failed to reach their quota of cotton or sugarcane standing on a barrel right near the Box—two hours on and one hour off. If you lost your balance, your time started over. I hoped they talked to Huddie, but I doubted it, given their situation.

I wondered how he would recover from that long in the Box. Beyond that, I knew he'd be weakened by the time he'd be released, so how could he reach his quotas? And if he didn't, how could he withstand the barrel or the whip—or God forbid, the bat—and be ready to get up and try again the next day?

On the seventeenth day, Huddie finally came into the cafeteria, this time at the very end of the line. His head was down, and he walked not so much with a swagger as with a limp. A kind of prison hush fell as he came in. Huddie gimped through the food procession.

When he got to me, I saw he had a fading shiner and a giant split on his lip that opened up like the skin on pudding. My eyes popped wide, but I didn't say anything.

He whispered through the bars, "It's gonna be fine" but I could see it was forced. His rage was just on the edges, making the egg whites of his eyes wiggle on hot grease. He looked crazy with it.

My chest burned for him, but I was trapped there, helpless to do anything to make him feel better. I looked down at my tin of dry cornbread, same thing they got each day. When I saw Huddie that way, I did the only thing I could do and snuck him an extra spoonful of margarine.

MUSIC IN TRAPS

A month or so passed without any personal interaction with the head cook, who sauntered by me without looking my way, as if I'd been soiled or something, which I reckon I had. I missed Huddie in the kitchen and felt deep anger at myself for having been the cause of him getting sent to the Box—a place no doubt haunted by evil spirits I could only imagine.

I wrote to Rhodie nearly every night to keep my mind occupied with something other than guilt over Huddie and fear of the head cook, who I knew must have my home address from my work file. I wrote to Rhodie about the crows I saw fighting over a bag of Grape-Nuts, about how pretty the sunset was, and what I thought might happen if sea otters ruled the world. I told her over and over how much I loved her. I never mentioned troubles with the head cook. She was my escape—the world I kept alive, even though I had been the one to kill it.

Then I'd burn those letters and fall asleep with my gun.

× × ×

As happens with all prison employees at the end of eight weeks, I met with the Warden to review my progress. I'd been tempted to bring up the head cook's *dislike* of me, but to what end? There was no position for me to move to in the penitentiary; this was the only job I was qualified to do. I couldn't leave. Going back to Midland meant going back to the place where Rhodie would be every Christmas, every spring break, every summer. I couldn't see her or I would fall apart. If anyone found out—and they would just by the way we looked at each other, I knew it—our fate would be sealed.

The Warden's office had a huge desk along one wall. Four low swiveling bucket chairs were set up around the room, in no order, and a card table with boxes of poker chips on top sat in the corner. On the wall behind the desk, a pin-up calendar featuring automobiles had the words "wife lunch" marked in red every Thursday. He had a radio, too. It was similar to Beauregard's, only there were three mesh parts in the front, each shaped like the rounded stained-glass windows you see in churches.

"How's your time here going then, Miss Dara?" the Warden asked after the guard who'd walked me over shut the door.

"Good, Warden. Thank you."

He had the kind of barrel chest that filled out the front of his shirts—maybe he'd been in the service. "Come in, sit down. Any one of those chairs."

I chose the swivel chair over by his desk, assuming he would want to sit down behind his desk. It sat a bit lower than usual, but with me being a bit taller than usual, it kept me at a good height for desk-to-chair conversation.

Instead, the Warden stood over by the windows that looked out over the endless fields. "It was my idea having you here—a woman in the kitchen. Thought it might tone down the violence some. I talked to the boys, and they say you're doing a fine job."

Me thinking he must have gotten good words from Beauregard and terrible words from the head cook, and decided to not listen to the cook.

He continued: "We didn't know how a woman would do here, but you're a strong one."

I sat there, not knowing what to say to that.

The Warden cleared his throat. Hissing honky-tonk music sang out from his radio.

"You worked with Huddie for a while there. One of our more *colorful* prisoners. Too bad he can't keep his fists to himself. I was rooting for him in the kitchen, but he's lost that privilege, as you know. He picked the wrong man to hit, to be sure. Just as well, since the field bosses were missing their best trusty."

The Warden turned back to me with a smile that made his eyes turn into quarter moons. He reminded me of Papa Bear. "Huddie's not only one of the biggest niggers, he can keep most of the rest under control. Not easy, with all those mosquitos in the wet fields. But those Negroes are strong—once you can convince them to work—much stronger than the white prisoners. Plus, the whites aren't usually in here as long, so they got less incentive to make friends in the fields, you see."

The Warden picked up a bottle of milk of magnesia from his desk and pulled back a big sip. A few strands of his hair—pieces of it almost orange from the sun—dropped forward. With one rough swoop of his hand, he pushed his hair back again over his head.

"Huddie was a big help in the kitchen," I said.

"Imagine he was—big nigger like that, especially with Jackson calling in sick with his *mystery* fevers. That man disappears like a blue jay on Fridays when it's hot."

I smiled.

We sat there for a minute.

"Bet Huddie misses the music we have in the kitchen," I said.

"I bet some of the people he *hurt* miss a lot more than music—bet some miss the sight of the flowers coming up and the smell of the fields and their children."

I looked down at the maroon carpet on the floor. "Bet you're right."

The Warden put a hand on his chest and held in a belch. His wedding ring was thick and silver. He turned and looked out his office window again, over the vast brownness of the yard against the thick stalks of the fields. We watched four men in a clearing encouraging a tired mule to carry a cart of cane to the mill.

"Music calms the beast," I said—not sure exactly why I said that, except that the emptiness between sentences had started to make me stupid.

The Warden walked over to his desk and sat down in his squeaky black chair. The prison-order clock on the wall behind him ticked away the seconds with a straight black hand. "I lost a guard the other day. There was a fight between three or four inmates and the guard stepped in, then one of them flung him back against the wall and his neck snapped. It can be just that fast."

I nodded. The ceiling fan whirled above us.

He sighed. "But what do they care? What do they have to lose? The convict who took down my guard is in here for life. There's nothing more to take away. You got kids?"

"No, sir."

"Well, remember back then to you being a kid. Once you didn't fear being hit, your parents lost their power." He took another swig of milk of magnesia, which left a thin white line on his upper lip—me thinking that I never lost the fear of being hit. "I'm just letting my mind wander about what you said about music calming the beast."

He paused for quite some time. I sat still.

"Rumor is, Miss Dara, that Huddie can play accordion and harmonica and piano and even things that aren't musical, like spoons and buckets and dirt."

"Seems that's his gift," I said, not knowing what else to say.

"Maybe I can use that to give the men something they won't want to lose."

With a quick slam, the Warden plopped down his milk of magnesia bottle and stood up. I followed his lead. He walked over and opened his thick wooden door.

He turned to me. "Oh, and you getting on good here then?"

"I am."

"Good," he said, and the guard stepped up. Clearly we were done. The guard walked me back to the kitchen.

× × ×

Next thing you knew, Huddie had himself a second-hand twelve-string guitar. The whole prison was buzzing with the news. At first, most of the prisoners didn't take too well to Huddie getting favorable treatment, but then Huddie started playing. When he played, even the weak-minded dropped it down a notch—including Old Redwood, the craziest of the crazy, who'd spend hours screaming at nothing anyone else could see.

During the relentlessly hot days, the captains let Huddie go from section to section out in the fields, playing his guitar for the men. It soothed them. At night, the prisoners would holler out topics to Huddie—like "Thunderstorms in Louisiana" or "Cigarettes and Whiskey" or "My Pretty Linda"—and Huddie would whip them into songs.

One day, I heard a white prisoner say in the chow line, "That boy tells deep stories about life."

The inmate next to him said, "He's a *nigger*, Jimmy."

"Yeah, but he ain't a *stupid* nigger."

When the colored inmates filed in, you could see Huddie shining with his happiness. Beyond the sheer joy of the music, that guitar also made him invincible in the prison pack—there was no way someone was going to hurt the only source of music they had. And the Warden's thinking was right; he could threaten to take that guitar away for misbehavior. The Warden gained power back over not just Huddie, but over all the convicts.

Huddie slid down the chow line. When he reached me, he raised his hand in front of my bars and turned it over to the pink and white of his palms to show me the bright red pads of his fingertips, whispering, "Calluses are coming!" as if he was talking about a train filled with gold.

"Congratulations," I said.

He nodded and hummed on down the line, me thinking that this man should not be kept in prison. A gift that powerful should not be holed up.

When I told Beauregard my thoughts, he fiddled with his mustache and turned in the bright kitchen to look right at me. "Maybe his gift is why he should *stay*," he said. "Maybe he's here to give these men a glimpse of genius and proof of God, something every one of them could use. Besides, his playing in here is surely lifting up the Negroes. Watch the way they walk in here now, with considerably more strut." Beauregard leaned across the counter. "Music like that is *made* in traps. This prison is making those songs."

"Maybe music is made here, but if it doesn't get out, it'll surely die here."

Beauregard turned back to wiping down his station. "You seem to know a little bit about how music lives and dies. You play?"

"No," I said, turning on the water, "but I know a thing or two about being trapped."

I turned the water off, and neither of us spoke for a minute. I wanted to tell him about Rhodie—that I had this love once and that it was beautiful—but it clearly wasn't the kind of thing you talked about.

"You planning a prison break to get him out?"

"I just might," I said.

Beauregard looked back at me over his shoulder. "I like your style, Miss Dara." He shook his head, smiling. "I like your style."

The head cook walked between us on the way to his office, carrying his clipboard as if he held the names of people who were allowed to pass through the pearly gates. "Shush. This ain't social hour."

I stiffened, wondering if he was going to ask me into his office again. Beauregard noticed, and I felt him notice, but I couldn't stop the response. He didn't say anything.

Later, though, he walked me to the time clock. When we were about to go our separate ways outside, he asked, "You OK?"

I looked at him and said, "I'm fine."

He twirled his mustache and looked off to where the sun had just started setting. "I think we have a different definition of 'fine.'"

"I'll let you know if I need help," I told him, though I knew I wouldn't for fear of reprisal against him.

"You let me know *before* you need help. You hear me, Miss Dara?"

I smiled and nodded. He lit us both a cigarette and asked me if I needed a walk home. I knew the head cook stayed an hour or so later to lock up, so it wasn't the walk home that worried me. I worried about what would happen at 10 p.m.. I worried I might sleep too soundly and not hear him break in. I worried that I wouldn't get him on the first shot.

I smiled as best I could, not being a very good liar. "It's a nice cool night."

Beauregard scrunched his eyebrows, unable to find the connection between my safety and the weather—and truly neither could I—but he let me have it, as any Southern gentleman would.

"It surely is. You enjoy it then, on your walk, and I will see you tomorrow."

Walking off, I forced myself to think about pie, rather than thinking about the head cook. I felt Beauregard keeping his eye on me until I turned the corner and he couldn't see me anymore.

THE WOOD

That next week, Huddie and I stumbled into a plan on how we could get a private moment here and there, some time to talk, as friends are wont to do. It started with me grabbing the basket of Wednesday tomatoes pulled from the small vegetable field at the *precise* moment Huddie came in from his time in the fields.

I hoisted the heavy wicker basket off the ground, to the front of my waistline, feeling the cords on the sides tearing into my hands. Then I tried dragging the damn thing, only it kicked up so much dust that it hurt my eyes. Finally, I figured I'd push it along with my feet—not the wisest thing to keep tomatoes from bruising up even worse than they already were.

"Dammit."

Sighing and in need of a break before my temper flared, I stood up and looked out into the dry, open yard. Dozens of men walked around, moving much slower than they do outside prison—why rush, I suppose. The yard had no rocks or places to sit other than the dirt. A guard on horseback ambled by, holding his gun pointing up on his thigh. Although there was only that one person between me and any prisoners in the yard, I felt safe. The area was so open that no one would risk causing me harm—unlike the closed office in the kitchen.

Somewhere far off, I heard the dogs howling at their dinnertime— the dogs they turned loose on anyone who tried to escape. It was easy to run off, there being no fences, but almost impossible to make it much farther unless you could swim across the Brazos faster than those dogs could hunt you down—and many colored folks didn't know how to swim.

I brushed a fly away, and it came back again, with a friend. The two of them sounded like electric static in the still air. I swatted and turned to my right and there, tuning his guitar on a rock, was Huddie. I stepped back from the basket, pulled out a cigarette from my sweaty bra, and was walking over to say hello when the guard on horseback rode over and intercepted.

"Stay back, miss."

I motioned to the basket. "I was coming to talk to you about getting some help moving those vegetables."

He shook his fat head and said, "Not possible."

"Huddie there used to be in the kitchen, so he knows the routine. Maybe he could just step out and carry the basket. It'll only take a minute."

The guard squinted and scanned me, checking to see if I was crazy or not. "Miss, it takes only *a minute* to get stabbed or slammed against a wall until your eyes shoot out blood. This nigger here needs only *a minute*, you got me?" He spit on the ground in front of me. "Seems to me you wanted to work in a man's kitchen, so go work in the kitchen."

Huddie didn't make eye contact with me. He kept his head down and hit the strings a few more times. I flicked my cigarette ash into the dirt. When I looked up, Huddie gestured with his eyes to the Wood—a piece of wood that had been one of the walls of a shed, when there was a shed. Now it stood as the place prisoners could go behind to relieve themselves.

The Wood sat maybe fifty feet into the yard. Luckily, there were enough cacti and guajillo trees to block me for much of the way. With one eye on the guard, who trotted off toward the fields again, I headed over.

By the time I got to the Wood, Huddie was already standing there in its shadow. He gestured as if he was urinating, but he wasn't. I walked up on the side, partly hidden by a tall jumping cactus—so named because it will stretch out to hit you if you walk too close.

"Miss Dara, how you been?" he asked.

"The kitchen's not as much fun without you. And no one can carry a tune, though Beauregard continues to try."

"Sorry about that."

"We *all* are, Huddie. How you doing?"

"Writing songs in my head nearly every day—no matter how tired I am. It's almost me sleepwalkin' through everything, until it comes time for me to get to my guitar."

"Well," I said, doing my best to ignore the urination pantomime, "you look good."

"The kitchen serves us some mighty fine food here, that's probably why," he lied, smiling. He leaned in. "The head cook?"

"He's keeping to himself. Heard his boy broke his leg, so maybe his mind is occupied."

Huddie's shoulders dropped a full inch, and his face relaxed.

"Huddie, I'm so sorry you got in trouble on account of me."

"It ain't you. It's this fire I got inside me. I can't control it. It's why I's here."

"But so long in the Box—"

Huddie looked hard at me. "Now if he does come for you, you cut him. You work in a *kitchen*—so cut him."

Off behind him, I saw the guard on horseback coming back around and Huddie motioned that we ought to finish our conversation.

He pretended to fix himself up while I scooted to the back side of the cactus and dashed straight ahead to the outside wall of the kitchen building, thinking: *I will.* I will cut that smug bastard if he gets near me again.

× × ×

The next Wednesday, I volunteered to haul in the tomatoes again, to which Beauregard, who also hated lugging that basket, said, "Far be it from me to take away something that gives you so much joy."

When I walked out, Huddie strolled over to the Wood. I slinked down along the wall of the kitchen building again and dashed over from cactus to guajillo to cactus like a thief. When I got to the side of the Wood he nodded, holding air instead of a penis in his hand, thankfully.

"I was hoping you didn't have to use the Wood for real," I said.

He smiled and looked around to be sure we were safe. "Now *that* would surely be a memory you'd take to the grave."

"A grave that might come sooner than expected."

"How's the cook?"

"Still minding his own."

"Cut him on the throat and pull across."

I put my hand up, not needing too much more of that advice.

Huddie smiled and nodded. We stood there for a minute. I knew I wanted to talk with him about life, but I didn't know what to say. Then I figured *what the hell, we only have a moment. So let's talk.* "You ever have a wife, Huddie?"

He nodded slowly. "Married Lethe Henderson when I was young. She was maybe sixteen—maybe eighteen, not sure. She worked taking her clothes off after she'd run off from her mean husband. We got together the first night I saw her and soon had two little ones then—only I's the kind of father who's best when he's not a father. And I's a worse man to marry. Lord knows how many kids I got total." He nodded down at his imaginary penis. "This thing has caused me some trouble."

The crack of the gunshot flew off, and Huddie jumped a full inch in the air. He whispered, "You best go!"

I took off toward the kitchen building, nearly brushing that sneaky jumping cactus on the way. Behind me, several guards shouted, and the dusty ground shook with bodies being thrown down on it.

By the time I pressed my back to the kitchen's wall, three convicts—two Mexican and one black—were being led to the whipping posts, their hands tied behind them. One white man stayed down in the dirt. There was so much blood on his body and in the dirt that it looked as if they'd dumped buckets of it on him.

× × ×

I didn't see him for another few weeks—him being mostly out in the fields in the daytime—but every now and again we managed some time. In those moments I learned about how he'd played in the red-light district and worked his way around the country loving more women than either of us could count; and he learned that I missed having coffee with my daddy and that I secretly wanted to be a singer up on a stage.

In this way he replaced my Rhodie, or part of her. He filled the emotional space in me that craved talking with someone about things we loved and things we hated. That connection. Me and Huddie only had small moments together but that made them even more special, the way pressure creates diamonds.

On the days when I couldn't meet Huddie, I still found a way to be with him. If the wind blew just right—and if we'd finished the noisy work in the kitchen—Beauregard would turn off his radio and we would work quietly and slowly, listening to Huddie's guitar like we were in church.

MY SOUVENIR

The head cook snuck up while Beauregard and two inmates were unloading a big shipment of rice bags from the loading dock. He dropped his coffee mug and it shattered right behind me, causing me to jump about a mile up.

"Nervous?" he said, his nearly white hair recently shaved around his ears.

I thought about hitting him in the eyes with a handful of soapy water. "No."

The head cook shifted his feet apart a little more and crossed his muscled forearms in front of him. "Clean that up."

I squatted so I wouldn't have to bend and started picking up pieces of the mug. He watched me, and I knew this was the kind of display he appreciated.

"While you're down there," he said, tugging at his crotch.

I palmed a thick piece of mug, then took my good God damn time cleaning up the rest of it.

"Come to my office later, before you leave—after Beauregard punches out."

"I'm meeting my boyfriend then. He's coming here to pick me up."

"*My office.*" As he walked away, he kicked a few of the smaller pieces of mug across the room. "You get those pieces too, now. And you be sure Beauregard goes on his way tonight. He hangs around, and he might find himself looking for work tomorrow—hard to find with a bad reference."

The rest of the day I was a bit absentminded. Beauregard noticed, him having an eye for the feelings of other people. I brushed it off as a headache does, telling him I drank too much coffee before bed.

"Do like me," he said with that charming smile of his. "Stick to champagne."

About ten times an hour I felt my pocket for that sharp piece of mug I'd palmed. When I took out the trash I practiced how I'd swipe at him—or *it*—when I got a clear shot. Dig under and cut up with a sharp pull of the edge. I cringed. Even though I'd cleaned more fish than were mentioned in the Bible, something about cutting open a penis made my stomach flip. Because, contrary to Huddie's advice to cut the throat straight across, I wanted to cut him where he'd really feel it.

That afternoon Beauregard walked by me at my station in front of the sink. "You sure look pale though—and not in a fashionable way."

"Headache does that to me."

"Get back to it!" the head cook yelled, and I dropped the big metal spoon I was cleaning.

Beauregard picked up the spoon and handed it to me. "Maybe you ought to go home."

My hands were shaking. "No, I'm fine."

Beauregard yelled back to the head cook: "Miss Dara here has a headache. She needs to go home. I'll finish up her part."

"That's not how we work here. She'll stay just the way everyone else with a headache, unless I need to make special amends for ladies. You think?"

I shouted back, "I'm just fine."

"You don't forget to come see me before you go. We'll talk about this headache of yours then." I heard his lips slap wet, even from that far away. "Now get to work!"

Beauregard ushered his wheeled tray back to where the last pile of food trays was, loaded it up, and pushed it with considerable strain on his lean muscles over to the wall. I was so distracted that I didn't thank him for offering to finish my shift; I just kept running my gloved hand along the sharp edge of the mug piece, memorizing where it was so I'd be sure to use the right side. Hopefully, the cut would send the head cook down hard enough so I could run out and yell for a guard to come get me. If not, the head cook would tear me up for certain.

The end of the day came, as it does.

"Going out into the wild yonder!" Beauregard said, snapping his tan-and-white suspenders as he hoisted them up from where they were hanging around his hips. He hung his white uniform shirt on a hook by the time clock. "You all right now, Miss Dara?"

"Goodbye, Beauregard."

Beauregard nodded and walked off. The door barely snapped shut before the head cook was calling for me to come join him in his office. "Bring you and that female headache of yours in here."

I pressed the sharp edge of the mug into my thumb, wondering if I should wear rubber gloves or not. I decided not to, in order to get a good grip. *Grab under and cut up.*

I stepped into his office. It never changed. A desk, a clipboard, a typewriter. No photos, no calendar, nothing on the walls. And it always stank.

"We're not strangers to this," he said, smiling. "Shut the damn door."

I did, only this time I didn't pin myself against it, but gave myself a good foot to move around. I wondered what would happen once I cut him. Would he die or would he kill me? Would he be fired or would I? Would he go to jail or would I?

The head cook walked over. "Took me a while to figure why a woman would take job in here. First I thought it was to tease the men, especially those niggers—given your relations with Huddie. That was at first." He reached out and touched my breast, pinched around, found the nipple, grabbed and twisted. I tried to stand still. He pulled his fingers away, dragging out my nipple a full half-inch before letting go.

"Now," he sneered, "I know what you are. And what you are is something that can be arrested. You could end up working the kitchen as an inmate in one of them women's prisons—though maybe you'd enjoy that too much."

He turned and reached back for a file folder on his desk. Smiling, he dumped the file upside down and a bunch of letters dropped out. I recognized Rhodie's handwriting. They were addressed to me at "Imperial State Prison Farm: Kitchen." *Dammit.*

"I'm the second person to read these," he said, "them having to go through our security and whatnot. Luckily the lady who reads is a friend of mine. I'm not sure how it was for her to get through, but for me, reading these was better than a dirty book. But don't let me decide on my own," he said, smiling a wet smile. "Let's read a few highlights together, you and me."

I wished there was a word beyond "queasy" to describe the kind of sickness that squeezes up from your guts and covers you inside out, like oil. I pressed my teeth together to stop the panic and the vomit and the screams. I knew my eyes looked wild and my breathing was coming out in harsh puffs, but I couldn't control it all.

He unfolded the first letter and read the first line: "'*My Dara— Why aren't you writing back to me? Don't you love me anymore?*'" He sighed. "This is slow startin', but it ends full on." His weasel eyes scanned to the bottom, where he read: "'*When I am in bed at night I think of you—many times. Love, Rhodie.*'"

My face blazed red. I ran my thumb over the sharp edge.

The head cook laughed and slapped the letter on his leg. "Good hot damn! This here's the kind of *pornography* that'll ship us straight to Satan's door—"

I grabbed for the letter but he held it up in the air above my head. "Get your damn hands in your pockets, you damn pervert."

I put my hands in my pockets. Hatred filled me, not just against him but against everyone, including myself, who thought I was filthy because I'd loved Rhodie. It boiled up inside me.

The head cook picked up a second letter, one I noticed that he'd starred, and started reading: "'*There is a dance next month. I'm on the decorating committee. I wish we could go together. You and I could dance with each other and no one would care, as long as we had other companions. I wish you saw that that life is possible. Please write, Dara. You are killing me.*' Aw, ain't she sweet? What did you do, show her love then leave her in the dust? You harlot."

He dropped the letter and stepped closer to me then opened his hand and ran it over my tender nipple again.

"This what you want to do to girls?"

"Stop it." My heart squeezed and stayed that way, curled up inside my ribs.

"How's your headache?"

I didn't say anything.

"If you are one of those sick girls who like other girls, then I'm about the best thing to happen to you." He smiled. "I give you a *blanket* to hide under so people don't find out your dirty secret. So let's get to it. I give you a cover and you give me what I want. Who needs romance when we are just here to serve purposes to one another?"

I held back the urge to knee him in the privates, since I knew that wouldn't stop him from getting at me before I could run off. I paced myself, waiting until I could cut that bastard wide open.

"It's filthy what you want to do, you know. *Filthy.*" He unbuttoned his pants and pulled out his penis. "Maybe you just never had a man before. This will wake up your parts. You a virgin?"

"No," I lied.

He flopped his penis in his hand. "Seems I might need some help getting started."

I panicked. It might be too challenging to cut him when he was all soft like that.

"I'll tell you what to do, and you'll do it because I am your *boyfriend* now."

Behind me I heard the kitchen door open and shut. The head cook missed it, since he was preoccupied with stepping back to give me room to kneel down.

I reached out for his penis and held the smooth, sad thing in my hand. The head cook put his hand on top of mine, moving it up and down. "That's good, but I prefer other things," he said, now half-erect. "On your knees."

My stomach rolled around, filling with heat. I'd never hated anyone so much in my whole life—a hatred that made me want to kill him.

Off in the kitchen, I heard Beauregard telling the guard that he'd forgotten to punch out. He was talking louder than usual. I heard his footsteps running across the kitchen, into the hallway, past the punch clock, and toward the head cook's office.

I yelled out, "Beauregard!" before I pulled out the broken piece of mug and slashed wildly at the head cook's member, missing but catching a chunk of flesh on the outside of his hand. The meat cut open and I was hit with a thin spray of his blood. He looked at his hand.

Nearly wild, I scooped the letters up and tucked them into the back of my underwear, under my uniform.

Shaking the blood off, he screamed, "I'm going to strangle the life from you!"

I turned and opened the door just as Beauregard ran up. "Is that blood?"

The head cook screamed, "That wretched creature cut me!"

Beauregard yelled into the kitchen, "Guard!"

The guard—the same jarhead who fed the horses—rushed back. He saw the head cook with his pants down around his knee-high socks, holding his cut hand. "Billy, put your–" he turned to me, then back, then—"Put a part of yourself back in your pants."

The head cook raised his hand. A thick line of red blood dripped off the edge of it. "My damn hand!"

"Now," the guard said.

Beauregard looked at the bloody piece of mug in my hand. "You missed," he said.

I smiled, even though I was shaky. "Those things aren't easy targets."

"I never tried to hit one."

The guard took him by the arm. "Billy, I'm sorry, but we need to see the Warden."

My eyes welled up. All that panic and anger had to work itself out somehow.

Beauregard and I moved into the kitchen, which glowed in the strange light of the moon through the window. The guard walked by with the head cook, whose entire body was red with rage.

"Bulldyker whore!" he screamed.

Beauregard stepped closer to me. "If he calls me that," he said, "why, just imagine what he'd call you."

I forced myself to laugh, knowing that I couldn't show that the head cook had hit a nerve. I didn't want Beauregard to see that I might be a bulldyker. We were tight, and I wanted it to stay that way.

Beauregard looked down at my uniform, where all the blood had splattered. "You want that laundered?"

"I want that burned."

I was careful to keep my letters concealed as I set the ceramic piece on the edge of the huge metal sink and wiped my eyes again. My body calmed.

Beauregard looked at the bloody piece of mug. "Huddie must have rubbed off on you."

"You think they'll need it for evidence?"

He wiped his forehead with his hand. "No. The Warden does all he can to avoid reporting violence under his watch. They'll move him on—right quick—but they'll be no trial."

I looked out the kitchen window while I wiped away a tear with my hand, thinking: *What will happen to the head cook now?* He could be let out tonight and come to my shanty and do God knows what to me. I had Dead Eye, but that was never any guarantee.

"You OK?"

I nodded. "What do you suppose will happen to the head cook?"

"Maybe they'll transfer him to another prison. I don't know. The Warden's a decent man though, to be sure." Beauregard straightened up and twisted his mustache. "You come stay with me tonight?"

"No, I'll be all right," I said, not wanting to be that kind of woman. It was bad enough I was crying in front of him. "Thank you, though."

He picked up the ceramic piece of mug. "You want to wash the blood off?"

"No," I said. "I want to leave the blood on it and put it on my bedside table, so I can see it before I fall asleep every night."

"Miss Dara, I've said it before but dammit, I like your style."

Beauregard walked me down the hot hallways and out into the sunset, him blotting his neck and face the whole way, saying "Whew" every now and again.

At the end of the walk out I'd stopped crying and the anger had gone away, leaving room for just the fear of the head cook's retribution. "Thank you, Beauregard."

"You don't mention it, Miss Dara."

He was about as decent a man as there was. A good friend. My heart swelled knowing how much he'd risked to help me.

Beauregard watched me turn the corner on my way home. I had trouble walking since my legs were shaking so badly I thought I'd fall over. I hadn't shook that badly since right before Rhodie's mother hit me on the side of the head.

I took in a deep lungful of heavy Texas air, thankful for the cool breeze coming by, and stabilized myself. As I walked, I worried myself nearly to death about the head cook coming to hunt me down—how many ways there were to get in my shanty. All those windows I'd appreciated before were now little pathways to my murder.

When I got home, two stray cats were hanging around more than usual, and I made the decision to take them in. Maybe the company would quiet me.

"Come on in."

The strange little things padded in right after me, sniffed the air and looked around, as if they couldn't decide if my place was *sophisticated* enough for them. When I sat down on my mostly green love seat, the little one purred at my feet, demure-like, while the big one jumped up on me with complete disregard for the amount of weight she hauled around. He damn near left bruises on my thighs. I decided to name them Cucumber and Pickle; a cucumber being bigger than—and yet related to—a pickle.

I dropped the stack of letters from Rhodie on the couch next to me. It made me angry to see them all ripped open and torn into. *That bastard.*

"I'd love to have some bourbon," I explained to the cats, "but I need to be *watchful* tonight. Either of you know how to fight?"

Cucumber responded with a deep, long meow.

I nodded. "I'm glad I can rely on you for help."

We sat still, me with my hand on the letters. Something scampered in a tree outside, and spikes of adrenaline shot through the middle of my body. Was that the head cook?

He's going to kill me, I thought. He's going to punch his way through my busted up door or my thin windows and he's going to beat me and kick me and strangle me and Lord knows what until I am defiled and, eventually, dead. I should have listened to Huddie and killed the bastard rather than going for the dramatics.

The wind blew. Of all the nights, there had to be wind that night. It scraped and gouged at my shanty, and with every little flutter I nearly went crazy with anxiety.

Pickle purred. He rested his narrow, soft head back down on Rhodie's letters.

"No sleep for me tonight, Pickle."

I set my gun down and stood up—disrupting my new brood—to get myself some coffee, then called the cats back over to my lap.

"These letters are from someone I love," I explained to them while they nestled down. "Her name's Rhodie. Rhodie wrote me all these letters while all I did was hide out, kitties, *hide out.* I tricked myself

into thinking I was the strong one, but that's not true. And look what
came of it: I hid out, but got caught anyway."

I pulled the stack of letters over and opened the one on top. Together, me and Cucumber and Pickle read those letters from Rhodie
until my face flushed pink from all my crying. To read all the longing
and the love in her words. Even while she'd been betrayed by me not
writing back, Rhodie hung on and saw the best; she hoped for the
best in me to come out again. She waited for me to reply. Meanwhile,
I'd been concerned only with myself.

Not writing to her was probably the worst thing I could have done.

"But then, if she'd have stopped writing," I told Pickle, "I wouldn't
be sitting here with you two—not that you aren't lovely, but you do
smell bad—and a gun, waiting to die. Why couldn't she just let me go?"

Cucumber meowed at me.

"I know," I said to him. "I hear it. I hear that I sound upside down.
I didn't tell her I wasn't going to write, so she kept writing, and then
I blame her for writing. Really, I blame her for loving me. That's it.
And now this is my penalty—this horseshit with the head cook is my
penalty."

The night clouds moved across the moon outside my living room
window. I leaned forward. The love seat scratched the backs of my
knees.

There, in the moonlight with my new cats, I burned all of Rhodie's
letters, one after the other. The room reeked of torched paper, but I
couldn't open a window or a door for fear of the head cook finding a
way in.

Eventually, the coffee can stopped smoking. I closed my eyes and
counted to ten, hoping to relax. It didn't work. I started over again—
one, two, three—then I heard another noise outside.

"What's that?"

I jolted up and cocked Dead Eye, looking around for the man who
was going to kill me—but he never came in. I held that gun until my
arm fell asleep, but he never came.

× × ×

The next morning, tired like I had the Black Death, I woke up to a crick in my neck so bad that I couldn't turn my head past center to the right. It was still early, but I didn't want to be in my shanty any more. Better to sit around at work, surrounded by people, then to sit here alone.

When I walked outside, carrying my other uniform—the clean one—I looked over and there, leaning back against the wall of my house, was Beauregard, sound asleep. He must've stayed there all night. That was probably who I'd heard creeping around.

I nudged his work boot with mine and he jolted up. "What? What?"

"Beauregard, you keeping post for me?"

He rubbed his neck and brushed the dirt off his black pants. "Who, me? No. I just had one too many at Maria's Roundabout and decided this looked as good as spot as any to rest up." He stood up.

I smiled. "Let's get to work."

We walked on toward the prison along the quiet morning streets. We didn't say anything during our walk, just enjoyed the misty pink morning on a day when I was still alive and in the care of a good friend.

× × ×

After we entered the kitchen building, Beauregard and I went our separate ways.

I walked out to the mailroom to ask that they return any letters that might come to me from the University of Texas, San Antonio. The woman running the window, presumably the one who read all of the incoming letters, shot me looks that said I was one step up from a dung beetle, but agreed with a curt nod of her tiny, pearl-earringed head.

She said: "Return them. Best to do that. *Best to.*"

"Thank you."

"Hmm."

I walked away with bigger things to worry about than her judg-ment. My stomach tightened up and soured from the stress of going back to that kitchen. *Would the head cook be there now?*

No one except Jesus with his cross ever walked a longer walk as I did that day, across the yard and down the hallway into the kitchen. With every step, I felt nearer and nearer to my death.

When I stepped in, Beauregard walked up to me, reapplying his mustache wax in the dull morning light. "No sign of him yet," he said.

I nodded and pushed some of my thin brown hair, damp with nervous sweat, behind my ear. I looked around, checking if the head cook's door was open.

Beauregard scrunched his forehead in concern. "You fine to work today?"

My stomach flipped and flopped, but I smiled. "I am."

"Let's go then. Coffee time."

Beauregard and I set it all up, precise as a clock. The entire time, I waited for the head cook to come in, but he never did.

An hour later, the Warden—his chest puffed out—walked into the kitchen. His boots made a steady clomp on the floor as he approached me over by the sink, where I was mashing corn for hominy.

He pulled me aside, next to a bag of onions that was almost as round as me. "Everything going well with you today?"

"Yes, sir," I said, not sure where to put my arms, so I tucked them behind my back in a soldier pose.

"The guard told me last night about how he found the head cook bleeding yesterday in his office, with you."

I looked at my shoes, then up again, determined to not take a guilty stance. "Yes."

"Well, that is not how I run my ship here." He scratched uncom-fortably at his right sideburn. "You won't be seeing the cook anymore. He's gone. Gone for good. You understand me?"

I let out a breath. "Thank you."

"He was taken away last night, with his family, and relocated under strict orders never to come to Sugar Land, Texas again. Not just the prison, the whole town. If he comes here or anywhere near you ever again, he will be arrested."

I nodded, relief softening me.

"He mentioned some strange things though. He talked about you and a woman named Rhodie and a packet of letters."

I prayed that I wouldn't blush—that I could hold it all in and tell this lie. "Letters?"

"Yes." He eyed me up. "Of a personal nature."

"Letters often are."

The Warden smiled. "Yes, they are."

"Did he have letters to give to me?" The more I talked, the easier the lie came. "Because I don't know anyone named Rhodie."

For a moment, I wondered if he would call my parents and ask them, if he would take this further. Then I reminded myself that I was in the adult world now, and there would be no calling of parents.

But what about the woman in the mailroom? No, the head cook wouldn't say he got the letters from her or she'd be fired and maybe sent to jail herself. I'm sure he said he found them or something.

The Warden sighed. "The cook had it in for you, as he probably would have for any woman I dared hire. He's no doubt telling tales out of turn to make a case."

I nodded, thinking that I had just experienced a miracle.

"Please accept my apology," he said in a very low tone.

To keep his privacy and keep myself under control, I only smiled.

The Warden gave a quick nod, turned, and walked out without saying goodbye, stealing a pinch of corn on the way.

All through the day I thought about miracles, how many happen that we just fail to see. Miracles happened to me all the time. *All the time.*

I wished Huddie was back on kitchen duty with me so we could share a few words about what had happened. Beauregard was a true friend, to be sure, but we couldn't really *talk*. He and I tossed around jokes and snapped towels and hid each other's keys, but Huddie and I had this unspoken sort of intimacy. I knew I could tell him what had happened with the head cook and my feelings about it all and he would understand. If Huddie were to ask me how I was getting on, I wouldn't just say "Fine," the way I did with everyone else.

In the breakfast line that morning, Huddie nodded and I gave him a slow nod back, letting him know that something had happened. He tilted his head and I shrugged a bit, telling him I was OK, despite what had taken place. I blinked hard, saying I had held my own. He bumped out a tight nod and I smiled back, acknowledging that yes, we would talk more about it at our next time near the Wood.

The following Wednesday we met at the Wood and I gave him the quick story, saying the head cook came at me with his pants down and I cut him.

"You sure can take care of yourself."

"I'm learning to," I said.

"Where's he at now?"

"They sent him away with threats not to return." I looked down at the dirt. "Gave me some terrible nights, though, wondering if he might try to come back anyway. But I don't think he will. He has family—a son he loves, Beauregard said."

Huddie nodded and eyed me up, seeing if what I said rang true, or if I was trying to keep him from getting riled up again. "Good. Good." He checked over his shoulder for the guard. "You lock up your house, now, just in case."

"I do."

"And you keep something under your pillow?"

"I do."

He nodded and pretended to finish up. "Good, then I can sleep better too."

I GO, YOU GO

In the beginning of 1924, Huddie played his first concert for the guards and the families of the guards in the yard. This is how the plans for his escape—and mine—got started.

The Warden had chairs set in family groupings with the guards sitting—or standing—near their wives and children, who were all dressed as if the Royal Family was coming for tea. I'd wished Rhodie could have been there with me to see it, her loving music the way she did.

On concert day, I leaned back against the warm wall of the kitchen building and lit a cigarette on my break. Huddie wandered up the middle of the crowd to the cleared area, his upper arm held tightly by a guard who matched his height.

"Hi there," he said to the crowd, smiling his sad smile under the hot sun as he took a seat on the graying picnic table that had been set up in lieu of a stage. His guitar sat in a case on the ground, like a casket, next to him. The scene was picturesque, to be sure—all grays and blues against the whites of his eyes.

The grass was Texas-brown and worn down with big spots where dust blew up. When the breezes came through, the women covered their mouths with thin handkerchiefs. I knew enough to position myself close to a wall so I could turn my head to one side to avoid the dust.

Huddie said to the crowd, "I's fixin' to start playing when the Warden says it's time and stop playing when the Warden says it's time." He opened his guitar case, pulled out his beat-up twelve-string, and turned the tuning pegs until the strings hit a certain note. "I know so many songs that unless you stop me, Warden, we could be here all week."

The crowd relaxed a bit, put at ease by Huddie's deference to the Warden.

"We looking forward to it, Huddie," the Warden said from where he stood off to the side, up towards the front. His back faced the sun so his shadow stretched out extra long in front of him on the cracked dirt.

Huddie nodded with his gap-tooth grin, wearing those gray, dingy stripes, his face shiny with sweat, his sad eyes looking out. He brought his hand up the neck of his guitar with such familiarity that he didn't need to look down when he started playing. And when he did, he changed—his face opened up, and his eyes took a joy in them. His neck got loose, and he straightened up a bit. And when he sang, he sang as if no one was watching.

Huddie's fingers moved over the fretboard. Sometimes he'd get playful with it and pull a note out by pressing and wiggling the string with his thick, dry index finger, bending the music. Sometimes he'd get low and gritty and hunch over, playing real close to his guitar—an intimate moment just those two were sharing.

His songs had stories to them. The stories were about heartbreak and dark rooms and running free. All the while, he strummed and beat that guitar along in the background, having more fun than I'd ever seen someone have while making music.

The side door clicked. Beauregard slinked around the building to join me. He lit his hand-rolled cigarette and nodded off to where the audience was sitting around the picnic tables, all watching Huddie.

Beauregard squinted. "Damn that man, huh?" He blew out smoke with his words. "Maybe you're right. Maybe his music *should* be free of this place."

I knew from his coded talk around the kitchen that Beauregard went to mixed-color joints to dance, so I assumed he meant that the music should be out there to change people's minds about colored folks—but I wanted confirmation.

"Why do you say that?" I asked.

"Well." He looked off. "What do you think those people thought when they first came here to listen to Huddie?"

"I think they were curious about what a Negro could do."

"Carnival-like?"

"Maybe."

"Now what you think they think?"

"I think they just look forward to hearing the music."

"That's right," he said. "Huddie got them to think past color, or maybe think about color a different way."

I nodded.

"If he gets out there— out past these walls —he could open a lot more minds," Beauregard leaned in. "Besides which, I've always wanted to be involved in a prison break."

We settled back and looked over at Huddie, sharing his joy—not to be generous, but just because he had so much that it had to go somewhere, or it would cause him to explode. At the end of the first song, the new head cook called for Beauregard and me to get our asses back in there.

"Presumably he wants the rest of us as well," Beauregard said.

"Presumably."

The new head cook was the polar opposite of the old cook—thin and nervous as a compass in a box of magnets. Old enough that the knuckles on his hands had started to knot up.

"Get moving!" the head cook shouted to us, not leaving the kitchen.

I stubbed out my cigarette in the dirt. Beauregard tapped out the lit head of his and put the stub in his pocket for later.

"You serious about a prison break?" I asked.

"You joking? They'd arrest me and put me in here where these Negroes would tear my handsome self up. *Animals*." He smiled.

× × ×

The next Sunday there were more people than the week before—
maybe even a Yankee or two among them, with their dark pants and
city haircuts. I stood along the kitchen wall, alone in the shade with
my cigarette.

Huddie started up some low, slow blues, and I closed my eyes. I
let the smoke float out of me. I knew the trash was buzzing near me,
but I didn't care. I just leaned back and felt the hot brick through my
shirts while I listened to that man do what he was built to do.

Huddie pulled a string or two in the middle of a chord so it sounded like two people playing.

"Whew boy!" someone shouted out, followed by a spontaneous
clapping of the crowd.

The Warden had wandered up, but I didn't notice until he cleared
his throat and I opened my eyes again.

"Oh, Warden! Pardon me."

"Far be it from me to pardon anyone—that's the governor's job.
That's him over there. The governor. Governor Neff, come down on
my invitation to see Huddie perform. Next week he's bringing the
whole family."

"Imagine that," I said.

"There's something driving his music, don't you think? Like it has
a mind and a soul all its own."

Not wanting to ruin the moment, I just nodded.

"All right, I best be going," the Warden said before he headed up to
signal that Huddie could play two more songs.

× × ×

A few weeks passed without much changing except the length of the
days and the treads on my work shoes. The new head cook, looking
as nervous as he always did, walked out from his office in his clean
white uniform and posted our monthly schedule on the door. Mine
had been the same since I'd been there, so I didn't bother looking.

Beauregard whistled when he looked at the schedule, then strolled over to cut up chunks of bread. "How did you do it?" he asked me.

I was busy measuring out twenty-eight cups of water to get boiling. "Hold on, I'm counting."

"Miss Dara, you got Sunday off!"

"What?" I dropped the metal cup back into the deep sink with a loud clink and raced over to the long schedule sheet. Sure enough, there it was—*Sunday off*. "How the hell?"

Beauregard asked, "You have something on the head cook?"

Just when he said that, the head cook walked out from his office with his budget sheets. "Might be she has somethin' on the Warden."

I ignored them. *Sunday off!*

"I lot damn!"

It took a will of mind to keep focused, but I went back to counting my twenty-eight cups and adding my special seasoning—two dozen shakes of garlic salt—to the water. I moved the pot to the stove and put a tray over the pot to get it to boil faster. In one hour or so, I could tell Huddie in line that I'd be able to see a full God damn show!

One hour.

Never in my decade at Imperial State Prison Farm did a pot of potatoes take so long to boil as it did that day. I pulled the tray off again to check.

"Stop checking on it, woman!" Beauregard laughed.

"I'm just adding some garlic salt."

"Why do you think garlic salt is going to fix every meal?"

"Because it does."

I waited a minute before checking on the mashed potatoes again. They looked done enough, dammit, so I moved them off the heat to get the process going.

The trick to making mashed potatoes at Sugar Land—on the rare time when we were allowed—was to dump the hot potatoes into the food prep sink and run water to cool them off, then pour on the milk *before* pressing them down. You wanted them cooled down before

you added the milk, otherwise—as I found out in the early days—
the lumpy starch takes over.

I wheeled the cart over, slid the hot pot onto it, and dumped the
potatoes into another metal pot in the sink with more splashing
than usual.

"Slow it down, Miss Dara, or you are going to be home Sunday
healing from steam burns!" Beauregard yelled.

I kept mashing. By that point, my right arm had grown larger
than my left from all the pressing down at work. I felt masculine—all
bulky, big, and sweaty—but it didn't bother me because in the prison
it gained me some respect and, as Beauregard told me on more than
one occasion, it eased the minds of his lady friends when they came
to pick him up. Clearly I was no competition.

When the potatoes were mashed, I scooped them back into the
original tin with a huge shovel of a spoon and wheeled them on to the
line, where the hominy usually went—only we'd run out of lye so we
scrounged extra potatoes.

I stood in the serving line to the right of Jackson, who hadn't had
a fever since that last heat wave, quickly scooping potatoes for all the
white men first. Jackson, meanwhile, scooped gravy as if this was his
first day on the line.

"Anyone love you, Jackson?" I asked him.

"What?"

"You scooping as if you got no one at home who loves you. Like you
want to stand here *all day* and scoop gravy!"

Jackson looked at me with his wimpy brown eyes and stuck his
bottom lip out. "You need me to hurry, you can just ask, rather than
casting aspersions against my family."

"It was a valid dang question."

"You are peculiar," he said—but he scooped faster.

Finally, the colored inmates—and halfway through, Huddie. He
took his time down the line, with that faraway look I had come to see
as the look of an artist composing.

"Those any good?" he asked of my mashed potatoes.

"I'm afraid they might be a little tough, but listen to what I want
to say. I have Sunday off!" I reminded myself to keep my voice down,
with nosy Jackson eyeing me sideways. "I'll be here to watch you play."

Huddie smiled the smile of a man who didn't get himself excited
about much. "Well then, maybe I's playing *two* special songs that day."

"Who's the other one for?" I asked, holding down my blush behind
the bars.

His wet eyes looked up, serious. "I've decided that the last song
will be an ask for a pardon from Governor Neff."

I scooped into the next tray. "Governor Neff promised not to pardon prisoners when he was campaigning—though if anyone could
get an exception, it'd be you."

"I surely will! And when I get out"—he turned to look me right in
the eye—"you need to go, too."

Jackson interrupted. "Move on down, boy!"

"Promise me."

"I'll get out someday," I said to Huddie, who stood there on the
verge of trouble until I said, "I promise." Only then did he move along,
humming low and bobbing his head.

THE GOV'NER

On March 13, 1924, Huddie walked across the patted-down dirt of the yard and over to the gray picnic table where he always sat to perform. Two guards flanked him—one who hid his eyes under his cowboy hat and one who clearly ate too many donuts. When Huddie walked by, a few of the women looked away—there were always a few—as if the sight of a man in dirty prison stripes touched them too deeply to bear.

Governor Neff sat at the center table, wearing a wrinkled mint-green suit. His genteel wife hung onto his sleeve, clearly feeling all the mercies of a woman who had it in her heart to believe that the good in every man will surface, if given the chance.

It had taken me two hours looking through my clothes so I could be sure to seem *casual* when I went to see Huddie that Sunday. I wore a dress, of course. It would have been possible to wear trousers, I suppose—if I had lived in New York City or dated some man that bought art, but here at Imperial State Prison Farm—which everyone had started calling 'Sugar Land'—I wore a loose dress just short enough not to drag in the dusty dirt.

My dress had sleeves that went down almost to my elbows. It was pale yellow with a wide white collar and white polka dots. There were two buttons—one on each hip—that I could button in to give me some dimension beyond a big girl in a bag. I didn't feel attractive or unattractive; I felt as if I would blend in.

By the time I got to the creaky prison gate, I smelled like yeast and heated-up rose lotion. Huddie had just started tuning his guitar.

I stepped over patches of gnarly grass struggling through the dirt like wire.

The prisoners weren't allowed to attend, of course, but we all knew they listened from the fields and inside the tanks. The guards loved working those Sundays, too.

The yard stretched out about half an acre or so until it sectioned off into plantation rectangles. I stood along the back between the visitors and the kitchen building. I didn't feel at home with the prison staff when I wasn't working, but I didn't feel at home with the visitors either. It was such a usual feeling, this lack of home and fitting in, that I hardly noticed it back then.

There I was, in my yellow dress, smoking and fluffing out the back to dry a line of perspiration making its way down my well-insulated spine when the Warden came up—his black shoes shining and his tan pants extra crisp. Something about him said he did his own ironing. "Huddie already wore down a few spots on that fretboard, didn't he?"

I nodded. Yes, yes he had. "Thank you for this day off."

"I got the idea to give him the guitar from you, so this is my way of thanking you—though my thank you can only be for the next two months."

"Two months!" I must have looked stupid being happy to have those Sundays off in order to come *back* to work.

The Warden laughed so loudly that he had to cover it with a cough. "My wife couldn't make it. She's sick at home with the girls." He shifted on his feet. "You got any family here?"

"No, sir."

"Call me Warden, Miss Dara." The Warden took in a deep breath. "Yes, ma'am, I'm glad I gave Huddie that guitar to play. Speaking of which, I need to go shake hands with the governor and all the family he brought. Enjoy your day, Miss Dara."

"I certainly will, Warden."

I watched him walk off, in those perfectly creased tan pants, and I thought, *he's not so tough.*

Huddie played his first song, about a woman who worked on a farm and had to carry around her sick child with her. He was telling all these folks with their delicate hats that there were people out there who loved their children but needed money and were forced to make decisions surely more difficult than whether to dress them in knee-high socks or tights. Huddie knew the limits, though, so he eased up and moved to a strong, thumping song about a man whose wife really enjoyed dancing—though mostly without him, if you know what he meant.

Huddie's hand glided up and down the fretboard between each lazy chord strum, moving the melody like butter in a pan. There was no hate and killing in that glorious music that he sang out those long stretches of road past the white prison building that made him look so small. He sang loud, with his foot stomping.

A group of five kids danced around in circles and most of the men clapped their hands on their thighs. I pulled a few pieces of tobacco from my tongue rather than spitting them out, waiting for the next song, the one Huddie told me he'd written for me.

I looked at him, and his white eyes looked back. He strummed quietly now, so the words could be heard:

Bars can brand a man, like cattle in the field—
Wherever you go, they see those lines,
And they always bring you back,
Back to the fields where the animals are.

That was what Huddie sang for me. With those words, he told me to get out of Sugar Land before I got branded as the woman who works in a prison, but he didn't know about the brand I was *really* afraid of getting.

Huddie didn't know what I'd done in a different small Texas town a few years earlier. He didn't know how I kissed Rhodie and moved my hands up the sides of her thin dress. The dress she said she wore for me, along with her butterfly scarf. He didn't know how we waited until her parents and her brother went to New Mexico and then we spent the night together in her room—a night with thunderstorms and lightning that lit up our bodies in the dark. He didn't know how grateful we were that the thunder covered the sounds we made that night from any folks walking by. That patch of freckles on the back of her knee.

Sweat gathered at the inside of my thighs. I was developing a rash from them rubbing together so much in that damn dress. I lit another cigarette. The sun was almost down. Someone far away, outside the prison walls, set off what sounded like a firecracker—or maybe it was a gunshot, or the whip.

I clapped as Huddie finished my song. He sang a few more while my mind drifted backwards—back to Midland and Rhodie.

Half an hour later, Huddie plucked a few chords and called out, "The last one of the day!"

Nervous, he cleared his throat more times than usual. He paused with his big hand resting on the part of the guitar shaped the same as the curve of a woman's body. This was the one for the governor, and it was a big gamble since he could risk pushing too hard and angering the man.

Huddie looked up, all deep creases and milky eyes. "This here is a song for you, Governor Neff."

The governor smiled one of those smiles that arrogant men with too much power smile. His wife snuggled up closer as Huddie started singing: "Please, Governor Neff . . ."

From along the wall it was hard to see the Governor, but I could see his wife. I watched her lean over to her husband and whisper in his ear. I watched her sit back then—as if she'd done as much as she could do. The Governor put his arm around the back of her white lawn chair and I got the feeling that he had made up his mind about Huddie.

× × ×

But afterwards, months passed without any word from Governor Neff. The prisoners teased Huddie, quoting the song he'd sung while they knelt on one knee saying things like: "Gov'ner Gov'ner, please oh *please* most kind sir. I'm a'begging!" and "I'll be a good nigger, you'll see!"

A few times this happened in the food line, and I felt his embarrassment that I was a witness—his embarrassment and his rage. Fighting it, Huddie shrugged and smiled his thin-lipped smile, going along with the God damn joke, making as if the mocking noises around him were nothing more than the buzzing of some thirsty mosquitoes.

Some of the guards even got to calling him "The Gov'ner." A pack of chickens pecking the weakest one to death.

Usually Huddie had a boast or two to come back with when people got on him—or a reminder that he often held the whip in the fields, but in this case, he stood mute, responding only with that thin smile and the anger I saw boiling up in his eyes. More and more, he sat alone in the dining hall or came in last so he didn't have time to sit down before the guards called everyone back. When he played his guitar in the yard, he stopped taking requests.

One Wednesday, a few months after he'd sung for the governor, Huddie looked up at me and nodded in the breakfast line, letting me know we could meet by the Wood again. I clicked my tongue to confirm and plopped a thick wad of gravy on another tray, wondering if it was the lack of dietary changes that caused near half of Sugar Land to always be suffering from stomach troubles.

For the rest of the day, I kept checking the clock, which moved slower than a snail on sand. Beauregard finally told me to "focus on being less obvious."

Doing my best to look innocent, I said, "What do you mean?"

He walked over, carrying one of the longer knives he'd been sharpening. "What I *mean* is that when you volunteer to carry the Wednesday vegetables, I look out the window and can see Huddie faking a bladder emergency that needed tending to at the Wood. So *be less obvious.*"

I gave him a sheepish look and said, "All right then," before sneaking another look at the clock.

Beauregard threw up his hands and gave me an exasperated, "Lord, woman!"

At 3 p. m. on the dot, I took my secret, strange route around the scraggly plants to where Huddie was standing, hand out in front of his crotch, pretending to urinate.

"How are you doing?" I asked.

"I know fighting will surely ruin my chances of getting out, if I have any." He gritted his teeth. "I's coming undone." He looked down at me in the shade of the Wood, his forehead wrinkling up and bags like mudslides under his eyes. "One more Gov'ner joke and I just might take a life."

"Keep going just a little while longer."

"They all want me to crack. They pushin' me to the edge."

"You know that anything you do is going to hurt *you* more than *them*."

Huddie shook off into the air, stood up, and got ready to go back out to the yard. "I's trying." He sighed and stared up at the sky, blue and clear.

With a flick of his hand too fast to see, Huddie threw a small flat blade made of some discarded metal. It landed in front of me, causing the smallest cloud of dust to stir up. I grabbed the blade up and shoved it in my pocket.

Huddie turned and nodded his thanks to me in the rectangular shadow of the Wood before straightening up and walking back out into that dustbowl of a yard.

WHAT SAILORS KNOW

No news came from the governor for ten full months. The heckling kept up, but more and more folks moved on to some new prey in the prison. Huddie got back to playing his guitar and, most important, he didn't kill anyone.

Then it happened. I picked up the newspaper that the new head cook always left for us to read after he'd finished with it, and there it was—the announcement that Huddie would be getting out early, and in only three days.

February 21, 1925. *Clemency. Mercy. Parole.*

Huddie was getting released. He'd done it. He'd gone a few years on a twenty-year sentence and got it cut back with a *song*.

When I told Beauregard he twisted his mustache and said, "Seems you'll have to find a new best friend."

I smiled. "Seems."

He wiped his hands on a towel hanging out of his uniform pocket and followed me into the kitchen to start our day. "That's the power of music for you. And he's got it—that power all the way through his black bones. You know what they are calling him around here?"

"Lucky?" I said.

"They call him Lead Belly. That's his singing name."

"He never asked me to call him that."

"He didn't give it to himself. People insist on giving you a name when they know you've become someone beyond the name you were given."

That day, I waited and waited for him through all the colored in-mates in the breakfast line. No Huddie.

Later, while Beauregard and I were cleaning up he gave me the news: "I just heard. Huddie's in the Box."

"What for?"

"For getting early release would be my guess."

"They putting him in for the full three days?" I asked, dumping a pot of water into the sink.

"Unless he reacts. He reacts, then Governor Neff will surely pull his pardon, and he'll be in the Box for a long while more. Plus he'll be back in here for his full sentence—and then some."

Three other prisoners helped in the kitchen that day. As usual, they said nothing, but I noticed them giving looks back and forth. I wondered if they wanted Huddie to get out. How would I feel if someone got out on a song, literally, while I was in for my full term? Plus, now their music would be gone.

I said, "He can do it."

Beauregard shrugged. "You sure are sunny side up on this one, Miss Dara."

He didn't know it, but I had something riding on Huddie's release. If he could go against his urges and keep strong and go on with a normal life, then so could I.

"I know he can do it," I said, though I honestly wasn't too sure.

× × ×

Those three days dragged on and I prayed for Huddie every night, hoping that the angels would watch over and keep him strong. Every morning Beauregard reported back to me that nothing had happened. Huddie held tight.

At night in my shanty, my mind created imaginings of what he might be enduring and how he might fail. When these thoughts overwhelmed me, I ate a piece of lemon cake. Then I focused on the cake—the way it damn near dissolved in my mouth, it was that good.

On the third day, with me a few pounds heavier, I looked up in the breakfast line and there was Huddie, leading the colored inmates in their procession. He walked slow but head high and back strong. His skin looked powdery, and his eyes sank deep into his thin face.

The pride I felt nearly split me open, to be sure!

He stalled in front of me as he waited for his tray. "They shined the light on me," he said. "I's out. This is it."

I smiled through the bars. "That's what I hear."

The inmates behind him gave him some time.

Huddie smiled, looking right into my eyes, and nodded. "Today then."

Then Jackson butted in. "Move on down, nigga."

"Jackson, you mind yours!" I said.

Jackson stood up a little straighter, that spineless monkey's ass.

"Life is more than stewed tomatoes," I said, and I turned back to Huddie. "I'm so happy for you."

Huddie lowered his head, not wanting my emotional outbursts to get me—or him—in any trouble. He slid down. Soon as he grabbed his tray, he turned around and leaned over so I could see him. "Now you get to leaving yourself."

I smiled and nodded, holding back the tears as Huddie walked out across the mass of gray uniforms with metal trays.

Later that evening, me wondering if they made Huddie wait all day on purpose, Beauregard ran into the kitchen as I was cleaning up. "Take out the garbage!"

"Now, Beauregard, you know this is your day."

"Take it out!"

"Oh shoot!"

I ran out to the cans, grabbing the first one hard by its metal handle, and got to the edge of the gate just in time to see Huddie walk off into the pink Texas sunset.

× × ×

Of course, Huddie was back in prison again come 1930—another prison, this time for attempted homicide. I don't say "of course" to mean that because he was a man or because he was a Negro that he was, *of course*, back in prison. What I mean to say is this: so let's say you're so blessed that you can sing your way out of prison—*then what?* Can you behave against the only way your muscles know how to move, the only life you know how to live?

The way I see it, Huddie reached inside and found his gift and he used it to make his life a lot better than it could have been. And given how strong the winds were pushing back, moving even a few feet is a miracle—any sailor will tell you that.

HAIRNET

The Warden, that big-shirted man with no ass whatsoever, had recorded some of Huddie's music before he was pardoned, when he'd played on Sundays. It was expensive to record, but the Warden said that anything priceless is.

After Huddie left, the Warden started to call me in a few afternoons a week after I'd packed the bag lunches, and we'd listen to Huddie's music. Neither one of us ever called him Lead Belly. When I would sit there with the Warden, sharing cigarettes and listening to Huddie sing, I'd remember how I promised Huddie that I'd get out of this prison—not knowing then, of course, that it'd be with the Warden himself.

See, I'd become comfortable in those walls. Somewhere along the line, I'd decided I'd rather live *unseen* than live in fear. So, ignoring my promise to Huddie, I stayed.

Most days after work, I'd walk back to my shanty, feed Cucumber and Pickle, maybe write a little to Rhodie or Mama and Daddy, soak my feet, and go to bed under the picture Rhodie drew for me of those two black circles with love in between. Some days, though, the routine would switch up, and I'd stay at the prison so the Warden and I could play evening cards—with surprisingly decent liquor, considering Prohibition and all.

Every now and again, a guard or two would join us, and sometimes I'd even get relaxed enough to take off my hairnet and sport my neatly trimmed haircut. Be a tiny bit of myself.

That's when one of the guards, a gorilla named Ken who said half his words as if they were sliding off a plate, said, "Whoa—now *that* is a hairstyle!" Telling me I'd be arrested if I weren't already in jail for daring a man's cut like that.

"It's *practical*," I said. "You work in the kitchen and tell me different. It's practical!"

The Warden, always a lover of the practical, shushed him. "Ladies come in all shapes and sizes and deserve our respect, Ken."

When he said that, it made it somehow all right for me to sit with my legs uncrossed. It made it OK that I didn't carry a purse. It made it OK that makeup felt like a colorful lie on my face.

"All right then, let's get out the bourbon and get to playing," Ken said, trying to make it better with the Warden.

The Warden made a good attempt at a smile and pushed back from his desk. "I got the best bar in the city right here, as you all know." He was trying to be funny, but his words were running slow and his skin looked gray.

"Warden, you all right?" I asked. "Warden?"

The Warden turned his back to Ken and me. In front of him, on the brown-paneled wall, was a huge, sun-bleached Confederate flag that he'd hung with four thumbtacks. He stared at it for a minute before opening his low cabinet and slowly mixing up our drinks.

We waited. Ken lit another cigarette in the already smoke-heavy room. He slouched across the wood table toward me, moving the ashtray with him.

"The Warden's wife passed two weeks ago," he whispered. "He didn't want anyone to know, so he made the guards swear secrecy. That's why he was off last week. It's just him and those two young girls now."

"I'm sorry, Warden," I said, trying to catch his eye.

He cleared his throat. "She went fast, but we knew—best of both worlds. Now, what's the wild card?"

"I call suicide Jacks," Ken said as he bridged the deck, me thinking that we couldn't stop death, but we sure could play cards.

The darkness outside the Warden's window was dotted by the new, ultra-bright prison lights, making it look as if we were floating in outer space up here. Inside some kind of space bubble.

Ken dealt the cards. I gave the Warden a side look that told him I was sorry for his loss and for what must be a hardship, raising two little girls so close to Sugar Land Prison.

The Warden nodded back to me, then threw in a penny. "Come on, ante up if you're in."

"I'm in," I said, chucking in a penny.

When that buffoon Ken leaned over to put a matchbook under the uneven leg of the table, the Warden smiled my way. "I'm OK, Miss Dara," he said in a low voice. "Thank you."

I looked past him and noticed a broom handle without a broom top, leaning up against the Warden's wall near his extra work boots and the trashcan.

"What's that there?"

"Oh, that's a weapon was used the night before last."

"Evidence?" I asked.

"If the man who used it weren't already in for life, I suppose it would be."

"That Concrete Bill's?" Ken asked, braiding his nickel through his fingers, the way he always did when he was going to bluff.

"Yes, sir."

"Who's Concrete Bill?" I asked.

Ken leaned forward and took a big sip from his drink. "Concrete Bill is a convict who decided to give one of the female-males in here a lesson." He smiled one of those greasy redneck smiles I always shied away from. "Fixed him up *good*."

The Warden, sitting in a chair facing the window, looked back over the dark yard below, lit in huge white circles by the prison lights. "There's no *good* that comes from assault."

I took a drag of my cigarette, feeling a spinning metal fist flipping around in the space inside my ribcage. I hoped that they'd hit that poor convict with the broomstick, rather than anything else—but

I doubted it. I nearly got sick to my stomach thinking about it. My head went dizzy, and I had to make sure to breathe quietly so it didn't show.

"Status in the U-nited States goes like this," Ken got to explaining. "White men are at the top, followed by white women, then coloreds, then men of any color that *act* like females." He'd been moving his thick arm down in notches in the air, and when he got to the men that act like females, he flipped his wrist up and down in the international sign for sissy.

I swirled my caramel-colored drink around, watching the bobbing cherry in it. My ears flushed hot with anger and shame.

"What did Concrete Bill *do* exactly?" I asked after I'd gathered the courage.

The Warden raised his eyebrows, and Ken stared hard at me. No one said anything.

"Oh," I said, thinking that the man must've made advances toward Concrete Bill and gotten a bad reply.

I knew of at least two boys in my lifetime who'd been beaten up for a similar offense. One of them got beat up so badly that his stomach ruptured. I was maybe thirteen when I overheard my daddy talking about it at the auto shop. I'll never forget it. He said, "If it were me, I'd've gone a few steps further. Best to rid ourselves of these insects."

Insects.

I asked Ken, "Where's the man now?"

"The female-man?" he said, pleased with himself. "In the hospital. They have him on a suicide watch now too. Apparently the boys had been using him—much the way the cabin boys spent their long voyages with sailors—when he tried to stand up to them."

"So let me get this correct," I said. "These men were doing acts *with* him, and when he tried to stop them, they attacked him for being that kind of man?"

Ken rolled his nickel all the way down the line of his fingers, like a magician. "Yes, ma'am." He said this with a strange certainty—with the conviction that this kind of logic made total sense to him.

"But they were being *those kind of men*, right? They were using him in that way, right?"

"Doesn't count in prison."

"Maybe that man isn't even one of those type of people," I said. The oh-so-worldly Ken sat forward again. "Oh no, *he is*."

I thought I'd done a good job defending that man by saying perhaps he wasn't homosexual. But, in retrospect, when I said maybe he wasn't "one of those kind of people," I was implying that therefore he wasn't *deserving* of this treatment—that he wasn't an insect to be played with because he wasn't really an insect, a homosexual. I used a line of defense that assumed, if he *were* homosexual, that he would be deserving—and, God dammit, I hadn't even realized I'd done that.

The Warden cleared his throat and drummed his hand on the table. "Ken, tomorrow I want you to make a point of bringing Concrete Bill up from the Hole to see me." The Hole—a new indoor room that had replaced the Box in order to satisfy some concerned citizens. "I'm going to explain how I am not doing anything with that broom since we are already knee-deep in paperwork, and it would only waste the court's money on a man who is in here for life anyway. You wait outside on account of then I'm going to have you walk Concrete Bill through the cafeteria and back down to solitary for *another* few days. Force only understands force by the time you're grown."

"Yes, sir, Warden."

"I'll show them all that I don't tolerate this kind of thing, especially since Two Foot Jake is going back into the population next week."

Oh God, I thought, aching for what that man would have to endure. "How long is he in for?"

"Two Foot?" the Warden asked. "Six more years, I believe."

The Warden filled Ken's glass, and I dealt the next round, forcing myself not to look at the broom handle in the corner again. It was so thick.

Sitting there I asked myself—and not for the first time—*what's the difference between living in this jail, under the watchful eye of danger-*

ous folks who are supposed to protect people in need, or living out there? Is the world just one big prison yard of varying sizes?

THE PREVETTES

A few weeks later—me going maybe a little too deep into the sad parts of my mind over Two Foot Jake—I got a letter from Mama that contained a formal invitation to the graduation of Rhodie Marie Prevette, hosted by Mr. and Mrs. Prevette. It took a minute for me to realize that the "Mr. and Mrs." hosting were Rhodie and her *husband*. To this day, I thank God that letter came to me at home, where I could buckle over and scream into my pillow in peace and quiet.

My response was unreasonable, of course, considering *I* had let *her* go—but reasonable or not, it happened. A part of me wanted Rhodie to stay single and solitary all the livelong days, as some sort of homage to the love we had once shared.

Mr. Prevette. With that name, I couldn't help but imagine him golfing in those golf outfits folks wore, shading his eyes and licking his fingers to detect any winds that might shift his luck. I hated him without ever knowing his first name.

Mr. and Mrs. Prevette invited me to come home to Midland and celebrate Rhodie's graduation from the University of Texas. It didn't say what degree she held now. It didn't say anything personal except the time and the place.

I realized then how little I knew about Rhodie, how much I'd stayed stuck in a jail cell in my mind, filled with memories of those three weeks we had together. Truly, in real life, it'd been four years, and I had no idea who she was.

The letter came on my day off—Monday. I had planned to wait until the next workday to see if Beauregard wanted to help me take my mind off it, but I just couldn't wait. After a full four hours reading and rereading the invitation, with its curly script practically stinking of a new house and a baby on the way, I walked over to the prison and waited outside the gate for Beauregard.

A few minutes before he was due to come through, a bright red Lexington Touring with white-walled tires drove up and came to a full stop right next to me. A woman leaned out the window on the passenger's side even though she was driving. Her sleepy eyes drooped, as if the troubles of the world would never have any effect on her. She wore a thin scarf of gold feathers that made her glow somehow, and I couldn't help but think how beautiful she was.

"Well, hey there!"

"Hi."

"You work with Beauregard, don't you?"

"I do. In the kitchen."

"I've seen you when I've come for him. What's your name?"

"Dara," I said.

She lit a cigarette. "Well, since you didn't ask, my name is Evelyn."

I blushed from being so rude. "Hello, Evelyn. Excuse me, my mind is in the clouds."

She looked up at the crowded sky. "It *is* pretty up there."

"Are you here for Beauregard?"

"Yes I am." She eyed me up. "You?"

"Yes—but he doesn't know it."

Somewhere behind all those clouds, the sun started setting, changing the direction of the light and the heat in the air. Behind us, the gate squeaked shut, and Beauregard strolled out. He saw us and waved, as if he'd expected to see the two of us talking together in the sunset.

When he got close enough, he said, "Miss Evelyn. Miss Dara."

Evelyn peered up at him through the window with her sleepy eyes. "I thought I'd extend my stay and take us out to Maria's Roundabout. I didn't know you had plans."

Beauregard, ever the gentleman, gave a slight bow my way.

"He didn't either," I confessed. "I just got a letter that disturbed me, so I thought I'd walk down here and see if he wanted to buy me a beer—in a friendly way!"

"That's the only way I buy beers these days," he said and winked at Evelyn.

Evelyn shook her head and opened the passenger door. "Hop on it. You too, Dara, in the back there. Just push my dresses aside. I need to get them cleaned, so don't worry about touching them."

The black seat sprung up and back when I sat down. I wished I'd worn something fancier than my yellow cotton pants and that silly sleeveless shirt with the bluebirds stitched on the collar.

"What's this about a letter?" Beauregard asked after he kissed Evelyn on the cheek.

"It's an invitation to a long-lost friend's graduation party."

Evelyn shrugged and pulled the car out from the curb. "Sounds fun."

"This particular friend might have been best *staying* lost."

Evelyn bit down on her cigarette. "We all have *those* friends, don't we?"

We fell silent, me knowing that they would have no way of grasping the depth of the problem since they didn't really know me or my troubles.

"You had a falling-out, I presume?" Evelyn asked, eyeing me in the rearview mirror.

"We did."

"Ah," she said to Beauregard. "Turn left here, honey?"

Beauregard pointed. "A left, then a quick right to the back parking lot."

"Sorry to hear about any falling-outs," Evelyn said, looking out for her quick left.

She parked around back. It was a good thing that Evelyn had driven up, otherwise me and Beauregard getting drinks might have started some talk in the prison. On the way in, she grabbed my arm and pulled me in with her, ahead of Beauregard who nodded hello to a few of the men standing close to the door. It felt fun having a girl-friend, even just one on loan.

Most of the folks sat around on stools, watching the small dance floor where a few daring—or drunk—people did their best. The saw-dust on the floor gave the place the smell of a barn, if the barn had recently been caught in a rainstorm of beer. We sat down on three bar stools trimmed with dark brown leather straps. Beauregard perched in the middle.

I looked around. In the back of my mind, this irrational fear sur-faced that I might run into the old head cook—that this was the kind of place he probably frequented every night after work and maybe he'd sneak back in to see old friends. I felt my pocket for that piece of mug, which I carried with me now whenever I left my shanty to walk the streets alone.

After asking our preferences, Beauregard ordered himself a beer and us two gin and tonics. I'd gone with whatever Evelyn wanted, knowing now was perhaps not the time to swig whiskey.

Evelyn leaned in, even prettier up close. "So, who's this friend who's not a friend?"

"Rhodie. Her name's Rhodie. We used to be real close but fell out."

The drinks came, and Beauregard toasted. "To Rhodie!"

Just as we clanked glasses, the Warden walked in with two field captains, who spent most of their days overseeing the fields. He saw us right off and walked over.

"This a kitchen night out?" he asked, smiling at me.

Beauregard smiled. "Impromptu, but yes, sir."

The Warden smiled at me. "You all toasting a good day?"

Evelyn raised her eyebrows at the Warden, clearly liking men with authority. "We are toasting some friend of Dara's who just grad-uated college. To Rhodie!"

Beauregard held up his glass again. "To Rhodie!"

I sat there while my stomach and other vital organs fell to the floor. Would the Warden remember that Rhodie was the name given by the old head cook as the writer of those love letters to me?

I raised my glass, but didn't repeat her name. The Warden stared over at me and I knew that he knew, him being clearly the kind of man who remembered details.

Without commenting, he tipped his dark brown cowboy hat to me. "Miss Dara." He turned to Beauregard. "Keep it light, Beau. It's going to be hot in that kitchen tomorrow."

"Light it is," Beauregard said as he held up three fingers for the bartender, letting her know to pour another round.

The Warden laughed—though without much feeling in it—and turned to join his friends. This was a man I'd come to deeply respect. I was overwhelmed with this feeling that I had let him down, that he thought of me as a liar now.

I watched him, but he never turned back, so I apologized to him in my mind, wondering how long I was going to keep being this person who betrayed people.

MARRY HIM?

Mama died in 1928 of heart failure. I took the train back to Midland for her funeral, saddened most that we never figured how to conversate the way I'd heard so many mothers and daughters do. I kissed her goodbye her all powdered up in the white coffin that Daddy'd picked out—and whispered to her, "I fell in love once, Mama."

Not a year later, I returned to Midland to set Daddy up in a home since he'd become too forgetful to live alone. The nurse said it was common for both parts of a couple to go—in one way or another—within a year of each other. And sure enough, as soon as I signed him in, he promptly forgot everything about this world and let his mind wander to places far beyond the walls of any of life's prisons. I wrote to him every month, but I doubt he knew who was sending the letters.

Sugar Land Prison withstood the crash of the stock market in 1929, while many folks in Sugar Land and other cities didn't. Our country grew accustomed to seeing soot-covered men walking the streets, offering to do odd jobs, while Sugar Land got $350,000 to upgrade itself.

In 1932, they—here meaning the inmates themselves—finished the project, which included a new concrete housing unit to replace some of those horrible wooden barracks at the work camps and twelve acres of fenced area with a meat packing plant and a cannery.

Then one day—a day that snuck up on me the way debt sneaks up on you—it was 1933, and I'd been in the Texas penitentiary system for *ten years*. A God damn decade. I couldn't believe it. Ten years, with more than my share of guilt at not having escaped, the way I promised Huddie I would.

For eight of my ten years at Sugar Land, Beauregard worked the prison kitchen. Then he married that dimpled Dallas girl, Evelyn, and joined her father's business. I sang at their wedding, with his brother on piano. He kept in touch afterwards by sending me strange little postcards with coffee cup rings on them. Over the years, they had two sons—he named one Beau and the other Regaurd.

Ken, that big ape, became my friend. Stranger things. He confided in me on more than one occasion about issues he had with his mousy wife and teased me about why I never took to anyone. The Warden, meanwhile, occupied himself by growing out his sideburns or his mustache or sometimes both. He never said anything about my lying to him about those letters from Rhodie, and gradually, the shadow cast by my guilt dissolved, as most things do over time.

Over the years, he and I talked about life—how he just wanted to live long enough to meet his grandchildren; how he wanted to be remembered as a good husband and a great father—in that order.

I had it good with my Sugar Land friends and our card games and Huddie's music. I even had it good in my steaming kitchen with that filthy window. It was like I'd married Sugar Land, and—as with any good marriage—I'd learned to love it even when I sometimes didn't like it all that much.

Everyone who lasted ten years got a nice pen and a bonus as part of a small ceremony led by the Warden. So, on March 4, 1933, I slicked back my hairnet, lumbered up to the portable stairs that had been rolled in, and walked up the small wood stage like Frankenstein in a gunmetal gray dress. I looked out at the two dozen or so guards—all who'd taken their hats off— who'd come to congratulate me.

Standing up on that stage like the winner of some pageant for awkward big girls, I'd resigned myself to being here for another decade. Maybe I'd get a higher spot in the kitchen—maybe, someday, even head cook. There were worse things.

I had no idea then that what I'd be getting that day was a husband.

The Warden stepped up onto the creaky cafeteria stage, looking nervous and overly groomed, with his hair so slick I could see the comb marks and his extra-stiff white collar rubbing red lines along his neck. The crowd clapped and smiled when the Warden stepped up to the fist-sized, silver microphone.

The Warden cleared his throat. "Ten years, is it?" he said.

The microphone shrieked with feedback. Someone in the crowd whistled out for me. I smiled.

"Miss Dara," he said, alternating between looking at me and looking out at the cafeteria, "you have lit up this place with your wit and wisdom and graced us with knowing exactly how much garlic salt to add to the short ribs we were all so excited to add to the menu last year."

More than a few people nodded to that last one.

"Here is your pen."

Everyone clapped and stomped their feet for me. I held my hand up in thanks, accepted my pen, and started to walk off. That's when the Warden pulled me back.

A gasp went through the crowd. Out of the corner of my eye, I watched their faces change from happy to shocked to confused.

"Warden?" I asked.

Then the Warden—a man who'd probably never made a showy move in his entire life, a man fifteen years my senior, a widower with two girls not yet teenagers—did the unthinkable. He knelt down on the stage and held out his hand for mine.

I dropped my ten-year pen. "What the hell?"

"I know you got ten more until pension, but marry me, Miss Dara. Leave the prison and come to my home."

My mouth hung open for a very long time.

Marry him? It had never really crossed my mind that the Warden had held any thoughts for me that weren't, well, brotherly—especially after learning about Rhodie.

Marry him? The Warden *was* a handsome man in his ironed khaki pants, to be sure, and many women would love to help brush his daughters' hair and go get them measured for bras—many *other* women.

Marry him? Well, he did make me laugh—and I always heard that was half of it. *Half.*

It was the clapping that snapped me out of it. I looked down. The Warden was still there, his belly sliding off his knee, holding out a ring. And I thought: *wonder if that belonged to his first wife.*

Beauregard, still as dapper as ever despite marriage, had driven in for the ten-year ceremony. I heard him cry out, "Do it, Miss Dara!"

I promised Huddie all those years before that I would get out of here, and this was my chance. It wasn't perfect, but it was damn good. I tapped the center of my breastbone, where I imagined a delicate metal box that held my secret love for Rhodie, and I put my hand in the Warden's.

"Miss Dara," he said, "will you?"

Truthfully, knowing that a man the Warden's age only had so many years left in his pecker made my decision much easier.

I leaned over him into the microphone and shouted, "Hell yes!"

The Warden—crunching knees and all—grabbed me and hugged me tighter than I'd ever been hugged, God love him. He took my hand and twirled me around like a sailor after months at sea. While I spun in the dizzy lights of the bright cafeteria, I remembered Huddie making music on that beat-up, second-hand twelve-string that constantly went out of tune, and I knew that, like him, I would do the best with what was given me to make something beautiful.

BOOK TWO

nana dara

I DID

It's odd that a *Warden* would be the one to take me from the jail
I'd set myself in, but that's how it happened. First, though—before
the marriage—we decided we should date a bit.

On our third date, the Warden made me dinner. When I walked
into his house and saw that he had put out five vases of flowers, all
different kinds since he said he didn't know which kind I preferred,
a happiness filled up inside me like steam—to feel that special, that
considered.

But the flowers also caused me to worry. A lot.

As the Warden stood there in his ironed blue shirt with flowers
all around him and a roast in the oven, all I could think about was
that I had no idea what I was going to do with his penis. There wasn't
easy access to books the way there is these days, so my lack of penis
knowledge—or girlfriends to consult—tormented me from that dinner throughout most of our short engagement.

As the summer drew on, I managed to deftly avoid his member
altogether—as was the way of many women back then. I'd felt it a
few times, banging against me while we kissed in his car or on my
couch after a movie. Once, when I let him reach up and touch my
breasts outside my blouse, I'd felt him push urgently into my leg.
Rather than be excited by the move, I was reminded of a disturbing
scene I'd witnessed when I was a teenager between my dog Roger
and a particularly curvaceous table leg.

Of course, I knew the overalls: his penis goes into my Venus fly-
trap, bumps around a bit, explodes, and then goes back to sleep. That

chain of events didn't cause me any alarm—indeed, if I'm being totally honest, I'd given myself more than a few private moments con-
templating just such a scene, despite my inclination toward women. It
was *the rest of it* that worried me.

How do I touch it? Do I help it find its way? Will it hurt if I squeeze it?

When I realized it sounded like I was talking about a beached
whale, I gave it all over and moved on to the other topic that plagued
me that summer of our engagement: my feet.

It was July. Since the Warden and I agreed to marry two months
earlier, we'd had ten dates—twice a week on his nights off. We saw
Duck Soup and *42nd Street*, ate pizza, went to a barbecue with a few
of the guards, and played a round of miniature golf that had tested
my patience on a cellular level. Until then, my feet had never come up.

"Whew," I said as I slid off one of my shoes, "my dogs are barking!
I sure miss my kitchen orthopedics."

Then and there, as the Warden stirred a glass of nighttime tea, he
set a tone for what he offered in our marriage: "Can I rub your delicate feet for you, Miss Dara?"

My feet? I blanched.

When you have been given a sturdy build, such as myself, and you
spend time on your feet, they work a lot. Working this much, your
feet do what any thing would to protect itself from pain and suffering: build a cocoon.

So, by that time, at thirty years old and after ten years standing in the Sugar Land slop hall, my fat feet rested on top of a solid
inch of brownish-yellow callus as strong as any horse's hoof. Every
few months, I'd take a pair of scissors to the callus and cut away at
it, then pumice down the rough spots, leaving an impressive pile of
waxy-looking shavings on my shanty floor that I swept out with a
wire broom. It was *managed*. Managed, that is, until the cracks.

What years earlier had been half a dozen small fissures on my
heels expanded, so by the night the Warden asked if he could rub my
feet, I sported deep cracks where the callus had split and pulled back,
leaving gaps as wide as a shoestring.

"Warden," I said, putting it off, "let's save that for later."

He smiled. "Yes, ma'am. I look forward to everything we're saving for later."

"Thank you."

He handed me my sweet tea. "You know," he said, "I had this moment a few years ago, Miss Dara, when I wondered what it might be like not to see you every day. That's when I knew I needed to see you every day. I needed to see you more than I saw you at work. I wanted to see you in the morning making eggs or out on the porch or bundling your sweater tight against the winds. I wanted to see everything about you, from your feet to your sleepy blue eyes. I love you, Miss Dara."

I smiled, thinking: *Dear Lord, I cannot let a man like this down.*

I knew I needed to get myself in order to be as beautiful as possible for our wedding night—from the feet up.

× × ×

In June, five days before the wedding—and the wedding night—I executed a massive trim on my feet. I decided to wait until the last moment so the calluses wouldn't have time to regroup, while giving myself a few days out to let the redness and swelling go down—my private science.

I sat down and cut away at the callus with my kitchen shears, despite what my mama had taught me about never letting them touch anything but food. In one or two spots, I was particularly stern, cutting down so far that the edges of my feet where the callus met the skin turned bright pink and throbbed.

There are injuries in war, I told myself. *Injuries in war.*

My forearms hurt from pressing the scissor blades together. My wood floor looked like it had snowed pieces of skin. My eyes watered from the strain—but I forged on.

An hour or so later, both of my feet were a mess of angry pink lines. I had made headway.

The trouble was, I couldn't really grind down the *center* of the callus, even with my pumice stone, so I hobbled into the kitchen, pulled out my cookie tin of tools, and got the heavy-grade sandpaper. I sanded and sanded my feet for half an hour, only to have the paper clog with callus residue.

I struggled back into the kitchen area and brought out the big guns: my potato peeler.

Even with its sharp steel blade, the God damn thing had no effect. It just dragged impotently across my feet. Clearly that tool was not meant to combat anything with more imposing skin than a potato. Sighing, I gave up for the moment, rubbed Vaseline on my damaged feet—especially in the crevasses that still remained—tucked them into thick wool socks, and went to bed, dreaming that I'd wake up with the feet of a queen.

Instead, I woke up with the feet of a peasant—but although the crevasses were still there, the overall foot felt a little softer, thanks to the Vaseline that had filled in the big gaps. That gave me an idea.

I wrapped my tender feet in gauze, put on my thick socks, and headed slowly to the local grocer for a big bottle of glue. With only a slight glance from the skinny adolescent clerk who clearly thought a stained sleeveless shirt was not a flattering look for a woman of my considerable heft, I purchased my glue and limped back to my shanty.

After pulling the curtain closed, I propped my left foot up on my wooden coffee table. With a towel underneath to catch any runoff, I squeezed the glue into my three widest fissures, blowing to help it dry.

At first, I left the twenty or thirty little cracks around my heel alone—knowing that if I kept up the scissors and pumice attack I could make headway with them—but when I saw how perfectly the glue had filled up the large cracks, I figured *what the heck*, and started gluing them all up.

My right foot required extra glue and extra drying time. It had massive cracks starting about a third of the way in on my heel and widening as they went up around the back—plain as day if I were ever to dare slippers, as any wife might. I was glad I'd been proactive enough to set the bourbon nearby.

"Here's to you, Warden!" I toasted.

After my right foot dried, I took another swig then pumiced my glued calluses down to a flat surface. I admired my handiwork. My feet were as damn close to perfect as this peasant was going to get.

"To my wedding night!" I said, drawing out another pull of bourbon.

Feeling some warm encouragement, I toasted my little shanty, which I'd soon be leaving—my quiet, unimposing home where I'd lived a simple life for ten years. Next, I toasted my nerves—that they would stay strong when the time came for me to meet the Warden's girls. Lastly, I toasted Rhodie.

"Rhodie," I said to the crickets and the stars behind the thin curtain out my front window, "I'm getting married. I know you already are. I hope you have those kids you wanted. I never had any kids, you know—even though I wanted them. Every time I see a baby, even now, I still think how beautiful you would've been holding a baby.

"A while ago, I thought that I'd been brave, but anyone can be brave for three weeks! What was true bravery was to keep writing me—to keep holding on to our love even when everything says it's not coming back." The bourbon burned the back of my nasal cavities. "You were always the brave one, Rhodie. *You* kissed *me*, remember? You were the girl who went to college when hardly any ladies did—and in a new city, no less!" I took another swig. "None of this matters much at this point, though. At this point, I'm just a simple woman with glued-up feet who finally understands what you might've known all along—that maybe you only get one soul mate, but that doesn't mean the rest is donkey shit."

I resisted the urge to scratch at my feet—a symptom, I'd learn later, of the glue stretching in the cracks—and took in another burning sip of Kentucky. "You were always smarter than me, Rhodie, or maybe I was just more stubborn, but either way I'm finally doing it—*I'm getting married*. And I promise you I'll do my best not to live a life of comparison. Like you told me before you left, 'You can't live in two places at one time without getting motion sick.'"

× × ×

The Warden and I had a short engagement, which is to say that we had a short time of dating before we tied the knot—a saying that the Warden told me was from the fancy way a man tied his tie on his wedding day, while I had always thought it was a play on the hangman's noose. The Warden had proposed on March 4, 1933 and on June 25 of the same year, we took a carriage ride over to the courthouse—my delicate, itchy feet thanking the Warden for that thoughtful gesture. He held my hands in his as we looked out the carriage window together, weathering the bumps and creaks of the road.

"Today's the day," he said.

"Yes, it is."

Sugar Land was still a very small town then, with only five streets connecting to create downtown. It had one carriage available on call, the one we were riding in. You knew when it came through that someone was getting married, so when we drove by, several women— almost all with children—stopped, shaded their eyes, and gave us a smile and a nod. One woman in a long blue dress even waved.

When we arrived at the courthouse, the Warden walked around to my side, unlatched my door, and helped me out of the carriage. He didn't seem to notice the disparity between my frame and the tiny black steps I was expected to navigate down. He only waited with his hand holding mine up as I steadied my footing and gingerly made my way to the solid sidewalk.

"New shoes?" he asked.

"Well, this is my wedding day!"

The Sugar Land Municipal Courthouse, a sign in the lobby told us, was founded in 1908. Ten years later, in 1918—just a few years before I first came to Sugar Land, the town had its first school, followed by a huge oil well at Blue Ridge that produced more than 450 barrels of oil. Oil—the blood of the South.

The Warden tugged at the tight white collar of his dress shirt. His auburn and white hair was combed so precisely it looked sprayed in place, like a doll's. His sideburns were trimmed and he'd had the barber shave up the back of his neck. With his black suit and all his proper grooming, I couldn't help but think he looked like a waiter in a fine restaurant.

I asked, "You ready to join the ranks of the imprisoned?"

He pulled at his collar again. "As long as married life comes with the promise of never having to wear this shirt again."

"We'll burn it on the same fire that takes my dress."

He kissed my cheek while we walked. "You look wonderful."

My dress was absurd. It had taken me two hours in Dresses for the Day, down near the wholesale book dealer, to find one that wasn't too fussy, wasn't too white, and wasn't too revealing. One that, as the lady helping me had said, "accentuated the positives" of my large frame.

The only one that hit all the criteria was a beige—"nearly bone"—dress with a lace triangle down the chest that went up to my neck and matching lace around the wrists. My dress helper thought "nearly bone" was my best bet given my "matron" status. In plain English, she was referring to the assumption that I was a widow or at least deflowered, given that I had just passed thirty. Neither one was, of course, true—not in the male-female sense of the word.

At any rate, there we were—me in an absurd dress with ridiculously long sleeves in the middle of the summer, standing by the Warden, whose face was getting redder by the minute.

The ceremony lasted six minutes from start to finish, including the signing of the documents. We took the waiting carriage to the Warden's house.

His house, I knew, maintained a sense of military life—thrown back from his youth no doubt. The walls were all white, except the living room, which was paneled in a red wood. All of his furniture

was either mustard yellow or olive green. The look wavered somewhere between "natural" and "camouflage"—a lot more colorful than
my shanty had been, I realized.

I then saw how folks would have seen my old shanty: a boring
shell to house someone who was getting by, but not really living. *How
could I have just gotten by? How could I have not made some kind of
effort into my surroundings?* I vowed from that point on to live a more
colorful life.

The Warden skillfully uncorked the champagne and took off his
tie. He brought out a plate of fruit he'd prepared ahead of time and
suggested I change to get more comfortable.

"Well, all right then," I said, like this was all perfectly natural.

The Warden kissed me gently on the lips. "I'm going to get this
suit off, too," he told me.

"You first," I said. "I insist."

I watched him head to the bedroom, then turned back around
in my chair, wondering if I should get truly comfortable in my loose
denim pants and old T-shirt or what. Perhaps "honeymoon" comfortable was a certain kind of comfortable? *Of course*, I chastised myself,
of course it must be. But what?

I did own one nightshirt. It was sleeveless with an orange ribbon
that tied in the front. It had been on sale, so I bought it—thank God,
I'd bought it!

I grabbed my glass of champagne and took a healthy sip. My hands
were so damp that I had to clutch the glass so I wouldn't drop it.

The Warden cleared his throat behind me, and I jumped. Flashes
of him in satin pajamas with a cigar flashed through my mind. I sniffed
the air, checking for cologne. I smelled something—not cologne, too
sweet.

As curious as any feline, I did an about-face to find out what the
smell was. And there was the Warden, in a short sleeve white cotton
shirt and ironed khakis, rubbing his hands together.

"Orange lotion. The woman at the shop told me it was a good
choice for a wedding night foot massage. How's your champagne?"

My eyes popped open. "I—Warden, it's just that—I, what I mean to say is that—Warden, I—I can't do a foot rub *and* your penis on the same night! It's just too much!"

I must have looked on the verge, because the Warden put down his lotioned hands faster than a pan on fire. He smiled. "Do I get to choose which one then?"

I couldn't help but laugh, despite the sweat stains under my arms and the throbbing glue spots on my feet.

"Either way might end in mortal embarrassment for me," I confessed.

"Well, speaking a bit candidly, Miss Dara, in either case you just need to sit back and relax. Let me do all the work."

I actually blushed. "OK then. How about I get dressed? You bring the champagne—with a little whiskey to give it some zing, will you?" My thought was to approach this like tearing off a band-aid. I gulped, visibly. "Meet me in the bedroom."

"Yes, ma'am."

The Warden walked over and collected the fruit and the champagne. It was then I noticed that he had bought me red roses and white carnations. I saw the details—the thoughtful flowers and the ironed arm covers on the mustard-yellow couch and the immaculate sink.

I walked down the dark green carpet of his short hallway and up to the plywood door to the bedroom. To push it open felt like leaving my past behind and stepping into a future with nightshirts and children and champagne. It meant being what was considered by most folks as *ordinary*. For the first time the idea of being somewhat ordinary didn't feel like a lie—maybe a small compromise for a stubborn lady such as myself, but not an all-out lie.

I turned the cold gold doorknob and pushed the door open.

He'd laid my suitcases on my side of the bed. The bed was covered with a white comforter that had small roses stitched onto it. At the bottom was a hand-knitted white, yellow, and green zigzag quilt. He'd opened the four drawers of a new white dresser he'd clearly bought for me, and already closed the white curtains of our one window for privacy, since the Guardtown houses had been built a bit close together.

I moved my three raggedy suitcases to the floor after I got out my nightshirt, grateful that I'd also picked up some matching socks so I wouldn't scratch the Warden with my feet while we slept.

A few minutes later, with me socked and standing by the bed— like a crazy Revivalist lady in my long nightshirt and early graying hair—the Warden came in. He was carrying our champagne glasses in one hand and the fruit in the other.

"Why don't you lay down on your belly and I'll give you a backrub to relax the situation," he said.

"If by situation you mean *me*, then that is a good idea." I clenched my fists in and out to try to warm them up and dry them off.

He noticed my socks. "And we can leave the feet alone for now."

"That mean you've made your choice between the two?"

He smiled.

The white comforter was cold and the room was so quiet with the curtains drawn. The only light came from the lamp on my side table, which looked like a giraffe with its long, skinny bronze neck and mustard-colored shade. I heard him rub his lotion-free hands together.

"You tell me if I am going too firm."

I almost said "All right, Daniel"—his given name—but felt that calling him by his name would be living a caricature of "marriage." To me, he would always be the Warden. Anything else felt forced and fake.

The Warden started with my neck, telling me that I was holding a lot of tension there. I nodded in agreement.

He asked, "Can I use some oil?"

"That'd be nice."

The oil filled the room with the scent of orange peels and lemons.

He moved my nightshirt down off my shoulders. I tried to relax, but not relax too much—or else I felt I would seem easy. He rubbed my back with his hands, then his knuckles.

"Your hands tired?" I asked.

"Relax now. I'm just changing it up."

It was hard to relax though, wondering if my large back and tight muscles were hurting his hands.

To my immense relief, he skipped my buttocks and my thighs, and moved down to my calves, which were exposed. Since the muscle of my calves was more pliable than my neck, the movements felt a great deal more intimate. He pinched the muscle up in big chunks then rolled it back down again—the oil making everything move as easily as the tides.

"You know, it's been quite a while, Miss Dara," he said when he got to my ankles and my socks. "It's been quite a while since I've—since there's been a lady in my room. And before my wife there'd only been two others. Those two were during my military days, so I'm not even sure if they count fully. But I want you to know, I'll do my best."

He was as nervous as me. Seeing that was both a relief and a burden.

"Warden, you seem like a man who always does his best. I'm not worried. Now"—I made myself brave—"I'm going to roll on my back and get under the sheet, so close your eyes, please."

He stood back up from my massage and let me wiggle out of my nightshirt and under the white sheets.

"Oh good Lord," I said, "will this oil ruin the sheets?"

I could hear the smile in his voice even though I wasn't looking at him. "No, ma'am."

I folded the white comforter down just under my collarbone. It smelled the way sheets do when they are line dried in the heat of day. "OK, you can open your eyes now."

He looked down at me with such open happiness that I felt beautiful, and I was excited for him to see even more of me. I liked this spotlight. I liked this strange sensation of feeling pretty.

"Now you close *your* eyes," he said, his sideburns looking darker in the dim light.

With my eyes closed, I tried to keep my breath even so I wouldn't get too nervous and sweat on the sheets. I hoped he didn't mind that

I kept my socks on. I wondered if his girls, Edna and Debbie, would be upset with me here in their mama's bed.

A quick minute later, I felt him snuggle down next to me, careful not to touch my body with his.

Before he told me to open my eyes, he kissed me. It was a tender kiss, and it woke up some places in me that were unaccustomed to the nearness of other people.

I kissed him back and—probably as much to his surprise as mine—pulled him over on top of me. I liked the feeling that I was giving something to someone who would enjoy it so much. And, it seemed, I might just enjoy myself too.

He grinned as big as I'd ever seen and kissed my neck. "This is going to be fun, Miss Dara."

"I think you might be right, Warden," I said.

I had been so frightened that I wouldn't respond the way I had with Rhodie. I assumed I'd been ruined after her—that I'd been put here on this Earth to love her and only her in the way we did.

When the Warden first entered me, I held my breath, fearing that he wouldn't be able to get inside—that I'd be too cold or resistant to let anything happen, not because he was a man, but because he wasn't her. But when he gently pushed, I found myself reaching up for his back and putting my hands on his shoulder blades and relaxing to let him know it was OK—more than OK, this feeling of submission and vulnerability, but also this heat and desire. Heat, desire, and soon after—pain. The Warden was not a small man, after all.

I gritted my teeth. "God dammit!"

"You doing OK?"

"I'm breathing through it!"

The official breaking of my hymen was harder than shoeing an oiled moose, to be sure. Maybe they get more solid the older you are.

I'll spare you the details of the precise moment, but it ended with me using every swear word I knew. I'm not even sure how our first sexual encounter ended for him, to be honest, but I do know that afterwards he held me all night long with his forearm as warm as butter on my belly.

× × ×

By the third night—three days before the grandparents were scheduled to bring Edna and Debbie home—we were in a groove. The Act had stopped hurting, and the Warden even stepped up and showed me a few new twists on the old bedroom dance, as he called it. These twists involved me on my belly and me arched up with a few pillows. To my surprise, I found myself thinking about those twists all day long, while he was at Sugar Land and I was making casseroles.

By the fourth night, the second to last night of our "stay-in honeymoon"—after we went to the annual car show, and I made him liver and onions—I surprised him by grabbing hold of the wheel, so to speak, and doing a little driving myself.

He smiled the whole next day, stopping to kiss me and saying things like, "I like this side of you," when he touched my backside.

With Rhodie, I was in the position of the admirer. Rhodie found me attractive, to be sure, but she wasn't blown away by me *on sight* the way I had been with her. She'd loved me after we talked and ran through the creek and I showed her the extra sod in the meadow that we could make into forts—while I'd loved her the minute she walked into the egg store.

The Warden knew from the moment I had my first talk with him—when he warned me not to leave the meat too rare—that there was something about me he wanted to see more of. In retrospect, he said, he could see that he loved me right off. I nodded, knowing that's how it had been for me with Rhodie—it took a while for my mind to figure out what my body already knew.

The Warden thought I was "gorgeous." It was nice to be in the other position, to be the admired one—plus it gave me a kind of confidence in the bedroom that made my early middle age one of my most *adventuresome* time periods.

FIVE ROSARIES

Before the grandparents brought his girls back home, the Warden thought I should meet them someplace neutral. We'd always dated when the kids were at the grandparents'. Looking back, it seems odd that I didn't meet them before, but those were different times— times when the likes and dislikes of children played a lesser role in the goings-on of adults.

"Meet your girls? Sure," I said, thinking that I'd rather pirouette in a pink tutu.

"Mamaw and Pappy can bring them by the prison tomorrow." He kissed me on the cheek. "Now I got to go tend to those roofing tiles."

I took in a deep breath. "Tomorrow."

"You'll be fine." He kissed the top of my head. "They're nice girls. Got to be tomorrow since they are coming home the day after."

He clicked the door shut. I stood there with my mouth hanging open and my guts bubbling up with panic. *Tomorrow?*

I needed some help here.

The dining room chair threatened to commit suicide when I lowered myself into it, but it somehow found the strength to go on. I tested it further by leaning back to grab a soft hand-sewn pouch I'd put in the drawer of the Warden's plate cabinet. It was the pouch that my grandmother had given to my mother when she got married and my mother had given to me when I left for Sugar Land—my first marriage of sorts.

I rolled the pouch around in my fingers before pulling out the rosary. It was constructed of ten rows of white Hail Mary beads that looked like suppositories. Sitting stoically in between the groupings, were perfectly round, pink beads for the Lord's Prayer. My mama had told me that those pink beads were genuine opals, one of the two birthstones of her mother's mother, the woman who first owned the rosary. A delicate silver chain connected all those beads.

The rosary was cold, as if it had been kept in the ice chest, but somehow gentle. The only part that felt hard was the crucifix itself, all pointy edges, especially where the nails in Christ's hands and feet stuck out. Even his body was pointy—his kneecaps and the crown of thorns and his thin ribs. I used to think that they made the crucifixes sharp so you'd have to hang them outside your pocket for fear of stabbing yourself, then everyone would know you had a rosary on you, like an ad for God.

The night before I was to meet the Warden's little girls, while he clomped around on the roof above me, I did something I hadn't done since I was nineteen: I prayed that rosary. The entire damn rosary, since I needed all the help I could get.

I offered my rosary up as a prayer to the Almighty that the Warden's girls would not walk up to me and proceed to make derogatory comments about my rectangular stature or my big feet or my closely shorn hairdo in front of the Warden. I knew he didn't see me the way I saw myself, but I worried that he might see me the way *they* saw me. So, despite the arguments in my mind in favor of bourbon over rosary, I moved over to the more comfortable light green chair in the living room, near the cactus, and prayed that rosary until my left butt cheek fell asleep—then I prayed some more.

I dozed off with the rosary and woke up to the Warden lightly touching my hair. It was morning.

"I didn't want to wake you."

"Aw, hell! What time is it?"

"There's no rush—we got forty-five minutes to be at Sugar Land. You get yourself some coffee, and I'm going to go have a cigar."

I got up without saying anything, annoyed that I could feel him smiling about it all.

What should I wear?

It wasn't a long decision; I only had my white Sugar Land shirts and two sundresses to choose from. *So, the blue one with the white flowers or the dark gray?*

I was glad then that Sugar Land was the chosen meeting space because, although I wasn't the prettiest thing going, next to tattooed prisoners with yellow teeth and hairy ears, I could hold my own. Besides, I knew also that the Warden was most comfortable at the prison. He thought of that place as a kind of retreat for children who had been beaten into dangerous adults, and therefore saw his role as part father, part drill sergeant. They were his extended family, even if they didn't know it. It made sense that his immediate family would be meeting up there.

I chose dark gray—the blue made me look like a giant hot-air balloon—and a pair of sunglasses with light yellow frames.

"It's funny," I said when I came out. "I have three times as many sunglasses as I do sundresses."

"You could wear some shorts."

I gave him a look that let him know what I thought about *that*.

"Well, all right then."

He held the door, and I walked through, smoothing down my hair. We strolled along Guardtown, him holding my hand. He smoked his cigar down, and I tried to keep myself calm so I wouldn't get sweaty.

"You all right?" he asked when we were almost up to the white buildings.

"Yes. You?"

"I'm just fine." He winked, and I thought that he did seem fine. *How could that be—didn't he see that he had married a giant piece of cement?*

So there I was—just a week after my wedding—back at Sugar Land. I rubbed my finger over my teeth, in case any of the light-colored lipstick I'd put on had rubbed off. It was my Sunday lipstick and, although it felt like one more thing to worry about, it was better than worrying about not having any.

"There they are!"

He waved over to where their grandparents had dropped them off. The only grandparents left were on his dead wife's side. They waved, but never made it over to meet me—not that day and not any day after. Maybe they thought the Warden shouldn't have remarried, or maybe it hurt too much to see their daughter's girls looking to another woman for care; I don't know.

The Warden walked back toward me, that big bear of a man hulking in the middle of his two wispy girls—one in pants and one in a skirt. They all held hands, strolling across the flesh-colored dirt at high noon. As they got closer, I wasn't sure if I should stay seated or stand or what. I wished I'd brought a cigarette.

A small plane flew overhead, and I looked up through my sunglasses, wondering how long geese feel the pull of the plane engines sucking them in before they lose the battle and get shredded. How much they struggle against a wind that will always overwhelm them.

"Miss Dara." The Warden cleared his throat. "This is Edna, who sleeps with the dogs, and Debbie, who sleeps with the cats." They had two wiener dogs from the same litter and two cats of nondescript parentage who would soon be added in with my two cats. Since they slept with them, the animals had also traveled over to the grandparents', who were dropping them by the house tomorrow.

They smiled up at me, squinting. Debbie curtsied, as much as a seven-year-old made almost entirely of hair can. She wore a pale pink skirt and white shirt with a blue belt in the middle.

"Daddy, can Edna and me have a race?" she asked.

Before he answered, Edna—in the blue sailor suit—yelled "Go!" and the two girls were off across the yard.

The Warden sat down. "Taking this in?"

"I am." I sat there with my legs pressed close together under the picnic table.

"I love you."

"I love you, too."

He nodded, then turned to watch his girls. Edna, the younger one, was winning the second leg back from the wired prison fence.

He called out to them: "Bring it on in!"

The girls pushed harder when they realized their Daddy was watching. They stormed up to our table.

"I won!" Debbie shouted.

"I *tripped*." Edna sulked. "You didn't win—I just lost. It's diff'rent."

The plane overhead was almost out of sight. I wondered why when I saw that plane I thought of the death of geese—why, instead, I didn't see people off to enjoy their lives. I vowed to begin seeing things on the light side and started by turning to Edna and saying, "The best winners are the ones that lose a lot when they're young. Life only gets better."

Edna looked around the penitentiary yard. She turned to me, cocked her head, and said the words that made me love her right off: "If this is *better*," she said, "I quit now."

× × ×

We went through the growing pains folks go through. I found out when I could reprimand the girls and when exerting my authority would threaten to paint a bright red circle around me as the one member of this family who didn't really belong. I came to know when I could remind the Warden that I came in late to the structure of all these people, and sometimes I just needed time to myself—and when such a reminder would sound like I didn't love his girls like I should. And I worked out when I could ask how their time was at their grandparents' house without sounding like I was trying to compete, which, truth be told, sometimes I was.

Then my second rosary came. Edna was just turning nine and was so skinny that we dressed her in clothes for girls much younger than she was, even though they were too short in the sleeves and too high in the dress line. Her hands were always dirty since she was a bright girl filled up with this drive to understand the world from grub worms up.

The Warden and I had told Edna that she could have three kids over for the night to celebrate her ninth birthday. Only she decided that two of the three friends she wanted to invite were boys—and the Warden told her flat-out no.

Edna shut herself in the room she shared with Debbie. I knocked and asked if I could come in.

She shouted in that way that only young children can, without care for the neighbors, "No!"

"Please."

"I don't want a birthday party!"

I stood with my hand against the door, as if I could feel something through the thin wood. After a moment, I walked in.

Edna, her thick brown hair in a mess, was face down on her bed. Her fourteen stuffed animals were off in the corner, all looking over at her with great concern.

She sniffed. "I don't want a party if the boys can't come."

"Do they want to come?" I asked.

She rolled onto her side, away from me, and said slowly, "I don't know."

"Why don't you just have your one girl friend over then?"

She rubbed her face against the pillowcase. "No one has *one person* over for their birthday!" She flopped onto her back and stared up at the ceiling, her face blotchy from crying. "Let's just cancel it. I'll tell everyone you won't let me have one."

To my shame, I felt a pang of dread that folks would hear that the Warden's new wife wouldn't let his daughter have a birthday party. I said, "Are you sure?"

"I just want to know what's wrong with me!" she shouted, crying hard, that deep kind of cry.

I stood up and pushed a few strands of hair behind my ear. Clearly this was beyond my experience.

To me she was a spirited, smart little girl, though there was something in the distance she had with the rest of the world that I understood. I stood by her bed. Edna sniffed an irritated sniff then lifted her messy head and handed me the pillow. She rolled over to cry into the bedspread.

"I don't want a party," she said, muffled and sad.

"Well you need to have one," I said, making the rookie mistake of caring more how other people saw me as a parent than how my stepdaughter saw me as a parent. "You'll have fun. I promise. I will invite those three girls, and that's that."

"I won't," she cried. "I'll sit there and not say a word the whole time!"

She went silent. After a few minutes, I left the room.

I did host that party. And it was horrible. The neighborhood girls came dressed in their finest regalia and brought fancy gifts and stacked them up in a pile while Edna, who had refused to wear anything other than her pants and a brown blouse, sat with her back to everyone, facing the wall in the living room.

That night—the night after her terrible party—I prayed another rosary that I wouldn't be such a selfish asshole. And after I was done, I went in to her bedroom.

Edna scowled at me from her sheets.

"I was wrong and you were right," I said. "I'm sorry, honey. So sorry."

Edna softened. We didn't hug or anything, but she nodded in a way that let me know that she had accepted my white flag. I left her room wondering how many people I would hurt because I cared what others thought.

× × ×

It wasn't until 1939 that I prayed the rosary for the third time since my youth. The subject of this rosary: *Debbie's junior prom.*

This time, I offered up my prayers not for Debbie's *tenuous* sixteen-year-old virginity or her safe transport to and from the dancehall, but that I would manage to help her with her make-up without her ending up like the Creature from the Black Lagoon. The only make-up trick I had was wearing sunglasses instead of mascara.

That night, a breezy spring night that made all the sheets on the line look like ghosts, I stayed downstairs and said the rosary. I prayed for the Almighty to intervene and endow me with make-up skills by dawn.

The next morning, I was greeted with proof that God did truly exist when the Warden surprised Miss Debbie and me by reserving a spot at the Sally Joan make-up counter for Miss Debbie to get her outer lids and the rest of it done professionally while I just stood there, complimenting. *Praise be!*

Who knows what became of Miss Debbie's virginity, but the way she looked when she left, I have no doubt it was the flag to be captured that night. It reminded me of that one time Rhodie asked me to dance, her holding her hand out, saying, "Dance with me. No one can see us."

Me blanching, "I can't. I don't know who would *lead.*" What a donkey's behind.

Miss Debbie adjusted her purple corsage after her date did his best to slide it on her wrist, "Daddy, you know Brian. And Brian, this is my . . . Nana Dara. My daddy's wife."

And that was how it happened—that was how I became Nana Dara. I wasn't her mother—never could be—but I wasn't really her stepmother either. I was *Nana Dara.*

Not long after, Edna and the Warden started calling me Nana Dara too, and then the folks at church. The name spread faster than crabs in an all-boys school, and within the year even the folks bagging up my ice cream were calling me Nana Dara. It matured me, this name and the status that went with it. I was no longer a girl from an egg store who left to cook at a prison, then became the wife of the Warden. I was Nana Dara, God dammit. I had my own place in this world.

× × ×

Two years later, the same year they bombed Pearl Harbor, I was pre-
sented with a situation that required I say the rosary for the fourth
time since my teen years. I said this rosary for the Almighty to give me
the strength to know how to console little Edna when she *didn't* go to
her prom. You need to remember, this was the 1940s, and prom could
turn you into a princess or a spinster overnight. Trust me on that.

On the night of the prom, the Warden huffed and looked off at
the pink clouds. "I'm going to head to the movies tonight."

In that moment, I knew how much harder it was for men sometimes. No matter what, they had to hold up the heavy walls of society
for fear that everything would otherwise cave in and hurt their families. They had to swallow their tenderness and let themselves sail
away from softness.

After he left, Edna and I sat on our unpainted porch swing, me
pressing up beside her with my hot body. I put on the radio and
pulled out a bottle of champagne from a cardboard box I'd put out
on the porch earlier. I popped the cork without too much trouble and
poured us each a mason jar.

"Nana Dara, I'm only sixteen," Edna said, her brown eyes looking
as intense as they always did.

"This is a special occasion. Tonight is the first night you and I get
to spend alone as grown women. And for that I am glad you didn't
go to prom."

"I wasn't asked."

I nodded, and she sipped her champagne in the yellow light of
our porch light. The crickets chatted about their day, and one of the
chickens from a few houses over came up to peck at the weed sprouts
in our front yard.

I wondered why Edna hadn't been asked to prom. Unlike me, she
had hair as thick as a horse's mane and perfect teeth and could sound
out almost any song on the piano. Sure, she could be full of fire every
now and again, but what sixteen-year-old isn't?

"Later on you'll meet someone special—like your father—who will recognize how special you are, Edna."

She nodded, clearly unconvinced.

I moved to the wicker chair across from the swing, pulled out the upside-down trashcan that we used as a table, and suggested we learn a little poker. Edna smiled so big and true in the afterglow of the fireworks that she looked like another person.

"Only if we can bet!" she said.

"That's the only way to play."

I shuffled loudly for effect and arched a fancy bridge.

"The trick to poker is the poker face, but it's also the poker *fingers* and the poker *feet*. You can't let your face or the other parts of your body reveal that you've told a lie. We all do it—we all want to get that lie out, so we tap our fingers or move our feet around or do something that lets other people know. The body and the soul—they want to be honest," I said. "You have to *work at it* to be dishonest. But that's part of poker. That's what we call bluffing. To be great at poker you have to lie with your *entire body*."

"I can do that," she said.

I spread out the cards and wrote down what hand beat what other hand on a sheet of paper for her to use.

First two games I won, both with aces high.

"Why don't I deal the next hand," Edna said, smiling.

"Now I'm not sure what you are *accusing* me of, but all right, your deal."

Halfway through our third game, and our second glass of champagne, we moved inside. I set the fans up in a way that wouldn't blow the cards around, and suggested we liven up the bets by a nickel—and liven up the drinks with a little gin.

"*A bite of it*, as they say."

"Well, sure." Edna shuffled the cards while I made us drinks. I heard her stop. "Nana Dara," she called out to me, "I *was* asked to go to the prom tonight."

I didn't turn around from the silver tray we called our bar. I just let her talk.

"I was asked by this nice boy who plays trumpet. But I didn't want to go. I told him I couldn't go. I, ah, it would've just felt too strange—I don't know how to say this, but to dance with a boy against this body . . ."

And there it was: my moment to come clean and tell Edna how much I understood, how I felt the same way. That my daydreams about Rhodie kept me going through the odd days when I didn't feel a true, deep sense of intimacy with the Warden. I could tell her that it would get easier. That there are moments of real love if you let them in—and that, after a few years, you might feel more and more true about it. That she'd learn somehow to do the dance or look for someone who didn't like to dance very often.

But instead I swallowed my secret again and handed her a glass.

"This here is a French 75," I said.

I felt her looking up at me with those nearly black eyes, wanting me to say something.

"You dealing?" I asked.

Edna took a sip. "Sure."

We were quiet for a minute while I battled out what to say. I knew she was thinking that I was troubled by her and that pressure made it harder for me to figure out what words to use. What I came up with was this: "All I can tell you is that I support whatever settles into you right."

Edna nodded real slow, keeping her eyes on the bubbles in her mason jar. She said, "I feel like there's been a great injustice done to me somehow."

"An injustice?"

She paused. I watched her thoughts move around behind her eyes as the fans clicked and whirled.

"But I guess there's more injustice in the world than fleas in the bayou," she finally said.

I nodded, not exactly sure what she was talking about, wondering if maybe it was the beverages causing her to talk crazy—and anyone who has had a French 75 can attest why I made that assumption.

An hour later, the Warden came home. In the crook of his arm was tucked a gorgeous bouquet of carnations and baby's breath.

"They call this a *nosegay*, Edna. You wear it on your wrist."

While he fiddled with the box, I slid our mason jars off to the side then hurried them into the kitchen. I don't think the Warden would've cared if we had a few, but my leaving the room with hidden mason jars sealed our night as a private moment between just Edna and me.

As I watched from the tiny square of linoleum that made up our kitchen, Edna stood up in her yellow summer pajamas and held out her wrist. Her father, all blustering and red—the way he got when the humidity was as high as it was, or he was about to be gentle, or both—slid the bouquet on her wrist. He pulled out the ribbon that had gotten wrapped around her thumb and made sure it was centered just so.

The Warden turned up our radio and held out his hand for a dance. Edna took her father's hand, and they waltzed around the living room. He spun his daughter around while I wiped away a tear or two. After a minute, I quietly shut off the lights in the kitchen and left them alone.

× × ×

Before you knew it, we had POWs being housed in the encampment at the Fort Bend County Fairgrounds, turning something so innocent and playful into a place for captured and caged humans. Before Pearl Harbor, folks around town would talk about the war as spectators, especially on Sunday when the thick paper came out. How Denmark surrendered *the very same day* it had been invaded by Germany, followed by Norway and the Netherlands and Belgium. How France had agreed to let Germany occupy its northern half, only to

have Italy invade its southern half. Basically, how the rest of the world
was falling like eggs in quicksand. Then Pearl Harbor happened, and
America came undone, too.

It was a new feeling, to think about being in America and being
in harm's way—but they'd blown up Hawaii, and now there were
spies everywhere. Even though the encampment was for POWs—for
folks we had *captured* and such—it constantly reminded us of this
new feeling of vulnerability. We had the enemy here with us in Sugar
Land, Texas, of all places. If they were here, they could be anywhere.

The prisoners in our POW camp who could work manned the
local fields and businesses, replacing our men who had gone off to
war. It was an odd switch to me and ruffled a few of the old birds
around town, them thinking these POWs might form some kind of
group determined to poison our lands and food supply. When it was
pointed out that they would then also be poisoning *their* food supply,
the old men would grizzle and say, "Of course!" as if the goal of every
honorable POW was suicide. *A very Japanese thing to say*, I thought
to myself.

Through it all—and years beyond—I felt satisfied knowing *we*, in
Guardtown, were safe. I doubted anyone would waste ammunition
blowing up a prison. But safety still didn't keep us from ordinary
death.

On September 8, 1949, the phone rang. I let it go two rings, as
was some odd custom I'd picked up along the way.

"Dara?"

"Yes?"

"It's Doctor Dixon here at Central Unit—the prison."

I leaned back against the wall, feeling its cold against my shoulder. "Yes?"

"It's the Warden, Dara. He fell down the concrete steps on his way
to the mess hall for his daily walk-through, and died."

"What?"

"The fall didn't kill him, though. It was another stroke. The stroke
caused him to fall. It ripped through the part of his brain that con-

trolled his body, which means that his heart probably stopped before he hit the last stair—if that helps to hear."

"*Another* stroke?"

Doctor Dixon paused.

"He's been having strokes for years now. You didn't know? He went blind in his right eye a few years back, and last year he started having trouble moving his right foot."

"I asked him about that," I said. "I asked him why his foot seemed to be dragging. He said it was just old age." I rubbed my stomach where it stretched out the fabric of my skirt. "He was blind in one eye?"

Doctor Dixon didn't say anything.

"And his headaches?" I asked.

"Those are from his condition also."

"So he didn't feel it? The fall?"

"He was probably out before he hit the first stair."

"Out," I repeated. "And now he's gone?"

The girls looked up from the dining room table, where they were pitting cherries.

Doctor Dixon's voice got low. "Yes, ma'am, he is."

I shook my head at Miss Debbie and Edna then turned to the wall to process it all—only my mind wouldn't stand still. *He had many strokes? He was blind in one eye? He fell and now he is dead?*

I hung up the phone without saying goodbye and stood for a while with my forehead pressed to the wall. When I turned around, the girls were standing there. They'd heard enough to know what I was going to say.

Miss Debbie's arms hung down at her sides. "What is going on, Nana Dara? Who was that? Who's gone?"

"Is it Daddy?" Edna asked.

"Your daddy has died. He had a stroke and . . ."

Miss Debbie started crying right away. I handed her a dishtowel that I'd tucked into my waistband. She used it to blot her face before she grabbed the phone and pulled it around the corner to call her boyfriend, Bo.

Edna didn't cry—not there. She nodded to me that she understood, then walked into the bedroom she still shared with her sister
and shut the door without making a sound.

My heart spasmed. I felt it skip a few beats, then swell and contract
back in my chest. I thought of a million things I needed to do—a list
of funeral arrangements and other miscellaneous things—in order to
keep me away from the tender spots. I wondered how the girls were
going to get through this. I tried to console myself that at least this
had happened after they were grown, Miss Debbie being twenty-four
and Edna twenty-two—but then I realized he'd never get to walk
them down the aisle like he'd wanted. Never rock a grandbaby.

My breathing tightened. I clenched my fists. I ran through more
lists: casket, notification to the paper, the wake, the plot, the headstone—I'd need to order it now.

I looked over at a picture of the Warden we'd had taken at the
Cherry Festival five years earlier. As instructed, we'd both put on a
cherry hat and toasted the camera with a tall glass of cherry juice. It
was on the table next to that damn mustard couch of his.

Every Sunday morning, when he'd iron his pants and his shirt for
church, he'd also iron the armrest covers on that damn couch. There
were punch stains and wine stains and cigarette burns on the couch,
but those armrest covers looked brand new.

And that's when I started to cry, in choking waves of tears—seeing
how much the Warden cared for things that other people might not
value. Seeing how he looked deeper than a few scars to see that this
was a *comfortable* God damn couch. It was just long enough for all
four of us to sit on without squishing up against each other too much.
It was used enough to weather a few oily spots from overturned popcorn bowls, but it was clean. It was loved. He was a man who knew
how to love—not just fall *in* love, but really love, even after something
isn't new anymore.

That couch had been long enough for him to sit on one end and
for me to lie down at a nice angle and get my feet rubbed through my

socks. He'd tease me about pulling off my socks, and I'd threaten to pull my feet away, as if him giving *me* a foot rub was a gift to *him*.

It was on this couch that I'd seen him late one night, in the third year of our marriage, slumped over, looking at his dead wife's picture, drinking gin and whispering. My guess was it was their anniversary. I never asked, just tiptoed back into bed and shut off all the bedroom lights.

That was the couch both girls slept on when they were sick, so the sick one wouldn't wake up the other in that tiny room they shared. I'd bring out a hot pan of water with rosemary floating in it to clear their lungs while the Warden would run out for whatever medicine we could use to make us think we were doing something. That couch held more than its share of dirty tissues and had soaked up buckets of cool water running from washcloths held on burning foreheads.

I walked over and curled up on it that night, where I prayed my fifth rosary since my youth. I prayed for the Warden. I said the rosary for the secrets of his soul. I said it as my way of greasing the doorman at the pearly gates, just in case the Warden had hidden some misdoings from me.

I prayed when all I could think about was how I would ever be able to sleep in our bed again. I remembered that he never said anything about me lying to him about my letters with Rhodie—that he loved me and left me my secrets. I remembered the smiling faces of the people in the cafeteria on the day the Warden knelt down on that creaky stage to propose to me, and the moonlight on our wedding night, and the way the fans blew that white ribbon around the flowers on Edna's wrist when he danced with her on her prom night—and I prayed.

I prayed the rosary because, God dammit all, I did love that man, after all.

THE KING OF THE
TWELVE-STRING GUITAR

The week the Warden died, in the fall of 1949, I was paging through the paper to make sure they had listed his obituary correctly when I came across a blurb on page three: *Lead Belly, Former Central Unit Inmate, Strums a Low Note.*

The article told how Huddie had built himself quite a name with folks like Woody Guthrie raving about his musical skill. The crazy Negro—he had made himself a reputation as a musical genius.

The focus of the article, though, was how Huddie had contracted ALS, or what had come to be known as Lou Gehrig's disease. The short of it: Huddie—the self-proclaimed and widely acknowledged "King of the Twelve-String Guitar"—was dying.

Well, shit.

I closed the paper right up. It was too much. I had just buried the Warden. And to add to it, I felt like I'd lost my entire family. Mama and Daddy were long gone, and my stepdaughters had turned their grief inside themselves, far away from me. Since the Warden died, I had sat in our home night after night having silent dinners with his daughters, the ones who didn't want my condolences—or maybe I was too lost in my own gray world to hand them out.

Huddie dying? I couldn't manage that right now, so I set the paper aside until I felt strong enough to handle it.

The next day, I opened it up again. The article called Huddie— Lead Belly—"one of the most prolific folk singers of the day, and also one of the most violent," having landed himself in jail for attempted murder or stabbing at least three times. It said that a few years after his first album came out, the doctors told him he had ALS, and that he would die from it:

> . . . Lead Belly's symptoms include tripping on stairs and, to his heartbreak, a decreased ability to make quick, accurate chord changes. Now, he's bedridden in New York City, with some difficulty swallowing due to muscle weakness . . .

I flipped the paper down and pushed my plate of spaghetti to the side of my gold TV tray. Two loud birds chirped at each other outside. I looked out across my small room. A force of blood moved through me with each breath I took.

The thought of my friend lying there, possibly alone, in bed, not able to play or sing, surged through my already damaged heart and broke it down even further. The Warden, God bless him, had left me a nice sum of money on his death, and I decided autumn might be a really beautiful time to visit New York City.

× × ×

The very next morning, me feeling deeply that he didn't have much time left, I woke the Warden's girls and asked them to have some coffee with me. Miss Debbie, her hair in curlers under a cotton hankie, said she didn't drink coffee—that it made her too aggressive.

"Oh, is *that* what does it?" I said.

She answered by putting a pillow over her face.

Edna, sitting up in the bed next to her sister's, folded her book over and said she'd be down shortly.

Five minutes later, we all sat around the dining room table, a small circular thing that the Warden's parents had given him after he got married to his first wife. I ran my fingers over the scratch marks on the rounded edge, where little Edna had decided to practice her fork skills.

"I have some news," I started. "Some travel news." I clasped my hands on the tabletop near one of the many vases of funeral flowers that had just started browning. "I need to see a friend . . ."

They sat there about as perky as starving soldiers on the front line. I continued, "In New York."

Coming to life, the girls gasped in stereophonic sound. Edna's eyes lit up—New York!—while Miss Debbie looked like she'd seen a vision of the end of the world. She held her hand to her throat. "Why on Earth would you go to *New York?*"

"My friend is dying."

Edna, all long legs and arms in her loose pajamas, leaned forward. Her wooden chair creaked. "You have a *friend* in *New York?*"

I resisted the urge to say who this friend was, not because he was colored and not because he was a musician, but because I didn't want to use his name to make myself seem more interesting to the girls. In short, I didn't want to brag—not that Miss Debbie would find the news of me being cozy with a womanizing, murderous Negro singer to be *braggable* in the conventional sense.

"I will be back in one week," I said. "Can I trust you two alone here?"

Miss Debbie rolled her blue eyes up toward her curlers. "We're *adults.*"

Edna looked up at me. "You want company on the trip?"

"Oh honey," I said, touched that she'd want to come, "I would love your company, but I'm afraid this trip might be a little much. He's dying, after all."

She stiffened up. "I know death."

"I know you do. But this death is a bit much maybe."

"Why's that?"

"Well, he's a colored man."

Miss Debbie leapt up from her chair and onto her righteously rigid legs poking out from her angel-wing-white nightgown. "What! A *Negro*—and a man! No, Nana Dara, you are *not going.* New York was one thing, but these are three things! *Strike Out.*"

Edna laughed. "This isn't baseball."

"No." Miss Debbie turned to her, hands on her hips now. "This is *life.*"

Edna leaned back against the wood rails of the chair back. "I think it's exciting. I didn't know you knew folks like that."

"Well, I did work in a prison."

"Oh my God!" Miss Debbie literally stomped her foot. "Is he an ex-convict?"

I put my hands out in a gesture of calm and placed one on each of their upper arms. "I will leave you some money for food. If there's an emergency, call the hospital number I'll leave you, and they can find me. I can trust you, right?"

Miss Debbie scowled. "Can we trust you? I feel like I don't know you at all." She turned away, loving her moment on the stage.

Edna shrugged and stood up. She pressed her cool hand over mine—a great sign of affection from her. "You ought to leave me the information, Nana Dara, for fear that Miss Debbie here might have the police called."

I smiled. "Good idea, honey."

× × ×

The trip to New York didn't move in exactly a straight line. I took buses and trains, and I even needed to spend two nights in a "roomette" on one of those new, lightweight Pullmans.

Not much for seeking out the company of strangers, I stayed mostly inside my little blue-and-green roomette, looking out the picture window in amazement at the changes in the countryside as we headed up north—watching all the farmlands get smaller and darker somehow while I waved hello to the cows, who didn't appear bothered in the least by the train's smoke and noise.

My roomette came with a sitting chair as comfortable as any on solid ground, a foldaway bed, a sink, and small toilet. All I could ask for.

In my mind, I planned what possessions I would take to live in one of these rooms if I wanted to spend my days on a train, seeing the world. I decided I'd bring my family portraits, a phonograph with as

many records as I could fit on a single shelf, Mama's old suitcase filled
with books—thinking I could also prop my feet on the suitcase when
they started throbbing—that picture Rhodie drew for me after our
weekend together, my bloody souvenir from cutting the head cook,
and a few of the artworks made for me by Edna and Miss Debbie
before they started getting dreams of their own.

Clearly my time on the rails—with the fields moving by and the
sky standing still—had turned me sentimental. Letting it overtake
me in the way that mood can, I decided to write some letters to my
long-lost friends.

First: that ape Ken. Ken who'd come by our house for barbecue
every so often with his mousy wife and their loud children. I wrote
and told him he's always welcome, even now that the Warden is
gone—*especially* now. I confessed that maybe I'd like to see him and
play some more cards—just me and him now. And though I knew
he probably wouldn't take me up on it, writing it down made me feel
like at least I was doing *something* to maintain connection, to be open.

As I sealed the powder blue envelope, a nice young man came by
and knocked on my roomette. He slid the door open and asked if I'd
care for more wine.

"Why yes," I said, "it's helping me write my letters."

He tipped his hat. "I do my best, ma'am."

"Only," I said, "why don't you make it champagne."

"I'll bring you a fresh rose too."

I smiled and thought that the world just couldn't get any nicer
than it was right then and there, in the cozy chair of my roomette.

After my tray arrived, complete with a linen napkin, an orange
rose, and the tiniest bottle of champagne I'd ever seen, I wrote to
Beauregard. I told him all that had happened with the Warden dying
and me heading off to see Huddie in New York City, riding a new,
aluminum train that shined so brightly I had to cover my eyes when
I stepped in. I wrote that I hoped all was well with his pretty wife,
Evelyn, and those two boys of his. I told him I remembered going
to get drinks with him and Evelyn and that it had stopped me from

my own internal madness after I'd gotten that notice from Rhodie. I thanked him and told him he'd been one of my best friends ever and that hopefully some day when he had the time—maybe when his kids had moved on—we could get together again. I signed it with love.

Even as I did, I wondered if I'd ever let anyone in. If I'd ever speak my truth.

I looked out the window. The sounds and bounces of the train were normal to me now, my body moving without resistance. A plantation of what looked like Christmas trees speeded by.

I saw that I'd been alone since Rhodie. For twenty-five years, I'd been alone. Even in a crowded room, even with a husband I respected and loved in my way, even with his children—I was alone. A loneliness that comes from settling for a love that won't ever touch your soul. From settling for your *body and mind* being tended to, while you tell your soul to *shush up*— to stop being so needy and wanting to be heard. To be grateful no one is trying to kill you.

Throughout my marriage I'd had that loneliness, one so dire that sometimes I'd find myself on the porch looking up at the sky long after the sun had set. On those nights, the Warden knew to leave me alone. He'd let me sleep on the porch swing outside, with my thoughts and my tears.

I'd hated myself for crying then. To dry up those tears, I'd remind myself of all the happiness I *did* have and the children he gave me— of how selfish and ungrateful I was being to question this life. And then, slowly, my soul would close its eyes and sink back down into the darkness inside me.

After my second glass of champagne and after the housing shacks along the tracks had faded into the moonlit fields behind them, I leaned back and decided to take a look at myself from the outside. To examine this person in front of me as if it wasn't me.

It took me a minute, but when I did, I sympathized with her. I came to understand that life isn't moments of going from *black* to *white*; it's letting the dawn come up as slowly as it needs, to until you realize it's a new day.

All these years, I'd silently chastised myself for being a coward—
for not leaving as dramatically as Huddie had. Now I saw that it just
wasn't possible at that time, in that place, being who I was. I did my
best, same as we all do. You simply can't make your legs longer than
they are. You can only take the steps that they allow.

I'd been a twenty-year-old small-town girl. Still, I'd shown bravery—and, dare I say, *prowess*—to unbutton Rhodie's shirt, to move
to the Imperial State Prison Farm for men, and then to leave and do
my best.

After all—and I do mean *all*—here I was on a train by myself,
in a roomette trimmed with gold paint and smelling of roses, sip-
ping champagne on my way to New York City. *That was something,* I
thought. *I am something.*

× × ×

I stepped off the train and caught a taxi over to the hospital that had
been listed in the newspaper article: New York Presbyterian. Tired
and stiff, I walked through the giant glass doors only to be told that
Huddie had gone home.

They gave me his listed residence—an apartment in Harlem.
To get there, I needed to take the subway and, one of the more
stern-looking doctors noted, a weapon.

The nurse leaned across the desk. "You would do best to hail a cab.
They come around in the circle out front every few minutes. Just raise
your hand or ask someone with a yellow hat to help you."

"Thank you kindly," I said, grateful that my large size gave me a
kind of presence that I doubted many would want to mess with.

I walked toward the door to where the cabs drove up. After all,
there was no way I was going to take a *subway*. I was not going
to walk underground into a metal tube speeding through the mud,
especially given how many mines collapse on a regular basis. *Crazy
city folks.*

When I walked outside, I got hit by wind so fierce that big chunks of my hair pulled up like tile in a flood. Torn between holding down my skirt or my hair, I opted for the most modest route and walked forward with as much dignity as I could muster, considering a plank of hair had fallen across my forehead. A nice young man in a yellow hat helped me into a cab, and I was on my way.

Not only did I get to Harlem, I got there unharmed.

I won't lie, though—I was scared the entire drive, seeing sights out my windows I'd never seen before: steam coming out of the street itself like nostrils of some terrible dragon, cars honking at nothing, women wearing next to no clothes, people sleeping on the street, Asians, men selling food and balloons on corners, all the lit-up signs.

To ease my nerves, I reminded myself that these sights were also blessed by God. God, my convenient friend.

The cab took me right up to Huddie's apartment building, but the driver didn't open my door or wish me goodbye or wait to see if I got in. He took off, and there I stood, shivering, hoping the address was correct—but also, from the look of the taped-up windows and cracking paint, hoping it might be incorrect. I steadied myself, repositioned my shawl to give me the look of confidence, and walked up.

The sky was grayer in New York than in Texas, or at least it was on that day. Kids played basketball in the street, same as we did, only they played dangerously close to folks' windows. The buildings—mostly brick—were set close together, even closer than Guardtown.

I rang the "Ledbetter" button near the huge entry door. A couple of colored men on the porch across the street raised their white mugs at me, saying hello. I didn't know if they were mocking me or not, so I just nodded and turned to face the door—making sure I didn't turn too quickly.

The woman who answered the door looked like a black version of myself—though while my dark brown hair had only a few lines of white here and there, hers was nearly all white, with only a little black on the frizzy tips. She seemed tired.

I was terrified as I stood there with her, clearly the only white person for miles around.

She looked me up and down. "Yes?"

I made sure my voice came out strong sounding. "I've come up from Texas to visit Huddie Ledbetter. Is he here?"

"That's my husband. And yes, he's here."

The woman held the cracked wooden door open. I doubted many white women visited Huddie—at least not white woman my age and *maturity*—and I wondered what she thought. She, his wife.

"I worked with him years ago," I said.

She nodded. "He's not well."

"That's what I read, so I came up here to see him."

We walked up the creaky stairs on stair treads that had worn down to dark blue threads in some spots. The hallways smelled like peppermint oil, and I wondered if they had a bad ant problem.

She opened their apartment door for me, and I stepped in.

"I need to get groceries 'fore the store closes," she said. "You go on in." She pointed to the back room, presumably the bedroom. "It's nice of a friend to come calling, rather than just sending word. So many of his friends are just sending words. Name's Martha."

"Dara."

Martha turned and walked back out into the hallway, leaving me there in their small, tidy apartment. A few cans of beer dotted an otherwise clean coffee table sitting in front of a sagging brown couch.

Not wanting to feel like I was prying, I turned my eyes down and walked back to the bedroom. The door was open a crack. I pushed in, so as not to wake him by knocking if he was asleep. There, on sheets the color of dry grass, under a gray military blanket, was Huddie. Propped in the corner, as dusty and dejected as a blind man's gun, sat his guitar.

I nearly cried, the sight of him like that, with not even enough breath to blow through a harmonica. This had been a man teeming with might and anger. A strong man with a wide chest and muscles all the way into his fingers.

Now, the bones of his face showed through his skin. He still had his hair—gray but there—and that big gap between his front teeth and that sadness, but so much else was gone already.

"You," he said, gagging a little for air.

I smiled and said, "You."

I sat down on the edge of his thin bed. Huddie moved his hand from under the gray blanket and looked over my wedding ring.

"The Warden," I said.

He nodded that he'd already heard, and smiled. "You got out."

"I kept my promise to you, though maybe not in a big way."

"You feel good with him?"

"As good as I could expect," I said. "The Warden's gone now."

Huddie nodded, not that he was sorry, but just that death happens.

"You OK?" I asked.

Slowly, pacing himself, he answered, "I got this room and I got Martha—best wife a man could hope for. Stood by through all this."

I looked around the room: a bed, a black dresser with most of the handles missing, a short stack of records on the dresser, a matching set of sand-colored suitcases with black straps, and that dusty guitar.

"Bigger than my other jail cells," he said before dropping off with a little bitterness, "Though I have learned that, for a black man, every room is a cell where he stays 'till they use him up."

"I'm sorry, Huddie."

He nodded. His tired eyes reminded me of a sick, lonely puppy. My glorious Huddie.

A roach crawled across the radiator under the window, down along the floor, and under his bed. *At least roaches don't bite*, I thought.

Huddie closed his loose, dark eyes again. This must be tough on Martha—helping him wash and change his clothes—and tough on him, on his dignity.

I took his hand, feeling the rough skin of a working man. "But we did get out, as much as we could, didn't we, Huddie? We pushed against those walls . . ."

"Yes, ma'am." He shook his head and smiled up at me. The dim sunlight hit the side of his face, and he let the anger go. "You loved him—the Warden?"

"In a quiet way."

"Well, good. So now you might be ready for love in a loud way."

I pulled back a bit, on reflex. I didn't know what to say. I didn't know for sure what he was saying, but I think I did.

He looked up at me. "I knew folks like you. Had to fight off scores of mellow boys during my time at Huntsville, 'fore Sugar Land—and more at Rikers Island. And in between, well, I played at all kinds of clubs, you know. *All kinds.* Along the way, I met lots of people, and I recognized you in a few of them, Miss Dara."

Huddie smiled up with the smile of the spirits—open and non-committal, so I told him the truth: "Once . . ." I said, my face hot. "Her name was Rhodie."

His eyes fluttered. "You loved once, so it's possible to do it again."

I nodded.

"Just talking science," he said, trying to smile again. "Pure science."

I exhaled and laughed. "Yes, yes, I hear you."

With his free hand, Huddie pointed to the short stack of albums on his dresser.

"Got three of mine left." He paused, then: "You take one, Miss Dara."

I walked over and lifted up the one on top: *Lead Belly and the Golden Gate Quartet.*

"They got me recorded other times too. In Austin, Minneapolis—" he struggled, but this was important—"All over the country."

"I'll look out for those recordings."

He closed his eyes. "Now, everyone's singing my songs—everyone except me."

"I'm so proud of you."

Huddie squeezed my hand with weak fingers that had once dug up foot-long weeds and worn down fretboards.

He opened his eyes and whispered, "Best go before it gets dark. Don't worry about me. I got Martha and I got five hundred songs in my head."

I held up his record, letting him know I had it. "Goodbye, Huddie."

"Goodbye, Miss Dara."

"Huddie," I said, mustering up my bravery again, "I love you."

He turned his head to me. His pink lips cracked a little when he smiled, and in that smile—that particular, soft kind of smile—I knew that he knew that we had loved each other. In this world I had known this man *truly* and without fear, and he had been my friend.

x x x

Huddie died on December 5, 1949. His death got front-page coverage in Sugar Land, him being a former resident of the prison. The paper even did a few follow-up articles on him. One article was about this white band by the name of the Weavers who recorded one of Huddie's songs a few months after he'd died—just *one*—and made themselves two million dollars. Two million dollars from a single one of Huddie's songs.

I hoped that wherever he'd landed, he wasn't angry over the success of that song—and all the others to follow. I hoped he wasn't bitter that he'd been prevented from having that kind of success with his own damn music. Instead, I hoped he saw the success of his music as a way to continue who he had been—a way for Huddie to escape his birthright and his color and even his death. His life would continue after his death.

This way, in his death, my friend showed me how to live right: to find the thing you love and be open to it, let it take you over—for him, his music—then let it carry you past yourself.

BOOK THREE

mrs. dara

THE BLAND OLD OPRY

After a bit of vacillation, I found the strength to make the decision to leave Guardtown and the shadow of what they by then called the Central Unit and set out on my own. I was determined to push the walls of my jail back even further and, at nearly fifty, it was about damn time.

Looking back now, I see the importance of that moment. That moment turned my path crooked and led to me find not only independence, but love and acceptance both from others and myself. At the time, though, I was so scared I broke out in hives all over my belly and my neck, which caused several strangers to shift back and ask me outright if I had poison ivy. No, I told them, just *fear*, which I don't think is contagious, though I'm not totally sure about that.

The sale of the house happened almost immediately since there was a long list of prison employees wanting to move from shantys into houses. I used part of the profit—much more than I had expected—to send Edna off to college in Dallas to study American history. She didn't stay there, though, instead moving to a new city every other year it seemed, including places that surely would have killed the Warden if he had been alive, places like Boston and San Francisco.

In some ways, I took Edna's disappearances harder than the Warden's death. There was a finality in *him* leaving, whereas with her, I kept hoping one day she'd stop back by. I was proud of her, though, the way she shuffled around, seeing the world. In my crazy daydreams, I even harbored a hope that, one day, she'd ask me to tag along, and maybe we could go see the Grand Canyon or pet the dolphins that swim right up to you in California.

In reality, I knew her moving was just another way for her to keep pushing away, like she did when she was a teenager and suddenly didn't want anyone to hug her. I gave her space, and when I got to worrying, I'd nibble on a few extra biscuits to calm myself.

I blessed Miss Debbie's engagement to Bo, who brought me flowers, but had no money, and never got his high school diploma. In an effort to connect with Miss Debbie, I offered to pay for a fancy shindig of a wedding. Turns out the offer was ill-timed.

Miss Debbie, ring finger wagging in front of her, announced, "It's too late. We eloped Thursday."

I folded my newspaper in half and slapped it down on the coffee table. "Who gets married on *Thursday?*"

"We do. We got wed."

"Where did you spend your wedding night, in one of Bo's cars?"

She stuck her lip out. "We are *saving* that part."

I raised a very doubtful eyebrow. "That so?"

She ignored me by flipping her hair and turning around to help herself to an apple on the counter. "But we'd still like to use Daddy's money for a car shop."

"It's not your daddy's money—it's mine."

"It's ours."

"He left you all your mother's jewelry, if you recall. The money is mine."

She crossed her arms the way she always did, and I couldn't help but smile at her spunk. "You're married now, huh?" I said.

"I am." She fiddled with her ring. "Bo'll be paying on this until he's seventy."

"You have an odd way to show your love."

She yanked her hand back, and I regretted saying that. *Why could I never say the right thing with her?*

I corrected myself. "I'm sorry. It's beautiful."

With a loud crunch, Miss Debbie started in on the apple. Despite her mouth being full, she told me her plan: "There's a garage for sale a county over, and above it is this little room where we can stay until he makes enough money to get us a house. Won't be long. He's already got customers."

I nodded, trying to look as thoughtful as possible.

She munched. "I want kids."

"Uh-huh."

"And you want grandkids?"

"If they come, sure."

"Then we need that garage." Miss Debbie put the half-eaten apple in the sink, a move that never ceased to infuriate me. She noticed, pulled it back out, and threw it in the yard through the kitchen window to be a treat for the nearby animals, the way I always wanted her to.

I said, "A garage?"

"You sent Edna to school!"

"And I'd pay for yours too, or your wedding."

She sighed loud enough for the neighbors to hear. "We eloped, and college is not my way. I hate reading."

"Who hates reading?"

Her neck got that angry tension in it. "I do! You know I do. Asking me that question for two decades is not going to make the answer change!"

"OK, now."

"Shoot, though."

I smiled. "I suppose we could call the money for the garage an *elopement* gift."

Miss Debbie literally jumped up and down. In her excitement, she raced over to hug me before that invisible barrier between us got in the way again, and she pulled back to a gentle hug with a bit less skin contact. "Thank you, Nana Dara."

I almost said, *Now be nice to him.* But instead I said, "You're welcome."

Later that week, I handed over the money for Bo's garage. Bo shook my hand over and over again, until I told him that I only had two of them, so he needed to go easy.

That house money sent Edna to college, got Miss Debbie and Bo to a place of being supported, and bought me a new house.

Thank you, Warden—again.

It only took me one day to find my house: a prefab mobile home with powder blue and beige siding that I dubbed *The Bland Old Opry*. She was timid yet bold, my new home. She had no yard to maintain, and each of her four windows had these tiny, built-on green fabric awnings to help keep the place cool in the summer. There was even a ceiling fan in the big bedroom. As someone who tends to run hot, I loved a good ceiling fan.

I bought it where I found it, in a mobile home park with an honest-to-goodness sidewalk and black lampposts and the most unusual display of mailboxes you will ever see. Mine was a coffee can flipped on its side that eventually rusted out. When it did, I replaced it with a metal Christmas cookie tin that I painted to look like a sleeping snake, but, if I'm going to be honest with myself, it looked more like a plate of intestines.

I took over the lease on the land, which I planned someday to buy outright, and paid cash for the mobile home. The older couple living there was being taken to Odessa to live in a complex near their three daughters.

"Out to pasture," the man told me.

"A pasture with a big swimming pool," his wife added.

I listened, hoping that, when the day came for me to go to pasture, I'd been mom enough for my girls to make sure I had a swimming pool.

× × ×

As I've mentioned, I'm what well-reared folks call "ample." My genetic calling to weight was with me since I was a youngster, but didn't branch into startling proportions until after the Warden passed on. By the time I bought the Bland Old Opry, I'd stabilized at a pleasant 260 pounds.

At first, I thought it'd be nice for a woman of my magnitude to have the whole place to myself, just me and the Opry and my cats— but then one day I got dizzy. For no reason I could fathom, I got dizzy and felt like I was going to pass out. There, in the midst of the Earth spinning around, I thought, *Who would find me if I die?* Miss Debbie was off with Bo, and Edna was running around trying to "find herself." I could fall and die and lie there in my own filth until the Angel of Death came, or the mailman smelled something rank. That would not do.

That day I understood that I was a living ghost. I wandered around, haunted a few places—mostly snack shacks—and drifted into my solitary space, waiting for a postcard from Edna. I lived on in her brief stories about working at bookstores and listening to poetry and taking boat rides. That needed to stop. I had to get some flesh-and-blood folks to be near me, otherwise I might start to doubt my own existence.

I decided to get myself a roommate. Someone who, at the very least, would find my dead body before it started getting funky.

A week later, a woman at the hair salon named Dorothy intro-duced me to my future boarder, the Fiddler. I'd been sitting in my chair when Dorothy, sitting next to me, said her third cousin needed to rent a room in a place of no judgment, where he could finish his "transforming" after he'd had some kind of run-in with the law.

Dorothy looked around. "Anyone know anyone? He's very quiet and helpful around the house."

"Well," I said, "I was thinking of bringing in a boarder—and I my-self have just finished transforming." I paused. "Menopause."

Dorothy nodded in unified sympathy.

I asked what kind of trouble her cousin had been in.

"He had this girlfriend—or maybe a few—and they were a bit too young for him," she said. "That kind of thing is frowned upon by some folks, though I know many girls who *invite* the attentions of older men, so I don't see why the bother."

All the women around us nodded their heads in agreement.

"Sounds fine by me," I said. "Give me his number, and I'll set up some time to visit with him and see if we might get along."

× × ×

The Fiddler—who'd yet to be called the Fiddler, but I can't remember his real name—met me for the Blue Plate down at Terry's: pork chops and coleslaw. The restaurant was nearly all booths, with three wobbly tables in the center that no one ever sat at, so the waitresses used them as ketchup and salt-shaker filling stations. When he walked in, I knew it was him by his bashful way of coming in—like he'd never been to the place before. He looked quiet.

I waved him over without getting up, and he smiled. I guessed him to be in his late thirties. He had a beard trimmed close to his face, long before that became fashionable, and kept his brown hair buzzed to fuzz around his neck and ears. His cowboy hat had a horseshoe painted on it and a leather band around it. He seemed peculiar—like a coal miner without a mine—so I knew we'd get along right away, me liking peculiar people.

As he slid into the booth, I commented on how evenly his beard was trimmed.

He smiled and rubbed his chin. "I use the same clippers I use on my head that I use on my face. Love those clippers. Can't shave down to the skin on my face because I get these terrible ingrown hairs."

"If you move in then, you'll want to get clippers with batteries since we lose power every few days in the Bland Old Opry, which is what I call my trailer."

"I already have 'em in a pair of clippers I invented myself."

"Oh, well then maybe you can see if you can invent a battery-powered TV."

"I'll surely try," he said, sealing the deal.

× × ×

The Fiddler moved in three weeks later, bringing one dirty beige suit-case with a belt wrapped around it and a small canvas bag that looked vaguely military and clanked with the sound of tools. I introduced him to my six cats—a number that grew every year—and warned him that they each had a cadre of their own pets, namely cockroaches that always got away and geckos who hardly ever did.

"You'll have to be on the lookout for the geckos, because just before they die they turn the color of the carpet."

"Yes, ma'am," he said as he examined the carpet down the hallway and into his room—the only other formal bedroom in the Opry.

"Go on and get settled in. I've made casserole."

"Sounds good."

He carried his bags down the narrow hallway, passing by a light that never worked. Seeing it, he put his bags down, stood on his tippy toes in his boots, and jiggled the base. "I think I can fix this if you want."

"Sure be nice to have a light when there's a cat fight in the hallway."

"I'll get on it."

And five minutes later, the light was working.

"How did you do that?" I asked.

"I just fiddled with it."

With that, I named him the Fiddler.

And fiddle he did. He was always taking things apart, then trying to reassemble them without their former squeaks or buzzes. By the end of the first year, I'd lost three clocks and two phones, and had to have the oil seal on my truck redone, God love him.

THE LAST LETTER

One cloudless day in 1952, I went out on the graying deck, side-stepping the termite slats, and sat down in my faded blue recliner to taunt the Fiddler, as had become my late-afternoon habit. He just made it so damn easy.

I was retaining enough water to grow rice in Arizona, so I clicked the leg part out on my chair to raise my ankles. The Fiddler, mean-while, pulled up errant dead shrubs from along the edges of the deck. His arms were redder than raspberry gum.

"What are you up to today?" I asked him while I shaded my eyes from the sun.

He held up his bony, hairy hands. They were cut up in spots from him pulling up the dry brush weeds on the hill behind and around the deck. "I'm bringing the brush back since I'm worried the wildfires will catch on to them and torch the Opry."

"The only fire we need to concern ourselves with is the one in your *loins!*"

The Fiddler stood up, sweat dripping off his red face. He looked angry. He clapped his hands down on his jeans, leaving big dirt marks, and grumbled, "Never mind."

"No, you keep on!"

"You best put some water buckets near the house, though, in case she burns. I'm done."

"Fiddler!"

Ignoring me, he walked over to the milk crate by the screen door, picked up the disembodied arm of my record player that he'd been meaning to fix, and walked inside.

"Don't be sore," I called out. "You know I'm just kidding you!"

But I'd said too much; he left for the bar.

The next day, late in the afternoon, the Fiddler called in my front door, "You in a better mood today, Nana Dara?"

"You just getting home?" I yelled back from the kitchen, which still smelled like my cinnamon sugar toast.

"Don't judge. I had steam to blow off." The front door clicked shut. "I brought a friend over."

"A *friend?*"

The Fiddler stepped into the kitchen, alone. He whispered: "She's a new friend who's leaving for Mexico in a few weeks, on account of leaving her job and wanting to get away."

I eyed him up and down in his black T-shirt and khaki shorts. "You're acting funny."

"I always act funny."

"Good point," I said, then, "I want to apologize—"

He held up a hand. "No need."

The Fiddler looked around. He scratched nervously at his in-grown neck hairs, and I thought that he must have a crush on this new friend. We walked into the living room together, and I could see right off why: she was beautiful in that sun-kissed, country way. She wore her blond hair in a bob and painted her dark, babydoll eyes with waves of blue eyeshadow.

"Joli," the Fiddler said, still scratching, "this here is Nana Dara."

She smiled. "Well, hi there."

"Hello," I said.

The Fiddler headed for the bathroom. "Be right back."

"All right," I said, then turned to Joli. "You a friend of the Fiddler's then?"

"We met last night. I'd had a few too many. Drinking away my sorrows over quitting my job down at the museum."

"Why did you quit?"

"That museum is so *dead* that everything on its walls has started to stink. I couldn't bear it one more day."

"The airplane museum?"

She rolled her eyes. "That's not even a true museum, is it?"

I raised my eyebrows and nodded. She had a point.

"But don't worry about the Fiddler," she said. "He was a true gentleman. He just tucked me in and fell asleep on the couch."

No doubt he tucked her in because he had no other interest in her sexually, she being older than his preferred age of eighteen years old—eighteen since his sexual *recovery*, that is.

"Hmmm," I said.

Joli looked around at the colorful plates I'd hung on the walls in the kitchen and the different-colored cactus pots I'd painted myself.

"When I was little my grandma took me fishing," she said with a small flip of her hair. "We'd use a stick and a piece of rope and a bright, colorful button that she'd soaked in oil. She loved color too. She would have *loved* this place."

I'm not sure whether that was a compliment or not, but I took it to be. "Thank you."

"My dogs will love it here."

"What?" I picked up my cup of hot tea sitting on the side table near the mustard couch.

"My pugs. They are right outside in the car there." She pointed behind her. "In the shade. Relaxing. They like to relax—well, mostly."

"Pugs?"

She smiled, showing off a charming gap between her front teeth. "The Fiddler said you couldn't resist a stray. Since I'm going to Mexico I can't take them with me, technically, they are strays!"

I blew on my tea. *Damn that Fiddler.* "Well, this just might not be the right place for your dogs," I told her.

"Why not?" She raised her eyebrows and looked out through the kitchen at the back door leading to a very dog-friendly backyard.

I sucked in a big breath, then blurted out, "This is a house of ill repute. You see, I'm a non-practicing lesbian."

"Well, I'm a non-practicing Baptist," she answered, without missing a beat.

Joli shifted her weight to stand with her hip out to one side, the way I'd seen cheerleaders stand. "You give up being a lesbian?"

"No," I answered, stunned that she continued the conversation. "My drive just went away one day." Though looking at Joli, I knew that this was not entirely true. She was gorgeous.

Joli leaned in. "The *change?*"

"Maybe." I coughed to hide a blush.

Joli nodded thoughtfully. "I do not look forward to *that* day, to be sure! I like desire." She stopped for a second. "Can I ask you something personal?"

"That's where we are."

"Were you ever *practicing?*"

"Once."

"Didn't you miss, you know, having *relations?*"

"We did have relations."

"No, I mean didn't you miss having sex?"

"What I'm saying is that we did."

"How'd that work?"

Did she truly just ask me that? "It just did. It worked. It was successful."

She smiled again, and I knew she got away with a lot with that homecoming queen smile of hers. "I often wondered about it myself."

A little surge of adrenaline came over me, followed by a self-condemnation—she was a good twenty years my junior! "I imagine folks do. You want some lemonade or sweet tea?"

"I'd like a little of both," she said, smiling again.

"Now you needn't charm me, I already said I'll take your dogs."

Joli paused and bit the edge of her lip. "They are *royal* dogs, you know, the kind the Queen of England has."

"Well, as long as they don't chase cats," I said.

Here she only smiled.

The Fiddler came whistling down the creaky, paneled hallway of the Opry, proud as a rooster in a hen house. "So you got some dogs now?"

I scowled. "You didn't need to get *vindictive*. I said I was sorry for teasing you."

"Why, Nana Dara, I truly have no idea what you are talking about."

"Dangit Fiddler," I muttered.

Joli spun around to face us. "You didn't tell me Nana Dara here is a lesbian."

Here he stood stunned, blood falling clear down to his toes. To his credit, he didn't say anything.

Joli continued, "I think that is just amazing. Here in Sugar Land. A lesbian." She shrugged. "At any rate, thank you for caring for my beautiful little pugs. We ought to get them in now, though, since the heat can flare up their anal glands."

I nearly choked on my tea. "Their what?"

"Anal glands."

The Fiddler chuckled.

"Don't worry," Joli said, "you can clean them yourself. But just wear gloves."

I felt faint.

"OK," the Fiddler chimed in, smiling bigger than I'd ever seen, "I'm going to drop Joli off. But don't worry, I made the pugs a little corner to sleep in."

"Where?"

"Right beside your bed," he said.

Joli headed for the door. "Oh, that reminds me. Don't feed them too many vegetables or protein. They get the kind of gas that can peel your paint right off, truly."

The Fiddler held the door for her. "Truly," he repeated.

× × ×

The Fiddler heaved in those damn pugs, then drove Joli to the train station—and all I could think was that that was one of the most beautiful women I'd seen in quite some time. I finally understood the trend to a tight waist and a high hemline.

Sighing, I shook my head. There was no more sense denying it: I liked women—not just Rhodie, but *women*, in general and in specifics. My wedding ring had given me a close chain to run on, but the desire had always rumbled below the surface. All the time, just below the surface. It wasn't Rhodie or anyone else; it was *me*.

Just as I was having these thoughts, the mailman came panting up my steps and dropped off several magazines and a letter addressed to me with my maiden name but no return address. The cancelation said it'd come from Midland, Texas.

When I opened it, a chapter of my life shut, finally.

Dear Miss Dara,

My name is Marigold. I am Rhodie Prevette's daughter. I am writing to tell you that she was in a car accident and she died. She left an envelope in her desk and told me years ago that if anything should ever happen to her that I was to open this envelope and follow the directions on her list. You were number two on a list of ten items. She asked me to "write to Dara Bernard at the Imperial State Prison Farm and tell her that I'm sorry for whatever I might have done and if I didn't do anything, to tell her that I forgive her."

My mother never talked about you, so I'm not sure of your history together. She once told me that she had a best friend that she lost touch with, who used to go bullfrog hunting with her. She said that next to having me and my brother and marrying my father, that this friend was her happiest moment. I think that friend was probably you, and I think she'd want you to know that.

The funeral was last month, here in Midland. I didn't get a forwarding address from the prison in time to have this letter reach you beforehand. I'm sorry. But I am writing now, and I hope what I've written you brings you some comfort in this sad time.

Sincerely,
Marigold Prevette

I went numb about halfway through the letter, so I reread it a few times to make sure I understood it all. Rhodie was dead. She forgave me, and now she is dead.

I always thought I'd get the courage to write to her and apologize, but I never did. I just kept sending letters into the fire and using her as a way to keep myself out of my own life. I'd been channeling all my affections and passions onto an image of someone that I'd spent a little less than a month with some thirty years ago. It felt stupid when I put it that way. Stupid and stagnant and fearful. Worse, my damn fear prevented me from ever sending her a letter and taking responsibility for what I'd chosen and how I'd wrecked such a sweet and gentle thing.

So I wrote her one final letter, hoping maybe she could read it over my shoulder:

My Sweet Rhodie,

This afternoon the mail came and, in it, a letter from your daughter telling me you'd died. I'm glad you had children and a husband and a life where people mourn you. I've been mourning you in my way for years, too many years.

Anyway, I never said I was sorry. I'm saying it now, and hopefully you'll get the message. I am so so sorry.

I should have written you from prison. I should have gone to your graduation—well, maybe . . . Either way, I left you when you stood up for me and when you needed me, and I am sorry. I left you because I didn't want to be those women in prison with my cousin Earl, and I left you because I didn't want to be the one the preacher sat in the entryway, away from all the rest. I didn't want to go to Hell, but really, I didn't want to *live* in Hell—and that's what I thought would happen. I was a coward about it and then, in many ways, created my own type of Hell.

I want you to know, though, that all these years later, Rhodie, you are still in my blood. You run around inside my body—in my mind, and behind my eyes, and through my heart. I will always love you, I think. I hope you are at peace. Sleep well, my beautiful, beautiful girl.

Your Dara

PEPTO DISMAL

In 1954, two years after my Rhodie died, I was visited by the cutest baby I ever saw. I wasn't a baby type, but this baby and I had a special bond, right off.

The father was a scrawny thing, with his hair too slicked back for his skinny neck. He wore a baseball cap pulled down so low that it shaded his face, and a scarf wrapped high up on his neck. The baby still had undecided blue eyes, though I had a feeling they might stay blue. The father didn't introduce himself. He just stepped up on to my porch—me wondering if he had some kind of delivery, maybe milk. With eyes lowered, he gestured that the Fiddler should take the baby up to me.

"What on God's earth?" I said.

The Fiddler shrugged and plopped the baby down on the bulge of my belly, a perfect bounce of blubber. The baby—who I felt was a girl— looked over at me with only a slight wobble of her head, sweet thing.

"Well, aren't you cute?" I asked her. "Why'd your daddy bring you here?"

The father didn't make a move, so I finally said, "You there, I think it best you come take your child."

When the father stepped up to take her back, he looked me dead in the eye. Those eyes looked familiar. Eyes that were almost black.

I looked up at him. There was something I recognized in the way this man stood. I'd noticed it walking up, his swagger.

And that's when I got it. With all the blood dropping fast to my swollen feet, I saw that this man standing before me was my stepdaughter—the one I thought I'd lost to her wanderings around the country: *Edna*.

"Tip your cap back," I said with a little quiver.

He did and yup, it was her.

Where has she been? Why is she dressing like a man? Is she in trouble with the law?

A tumbleweed rolled across the empty space inside my chest. It hurt, that spiky thing inside my ribs, and made it impossible to speak. I just sat there, dumb and fat, as my stepdaughter turned with the baby and walked back down the gravel that led up to my double-wide. I watched her go, thinking I must be wrong, but knowing—as a mother, even a second mother, does—that I wasn't wrong. That was her.

"What's going on, Nana Dara?" the Fiddler asked.

Still too stunned to talk or move, I stayed where I was and thought through it. Edna wasn't the sort to be in trouble with the law—Miss Debbie, maybe, but not Edna. She was too logical for all that. *So why was she trying to be a man?*

My mind played out a montage of memories, all the times that added up now: her wanting to play baseball, not softball; her refusing to cross her legs or carry a purse; her always playing with the boys—that birthday party when she'd wanted the boys to come but I didn't allow it. I even caught her once strapping a scarf tight around her breasts before she went out. She explained to me that it was because they played rough, and she wanted to make sure she didn't get injured. At the time I was just happy not to have to worry about her with boys, like I had with her older sister.

Then the big memory hit me: *her prom*. She hadn't wanted a boy's body to press against hers. She asked me what was wrong with her, and I did nothing to ease her mind. I just left her hanging there with all her doubts.

Edna's figure got smaller and smaller down the street until she turned and disappeared. I sat there, wrapped in mystery and confusion, unable to call her back. The Fiddler tapped my shoulder and

told me that Edna had given him a note when I was playing with the
baby.

"Well hand it the hell over!"

"Here you go," he mumbled.

I unfolded it faster than a child tips a Christmas stocking.

Nana Dara,

I'm leaving tomorrow for quite a while. It's just too tough. The baby
is mine. I wanted to bring her to meet you since I know you and
Miss Debbie are often on the outs, and Miss Debbie is going to
adopt and raise her. She will be a great mom.

That this baby came from me has to be kept a secret.

The baby will still be your granddaughter this way—and I'll be her
aunt. My life can't be the kind a baby grows up in.

She sure is sweet, though. I want her to have a good mother. I can't
raise a baby and stay sane. I don't expect you to understand, but I
hope you will try.

—E

The thing my eyes settled in on was the line: *That this baby came
from me has to be kept a secret.* I cringed, knowing that secrets have
a way of working themselves out of tight spots, of popping up somewhere else where the dirt is softer. Maybe since my secret didn't see
the light of day all those years ago, I passed it along to this child. I
should have been honest and told people that once, back in 1923, I
loved a girl who loved me back, and it changed everything. I should
have told her that, despite preferring the company of woman, I didn't
live a false life with her daddy—it was just like having hamburger
when you want steak. I should have said something.

I sighed and held the letter in my hand until the paper softened. The night grew dark. The light flickered behind me near the overpopulated fly strip. An owl hooted with that hollow sound they make on quiet nights. And I knew what I had to do.

"It's time we deal with the consequences of secrets," I said to no one.

"Fiddler!" I called out. "Did you put the radio back in my truck? I'm going a full county over, and I don't feel like making that kind of drive without a little music."

× × ×

Nearly an hour later, I heaved up to Miss Debbie's trailer and rapped on her aluminum screen door. "Miss Debbie, you get yer ass over here right now and open this door!"

"Nana Dara?" Miss Debbie shuffled to her door like a Chinese woman on bound feet. "Shush! The baby is sleeping."

And that's when it truly became real—not real in my mind, but real in my *emotions*. There was a baby. She was here. I was a grandmother.

"When were you gonna tell me about the baby?"

"You haven't come out here to visit me in three years since that whole misunderstanding with me calling you plump, and *this* is all you can say?"

"Roads move two ways, Miss Debbie!" I put my arms out firmly, hands on hips. "You ever seen the inside of my Opry?"

She chewed her gum as loudly as ever in that pantsuit that clung to her thighs like brown Saran Wrap. "I know Eddie wrote you a note."

"Well, we could talk too. You think about calling me? We have these things called *phones*." I stopped. "By Eddie you mean Edna, right?"

"Do you know after Daddy died and I got married I've only seen you maybe a handful of times. Now you want *me* to keep *you* up on what's going on?"

"Stubborn," I muttered.

"Kettle," she shot back. But then she softened in a way I hadn't remembered her softening before. She sighed and bumped the door further open with her hip. "You can come look at her, but don't touch—it took me a solid half hour bouncing her up and down and making choo-choo noises to get her down. And yes, Edna is now going by Eddie and dressing the part—much to the Devil's delight."

I stood in the doorway like I was making a statement—no one is leaving here until we settle this!—so Miss Debbie's sudden invitation to come see the baby made me feel a little ridiculous. I tried as best I could to switch from crazy country woman to stable grandma.

"She sleeps in the nook here—the crib fit perfect. Eddie found it for her."

I relaxed my stance a little, wondering how I'd let so many years go by. But I knew. I wrote Miss Debbie off long before the Warden had died, sometime between her first cheerleading practice and that weekend she took the Warden's car and drove off to Georgia with her boyfriend. I let her go since she needed authority, and authority was the Warden's terrain, while I drifted back and forth between being stepmother and babysitter. And, of course, it didn't help that she pulled her trump card on several occasions, reminding me that I was not her "real mom" and never would be.

"All right," I said.

I looked at Miss Debbie now, her eyes smiling somehow, and I wanted to reach out and tell her that I was sorry I'd been so distant and caught up in what it meant to be a mom like every other mom—a woman like every other woman—so much so that I felt like I was pretending all the time. But I just couldn't make myself move that quickly, so I nodded to her with a small smile and stepped in from where my big body had been blocking the doorway.

Miss Debbie's living room looked a little different than the last time I'd seen it—she'd replaced her big, glass bulb lamp with a lamp that looked like it had a puffy skirt for a shade. The shade was wider than the two-tiered side table it sat on. Strange.

She also got herself a new white-and-red floral couch. I use the term "floral" loosely here, since those flowers were crazy elongated things, like what might grow in some prehistoric era when the oxygen was too high.

I said, "So, Edna stopped by to see me, with the baby."

"Eddie," she corrected.

"*Eddie*, right." I cleared my throat. "Oh—and why is she dressing like a man? Is she hiding from something?"

"Only God's good graces."

"What?"

"She pretends to *be* a man."

I stepped back. "Oh."

"Tea?" she asked, letting me know that the subject had just been dropped.

I nodded, dumb as a cow. "Three sugars."

"You go on and look at her while I get your tea."

I walked over and looked down into the crib. Bumper stickers from different states were plastered over the solid pine headboard part. The baby was sleeping peacefully with her arms outstretched like Jesus himself. She had a rash on her forehead, poor thing. Miss Debbie had wrapped her hands in tiny mittens so she wouldn't scratch at it.

Even with that rash, she was beautiful—so beautiful that she didn't seem real. She looked like one of those perfect babies they put in ads, like a picture taken in a perfect house with a perfect family somewhere, not here with all us misfits.

"Isn't she gorgeous?" Miss Debbie asked as she walked up, looking as close to peaceful as I'd ever seen her.

"She is."

"You know she's *mine*, right? That's all she ever needs to know. She doesn't ever need to know that Eddie gave birth." Miss Debbie squinted her blue-shadowed eyes in that threatening way she could do.

"I get the gist. Only how—"

She grabbed her highball glass off the counter. "Come here, outta earshot."

I followed her back into the living room. "Eddie dated this man but only one of them was serious—and you know it wasn't her. Well, he was leaving for basic training and she decided it would be all right to give him a send-off. One time. No harm."

I nodded, still dumbstruck by all of this.

She continued on: "You know I can't have kids on account of my female troubles. And Eddie can't have a kid on account of needing to be something unnatural—which, I can assure you, I am *not* OK with from a religious perspective—but it got me this little one here. That's the deal. Eddie, deviation though I feel she is, can stay involved as 'Aunt Eddie' as long as the secret stays kept."

"How does Bo feel about it?"

"He couldn't be happier. He's down at the car shop right now, says he's gotta work even harder if he's gonna put this one in good shoes. He thinks bad shoes are the root of a lot of adult difficulties."

"He's a smart man," I said. "Is Edna all right then?"

"Eddie, Nana Dara, *Eddie*. And yes, she's all right." Miss Debbie lit a menthol. "If by being 'all right' you mean selfish to the gates of Hell."

I sat down and gestured for the Warden's eldest daughter—the one he thought might go to secretary school someday—to pass over her cigarette and, ignoring the bright red lipstick on it, took a deep drag. My whole body laid back and relaxed with the exhale.

"PD must *never know* who gave birth to her."

"Wait now, what's her name?" I asked, trying to slow down Miss Debbie's aggression.

"PD."

"What's that mean?" I handed her cigarette back.

"Patricia Delilah. Eddie says it stands for Pepto Dismal on account of her warped sense of humor. Says she was so sick during her pregnancy that she decided to call her that. I, of course, changed *that*."

"Ha!" I laughed. Edna and that weird sense of humor she had. My chest felt heavy with how much I missed her then.

Leave it to Miss Debbie to break the mood. "Nana Dara," she started in again, "to be clear, PD is *mine*. She is *my* baby. I love her like mine—I love her because she *is* mine, and she can never know. This baby is *mine*." She put both hands on her hips. "I need you to understand that."

I looked across the living room at the ceramic Santa that had been in a bowl on Miss Debbie's end table for years now. One of its white-gloved hands had broken off. The other one was held on by fraying scotch tape.

"Nana Dara, you with me here?"

"These secrets are bad, I'm telling you." I leaned back.

She shrugged.

"What I don't understand is why Edna isn't raising her own daughter?"

"She's *my* daughter!"

"Calm down, Miss Debbie, before your hair falls."

"Can you imagine, Nana Dara, *can you imagine* not wanting to be fully in a girl's body then finding out that body is pregnant—the most feminine thing a woman can do?" Miss Debbie crushed out her cigarette and looked at me like I had no feelings whatsoever. Like I was an alien, which I just might be.

"I can understand that— as best I can. But my question is, why can't Edna—Eddie—why can't Eddie just be Eddie and be her mother?"

"Because we live in a small town in Texas. Because this is 1954. Because loving this *girl* would mean Eddie never loving a *woman*—if you get me. If anyone found out they would take Eddie to jail and take sweet little PD away. Bad enough she had PD out of wedlock."

So Eddie turned out like me.

"What a mess," I said, shaking my head.

With fire in her eyes, Miss Debbie lit herself another cigarette. "*Mess!* This baby is a *blessing* from God, not a mess. He's given me what I cannot have. I think of it this way: Eddie is getting herself the life she wants, and I'm getting myself a baby. Praise the Lord!"

"When did you find the Lord, anyway?"

"He was never lost—*I* was. The Lord helps me keep on the straight and narrow path in my abiding love for Bo and for the simple pleasures in small-town life."

The thick brown stripes on Miss Debbie's pantsuit made her look even harsher than she usually looked. I don't know why she grew up so harsh, really I don't.

"Nana Dara, are you even *listening* to me?"

"Now who's gonna wake the baby?" I said, using my low voice. "And I am listening. But now you listen—I am not going to lie. If that baby ever asks me who her mother is, I'm going to tell her. Nothin' good comes from lies!"

"What do you know of them?"

"Maybe more than you know," I said.

"A lie is a lie. A secret is just a secret. This is a secret."

"I'm not going to argue with you. I am not keeping a secret. I am not lying. Either way, it ends here."

At that point, I thought it would be dramatic to rise from Miss Debbie's pink velour chair and see myself out, only I didn't count on the chair having such a sinking cushion, so when I tried to get up I found myself stuck. Miss Debbie tapped her ashes on the carpet and smirked over at me struggling to stand up.

"Jesus. Look at us!" she laughed. "You're too damn fat to get up from a simple chair, and I am acting like a scared cat."

Miss Debbie flashed her mostly straight teeth at me, and I knew something was up—she was being too damn nice. She walked over to me as I settled back down into the velour and offered me the last drag of her cigarette.

"So let's tell her the truth. Only thing is—" she fake-frowned— "we'll have to be *sure* PD doesn't tell any of the kids at school. I mean, how would *they* understand? Even if we *could* get a four-year-old in PD's future kindergarten to understand the complexities of intimate human nature, would her friends understand? The church? Would she be shunned out there?" She paused dramatically. "Well, you know the folk in town, what do *you* think?" Before I could answer, she continued: "So we can tell her but then she'll have to keep the secret or have an impossible and friendless life."

"I'm not blind," I said. "I see."

Miss Debbie sipped her drink. "So that is the choice: we keep a secret *from* her, or we tell her—and then we make sure she keeps the secrets from her *friends*."

I thought on it. *Dammit, she had something.*

Miss Debbie smiled and blinked her blue eyes several times. "Think about it, Nana Dara. That might very well be the first big thing she learns from us—how to lie to her friends."

Just then, as if that sneaky stepdaughter of mine had it all rigged, baby PD let out a thin, frail cry.

"You ponder that," Miss Debbie said, smashing her cigarette out beside a few half-burnt candy wrappers. "I'm going to go feed your granddaughter. If you want to, you can stay and hold her."

I'll give it to her, Miss Debbie sure was good. "Of course I want to hold her."

"I'll be back in a second to help you up."

So I let it go, but even as I did it—even as I knew I was doing the best I could in the moment—I felt like I'd just poured a little water on a dangerous seed just looking for some place to pop up.

FASHION

Eddie disappeared for a few months after leaving us with PD, no doubt to grieve. But then she stopped by. She was about to take off on a project to help administer the new polio vaccine in schools all around Texas. She ran the statewide project, doing the scheduling and lining up the nurses and whatnot. It felt nice knowing that, partly thanks to my stepdaughter, there would be fewer children who would grow up like President Franklin D. Roosevelt, whose young legs had been crippled up in the big outbreak of 1921. Thirty-five years later, and we were finally vaccinating against it.

Eddie looked very dapper when she came to see us—if that word can be used for females. She wore a suit with an ascot and carried a new black briefcase filled with alphabetized school lists. Her spunk reminded me a bit of Rhodie, though still I worried about her dressing so manly.

I thought about how the word "pervert" had become the word "invert" in open-minded circles, of which there were few that I saw in Sugar Land. Outside Sugar Land, I hoped that the change of word came along with a change of sentiment—and it wasn't just folks were just being more polite about it all.

"You seem distracted today, Nana Dara," Eddie said.

"Just ate too much beef last night. Always leaves me feeling separated from myself the next day." I looked over at her, leaning forward in my wobbly chair. "You all ready for your trip?"

"They got me that car out there," she said, pointing to a long white automobile that was hers for the duration of the project, "and a string of nice hotel rooms, so I'm set."

"Sounds exciting." Me thinking: *you are out there caring for all those children, but you leave your child with someone else.* Then I mentally slapped myself for thinking that. *Asshole.*

"Not sure if lines of crying children are *exciting*." She slicked back a piece of her hair.

At the time, I knew that if there had been a homosexual vaccine like the one they developed for polio, I would have gone around to schools poking children with needles so they would grow up and fall in love with who folks thought they should fall in love with. Make life easier. Of course, now, I've come to believe that each and every life has the number of trials it is destined to have, and, if you take one away, another one fills its place. Your life is your response to these trials. No life is easy, and no life is hard; it's just what adjectives you choose to use to describe it.

"You write me when you can," I said.

"I will."

"Try to send me a postcard with the picture of the town on it. I'll collect them and hang them down the hallway or something."

"I don't know how you'd fit anything else on your walls."

I smiled. "I have my ways."

"'Bye, Nana Dara."

"'Bye, Eddie."

With a professional's nod, she pulled up her heavy briefcase and walked out to that white car. I stood at the door with a few cats winding around the loose fabric of my housedress, amazed that this girl I'd helped raise had the independent spirit in her to go out on her own and earn her way all by herself—and in a man's hat to boot.

NEW PICTURES OF MY GIRLS

A full season later, Eddie knocked on the clacking door of my Opry. The rains had started, making Texas bloom as only Texas can—with waves of endless wildflowers. Flowers pushed up through the planks of my deck and in between the gravel on the road and around the wooden poles of everyone's crazy mailboxes. No one minded if the dogs tinkled all over those flowers, or if kids picked them in greedy handfuls since there were always more. Miles and miles of them.

I opened the door to Eddie wiping her tiny feet on my shredded welcome mat. With those flowers behind her, she looked like a painting from one of those Impressionist painters—the ones who used dots of paint to give everything life.

"Eddie! Hello. You done with your project?"

"Nearly. Just working my way to this part of the state. This is my day off. I get one a week."

"Well, I'm glad to see you. Come on in."

I waved her and her briefcase—looking much less shiny now—in. The door dropped back a few times and never did latch itself shut.

"How are you?"

"I'm good, Nana Dara. I'm good. I just came back from seeing PD and Miss Debbie. That little girl is so sweet." She looked up with those deep brown eyes of hers. "I came by, though, because I have a favor to ask. Do you have a minute?"

"I have several of them—enough to be strung together into a full day."

"I only need a few."

She nodded and moved past me, wearing a pair of blue men's pants and a yellow button-down, tucked in with a somber belt. I smelled some tangy cologne and wondered if she went to a barber to get her hair shaved up the back of her neck like that.

I moved past her to the couch, gesturing that she take a seat in the empty chair near the door—the chair that had been in the Warden's house. "Careful, you might remember that it used to twirl. Now it just sort of *careens* from side to side when you sit down."

"Thank you."

Eddie looked at all the knick-knacks I had on my wooden shelf and the paintings on the walls. She pointed to some old magazine images of sunset that I'd framed in green wooden frames. I'd hung them in what *Good Housekeeping* called a "grouping."

"New?"

"I like to keep it fresh."

"You surely do," she said.

She sat down in the yellow chair, looking tired. The pugs ran by, wheezing while they were chasing each other, letting out a pitiful yelp every now and again as if to prove they really were dogs.

"So, Nana Dara . . ." she said, rocking forward.

"Shoot."

"You know that I—that I have an unusual sense of fashion."

"I can see that."

She blushed a little. "It's how I'm comfortable."

"I understand," I said, then I asked her what I'd been dying to ask her for some time: "But isn't it hard for you?"

"It's hard for me with other people sometimes, yes, but it's easier for me with myself. And in that way, then, it's ultimately easier with other people—since I am being myself. Is that making sense?"

"Mostly."

She clasped her hands in front of her, on her knees. "When I see pictures of myself when I was made to behave and look a certain way,

I feel angry. I hated myself so much in those dresses, with my hair in ribbons, that even now it is too much to look at."

I gulped and held back a wave of hot guilt for not having stood up for her against the Warden's very strict demands that his daughters dress like proper southern ladies. Indeed, if I'm being honest, I might have pushed on Edna a little hard myself, hoping that she wouldn't turn out like me. I remembered tying ribbons in her hair while she stared straight ahead in the mirror, sometimes with hate-filled tears rolling down her cheeks and sometimes with eyes as dull as death. I remembered all those fights over shoes and stockings and haircuts. More than once, the Warden had even taken her over his knee to tame her—not that that ever truly works, it seems.

"I'm sorry," was all I managed to say.

"I understand now why you did what you did. It's OK. But that leads me to my favor . . ."

I nodded.

"Can you take down any pictures you have of me when I was Edna? I'll give you new ones."

"Consider them stowed."

Eddie let her breath out and relaxed back in the wobbly chair. "I'll send you a picture or two of me out in the field, with the nurses."

Here I raised an eyebrow, but held my tongue. *The nurses?*

"I'll take the photos I have from the frames, but leave the frames ready for those new pictures."

I totally understood her position. Before I'd fully embraced my destiny as a large woman, I'd tried dieting. And every time I did, I asked the Warden to take down those pictures he had of me when we were first married and I was trimmer. Those images showcased my current failure—how far out of control I'd let myself go. Eddie was trying to form who she was now—not who she was as compared to who she used to be. Basically, Eddie did not need her skinny pictures up.

"Thank you," Eddie sighed.

I smiled a teary-eyed smile, experiencing one of those rare moments when I really felt like someone's mother and not just the person who supported the Warden in his love of *his* children.

"You know what?" I said. "You inspire me."

Eddie turned her dark eyes down and blushed again. "Really? I couldn't tell how you stood about my . . . fashion choices." She cleared her throat, clearly about as good in emotional situations as me.

"I'd like you to come by again when your project is through and sit for a while. Have some sweet tea. What do you think?"

She brushed a piece of hair behind her ear. "I would love that, Nana Dara."

I realized then that I'd never really asked Eddie over. Maybe if I want folks to visit, I ought to ask.

I looked over at her then, and I *saw* her. I didn't see my stepdaughter wearing some kind of costume; I saw who she had become, ugly belt and all.

"Bring me those pictures yourself."

Eddie stood up and smiled. She adjusted her button-down to be sure it didn't blouse too much. "Will do."

After she walked out, with a wave and a slap of the door behind her, I moved around the Opry taking down pictures of Eddie as Edna. In one of them Edna had been maybe fifteen years old. She was sitting on our old porch swing, looking off after a long fight with the Warden to get her into the pink get-up he'd chosen for her to wear to the VFW. I took the picture because Edna had been one of those young girls who could be so beautiful when she was angry. I ran my finger over it, knowing now how many different ways there are to be beautiful.

× × ×

The next day, the Fiddler came home from a day-labor job—painting some bridge or another.

"Howdy, Nana Dara," he said on his way in, sweat rings like lazy polka dots on his gray work shirt.

"Fiddler."

There was something easy but nervous about the Fiddler that made our relationship easy but, well, *nervous*. He always needed my permission to do anything—maybe because I had the power over his housing situation or because he didn't trust his own mind or because he'd had the kind of childhood that seemed to include shoes and lamps being thrown at him across the room.

"Let's have margaritas," I said, making my way over to the kitchen.

The Fiddler smiled and moved from nervous to easy, now that he knew what was expected of him, which was to make margaritas.

"You know I make a good one," he said, rubbing his unrelenting beard the way some folks rub a cat's head.

I smiled and redirected myself back to the living room, where I plopped on the couch with a thud. Unlike some, I didn't go in for thin couches on peg legs, no matter what the trend. I still loved that sturdy mustard couch from the Warden. The sun drifted down behind my recently tie-dyed curtains, and, when I looked over, I could almost see him sitting there with me again, teasing me about my socks. Then, like steam in a breeze, the Warden disappeared.

The Fiddler asked me, "You ok?"

I yelled over the noise of him breaking ice up in a dishtowel on the countertop. "Eddie stopped by today and asked me to take down the pictures of her in those dresses we always put her in."

He pounded away. "All right."

I yelled, "*Eddie* doesn't want to be reminded of *Edna* right now. So I took the pictures down since she asked, but I doubt Miss Debbie will take *her* pictures down."

I smelled the limes in the air after he cut them up. That smell always made me happy.

The Fiddler shook the ingredients together in his antique cocktail mixer. "Why not?" he shouted back.

"The simple answer? Because Miss Debbie is Miss Debbie."

The Fiddler walked in with our margaritas, his cowboy hat tipped back now. He sat down carefully, adjusting to the way the chair tilts before it settles, and sipped his drink, crossing his long legs out in front of him.

"What can you do about it?"

I sipped. "Not sure really."

The Fiddler looked over at me with a hopeful glint in his small eyes. "Maybe *nothin*'?"

"Nothing?"

"This might be between them—these pictures and where they should go."

"I want to help Eddie."

The Fiddler leaned back after testing to be sure the chair wouldn't give way, and sipped again.

I, meanwhile, had an idea. An idea I would have never entertained in my youth, but now I was an older lady—a widower even—I felt somehow above the law. "I'm going to sneak in and take the pictures down."

"This is criminal behavior we are discussing here."

I tsked and pulled up the leg of my coveralls to scratch my knee. "This is just the removal of a few offending photographs."

"Breaking and entering and theft."

"How else can I get Miss Debbie to take those pictures down?"

"Call her?"

"When did *talking* ever get me anywhere with Miss Debbie? Do you know once, when she was maybe fourteen years old, we spent an hour discussing how skirt length can define a person, and you know what she did? She said 'yes, ma'am,' the way people do, then I watched her through the front window go out to her friend's truck, open the door, take a pair of scissors from her purse, and cut that hem up a full three inches before hopping in the truck and skidding down the street. *Call her?* Clearly you don't know Miss Debbie. Talk is just that."

I sensed the Fiddler growing nervous at the mere hint that I might want to do something against the rules.

"You want me to top off your drink?" he asked.

"Is a penguin the butt of a bad joke?"

The Fiddler stood up on his scrawny legs, took my glass, and walked in to top us off. He called back to me, "Maybe you could ask Bo to take the pictures down?"

"*Bo?* If that man had a backbone when he met Miss Debbie she has long since driven it out of him."

The Fiddler walked back in, focused intently on not spilling our drinks, and handed me my glass.

The kind of indignation that is fueled by liquor took hold of me. "It's just not right that Miss Debbie would cause Eddie such *grief.*"

"Do we know she has?"

"We can *assume.*"

The warmth of the margaritas gave me a strange kind of clarity.

"It would be torture to go over and see yourself in what you think are your worst moments plastered all over someone's trailer."

The Fiddler nodded in his beat-down way. I knew he knew there was no point talking to me, but still I continued to convince him since I needed his help.

"Tell me you see my point!"

"I do, I see your point." He chewed an ice cube.

"She and Bo are polka dancing tonight and they dropped PD off at Bo's crossed-eyed cousin's place, so we can get in and out." I was so excited by the plan that I didn't pace that second margarita and drank it like water. "We're going to sneak in there, Fiddler, you and me, and get those pictures—for Eddie! Miss Debbie always keeps a spare key in the boot out front. It'll be easy."

The Fiddler didn't say anything as he walked to the kitchen to refill our glasses.

"You hearing me?"

"All right," he said, with his back to me. "Tomorrow."

"No, *now.* I could be dead tomorrow. You can't deny an aging woman her dying wish!"

The Fiddler, charmed by my infallible logic, got a little twinkle in his eye. He swigged down his margarita and said, "All right, let's get them pictures."

He held the door, and we wobbled to my truck. I bent over as gracefully as I could, set the nearly empty glass on the edge of my porch steps, and gestured to the truck with wide arms. "And we're off!"

Forty-five minutes later, after a few rousing renditions of radio favorites, I clicked off the truck lights and coasted stealthily up the gravel to Miss Debbie's trailer.

The Fiddler whispered loudly, pointing to his gray work shirt. "We should have worn *black*."

"These are fine," I said, patting my dark blue coveralls.

It must've been 10 p.m.. Music played out from nearby trailers and more than a few lights from TVs lit up the night, but not a soul outside. Perfect.

We crouched over and slinked up to the porch. I reached inside the boot—no key. I turned it upside down and slapped it against my leg. Nothing fell out. *Dammit*.

"She must've taken the key," I whispered.

"OK, let's go home," the Fiddler said.

"No! We're breaking in."

I took three steps to the right and tried the front window. Locked. I tried the two on the side which were hidden by six-foot bayberries, but no luck there either.

"Nana Dara!" the Fiddler called from the front edge of the property, refusing to go past the front yard.

Ha! One of the windows on the other side sat open a few inches. That would have to do.

"I need more height—get on over here!"

He backed away, toward the truck. "No, ma'am. This could be jail for me."

"Oh for heaven's sake, grow a set!"

He just shook his head and opened the driver's side of the truck.

Alone but determined, I drug over a rusted metal basin Miss Debbie used for bobbing for apples at Halloween. Overcoming my fear of falling right through the thin metal, I stepped up and shoved my arm in the window to knock the stick down that was keeping it from being opened any further. A redneck lock.

For those of you who don't know, there's a section of a woman's upper arm—especially a woman such as myself—that abruptly bulges out. It was that bulging spot that got wedged in the open window. I tried to bend up and wiggle my fingers to knock down the piece of wood, but I couldn't. I was stuck.

"Fiddler!" I yell-whispered. "Fiddler!"

No answer. *God damn coward*, probably crouching down inside the truck.

I feverishly tried to nudge the wood down with the fingers of my stuck arm—only to realize that my arm fat had caused the window frame to push up even tighter against the wood stick. Now *firmly* jammed in place, my arm started turning blue. On top of it all, I was sweating like a whore in church.

At that point, I heard Mrs. Jimmy James, Miss Debbie's neighbor, open her door. She owned a pair of Rottweilers so big you'd think she was in league with the Devil.

"Come on you two," she said to the Devil-dogs. "Don't shit in the front yard."

Obediently the beasts waded right through the bushes along the property line and into Miss Debbie's yard, where the window held me tight. Not having been taught the boundaries of their property, the Rottweilers came at me with fangs exposed, barking up a storm. Panicked, I struggled to free my arm, which caused my slicked-back hairdo to flop out in hairsprayed bunches.

"José and Righteous," Mrs. Jimmy James yelled from the stolen pebbles in front of her door that she called her patio, "where are you two?"

They were up on me now, both dogs, black as night, staring up with those mean white eyes. In my frantic attempts to free my arm and keep back from the beasts, I stepped too hard on the metal basin, and one of my feet dropped clean through it.

The Rottweilers took that as a sign of aggression and lunged at my overalls. Luckily I was never a woman who believed that tight clothes were slimming, so I had a little give for them to pull on. Just as one of those wretched creatures tore my overalls off at the upper thigh, exposing years of neglected inner-thigh grooming, Mrs. Jimmy James raced around the bushes in her nightgown, armed with a broom and a can of insect spray—or at least that's what it tasted like when she started shooting it in my face.

Despite my blurred vision, I screamed, "I am Nana Dara!" but it couldn't be heard over the dogs barking and Mrs. Jimmy James calling out for the police.

Lights went on all around me as all of Miss Debbie's neighbors opened their doors to investigate.

Finally, in the fury, my bruised, blue arm came free.

Then—freed—I fell backwards, my foot still stuck in the basin. Mrs. Jimmy James clobbered me several times in the head. Clumps of broom straw lodged themselves in my already shameful mess. At one point, the broom itself got stuck in my defeated coif. On the upshot, the smell of the insect spray kept the dogs at bay.

Mannie Johnson, the sign painter who lived across from Miss Debbie's trailer, ran over with his shotgun. He guided Mrs. Jimmy James away from me.

All sunburned and aftershavey, Mannie stepped up to my metal basin, which was now wrapped around both of my feet like a skirt. His eyes widened. He pressed the tip of his rifle into my doughy stomach, where it had peeked out between my upturned shirt and overalls.

He cocked the trigger. "What's going on here?"

As I turned my head to answer, I realized that I was lying in the exact location the Rottweilers visited every evening to relieve themselves of what clearly must be high-fiber meals.

I lifted my soiled, patchy head. "I'm Nara Dara, Miss Debbie's mother. You know me, Mannie."

"Whew—Lord! Is that dog doo in your hair? My goodness." He lowered his rifle and raised his hand to cover his mouth.

"I'm trying to get in the house here," I stammered.

By now, the moon shone down on me like a spotlight. A few more people walked up behind Mannie, took a peek at me, shook their heads, and retreated back into their houses.

"We keep a spare key in case Miss Debbie locks herself out. I'll— I'll go get it for you," he said, stepping back.

Mrs. Jimmy James didn't apologize. Instead, she consoled her dogs on what must have been a terrifying experience for them, and left me there with their poop.

I struggled up and stepped out from the basin. Mannie Johnson met me at the front door with the key. He handed it to me at a distance with an outstretched arm, suggested I wash down.

"Thank you, Mannie—I hadn't thought of that."

Holding my disheveled and discolored head up high, I walked— limping only slightly—to the truck. I banged hard enough on the door to scare the pants off the Fiddler who was, as I had suspected, crouched down in the front.

He looked up at me from the patchy floor. "That you I smell?"

"Unless it's the scent of *coward*—then that'd be you."

"I'd be a coward and a free man any day."

"You are not going to jail. Dammit, Fiddler. I got the key. Let's go in."

The Fiddler poked his narrow, scared head up and—seeing the coast now clear—he edged up on to the seat and out of the truck. I looked down, amazed he could fit his long body in such a small space.

We walked in silence up to the front door. I resisted the urge to itch at something stuck in my hair.

"I feel like people are watching us."

"For once," I said, "you might be right."

The key slid in easily. We opened the door and clicked on the light. There on the photo wall behind her white-and-red flowered couch were five rectangles where the paneling looked darker—five spots where pictures of Edna used to hang. They'd all been taken down.

Looks like Miss Debbie had done a bit of changing herself over the years also.

"Don't you say a word," I mumbled to the Fiddler. "Not one God damn word."

THE TWO-TON MONSTER

With the patience of a brain surgeon, the Fiddler lifted dripping bacon—piece by piece—from the skillet to a plate with a paper towel on it. He sucked on his toothpick with those little hamster noises he made.

I shouted out, "What are you diggin' in your tooth for—gold?"

I dropped down on the mustard couch and felt the fabric of my housedress stretch at the hips, where it always scrunched up against my girth. The dress had softened after years of washing and wear. The fabric had faded to nearly see-through. I think, at one time, there were small pink roses printed on it, but they faded away completely. "The tiny print," Mrs. Lynne, my dressmaker, had told me, "will draw less attention to your curves."

Now, I wondered, *without any tiny print left, are my curves in the forefront?*

I wiggled to find a comfy spot on the cushion and, just like that, my dress ripped.

"Hot holy hell!" I said.

The Fiddler nodded his head at me from the kitchen. He slouched his thin body against the white edge of the sink. When he raised an arm to scratch his beard, a considerable puff of underarm hair sprang out of his cut-off flannel shirtsleeves. Looked like he had armpit afros.

"Time for a new dress anyway, isn't it?" he asked as he pulled out another toothpick from the front of his jeans.

"You got a problem with those toothpicks," I said, and made my way down the hallway into my bedroom and up to my closet, with my right hand holding the side of my dress together.

That winter, I'd dyed my bedding in a tie-dye method that little PD showed me. Something she learned in her kindergarten. We stood out there with three buckets, all the plain fabric I could find, a box of rubber bands, and three boxes of various dyes. Her brown hair was still straight as ever and still in ponytails. Miss Debbie had painted her nails, and PD was particularly proud of them. That was how I convinced her to put some rubber gloves on before dyeing. I warned her that otherwise the dye might ruin her nails.

"I love my nails," she said, smiling with those teeth coming in crooked.

"Well, Peanut, you have to protect what you love. So wear them gloves."

She shrugged that same cute shrug she'd been doing since she could walk, and put the gloves on, even though they were huge on her. I rubberbanded them onto her wrists, and we got to twisting and tying all the fabric, starting with my bedspread. It came out with circles of purple and red, with muddy greens that looked like a salad had melted on it. Still, it always brightened my days—all that color.

The walk to my bedroom with my ripped dress wore me out. I dropped down on the edge of my bed and slid my closet door open with my foot to survey what I had hanging in there.

"Dresses, dresses, dresses . . ." I muttered, scanning the hangers, most of which were holding extra blankets and drawstring bags filled with old rags I thought might be made into rag carpets someday.

One, two—*two dresses*. I had only two fall dresses left.

I remembered using one to clean up some cat mess back in December, then deciding it was best to toss it, and I remembered that another had gotten a little tight at the end of the season, so I had given that to the church. Did that really leave me with only *two* dresses?

Fiddler was right—I needed dresses. It was October already. I needed fall dresses, and quick.

I changed into my best underwear and one of my two remaining dresses, grabbed my truck keys, and headed to town.

This is the thing about my dressmaker: she knew me. Me and Mrs. Lynne had developed a kinship supported by our mutual love of fried cheese and dogwood trees. We also liked the same kind of dress—tight on the top and on the hips, loose everywhere else. We *understood* each other.

Imagine my horror when I drove around the corner to see a giant "CLOSED" sign on Mrs. Lynne's door. A table of her goods sat out front, and some young man, no more than twelve years old or so, was selling everything off to a crowd of eager ladies.

I pulled my old Ford, popping and clicking the way it does, up to the curb, and yelled out the passenger window to the boy. "What the hellfire is happening here? Where's Mrs. Lynne?"

"Heart gave out, ma'am," was all he said before he turned to a woman who was asking about the price of Mrs. Lynne's huge white scissors.

"Her heart?"

"Yes, ma'am," he said over his shoulder. "You can try Mrs. Tanya May Rogerton down two blocks. Most of Mrs. Lynne's folks have gone over there, I hear."

He hadn't done anything wrong, but still I drove off without so much as a thank you.

Poor Mrs. Lynne. Hearts are tricky things. Sometimes I feel like they have timers inside, and when your time is up, it's up. *And who the hell is this Tanya May Rogerton?*

I lit up a cigarette. "Dammit."

I parked behind another truck, this one with a coat of primer and stickers on the back that gave us the full character of the driver in five words: *Speed Demon* and *Join the Army*.

Mrs. Tanya May Rogerton's dress shop was clearly identified by a white mailbox that had a picture of a woman wearing a tea dress painted on it. The woman was painted in red, making her seem patriotic in color and style. Big florets of jade grew on either side of the mailbox, indicating that this place was well maintained—that this dressmaker had an eye for detail. She cared.

I headed up the cobblestone path and into Mrs. Tanya May Rogerton's tiny and tidy little dress shop. A bell jangled when I shut the door. It smelled like lilacs inside and had the low lighting of someplace sacred. Ahead of me was a mother-daughter duo, talking wedding dresses. *This is going to take all God damn day,* I thought, when out from behind the mother-daughter duo walked Mrs. Tanya May Rogerton, her hair as white as Cupid's diaper.

"Can I help you?"

"I—Ah . . . I only have two dresses left."

She smiled. "Well bless your heart, that won't do."

Mrs. Tanya May Rogerton gestured toward one of two antique chairs set up in a spot in the corner near the tall front window. I hoped I could fit. A book of fabric sat on the dark wooden table between the chairs, with a mason jar of white roses near it.

Without her slightly heeled shoes, Mrs. Tanya May Rogerton was probably a good three inches shorter than me, but the way she carried herself—chest out, head up, smile on—added height. She looked like she might have done pageant work in her younger days. Her white hair was done up in the shape of a perfect upside-down U and her nose was dull the way someone's is when they know the secret art of powder application.

I was glad I had changed my drawers, but would it have killed me to pay a little more attention to my hair?

"Why don't you pick out some fabric, and I'll be back to take measurements."

"Oh no, I know—I know my measurements."

"Just in case. Don't you worry. I have a back room and am very discreet. Would you like some lemonade?"

"That would be lovely."

Mrs. Tanya May Rogerton walked quietly across the various Victorian carpets she had laid around the floor to a pitcher of lemonade

near the mother-daughter. I watched as she poured me some, adding
mint with silver tongs that were sitting in a white bowl of fresh lemons.

Measurements? I groaned to myself.

When she handed it to me, I noticed her wedding ring. It had a
tiny diamond on a gold band that grew up and coiled around the diamond to make it look like the center of a snake eye. She noticed me
looking and simply said, "Art deco, hon."

I nodded and directed my attention to the fabric book as Mrs.
Tanya May Rogerton walked over to help the mother-daughter. After
a few minutes, she insisted that they take the wedding fabrics book
home to look over before they made their decision.

"Don't show the fiancé, of course!" She smiled, shutting the door
behind them and dropping her reading glasses from the tip of her
nose to hang from her neck on a white ribbon.

"Thank you, Mrs. Tanya May Rogerton!" the daughter called back.

It had been a couple years since I'd had any strong attractions, but
I woke right back up again at the sight of Mrs. Tanya May Rogerton's
breasts snuggled up inside her tight white cotton top. She was a woman of advanced years, but she knew how to perk herself up, to be sure.

The heat from the October sun through the window beat down
on the back of my old yellow dress. I looked down at the fabric book
and noticed that my nails were lined with dirt from my time weeding
yesterday. *Oh God.* And I'd forgotten all about that barbecue stain on
the front of my dress.

Here was this woman, about the same age as me, but just *look* at
the two of us.

I pulled my dirty hands back when she sat down across from me.
"How about you pick the fabric?"

"Well," she said, looking into my eyes, "you've got pretty blue
eyes—I would kill for that color—with your fair skin. Hmm. Peach
colors, bright blues, maybe a bold green. Avoid whites."

There was no judgment in her tone. No "you're too fat for white."
She was only offering her impartial, professional opinion.

"I dare to wear white because it makes my customers think I can keep something this white this *clean*, and if that's true, then I can handle their wedding gowns and alterations on their great-grandma's silk party dress from the turn of the century." Her breasts, followed by the rest of her, leaned right by the roses. "Truth is, I keep this outfit here in the shop. I'd never be able to keep it clean if I didn't."

I smiled and curled my fingers in while I sipped my minty lemonade.

She stood up easily and waved me to follow her. "Let's go take those measurements."

Her shop was basically a square, with a short, three-step hallway off the main room that led to a closet or "a quaint measuring room," as she called it.

"OK, now, so you go in there. Pull the string on the lightbulb and it'll click on overhead. Be ready—she's bright! Then undress down to your basics."

She turned the bronze doorknob to the slender door and held it open for me. The room was narrow and not too deep. I had enough room to barely stand akimbo, but that was about it. Luckily I could slip my shoes off and didn't have to bend over.

"Knock when you're ready!" she called through the door.

When I stood up, I looked at myself as if I were looking at a stranger. Staring at my stockinged feet, I examined myself up from my thick-but-muscular calves to my thighs, which had bags hanging off them in the middle, where there were obvious signs of chafing. I cringed at my saddlebag of a lower belly, and my doughy upper belly where oval-shaped, pink-nippled breasts rested. Everywhere, there were stretch marks to document my journey to obese.

Surely that wasn't me. Surely I hadn't let me become her.

Mrs. Tanya May Rogerton asked if I was OK. I wanted to say, *Sure, if you like being a melting snowman with nipples like saucers of pink milk*, but instead I said, "Yes, ma'am. Come on in."

She clicked open the door with the greatest care. Her tortoise-shell reading glasses were perched back on her nose. The light was so bright above that my belly cast a shadow over everything from my mid-waist down. I closed my eyes as she unraveled her tape measure.

"My apologies. That is one bright bulb," she said, "but I need it to read my tape numbers."

I felt Mrs. Tanya May Rogerton hold her arms out and realized to my horror that she couldn't get them around me.

"Can you do me a favor and hold this end while I take my measurements?" she asked.

I opened my eyes. "Certainly." I tried to sound upbeat, despite the fact that it took two grown women to get a proper number of my circumference.

She measured my breasts, waist, and hips.

"52-53-54."

That's not the weekly weather forecast for Alaska—those were my measurements. *Dear God.*

I stood there in her transformed hallway closet in my "good" underwear—the only pair without holes—and my eight-year-old bra that was held fast on the left side with a safety pin, and listened to her read out my measurements as she wrote them on her hand.

52-53-54. The numbers got bigger, as if I were sliding down—a mud flow off a mountain.

Mrs. Tanya May Rogerton wound her tape measure around three fingers and clipped it together with a paper clip. Her nails were painted an even, unchipped pale pink. They were filed short, professional but pretty.

She stepped back a few feet, fully exposing the lightbulb overhead again. "Get dressed, and I'll see you out front."

The measuring room had been painted sky blue to make it feel bigger, but still I could barely breathe. When Mrs. Tanya May Rogerton shut the door, I stared into that mirror under that aggressive lightbulb, and I saw myself again without any filters. I saw a woman who hadn't really allowed herself to *be* a woman in fifteen years—maybe more.

I saw a belly rising like too much yeast and breasts that weren't so much lifted by my bra as stopped from flowing onto my belly. I saw a flap of blubber falling over the front of my beige underwear, directly blocking access to my lady bits—should access ever be wanted. Even my elbows were fat, with sacks hanging from them like chins.

At first, I tried telling myself that it was the light, but there's only so much you can blame on light.

"You all right in there?" Mrs. Tanya May Rogerton called out.

"I am."

I grabbed my old dress off the bistro chair in the corner of the closet, dressed—careful not to tear the fabric—and walked out.

"You look pale, are you all right?"

"I've let myself go," I said.

"Parts of us go as time moves on, to be sure."

"I can't think of one part that has *stayed*."

"With eyes like yours, you don't even notice," she said.

The delicate bell tied on the front door rang as a new customer came in. Of course that woman looked like God damn *Jean Harlow*.

"Have a look around, I'll be with you in a minute!" Mrs. Tanya May Rogerton called out to her. She looked me up and down in a business-y way. "You want the same style dress?"

"How about I let you decide that."

"Well—" she stepped back and eyed my dress again, squinting—"that one suits you, but maybe we could raise up the length a little—show some calf."

"OK."

"And fabric?"

"How about—"

"Oh right, you're letting me decide."

"Yes, ma'am."

She looked up and smiled. "Will do."

Jean Harlow the Second interrupted from across the quiet shop. "Do you do coordinates?"

"I certainly do," Mrs. Tanya May Rogerton told her, as perky as static cling.

Jean Harlow the Second gestured to the two big brown bags she was carrying. "Mind if I set these down?"

"Not at all. Right on that chair there would be fine."

She lifted the bags and plunked them onto the chair. "I found the most *amazing* things down outside Mrs. Lynne's old shop. I'm always on the hunt for a good sidewalk sale."

"They must be making out well down there," Mrs. Tanya May Rogerton said.

The woman helped herself to some lemonade, obviously taxed.

Mrs. Tanya May Rogerton readied her pen and looked up at me. "So, your name?"

"Folks call me Nana Dara."

"And how many dresses?"

"How about four?"

"Four. All right then, Nana Dara, I'll see you in ten days with four dresses."

Not knowing what to say—not that there were many things I could have said—I nodded like a fat sheep on the way to the abattoir and walked out to my truck.

I blotted my forehead with the back of my hand and started her up. Exhaust came in the windows as I shifted and moved ahead, not looking at the dress shop in case Mrs. Tanya May Rogerton was looking out.

I thought about her while I took the slow right past the pumpkin patch. *How could we be so similar but so different?* Those thoughts led me back to think about how I looked in that mirror. It'd been years since I'd seen myself in full view like that, and it struck me that I *behaved* as if I didn't look that way. There was a confidence to me—a way I took my place in a room. Until that moment in the mirror, I saw myself as a large, middle-aged lady who made people feel comfortable. But now—thanks to that mirror—I saw myself the way other people saw me: a fat woman with a flap of blubber and three chins who looked a little like a huge baby doll in a crazy dress. People felt comfortable around me, sure, but maybe it was because I proved—as I once had with Beauregard and his ladies—to be no *competition* in any way.

The revelation of how I appeared shocked me so much that I played it over and over again in my mind for the whole drive, missing a stop sign or two along the way, not that there was ever anyone around to mind, except maybe a wayward rooster.

I lit a cigarette and blew smoke out the window. At least I had the title of "widow." I could barely tie my shoes and my fat behind had ripped through dresses, but I was a widow. I had *proof* that someone had loved me once upon a time.

When I walked into the Opry, there was the Fiddler, leaning back against the sink, eating peanut butter from the jar with a spoon.

"You get some new dresses?"

"What I got was a hard look at reality, Fiddler, and it is *ugly*," I said when I walked by him to my room. He knew better than to follow.

I clicked on the radio, fell down on my bed, and pulled out one of my secret stashes of treats: a marshmallow rolled in sugar. Every time I ate one, I hated myself for eating it, but I couldn't stop. The taste made me feel good for a few minutes—and then I needed another taste to bring me back up again. This reminded me of how it had been after the Warden died and Edna—Eddie—took off.

I tried to eat slowly, but knowing I had more marshmallows to follow caused me to speed up. Before you know it, I'd eaten all twelve. The sugar coated my teeth, and I wanted more. I went to my second stash: a tin of malted milk balls.

Usually when I eat a malted milk ball, I bite it in half, then suck on each half, letting the inner malt melt away. But, that day, I popped them in two or three at a time and chewed them with an emotion that was part anger and part greed—gluttony maybe.

I stuffed myself until I couldn't eat one more bite. Then I sat there, feeling fatter than ever, and I accepted my fate. My fate was to eat until

I got so huge that I could barely move. I would die in bed and have a recovered pedophile find me. That was my future in one sad sentence.

I'd always wanted a family who loved me for who I was, and who I loved for who they were. A *true* family. My parents loved me as their child, and the Warden loved me as his wife—but no one *truly* knew me, except maybe Rhodie and Huddie.

So the two folks who ever knew me were dead. *Perfect.*

Somewhere in my mind, I realized, I held this dream that me and the girls would be like a true family, able to talk about everything— not just the comfortable bits. I'd be able to say, "I met this woman today, and she was so pretty that I was embarrassed about my weight." But then I chastised myself for being a damn fool, grabbed a bottle of pop from beside my bed, and guzzled it down.

× × ×

I only left that stuffy room once over the next three days, to go to the store and fill up on snacks. Now I knew how I *truly* looked with that cart filled with candy and ice cream and breadsticks dipped in chocolate. For the first time, I saw it reflected in the eyes of that skinny girl who took my money. Maybe that look had always been there when I made my secret runs, but I hadn't noticed it. Before, I'd cheerfully handed over my money after unwrinkling it, and I'd said something like, "A little something for my sweet tooth," or, my standby, "Poker night treats," and she would smile back at me. I'd never seen anything except a genuine smile before. What a flabby fool I'd been.

As the girl bagged up my things for me, she snuck a look to the other cashier—a boy with blond hair sculpted to a flattop. They exchanged looks over me, the fat lady with all that fat-lady food.

I held my head up as I picked up my three bags and walked out to the truck, past a few other people who gave me looks in the parking lot. They gave me looks without even knowing what was in my bags. They gave me looks just because I *had* bags—like a big lady wasn't supposed to eat at all!

I prayed that, when I slid into my truck, the front seat wouldn't give that awful shriek that the springs sometimes gave when I sat down. But it did, and they heard. The tall girl laughed, and her friends joined in.

I wasn't even out of the parking lot before I broke into my Sugar Daddy caramel lollipop, chewing on that thing like I didn't give a good God damn about my fillings or my teeth or anything else in the world out there.

× × ×

By the end of the week, that one dress that still fit me was tight in the belly. I was imprisoning myself in fat, shrinking the prison walls I'd worked so hard to push back. But I didn't stop.

On day ten, I asked the Fiddler if he would mind taking the truck into town to get my dresses. I didn't want to see Mrs. Tanya May Rogerton. I had the cash, if he could pay.

"No trouble," he said, chewing on another innocent toothpick, his nervous habit quickly becoming a full-time hobby.

I motioned to the keys, hanging from the key peg by the door. "The shop is a few blocks from Mrs. Lynne's old place. You can't miss it—there is a red woman in a red dress painted on the mailbox."

He nodded and headed out. "Need anything at the store?"

"You know I don't," I said, thinking: *I have enough food stashed to last through the winter.*

He held up his hands. "All right now, dang!"

For years, I'd been fine with the way the Fiddler whiskered up the sink, scraped dog doo off his boots using the edge of the deck so it got hot and stunk up the whole area by day, and how loudly he cleared his sinuses every morning. I'd been fine with his odd need for raw goat's milk, telling me some craziness about how it reminded him of his mother, who'd raised him on it. Trouble was that anything I had in the ice chest near his open jar of milk tasted goaty, which is to say it tasted like scrotum.

That week, I grew to hate all of it. Every breath he took rattled my strings. When he dropped and dented the trashcan lid, I was so angry that I asked him if he'd ever been tested for mental disease. The worst part of it was that he just took it—and that made me even more aggravated.

About the only time I wasn't aggravated was when I was snacking. And since the Fiddler was always around, I was forced to do most of my snacking in my room, where the sheets were now sticky with sugar. I grew tired of hoarding wrappers in a bag in my closet. My room stunk.

This anger inside me was poisoning the area *around* me, but I couldn't stop it. I ruined everything for five minutes of feeling good with a snack—and I knew it—but I just couldn't stop it.

My mind just kept spinning: I was the horrible person who'd broken Rhodie's heart, and the horrible mother who'd let my child grow up alone and angry in doll outfits so I'd look normal. It was my fault that Eddie then got herself pregnant—by someone I never even met—and, even worse, my fault that she'd given up her own child, my sweet little PD.

Beyond that, I knew I'd never be truly known and loved. I would die a fat, loveless, unknown lesbian in a tie-dyed room that smelled like rotten cream and bologna.

The Fiddler retrieved my dresses while I ate and smoked and thought about what it would be like if he weren't here—if I could just get fat and eventually die in peace. The picture wasn't a pretty one: me being able to yell at the evening news and leave the bathroom door open so I could be comfortable on the commode and keep my Milky Ways in the freezer, the way I liked them—things a timid, skinny man in recovery would never understand.

An hour later, the Fiddler carried the dresses in—each one on a hanger, with the hangers tied together with the same ribbon on the little bell on Mrs. Tanya May Rogerton's door. Sweat dripped from his underarm afros down his tan arms.

"Dammit, don't sweat on them," I snapped.

"Sorry," he said and dropped them over the red vinyl chair in the kitchen. "Goodness, you are in a mood."

"I'm in a *state*."

"Well whatever state that is, the taxes are too high," he said and stomped to his bedroom, chewing another toothpick.

THE MANY FACES OF HELL

By the first week of December, none of my four new dresses fit. *Not one.* I'd get them on over my head and shoulders, but then they'd get stuck either at the breastline or around my belly. Not a *one* made it to my thighs.

I stood in my bedroom, buck naked, looking down at all my new dresses in a pile on my bedspread. She'd chosen some gorgeous colors too, Mrs. Tanya May Rogerton did. Just like she said, she made one with a bright peach and one with a bold blue and one with zigzags of green.

I sat down next to the pile in my hot, stinky room and wondered what to do next. I had nothing to wear. Not one God damn thing.

I rifled through my closet. My old white cotton robe—the one the Warden gave me on our third wedding anniversary—was about the only thing I could get around my girth. I was about to put it on, ready to do my best to act casual in only a robe, when I remembered that I had a T-shirt from the chili cook-off, where Miss Debbie's Bo had placed second a few years earlier. I put that on with my pajama bottoms that had the elastic waist, and I was ready to leave my room. On the way out the door I decided to jazz it up, so I added a silk scarf around my neck.

Listen, I told myself, if women those days could wear dresses that looked like boxes and pants that used to be quilts I could wear my *Watch Them Beans!* T-shirt from the *1953 Hotter Than Hell Chili Cook-Off.*

When I was younger, I vowed that if my stomach ever protruded past my breasts, I would make some weight-loss changes. That was twenty years ago. I had done nothing for those twenty years but watch the race between my breasts and my belly, which my belly had clearly won. Now there was a better chance that bears would dance with bunnies than that my breasts would ever catch up.

"Oh, well, uh, where's your dress?" the Fiddler asked when I walked down the hallway in my unique outfit.

"Where's your tact?" I answered.

The Fiddler threw up his hands. "You've been riding me for two months now, Nana Dara, and for no good reason that I can tell. I'm *sick* with all the tension. I'm chewing so many toothpicks that I'm worried about wood getting stuck in my stomach."

"I'm sorry," I said, then: "Come on. Let's sit a spell."

We walked out to the deck. Thankfully we were deep in winter so I could leave the robe on.

The Fiddler, all elbows and sad eyes, sat down. "You don't like the dresses?"

"I wore them before— two weeks ago— didn't I?"

"Yeah."

"And I *said* I liked them, didn't I?" I swatted at spider webs I wasn't sure were there.

"You are growing too mean. I am nothing but nice to you, and you are growing too mean."

I leaned away from the Fiddler. "Seems I am *growing*, that's for sure."

He nodded like this was no news to him.

"Is it that obvious?" I asked.

"I noticed."

"Well, damn, thanks for telling me."

"That's not right fair."

"Just take your redneck ass back in the house and leave me be!"

The Fiddler walked off the deck, through the kitchen, and out the front door. He wasn't around for the rest of that day—or the next.

I'm not sure where he went, but he didn't come back for two days, and when he did he smelled like the armpit of a French harlot.

"Fall asleep on the floor of a distillery?" I asked, without looking up from my crossword puzzle.

The Fiddler, in the same jeans and flannel he left in two days earlier, stepped past two of the cats, who were sleeping together on a sunny square on the floor, and walked to his room. Just before he went in, he stopped and turned to face me. "Ever given any thought to why you suddenly care about your weight?"

"What?"

"You didn't care what I saw or what your family saw. You only cared what *Mrs. Tanya May Rogerton* saw."

I felt a rush of panic and wished I could backpedal somehow out of the room. "What now?"

"You are having sinful thoughts or inclinations toward Mrs. Tanya May Rogerton, and so you're hatin' on yourself."

I looked him dead in the eye. "What?"

"You are *overeating* because you are *hating* what you are. What you are is sinful, that's true, but I don't want to see you kill yourself over urges of the flesh that can be overcome."

"Overcome?"

"Like I did."

I stood up from the couch in the same motion that forms a tidal wave. The Fiddler took a small step back but held his ground.

With a fierce tension in my voice I said, "I am not you, Fiddler. My *adult* love is not your lust for young girls."

"What you feel and think is wrong. It ain't right. It's wrong."

I took a step toward him. The muscles in his face strained so much that they actually bulged out at the end of his jaw, in front of his ears.

"I had a friend once named Huddie," I said, "and he told me that he was the way he was because he couldn't hide the color of his skin. Well, looking back, I wish to God I couldn't hide. I wish everyone looked at me and saw right off that I am a lover of women, God dammit! Maybe that way I would have been forced to step up and find myself someone to love. Instead, I'm sitting here with you and getting told I'm a wrongful person, when I am so sad about it all that I'm eating enough to explode. God damn you, Fiddler!"

The Fiddler looked down with his forehead all scrunched up the way he did. His hair was fluffy on top, on account of him needing to get a trim after the past few days. I watched him struggle with what to do.

A minute in, he straightened up and said the most words I think he'd ever said in a row: "It might be wrong to me, but I don't condemn what you are thinking of doing or might do with another woman. I just can't live with all this *anger* about it. Maybe you hate the world for being the way it is toward folks like you. Maybe you hate me for feeling similar. I don't know. What I do know is that you treat me poorly, and I'm sick to my stomach nearly every day. It's making me feel like going to the places I've worked so hard not to go to. I see you eating yourself to death, and I want to throw it all away too, and give into my temptations. I am sorry I judged you and said some things, though I'm even sorrier to say that I got to *go*. It just ain't safe for me here."

I shouted, "Fine!" then I pushed by him down the hallway and slammed my bedroom door. I plopped down on my colorful bedspread and cried for a full hour, unsure what to do.

Through the door, I heard the Fiddler dragging his army bag of clothes and his suitcase behind him. He banged down the hallway, each crack reminding me how hollow my walls were.

"The stress here is causing me to get into a state of temptation when I promised God I never would," he shouted out with a hoarse voice, "but we were close—real close, Nana Dara, and that's what I'm going to remember."

I didn't want him to hear my messy crying voice, so I didn't say anything.

He yelled back down, as much as he ever did yell, "You were my friend, and I'm sorry."

In response, I threw an empty bottle of pop at my door.

Ten minutes, later someone pulled up on the gravel—probably someone from his recovery program since he really didn't have too many folks I would consider friends, except me, the cats, the pugs, and a few drinkers down at Maria's Roundabout.

When he left, the hurt came on me so strongly that I was afraid I'd start to eat everything there was to eat and not stop until I popped. He'd been as close to true family, by my definition, as I'd ever had. He lived with me, he loved me, and he knew nearly everything about me—though, in the end, he turned that knowledge *ugly*, the thing I most feared.

"Damn him!"

Then I got angry again. Angry with him for what he'd said and how he left, but also angry at Mrs. Tanya May Rogerton for how she'd never love me. She and I would never split the head and foot of the dinner table, with my stepchildren and my granddaughter seated between us. It was a pipe dream. Maybe, in this life, this was as far as I was meant to go.

I breathed in slowly to calm my thoughts and sort out the hurt from the anger from the fear from the sadness. Not an easy task. I wiped my eyes and looked up at the low ceiling of my Opry, where it was yellower than the rest from me smoking in bed.

Now I'd lost my best friend, who thought I was horrible and sinful. I sat there with that, letting myself feel what *that* meant. It caused me to ache all over, like pneumonia.

Overall, I just couldn't make sense of the mess of pain and shame and anger about love and who I was and what that meant to other people. It was like running in a maze in the dark.

I focused on the Fiddler. The fault, I decided, was 85 percent mine on account of me being mad at the world and my fat self, which came out mostly on him since he was the most *nearby* part of the world. The remaining 15 percent was on him and his opinion that my predilections were, to quote the head cook all those years ago, *filthy*.

That last bit—the filthy bit—made me want to punch myself in the stomach, so I didn't stay with that feeling too long.

With the Fiddler, I knew that I'd been a lunatic carrying all kinds of angry, and I'd made his life miserable. He didn't leave because I'm a non-practicing lesbian—he left because I was angry with him for nothing he did wrong. That was the black rock in the swamp, and I let it wash over me: I'd chased my best friend away—one of the simplest, truest friends I'd ever had.

Somehow I made him say to me perhaps the things I thought of myself. I hurt him to hurt me. *How could I be so horrible, to all of us?*

Truffle, my dark gray cat, came up to say hello, but I couldn't be bothered. I shooed him away, grabbed a candy bar from under the bed to calm me, ate it, then slept a sad, hopeless sleep for thirteen hours.

× × ×

Several days passed since the Fiddler left, and I wallowed and spiraled. Seems the Fiddler kept me stable just by being there. Maybe I did the same for him, and that's why me coming undone on him like that shattered him so much that he was afraid he'd go back to his wicked ways, as I'd done with my food urges.

I missed having someone to tease in the morning, and eat sandwiches with at lunch, and share beverages with at night on the porch. All my margaritas were too damn sweet with irregular salt rims that slunk down into the booze and ruined everything—besides, who drinks margaritas alone? Bourbon, sure, but not margaritas.

I missed the Fiddler every minute of the day, and I hated myself for not being able to be settled with my title of "widow." If I'd have closed off my romantic heart and not had secret thoughts about Mrs. Tanya May Rogerton, I would have my best friend here now. *Why did I need this kind of love?*

As I was thinking, up drove Miss Debbie. I heard the gravel fly off in a million directions, followed by the characteristic creak of her car door. She walked right on in before I could even get up, calling out, "You got anything to cool me off?"

"Hello to you too, Miss Debbie."

She sniffed the air like I used to sniff the Fiddler's goat milk. "What stinks?"

"Probably something from the cats."

She looked inside the small drawer on my side table, where I kept the tools to keep my callused feet under control. "What's all this?"

I redirected. "Gin and tonic?"

She shut the drawer and cracked her gum. "Two lime wedges— give them a squeeze first."

Miss Debbie's legs were lean and strong, accented by her white clunky shoes. She wore a tight-fitting paisley skirt and a long-sleeved yellow blouse with way too many bracelets. That woman always looked good, even with a blob of melted crayon on her back.

"Come with me," I said, and we walked into the kitchen area.

"Where's the Fiddler?"

"Gone."

"That T-shirt scare him off?" She pointed to my *Watch Them Beans!* shirt.

"It was just time."

I unscrewed the tonic water in the sink, in case it exploded. One of the pugs wheezed past me, his tongue hanging out the side of his mouth. He fumbled over to collect some attention from Miss Debbie, who had no interest in dogs.

I yelled over my shoulder, "I don't have lime."

Miss Debbie ran a finger along the edge of her mascara while the pug sat sideways on the floor at her feet. "You have lemon?"

"No."

"Orange?"

"No."

"*Any* fruit?"

"No."

"You always have fruit."

"The Fiddler had fruit."

"You have marshmallows—and clearly," she said, finally taking off her rhinestone sunglasses to look me over, "lots of them."

The pug gave up and wandered into the back room, no doubt to jump up on my bed—an action that required considerable effort from that plump little thing.

She asked, "So what happened with the Fiddler?"

"Gone."

"All these years, whenever I ask you questions of a personal nature you answer impersonally."

She was right. That's how I operated.

I thought about the Fiddler and wondered if things would have been different if I had confided to him my troubles with food and my attraction to Mrs. Tanya May Rogerton before that secret became a boil. I should have tried—the worst that could have happened happened anyway: I lost him.

I took in a breath and gave it a try. "The Fiddler said I'd gotten overly angry of late, and that it was too much for him to be around, me nitpicking and whatnot."

"What are you angry about?"

I wasn't ready to go into all that just yet, so I simplified. "My weight."

"That must generate quite a bit of anger then," she said with her eyebrows raised as I walked over.

I jammed the glass into her hand. "Here."

As usual these days, she was carrying the biggest vinyl bag I'd ever seen. It was white with black curved handles that fit over her shoulder.

She pushed her finger into my side. "You are really putting it on, Nana Dara."

"Didn't I ever teach you manners?"

"You told me not to lie."

"There are such things as *omissions* in polite conversation."

"Since when are we polite?"

When she leaned back something crinkled. She reached her hand behind the seat cushion and pulled out a big bag—not the little bag—of nougats, empty.

She shook the bag in the air. "Evidence!"

"If you are going to talk about my weight, you might as well go." I started to stand.

"No more mentions of weight, I swear!"

Miss Debbie dropped the nougat bag on the floor and started in about how much she and PD are loving to sing together lately and how Bo plays guitar and PD bobs back and forth, messing up the words to anything by Elvis.

"She's cute as a bug!"

"I know she is." I smiled. "And how's Eddie?"

She sighed. "Still living a book written by the Devil."

"Eddie been by to see PD?"

"Eddie travels to El Paso a lot now—*for some reason.*" Miss Debbie let it go at that. "But she makes sure to visit PD every week if she can."

"You think it's hard on Eddie?"

Miss Debbie stiffened up, the way she does. "Maybe from time to time. But that was the choice she made. She made her *choices.*"

"You think she made the choice to be the kind of woman who can't raise her own child?"

"Let's be clear here: she could have raised her own child if she'd stop dressing like *the Mayor.*"

Eddie was here on this road in life for a reason, I told myself, and so was I. Maybe we were put together to help each other through our circumstances. So I asked Miss Debbie, "Now what if I told you that you had to start wearing men's suits, and I told Bo that he needed to slip on a dress?"

"If everyone else was doing it, I imagine we'd hop right in line." She puckered her lips a bit. "Besides, I can make any outfit work. Nana Dara, Eddie lives a selfish life. Simple as that."

"By *my* way of thinking, Eddie did the most selfless thing a mother can do—she let her child be raised by someone else to spare the child any pain."

"Pain caused by the mother."

My neck got hot. "Do you think it's possible for folks to live a happy life without the love of a spouse, if they are able to get themselves a spouse?"

"It's possible."

"So you'd wish for your sister to die alone?" I said, thinking: *For me to die alone, too?*

"She'd have had PD."

"Until PD got married."

"This is someone who first got herself *pregnant*, then handed her baby over so she could pretend to be a man!"

Miss Debbie got so angry that I was afraid she'd crush the glass in her hand. This seemed about as close as we could sidle up to the whale without touching it, so I let it go.

"Calm down now, Miss Debbie. I'm just trying to practice some of those Christian values you are always preaching."

She smiled one of her fake smiles, the kind she reserves for bad waitresses and adulterous men in church. "Let's agree to disagree. Better, let's agree to bury this subject. It is *dead*. Agreed?"

I didn't say anything.

With some clear effort, Miss Debbie relaxed. She took a big sip of her drink and breathed deeply, shifting back to a stable mood. "You need to come see PD more often. You are her *grandmother*. And that's why I'm here—to invite you out for New Year's."

"I thought that invite was standing each year."

"It is—I'm just reminding you."

"And leaving PD with Bo?"

"Can't I come see you every now and again without it being like this?" Miss Debbie paused, then looked me in the eye. "Now about New Years. Answer me, true—can you drive anymore?"

"What?"

She rolled her eyes. "Can you *fit* behind the wheel?"

"Miss Debbie!"

"Nana Dara, I am being serious now. If not, Bo can come get you."

I didn't answer her. *Of course I could fit!* Though it was getting a little tight.

I crunched some of my ice with my teeth. "How is Bo?"

"Loving his cars. If it weren't for PD, he might sleep down at the shop every night."

I raised an eyebrow but didn't say anything.

"He's good. He's good. You know he is," she said.

"All right, well, we're caught up with how everyone's doing, so you best get going." I felt an urge for some cookies.

Miss Debbie slapped her knees. "Nana Dara!"

"Now I know you'd love another gin and tonic, but you need to go have dinner with your family."

"They are *your* family too. Besides, it took me an hour to get here!"

"I'll fill up your glass and you can take it back with you."

"All right. I'm worried about you, you know." She stood up and smoothed out her paisley skirt.

"I'm OK."

I filled her glass with mostly tonic and walked it back to her just as she slid her sunglasses back down from her hair.

"Sincerely though," she said, "it stinks in here. You best look around for lost food items."

PINNED IN,
SAWED OUT, LIGHT SEEN

Sunday morning I woke up and smelled the funk Miss Debbie had complained about. I sniffed around until I figured it out. That stench was coming from *me* or, more specifically, from inside one of my rolls of stomach pudge where my sweat and some crumbs got trapped. When I flattened out my roll, I saw a red patch of irritation. On closer inspection, I saw lines of gray smudge that had a smell to them.

I was molding.

Horrified, I climbed into the tub and did my best to reach all my creases, but to my shock, I could no longer reach my backside—the biggest crease of them all. I had grown too big to wash my own ass.

× × ×

By the day of New Year's Eve, a week later, I had to call and cancel on Miss Debbie since I was having trouble getting behind the wheel of my truck.

"But I drove out there to ask you in person!" was her first response, followed by, "And PD is looking forward to seeing you. Plus I just put fresh butter in the butter bell."

"I can't make it. I have to do something."

"What? You have hardly any friends, especially with the Fiddler gone. I still don't understand that one." She paused. "Unless you can't drive. Are you too big to drive now? Wait, don't answer that. I'm going to have Bo get you. He won't mind. He has a new engine he wants to test out anyway. Bo! Bo, baby, can you get Nana Dara? She's unable to drive herself." I knew she was gesturing to him that I was too fat to squeeze in behind the steering wheel. "OK, he said yes. Put on one of your nice, new dresses and bring some acorn squash," she said, like I just had acorn squash on hand. "And ice." She hung up.

My head spun trying to figure out how to get out of this. I walked out to my truck, opened the door, and held my breath in as deeply as I could. I grabbed my chub with my left hand and held it up, pressing up against my breasts, and tried to slide in. For the third time in two days, I checked to see if the seat could move back any further. It couldn't.

I exhaled, and my fat fell down on the wheel. I was in, mostly. I could do this—so long as I didn't need to make any hard lefts or rights with the steering wheel. I struggled back into the Opry and called Miss Debbie, who said I was in luck—Bo hadn't left yet.

"Good. I'm driving myself over."

For those of you not from the rural South, sometimes the driving can be fast, with empty roads and bright blue skies—or it can take forever, with deep potholes and cotton trucks and big green tractors. I'd gotten a long driving day when I had to stop for some rodeo cowboy hell-bent on crossing ten steer on a single rope.

While me and my weighted-down Ford idled, the heat came up from the truck's guts under the metal hood, despite the chilly day. The clouds gathered and I hoped for rain to cool down the engine, but no such luck. Meanwhile, those steer took their good God damn time crossing with Jimmy Cowboy tugging the gentlest of tugs and chewing on turnip greens.

I stuck my head out the window. "Can you get them moving? I'd like to see midnight tonight."

"Sorry, ma'am. You just can't rush 'em."

I couldn't wait one second more, so I swerved around the cattle and pressed the gas down—then ran straight into a hay truck. I heard the crash before everything got dark on me.

× × ×

The nice folks at the hospital took a slew of X-rays and settled me into a room. I'd been there for about ten minutes when PD, still as sweet as pecan pie, walked in hand-in-hand with Bo, who was graying even more around the temples in that handsome way some men grow old.

Little PD was apparently wearing the clothes she wore for bug digging, which let me know that this was serious since Miss Debbie had rushed over before she made sure her little girl didn't look like a little boy. Behind them Miss Debbie stomped in, wearing those sunglasses that were as big as the fish bowls you could win at the carnival for three bull's-eye ring tosses.

She cried out, "Nana Dara, first Daddy then you!"

Bo waved to the nurse in the corridor, saying it was OK—Miss Debbie was just a little passionate, is all. He closed my hospital room door.

I sat up as best I could. "The Warden had a *stroke*. I had an *accident*. And, in case you haven't noticed, I'm not dead."

"You need to get your life together," she said and stood over my bed like the messenger of death herself.

PD looked up at us and smiled. "I drew you a sun," she said, holding out a piece of binder paper with a yellow smiling sun on it.

Miss Debbie sucked in a breath. "She's so good she can even draw in the car."

"Though that car is pretty smooth," Bo said, putting his hands on PD's little shoulders.

Miss Debbie sighed. "Now is not time for *car talk*, Bo."

"Nor is it time for Hell talk," I said.

"What the heck is the matter with you!" Miss Debbie pulled out a cigarette from her bra but didn't light it. "You are killing yourself!"

Bo asked PD if she wanted to go look at the fountain in the middle of the hospital yard and PD, always one to be fascinated with the workings of water, nodded her head up and down. She waved to me as they left.

Miss Debbie watched them go, holding her smoking-arm elbow with her free hand like a fashion model. I looked over at her, and I understood that she was stuck in a place that would never support her being what she could be—some style-minded woman in a big city somewhere, with places to *go*. Her life would always be too small.

"Your truck is *totaled*," she said. "They had to saw it open because you were *too heavy* to just come out the window."

"What?"

"They cut the doors off and drug you out, Nana Dara."

"Where's Eddie?" I redirected.

"*What?* How the heck should I know?"

"Did you call her?"

"I sent a carrier pigeon," she huffed.

My nurse—a short thing with a ponytail left over from high school some decades earlier—came in and asked if I wanted anything to eat.

"Jujyfruits," I said, just to gouge at Miss Debbie a bit.

"Nana Dara!" she squawked.

The nurse didn't look up. "We have catfish."

"That'll do," I said, ignoring thoughts about how it must have looked with them dragging my fat body from that cut-open truck. *Lord.*

Miss Debbie rifled through the one cabinet in the room like the nurse wasn't there. The nurse watched her, waiting for Miss Debbie to notice and stop, but she never did, so she turned back to me. "Catfish. OK. You get well." She squeezed my leg through the white blanket and sheet. It felt comforting to be touched. It'd been so long.

"Can we smoke in here?" Miss Debbie asked me.

"Only if you don't mind your face being blown off by loose hospital oxygen."

She set her giant vinyl bag down on the guest chair by my bed. The chair looked like tweed, which made me wonder how they could possibly keep it clean in a place that specialized in bodily fluids. She pulled out a pack of menthols to hold.

"What are you going to do now?" Miss Debbie asked, as if I had just attempted to climb a hill and rolled back down.

"Save money for a new truck."

"I imagine that's a start."

"I could go back to making birdhouses. I make the best birdhouses."

She softened. "I remember."

"I could sell them down at the market."

"That's a lot of birdhouses."

"You here to cheer me up?"

Miss Debbie scratched her forehead. Her nails were bright blue with New Year's stars painted on them. It always amazed me how she never damaged herself with those talons.

I looked around the white sanitized room, wondering how I'd let it go this far. I truly could die, and that frightened me so much I almost left a gift on my clean hospital sheets.

"I'm going to start walking to get this weight off," I said, something inside me clicking on. "I'm going to wrap myself in plastic and start walking. I need to make some serious changes. My life will never be like this again."

Miss Debbie let out a sigh and nodded. "Good. But start with short walks, like once around the Opry. You are *big*, Nana Dara, so start *small*. And you can't seriously wrap yourself in plastic."

"Extreme is needed."

She held onto her menthol pack. "I'm so worried about you. You— you are my second mama, you know." She smiled and cried a little, not caring that her tears were destroying her carefully laid makeup plans. "I'm just so worried."

"You're going to be more worried in a moment."

Miss Debbie paused, then lit a cigarette from the pack she'd been squeezing. "How's that?"

"Stand up near the door there," I said.

She moved over to the door and crossed her arms, making sure the cigarette was out of the way of her vinyl bag.

"You ready?" I asked.

Her hand shook as she took a deep drag on her cigarette. "Yes."

"I'm saying this because I want us to be family—*real* family. I want you to know me for who I am so maybe someday we can talk. Love is important, you know, and so when we leave it out of conversation, it leaves a hole."

"Are you feeling dizzy?"

"Miss Debbie, I'm a non-practicing lesbian. Always have been."

Miss Debbie wiped her eyes and yanked open the door. She hollered out the door: "Come quick, she's having a stroke or her mind's being overtaken! She must have hit her head—hard!"

"Miss Debbie, calm down." I tried to sit up but was too afraid of jostling the monitors on me. "I am not having a stroke, and I am not crazy. I have always been a lesbian—though I did love your daddy."

"I cannot hear any more of this." She let the white door close behind her and looked toward Heaven. "God is sending me more tests than Job." Miss Debbie glared at me and dropped her sunglasses down from her auburn hair. She stubbed her cigarette out in the plastic vomit tray sitting on the cabinet. "You need to get some sleep and get your shit together, Nana Dara. *Get your shit together.* Praise be his name."

Miss Debbie tried to make a grand exit, but when she yanked the door, it wouldn't pull open fast enough, and her vinyl bag dropped from her shoulder. She fell a little to one side, stumbling on her clunky heels. "Well, hell!" she yelled just as she got the door open and crashed into the hallway. "If you need me, I will be at church—*praying.* You know the way."

Her sunglasses fell, and she kicked them out of the way, so as not to be distracted as she stomped out on her righteous path.

BEING AVAILABLE

Bo drove me home from the hospital. We hardly said two words the whole trip. *I* knew that *he* knew what I'd confessed to Miss Debbie, and I knew that he didn't want to discuss it. I could just see Miss Debbie railing against me in that loud whisper she had, periodically covering PD's little ears to keep her safe from the topic. The topic being *me*.

Out of respect to Bo, I didn't ask him any questions. I didn't get him in the middle. I just sat there, letting the remnants of a terrible Connie Francis song trail through my brain like a punishment.

Two days later Eddie, raced up to the Opry. She raised her hand to her forehead to cover her eyes against the bright sun and peered in the front screen door. "Nana Dara? *Nana Dara!*"

"I'm alive! I'm just on the couch. Come on in."

My stepdaughter pushed open the door. I watched a moment of realization pass through her as she saw how big I'd gotten—my size no doubt highlighted by my yellow T-shirt and matching sweat pants. It must've looked like I was merging with my mustard-colored couch, as if it was just a puddle of me.

Eddie's hair was a little longer now and could maybe be a bob if she didn't keep it so far back behind her ears. It made me wonder if she did that in case there were times when she had to wear a bob to feminize herself. It's tough living so *consciously* all the time.

"Come on in."

She took a few steps in and looked around as if she expected to be attacked by a giant pan of fudge.

"Don't worry. I'm working on my weight—I'm turning it around."
I took in a breath. "And I want to tell you something I should have
told you all those years ago on the night you didn't go to your prom."

"*Which* prom that I didn't go to?"

"The first one."

"All right."

"Ah . . . well . . ."

While I stammered, Eddie sat down on the rickety chair with her
legs spread and her hands locked in the middle, like she was watching football. When she looked up at me, she broke out in a big smile.
"Why don't you let me guess what you are going to tell me?"

I lit a cigarette. "Sure."

"You're a lover of Sappho."

"What now?" I asked.

She clarified, "You're a lesbian."

I nearly dropped my cigarette. "How did you know?"

"Other than the shoes you wear? Miss Debbie."

"That girl leaks more than a wooden bucket of termites."

"She called and read me the act—said it was my doing, that I had
'poisoned the waters of our family well.'"

"Lord." I leaned back.

Eddie smiled. "She goes crazy sometimes, Nana Dara, usually after Bible study or her third gin and tonic—or both."

"Eddie," I said, staying on track, "all of your pain is *my* fault. I
should have been there for you. I should have been a role model for
you. It's my fault you suffered."

"What?"

"I had chances—like prom night—to tell you about me so you
wouldn't feel so alone."

She sighed. "That is even crazier than your rampages about aliens."

"Well, they are breedin' with us—"

"Oh, here we go! Between you and Miss Debbie, I'm looking like
the sanest one out there—me, a woman with a bow tie collection."

Eddie had a new ease to her, I noticed. She even smiled without hiding her teeth and just made a joke about her ties, something we never even addressed before, much less joked about. I hoped there was someone out there thinking about her right now.

"Seriously now, I should have told you earlier. I should have said something. Instead I made you hide and be someone you weren't, and then you did dangerous things and got pregnant and had to give up your baby—"

She looked down at her trimmed, plain fingernails. "You really taking all that on, Nana Dara?"

"Yes. Yes, I am."

Eddie took the cigarette from my smiley-face ashtray and sat back down. "*I* did what *I* did. I didn't love the man who got me pregnant, but he was fun—and when my friends and their boyfriends went out, I had someone to take along. Then he enlisted. I slept with him because I *wanted* to, not because of anything you did or anyone I wasn't yet able to be."

I nodded, unconvinced but trying to look the opposite.

Eddie stared down through her knees at my stained and worn carpet. Her face grew dark. "But I will tell you this—the pregnancy sealed it for me. Made it all clear what I could and could not do. I love PD, you know I do, but I hated it, Nana Dara. I hated being pregnant. I didn't really want the body I'd been given, and there I was, with it in its highest female form. And the doctor visits. Do you know what they *do* to check on the baby? Oh, I could barely handle it. And I was alone."

"Honey, I'm so sorry."

"I finally told Miss Debbie in the second trimester. I told her because I didn't know if I could keep on going. I didn't know if I could do labor. I needed some reason to keep on."

I tried to catch her eye, but she kept her head down.

"Once I told her I wanted to give her the baby, she drove me to every doctor's appointment and bought me all my clothes and didn't say a word when I cut all my hair off, she said I was in 'the crazy point' of pregnant. She'd read it in a book."

I smiled. "If you got Miss Debbie to read, you *know* it's serious."

"She told me all about the stages and made me write down what I was eating every day. It was Miss Debbie in the room with me when I found out it was a girl. We had some wine later that night to celebrate, and I asked her if I could name the baby. At that point, I could have told her I wanted everything she owned—and her husband—and she would have given it to me."

"You could probably still have him, I imagine."

Eddie met my eyes. "Nana Dara, we both know I'd never want him."

"Me neither."

She smiled—beamed really—and took another drag off my cigarette.

I said, "Can I ask you something?"

She nodded.

"I don't quite get how you don't want to have a woman's body—I mean, what does that *mean?*"

"It took me so many nights, many of them more than a little dark, for me to come to understand that. And by understand, I am not saying that I understand but, rather, that I just accept. It's like what you learn in Eastern religions, like Buddhism."

"What now?"

"Buddhism." She smiled. "I learned about it when I was in California. It's just like a different religion, only they don't like to call it a religion—they call it a philosophy."

"All right," I said, wary.

"Buddhism teaches a lot about self-acceptance, or at least that was the focus when I was studying it, seeing that I needed a lot of self-acceptance. I learned to stop asking 'why' and start accepting the fact that I have these strange yearnings, which put me somewhere between the two genders, and having something is enough—you don't always need to know why."

I didn't say anything, my mind playing a tug of war between how I'd been raised and how I truly felt.

She went on: "There's a saying I repeated to myself fifty times a day, every day, for three months: 'What you are is what you have been. What you'll be is what you'll do now.' Buddha said it."

"Buddha?"

"He's like Jesus—actually a lot like Jesus, only not Jesus."

I smiled. No one in Sugar Land that I know sits around talking about an alternative to *Jesus*.

"Nana Dara, the way I've come to love myself, as I am in every moment, is the way I want you to love yourself. Start by giving away all those notions that who I am is your fault. Maybe even thank yourself for who I am."

It hit me then—the same way it hit me all those years ago in the prison when I defended the man who'd been assaulted with the broom by saying that maybe he wasn't a homosexual: I had just apologized to Eddie for being the way she was, which means that I thought her being this way was wrong—but I didn't, did I?

"I'm just sorry you felt so bad for so long."

"I know." She smiled like someone who didn't mind waiting five hours on a lake for one measly bite. "Thank you, Nana Dara."

I took in a breath and recollected, hitting the maximum of new information I could process in one day. I pulled us back to our original topic, letting Eddie know she had to ease off or my head would pop. "OK, so then you had PD . . ."

She nodded, telling me she got it. "Yes, ma'am."

"Was that hard for you, given what we just talked about?"

"I came to think of it like this, Nana Dara: It's what needed to happen, for a million reasons. A million."

"That's a big number."

"Yes." Her dark eyes dulled to a faraway place. "Yes it is."

"Oh honey."

"And now there's PD."

I said, "Yes, yes there is," all the while wondering if she gave up California and their crazy philosophies that seem to suit her so she could be near PD.

"Well," she said, clearly also at her limit for the day, "it's time for me to head out."

I pushed myself up with arms that were getting stronger every day. "You think you might want to have a visit again some time this week?"

"Yes, ma'am."

"Good," I said.

"Are you fine with Miss Debbie—with the way her mind goes?"

"I just hope it passes."

"Most storms do," she said.

"Even on Jupiter."

Eddie tucked her shirt in and headed for the door. She turned back to me. "So, you have a girlfriend?"

"*What?* No, no."

She laughed. "Why not?"

"I'm an old woman!"

"So?"

"So, that's nasty."

She stepped outside. "That so?"

"No," I said, taking a minute in our safe space to consider the words I'd just used. "No, it isn't nasty. It's just not *available*."

"Well," Eddie said, looking feisty and proud, "I've found that it's more available than folks think."

A NEW DRESS

Eddie and I visited quite a bit, with her keeping me occupied while Miss Debbie held her distance. Then, two months later, Miss Debbie started calling me up, her acting like no time had passed and nothing had changed. She called me every day at noon, telling me she was just making sure I was still breathing, asking if I needed anything.

If I needed wood for my birdhouses, she'd send over Bo, but most times she'd come over herself to help me out—and usually she'd bring my little peanut, PD.

The phone rang again at noon, right on time.

"Hello, Miss Debbie," I said.

"You want me to come by to get you out for your errands?"

"No, I'm trying to walk."

"You miss that truck, huh?"

"You bet I do. But the weather's nice, so it's not so bad. And it forces me to move around."

"Glad you are walking because you know that weight is going to kill you."

"How's your gin?"

"Gin don't kill." She paused to yell at PD to be careful with her juice cup. "*People* on gin, however . . ." She recollected herself. "How'd the birdhouses do this weekend? Eddie said you emptied her trunk."

"Sold left and right at the Saturday market. Baptists love birds, it seems."

"Mm-hmm."

"I'm going to start making dollhouses, too. There's a demand for them."

Then Miss Debbie finally breached the subject. She started in easy: "Nana Dara, you had a crazy spell in the hospital. Do you remember?"

"I do."

Her voice hushed on the phone. "Do you take it back?"

"I do not."

"Then we are needing to *talk*. I'm bringing the water."

"The water" was a small vial of holy water blessed by the pope himself. While Baptists push back against such notions, believing things like holy water are too close to magic, Catholics—like Miss Debbie's grandmother—believe the more magic, the better. The vial had been left to her after her grandmother died. It was the biggest gun Miss Debbie had, and that's saying something.

"Miss Debbie, I assure you there is no need—"

"I am coming over." She clicked her tongue, then yelled, "PD, don't take your shirt off! Nana Dara, I have to go. She just can't keep her clothes on."

"Like mother, like—"

"I'll be by in an hour." She hung up.

I sat on the couch, propped my feet back on my thick heels, and closed my eyes to do some relaxations that Eddie taught me. When I inhaled, I thought of a sunny field of dandelions. When I exhaled, I imagined blowing across the field and sending all those seeds flying like fairies in the light.

I stayed calmed for about an hour—then Miss Debbie rapped on the door, causing it to clack every time.

I yelled out, "Just come on in like you usually do!"

I sat up from the soft back cushion, conscious of the tightness of the special socks the hospital had given me to get blood flowing in my ankles.

That cutie PD ran in, her doll even rattier than before. "Nana Dara!"

"Looks like dolly could use a hair wash."

"So could you," Miss Debbie said, lighting a cigarette while she held the glass tube of blessed water in her tight fist. "PD, honey, you go find the kitties now. Remember, no cutting their hair."

PD kissed me on the cheek without being asked to and was off through the flapping screen door. I had a vague worry that she would hit the cats with her doll, but they were pretty fast felines, despite the ice cream I used to feed them.

Miss Debbie shouted after her, "You call me if you need me, PD!"

She hadn't brought her oversized bag this time, just her cigarettes, her bright red lighter, and her holy water. She'd used a very pale lip gloss that morning, not her usual harlot-color and give more pious weight to the ceremony.

"We are not to talk about the words used at the hospital. Those were wrong and wicked, and if you ask me, they are somehow responsible for Eddie dressing like a salesman."

I sighed from the couch, my legs hurting from my morning walk. "By saying 'wicked' you realize you are calling me—"

"I am doing no such thing. Love the sinner, hate the sin." She sucked on her cigarette and pulled over the red vinyl kitchen chair without asking. She didn't like sitting on the rickety chair.

"Miss Debbie," I said, "I don't take kindly to you hating what it is that makes me feel love in the romantic—"

"*Shush!* Even without your twisted thoughts, you are nearly a sixty-year-old woman, so there is no need to discuss such things."

"Will *you* be talking such things when you are sixty?"

Miss Debbie sighed, unable to understand what she could have done to cause God to betray her like this. She unscrewed the lid to her vial of holy water. "Here, dab this on yourself while you make the sign of the cross. You need to ask God, Jesus, and the Holy Spirit to help you fight these demons."

"This is too much now."

Miss Debbie stopped mid-drag then exhaled slowly. She set the water down on the gold-rimmed TV tray next to her.

I felt my face getting red. "Don't you think I tried praying? And after I fell in love with a girl, I prayed harder and harder. I locked myself up in prison *and* I got married, but still it lingered. Do you think that might have been God's way of showing me that there's nothing wrong with me?"

"I think—" she proceeded with caution—"that the Devil wears many disguises."

I flopped back into the couch and stared hard at her. "You think?" I calmed myself. "I've romantically loved three people in my life, and your daddy was one. Not meaning to bring up things, Miss Debbie, but given your record, I hardly think the judge's robes suit you."

"You are *family*. I have every right to opinionate."

Maybe knowing Eddie and I were together on this gave me strength. Whatever the reason, I let her have it. "The world has enough opinions. The world defiles and beats and imprisons and sometimes *kills* folks like me! I want my family to be better than the world. I deserve that—I do!"

Miss Debbie puckered up her lips. "You reap what you sow, Nana Dara."

"You deserve infertility?"

She huffed. "That's different! Those are uncontrollable things! You were with Daddy, why couldn't you just be with another man after him?"

I settled my eyes on hers, to make sure she heard me. "Because a secret that deep grows around you like a cocoon will eventually makes you choose—either emerge as a butterfly or die in a thick, brown coffin of your own making."

"Aren't you a little old to be a butterfly?"

"You saying I'm not too old for a coffin?"

"I didn't say that!"

My face flushed so red I felt it down through my chest. "You love the way other people see our family *more* than you love the way I feel."

"That's a big, awful lie!" Miss Debbie stomped into the kitchen to put some water in a mason jar for an ashtray.

It got quiet for a minute. I practiced imagining my fields of dandelions.

Miss Debbie slowly walked back in. She looked so old all of a sudden.

No one said a word—a stand-off.

"You ever try chewing tobacco?" I finally asked, knowing the best thing to do when you hit a wall is stop running into it.

"What?"

"*Chew.*"

"Good heavens, no."

"Why not?"

"Ladies don't use chewing tobacco."

"In some countries, ladies do. And in others, they have to wear bags on their head—for religious reasons."

"That is done by tribes who are not following the one true God."

"That's what they say back at us."

Tired, Miss Debbie dropped her cigarette into the water. "Nana Dara, please."

"I'm just saying that I have been questioning things a bit these last forty years. We have lots of silly beliefs—all of us."

"Well, I will stick to what has been believed for *two thousand* years, not what you have thought on now and again over forty."

"To each their own."

PD slammed in through the back door. "Mama!" She was crying, holding her doll in one hand and her face with the other. "The kitty scratched my cheek!"

Miss Debbie stood up, gave me a look that said my cats were also the Devil's, and walked with PD into the kitchen. "PD, sugar, because the kitty can't talk, he needs to let you know when he's scared or feeling that someone is being too rough."

"I was just showing Mr. Honky Tonk how to walk on the top of Nana Dara's easy chair."

"Band-aids?" Miss Debbie yelled over the sound of water from the faucet.

"Try the junk drawer."

She pulled and pulled, finally yanked the over-stuffed drawer open. "You got a bike in here too?"

A few minutes later PD, with a fresh band-aid on her cheek and about an inch of red around her eyes, walked back into the living room with her mama.

"You OK, baby girl?" I asked her.

"I am."

"It shouldn't scar," Miss Debbie told us.

I leaned toward PD. "But if it does, it'll make you look tough."

PD smiled a little. Miss Debbie rolled her eyes, took PD's hand, and walked out. "Really, Nana Dara?"

"Calm down now, Miss Debbie."

"We got to be going."

They moved so quickly that I didn't have time to get up and walk them out.

Miss Debbie turned to face me through the damaged screen of my door, giving me the look you give animals when you aren't sure if they are feral. "I don't get you or this thing. I was willing to blame the medications, but you had to push. Why couldn't you just let well enough be? Why can't *anyone* just let well enough be anymore?" She pursed her lips until they were white. "From this day forward, there is to be no mention of this, or I will cut off the blight that threatens the branch."

And she left, PD turning around to wave bye-bye to me on their fast walk to the car.

× × ×

Despite the threat, I tried a few times afterwards to bring the subject up with Miss Debbie, but she shut the conversation down with an impressive string of smoker's coughs, her convenient and temporary emphysema.

So went the next few months, with my body gradually getting strong by doing exercises like lifting sacks of rice from the ground to my waist then up over my head. I repeated "What you are is what you have been. What you'll be is what you'll do now" fifty times a day. In my free time, I made birdhouses using some tools the Fiddler left and sold them at the market with Eddie when she was in town. Seemed she had a lady friend in El Paso.

"Sometimes you seem sad, Nana Dara," she said on one of her visits.

"Truthfully, losing the Fiddler took its toll. The Opry feels so big now."

"Well, what makes you happy?"

"I used to enjoy singing in the church, like I'd done before the Depression."

"Then you ought to do that again," she said.

I nodded, knowing I needed to do something to keep this weight off—knowing sadness drives me to eat. So I went to church—and that's when I saw Mrs. Tanya May Rogerton again, sitting with a grouping of nondescript, widowed church hens all wearing bold glasses like they were at a fashion show. *Was she a widow?*

When I saw that she saw me seeing her, I nodded and blushed like a high school boy. It was awkward, but her smile told me that she found it charming, and I felt a bit of my old pre-changing-room-mirror confidence swelling back.

From up in the choir loft, I watched Mrs. Tanya May Rogerton more than I watched my hymnal, especially during the homily, which was about the "new promiscuity" that was taking over America like "a pestilence." Mrs. Tanya May Rogerton sported what Miss Debbie called a "gaucho," which is to say a baggy one-piece pantsuit. Hers was bright red with extra-loose pants that came mid-calf and cinched in at the waist. The shirt portion held on a little tighter with a U-shaped neck and sleeves that came halfway down her forearms. It was so well tailored that you forgot how daring it was to wear to Sunday service. I assume she added the pearls to tame it down.

When she saw me coming down the staircase from the church loft after the service, she made her way through the powder blue ties and white bonnets and flip-dos to me.

"Why, Nana Dara," she said, her smile shiny with those perfect white teeth of hers. How anyone can have perfect white teeth and be a Southerner, tempted at every turn by tobacco, coffee, and tea, is beyond me—but she did.

"Mrs. Tanya May Rogerton."

She looked me up and down. "That's not one of my dresses, I see."

"Sears," I confessed.

She held a hand to her chest, grabbing for her pearls. "You dare say that in a place of *worship*."

I smiled back. "I needed bigger seams."

"Is that why you haven't come in for any more fittings?"

"Sadly."

"Bless your heart, but that's my job." She leaned in. "If I lost every customer that needed seams let out, I'd be out of business, for sure."

"Well, you sure don't seem to need your seams let out," I said, with immediate regret.

"That"—she leaned in—"is the optical illusion that a good seamstress makes happen." She stood back up again. "How you been treated?"

"Oh, me? Good."

She turned her head down for a minute and looked me dead in the eye. "When seams stretch, it is either because someone is being treated too well or not well enough, but never just 'good.' So which is it—you having grand times or scant times, Nana Dara?"

"Scant," I said.

She let out a satisfied breath. "These times come and go, you know."

"That's the rumor." I stood there for a minute, not sure what to say. "How is life treating you?"

"Well, I have three weddings coming up, one with nine bridesmaids—*nine*." She leaned in again. "The bride's family are Imperial Sugar people."

"Very nice."

"Let's hope."

PD saw me and ran over with her doll in the air, its hairpiece now half-melted and its dress stained purple on the one side. She was still a tiny girl, skinny like Eddie had been, with those nearly black eyes of hers and that straight dark hair—no doubt to Miss Debbie's chagrin. I can hear her now saying, *Nothing a permanent won't fix.*

PD stopped just in front of me. "Hi, Nana Dara. I think I could figure out which voice was yours up there."

"You have a good ear then," I said. "PD, this is Mrs. Tanya May Rogerton."

PD held out her petite hand, and they shook. "Hello."

"Why, hello."

"PD, honey," I said as she gave my leg a hug the way she always did, "how you liking school?"

She looked up at us, making her big eyes look even bigger. "I love school!"

"Good," I said. "I loved school too."

PD turned to Mrs. Tanya May Rogerton. "You look like an angel."

"It must be my white hair."

PD tipped her head, her ponytails flipping as she did. "If I had two wishes, one of them would be to be an angel—only not dead."

Mrs. Tanya May Rogerton smiled. "And the other?"

"A donut the size of all of Sugar Land."

"Yum," Mrs. Tanya May Rogerton said.

Miss Debbie called out for PD across the room. "Come on now, PD! Your daddy's got a customer coming by. Let's go, Nana Dara. Hup!"

PD tucked her doll under her arm, and I wondered how much longer she'd be carrying it around. Poor stinky thing.

"Nice meeting you," PD said to Mrs. Tanya May Rogerton. Then she held her badly damaged doll up for her to kiss its melted head, and God as my witness, she did.

Tired of waiting, Miss Debbie and Bo, in his tight bolo tie, came over to get PD and me.

When they walked up, I started the introductions. "This here is Miss Debbie. Miss Debbie, this is my dressmaker, Mrs. Tanya May Rogerton."

"*Rogerton?* Was Billy your husband?"

"For twenty-six years."

Miss Debbie stopped in her tracks and took Mrs. Tanya May Rogerton's hands in hers. "I'm sorry for your loss."

"It's OK. It's been quite a few years now."

"Your husband bought several cars from my Bo here."

Bo nodded while I was busy thinking: *Hot damn, she's a widow!*

"Oh yes!" Mrs. Tanya May Rogerton flashed her smile. "I know about you, Bo. Billy loved his Mustang. He'd take that thing to town more than he'd take me, bless his heart."

"Can't separate a man from his car any more than spider from its web." Miss Debbie dropped her hands. "I love your outfit. Did you do that yourself?"

"All you need is a pattern."

"All I need is a pattern and a bona fide miracle to make that happen. I would love to meet with you about some new clothes."

"Miss Debbie," I said, "you'll need to get Bo to build you a shed out back if you get any more clothes."

"He *is* handy with a hammer." Miss Debbie leaned in to Mrs. Tanya May Rogerton. "I am coming to see you, *mark me.*"

"I look forward to it."

"Come on now, Nana Dara."

They went ahead without me. PD skipped alongside them as Bo reached out for Miss Debbie's hand.

Wanting to keep talking, I gestured to my Sears dress. "This flower pattern too big for me?"

"They make a statement."

"That was my goal."

"Well, you met it."

"I'm going to drop more weight soon, and then I'll come get fitted."

One of her widow friends came over and pulled her away, but not before she said, "Don't lose it all. A little weight looks good on you."

× × ×

A week or two later, a box arrived at the Opry. The return address label was stamped with the same red woman in the same red dress that Mrs. Tanya May Rogerton had painted on her mailbox. I nearly tripped over my little black cat, Licorice, racing back into the Opry with that box. I cut through the Scotch tape with my long thumbnail and wiggled off the lid to find a beautiful pale blue dress wrapped in white tissue paper. On a piece of cardboard with the red woman stamped on one side, Mrs. Tanya May Rogerton had written:

Nana Dara—

Here is a brand new dress, with a guess at measurements—it is my gift. You can thank those nine bridesmaids. When you feel right, come see me. I have a fabric that would look nice on you for a second dress, too.

Mrs. Tanya May Rogerton

I put that card in my icebox—in the empty spot where my ice cream container used to sit—to encourage me when I wanted to fill that space again. *Mrs. Tanya May Rogerton!* Imagine that.

After putting the card away, I lifted a few more bags and did laps around my yard, but I was still fidgety. Since it was only 8:30 p.m. I decided to call Eddie. It rang twice.

"Eddie?" I said, coiling the sticky cord of my phone around my finger.

"Nana Dara?"

"All right, now that we've settled who is who, I wanted to call and tell you that I am down another thirty-five pounds so far."

"Nana Dara, I am proud of you."

"Why, thank you."

Eddie cleared her throat. "So, what are you up to?"

"I'm in the choir."

I paused, wanting so badly to talk with her about Mrs. Tanya May Rogerton, but just unable to make the words come out. Even though I had a kindred spirit in Eddie, all those old fears rose up again and closed my throat. I saw then—again—how much of this really had to do with me more than everybody else, not that some didn't play their part.

"You like the choir?"

"I love singing."

"I remember you singing in the backyard all the time."

Pillowcase, the cat I'd named on account of having found her in a pillowcase by the side of the road, purred up next to me and rubbed her face on the phone.

Eddie asked, "That a cat I hear?"

"Only other thing here except me and those damn pugs." I sipped my seventh glass of water, to keep the fat moving.

"Anything else on your mind?"

My nerves were tense, knowing I was about to start a casual conversation about something that has never been casual in any way. "I, ah, think I might like someone. But she's a widow."

"So are you."

"That's different."

"You think everything is different."

"It is," I said, feeling flimsy.

Eddie chuckled. "You ought to ask this woman out on a date."

Just the thought made me a nervous wreck. "I'm not sure she'd approve."

"That's a common condition of our situations. We're never quite sure."

"It's just too risky."

"The Nana Dara *I* know killed a rattlesnake by getting it right between the eyes with a knife when we couldn't find the shovel. You remember that? The Nana Dara *I* know beat all Daddy's friends in poker—*three times.* You just make sure that widower woman knows you are *that* Nana Dara, and you are taking her out."

"I got that snake on the first hit."

"You sure did."

"Then I cooked it up that night."

"It was damn delicious," Eddie said.

I had forgotten those things about myself. In the wreckage of shame and remembrances, I'd whited out those bits. But Eddie didn't. She easily could have dwelled on some of my lesser moments and made those grow and grow until my better times shrunk back in their shadows, but she didn't. Eddie had held on to who I was until I was ready to see myself again.

"She makes dresses," I said.

"She make suits?"

"Ha!"

"It gets easier, you know," Eddie said, "talking about things the way folks talk. Talking maybe like it's normal, though it truly isn't."

"It's nice to have someone to listen."

"Right here in the family—we got each other, me and you."

"Yes we do," I said. "Good night, Eddie."

"Good night. Now you go get her, tiger."

THE OSCAR WILDE WAY

By Easter time, I could walk nearly to town and back from the Opry with only the most reasonable amount of aches and pains. I'd lost seventy pounds. Seventy God damn pounds!

I'd managed to save a chunk of money, but I still had a long way to go, so I decided to start making custom picnic tables in addition to birdhouses and dollhouses. I painted the tables whatever color folks wanted and sealed them tighter than Grandpa's lips when asked about his moonshine.

The new dresses from Mrs. Tanya May Rogerton fast became what motivated me to walk by the snack shacks rather than walking in. I couldn't bear to disappoint her.

I'd gone in to see Mrs. Tanya May Rogerton for measurements three times—our "checkups." I never did ask her out. That seemed less possible than making it to the moon. Still, it was nice feeling so alive around her—and maybe that would be enough.

Then, on our third measuring, I looked into her mirror and saw something I hoped I wouldn't: sagging skin. Seems I wasn't losing weight so much as I was *deflating*.

My skin hung in wrinkled groupings, almost like pie dough that needed rolling out. I pinched the place where my body actually started and imagined slicing off the excess with a pair of scissors. Of course I couldn't do that, given all the veins and nerves and whatnot, but I wanted to. Truly, I might have risked it, if only to avoid Mrs. Tanya May Rogerton seeing me like this.

She knocked on the door. "You ready, hon?"

"You need an assistant."

"What's that?"

"I said, you need an assistant. I don't want to be measured by you. I don't want my friend to see me looking all saggy and misshapen."

Mrs. Tanya May Rogerton opened the door discreetly. She eyed me up and down. "Oh, *that*. That happens."

"What am I going to do?" I cried, holding a bag of limp skin in my hand. "I don't know which is worse, being big or—"

She took the tape measure from her teeth. "*Skin* is not going to kill you like that weight will. Besides, you can get that cut away."

"You can?"

"It's not cheap, but they do it in Dallas—where they do everything. Meanwhile—" she got back to measuring—"moisturize with aloe. You have a plant?"

"At this rate," I said, pinching my sagging underarms, "I'll need a *farm*."

"I don't have a farm, but I do have a nice plot of aloe out back. You go help yourself when we're done here." She rolled up the tape measure and paper-clipped it. "47-49-48, and I think some of the waist is your excess." She tucked the tape measure in her seamstress pocket. "This week, on account of your halfway mark, I'm going to make you a pantsuit—break you from those dresses. If you don't like it, you only have to wear it for two weeks."

"I always wanted to wear pantsuits, but by my mid-thirties they got too hard on my form."

"That's what ladies think. They think that, if they are big, they should wear big—but the opposite is true. Besides, you have a sturdy form. Show it off."

"Perhaps when I'm a little *less* sturdy."

"It's good to be sturdy." She flashed her smile and told me to take my time getting dressed.

I buttoned my dress up, clicked off the light, and helped myself to some aloe in the back on my way back into the store. Mrs. Tanya May Rogerton was just turning the OPEN sign to CLOSED.

She asked, "You want to get lunch with me?"

"Where?"

"Here."

Without waiting for my answer, Mrs. Tanya May Rogerton—the sun making her hair look even whiter—walked behind the counter and pulled out two chicken-salad sandwiches.

"I thought you might say yes," she said when she handed one over.

We sat down in her sitting area. The fan made a low whirling noise. I was going to make a joke about how typically folks see you in your underwear *after* you've eaten together, but stopped myself.

She poured us both some strawberry water from the pitcher on her counter. The sunshine on the rug looked like a slanted window on the floor. For a minute, it seemed as if we were in a living painting— some kind of frozen moment. I knew I would remember her standing there in her loose, off-white dress pouring water from a pitcher filled with ice and strawberry slivers for a long time. Maybe forever.

"You ever go to movies?" I asked.

"I do," she said.

"Maybe you'd like company?"

"It just so happens I would."

"It's seven miles to town from the Opry. How about I walk here, then I drive us in your car? That would give me quite an incentive to exercise."

She handed me my strawberry water and sat down. "What would?"

"You would, Mrs. Tanya May Rogerton," I said, blushing against my will.

"Well." She smoothed out the embroidered napkin on the table between us.

I recovered. "I would like you to see me more often when I'm dressed."

"And that is how I know you are a Southern lady, not pulled in by the politics of the time. Although—" she leaned in—"there are a few of the modern politics I agree with—at least in principle."

I didn't know then what she was alluding to, so I got nervous and ate a big bite of my sandwich before asking if she could give me the information for a Dallas skin doctor.

"I have someone I can ask."

"You seem to know a person for everything."

"People *undress* in front of me," she said. "It makes for personal conversation."

I nodded and took this to mean that she was personal with me only because she got personal with all her clients. Going to the movies was just two widows passing the time. That revelation of not being special to her weighed heavy on me. I'd hoped maybe she fancied me, but I suppose she needed to seem like she fancied everyone in order for them to feel comfortable stripping down and revealing all their bad sides.

"You OK?" she asked me, laying her hand—as cool as lettuce—on top of mine.

"I'm just tired today."

"Poor thing," she said before pulling up the napkin from near my hand and dabbing her mouth, as if she were headed for the napkin and not my hand the whole time.

× × ×

Mrs. Tanya May Rogerton and I saw *Psycho* and *The Magnificent Seven*—and then we did something that changed my life forever. We drove three hours in her spirited Volkswagen fastback to Austin where we decided to go crazy and see *The Trials of Oscar Wilde* since the movie had been banned from Sugar Land.

The gorgeous old theater got as crowded as a Good Humor truck in the desert. It smelled like popcorn and Old Spice and strange new scents I'd never smelled before. The red velvet seats squeaked when we sat down, but they were comfortable enough. My armrest had a bit of residue on the edge from the person before me, someone who clearly enjoyed toffee. I wiped my hand as casually as possible on the back of the seat in front of me while Mrs. Tanya May Rogerton figured out where to hang her purse where it wouldn't touch the floor. We looked to be the oldest folks in there and had the tamest fashion of anyone, even the men—*especially* the men. It was like traveling to the future.

Just as we settled in, the screen went dark, and the slim lights lining the side walls dimmed. It felt as if I was falling asleep in a dreamworld with Mrs. Tanya May Rogerton right there beside me. The music crackled on and the film started.

Everyone stayed calm during the film until reference was made to Oscar Wilde's "gross indecency" for having an affair with a young man named Lord Alfred Douglas, Lord Queensberry's son. At that point, a man in the theater whistled and yelled, "Three cheers for indecency," leading a legion of other whistlers and clappers.

I slinked down in my seat, readying myself for a wave of opposition from the rest of the crowd, but none came. Mrs. Tanya May Rogerton, smiling in the glare of the movie lights, quietly threaded her arm through mine.

"You liking this?" she asked, leaning in.

Not sure whether she was talking about her arm or the movie, and not wanting her to move her arm, I just nodded.

"That young man was twenty years younger than Oscar Wilde!" she whispered. "That sort of thing happens all the time with older men and young ladies—but that's not really the issue at hand, now is it?"

A young man in front of us turned slightly to let us know that Mrs. Tanya May Rogerton's commentary was not increasing his enjoyment of the film. She nodded curtly, but kept quiet.

The movie went on, with a few rowdy folks in the audience yelling back to the screen when derogatory bits were said against Mr. Oscar Wilde, making me wonder if they hadn't snuck in a little something stronger with their pop. The theater buzzed electric that night, with a kind of tension *and* release. A man near the front with dark peg-leg pants and a bright red turtleneck, who looked like he fell asleep each night with a book on his chest, smoked and hollered that Oscar Wilde should have been sainted.

"Amen!" someone responded from the back.

Maybe it was being inside that bubble of a theater or maybe it was a gathering of all the lessons of my life to date, but either way I blurted out, "You know, I kissed a girl once—when I was also a girl."

Mrs. Tanya May Rogerton's face broke out with the smile of a gossip who'd just hit gold. She gasped and pulled me to her. "*What?*"

Two people in front of us turned around, looking more agitated than worms in a bait cup.

Mrs. Tanya May Rogerton barely cared. "Tell me!"

"I'll tell you afterwards," I said and pointed that she turn her attentions back to the screen.

"Afterwards?" She took her arm away. "You, Nana Dara, have a cruel streak."

As soon as the credits started Mrs. Tanya May Rogerton whispered, "Let's get moving. We have a long drive back—just enough time to hear the secret details of your youth." She grabbed our empty cups and scooted in front of a few people who were reading all the credits. I'd never seen her be so impolite.

I squeezed down the theater row after her, grateful I'd lost as much weight as I had but also painfully aware of the amount I had to go, as I felt my buttocks grazing head after head like I was going over bumps made of hair.

× × ×

Thankfully she'd parked close to the entrance of the theater because Mrs. Tanya May Rogerton practically sprinted and, despite my elevated exercise, I would not have been able to keep up much longer.

Red-faced and feeling for my pulse on the right side of my neck to be sure I wasn't going to have an attack, I said, "You are walking so fast that I almost took these secrets to my grave!"

"You would have been good on the stage," she said.

I walked around to the passenger side and unlocked her door. "And I'm driving back. We almost died a dozen times on the way over."

She tossed me her keys. "I like it when you drive anyway, hon. Gives me a chance to put my feet up."

A black couple with hair as puffy as Q-tips walked by holding hands. They were so unlike Huddie and the black folks I had grown up around that I had to smile. Made me wonder what the 1960s had in store.

I slid in, moving the seat back a hair, and we were ready to go. "Don't ask me about my past until I'm out of this parking lot," I said. "You know how I feel about parking lots—they are death traps to be sure. I need to *focus.*"

"I will try to be patient," she said, wrapping a red-and-blue silk scarf around her hair so she could roll the window down.

I drove out onto the road headed back to Sugar Land. Unable to hold it in a moment longer, she said, "OK. Now spill it."

"I wasn't really a girl—I mean, I was nearly twenty."

"Loretta Lynn was celebrating her seven-year anniversary by then."

We turned onto the freeway, chugging down the on-ramp before I took my spot in the slow lane.

"You were twenty. And she was . . ."

I cracked my window to stop Mrs. Tanya May Rogerton's window from whistling. My neck felt numb from an anxiety that was multilayered. First, I was nervous speaking about my wanderings of years ago, fearing Mrs. Tanya May Rogerton might find it too much to handle in the end. Second, I worried that talking about my time with Rhodie might change it somehow, or might even be a betrayal of her. Third, it was plain difficult for me to talk on that level of personal. It was frightening, like when you first try walking in heels in public—something I did only once when I was sixteen for my cousin June-June's wedding. The results were tragic, let me tell you.

I took in a breath and started. "She was twenty also, and heading to college."

"And her name?"

"Her name was Rhodie."

"And where did you meet?" She waited, then sighed. "As God as my witness, you are the world's worst storyteller."

"We met at the egg store where I was working."

It got silent.

"I'm not asking any more questions. I will simply sit silent in this car until you start telling me the wheres and what-fors of this tale." Mrs. Tanya May Rogerton opened her glove compartment with a loud cracking sound and brought out a box of figs to snack on in the silence.

"I'm sorry," I said after a few minutes. "I don't know how to talk like this."

"You just tell me what she looked like and how you became friends and then how things progressed as they did."

"Does this upset you?" I asked, my throat clenching up so hard it hurt.

Mrs. Tanya May Rogerton sighed and closed her fig box. She set it on the floor at her feet and turned to me, with one leg tucked under her.

"My husband died nearly a decade ago," she said, "bless his heart. We had a strong marriage. A good one, although we had never been blessed with children, as you know, on account of an injury he got hunting. Everything worked but didn't work at the same time." She paused, then got back to it: "About fifteen years in, I met a woman at the VFW. We both did dress work and got together on a project to upgrade the church robes. She did this beautiful embroidery work. On every one of those gowns she'd stitched the Lamb of God. They were so gentle, those little lambs.

"Over that year working together, we got close, and she confessed to me that her husband shopped around a bit. Might have even had another child a county or two over. Anyway, her name was Barbara, but everyone called her Taffy—I don't remember why. Taffy had three kids that she loved. For her, she'd said, that would do.

"Her husband started staying away more so more and more, and I went over there helping her with the kids, since I couldn't have any of my own. Well, one night we were sitting on the porch, drinking some redneck lemonade, when I leaned over and kissed her. I have no idea why, but I did it."

I nearly swerved off the road. "What'd she do?"

"She kissed me a little, but then she pulled away and told me it was time to go check on the baby. He had croup."

"And?"

"And we never talked about it again. We finished up the project, and she told me she was getting too busy with raising the kids while her husband was away nearly every weekend. After a few more months, she started going to Saturday night services and I just never saw her again. Somehow, I just never saw her again."

I had no idea what to say.

Mrs. Tanya May Rogerton grabbed her fig box again and popped one in her mouth. "Now *that's* how you tell a story. Get to it, Nana Dara."

So I did. I told her everything—right down to the time Rhodie drew hearts on my arm with berry juice, and it stained so I couldn't wash it off for three days and had to wear long sleeves. I told her about our one weekend together, when her family drove to New Mexico, and about the thunder and lightning storm that happened then and how it felt so natural. I told her about her mother finding us and slapping me on the side of the head, and the deep fear and shame that slap burned into me. I told her about my cousin Earl and that other officer who had defiled those four women in jail. I told her about the pastor who set me apart from everyone in the entryway after Sunday service, and about my crazy, selfish decision to break Rhodie's heart. I told her that Rhodie died before I could apologize.

"You are too hard on yourself," she said. "You were a young woman—a scared young woman."

"I've recently come around to giving myself that forgiveness, mostly—to practicing what Eddie calls self-acceptance."

I put on my signal and changed lanes to pass a truck loaded down with hay, some of it flying off and hitting my windshield.

"Hmmm," she said, waiting to see if I had any more to say.

I took in a deep breath, preparing to tell her about the head cook. This was something only a few people knew about, and something that had never been thoroughly discussed. Both Beauregard and the Warden acted like the matter had been shut when the head cook got sent off after that night with me and him and my piece of mug. In their polite avoidance of it, I allowed that night to somehow make *me* dirty—like they were kind enough to overlook *my* dirtiness because they loved me. Messed up but true. It's just how my mind works sometimes.

I started in, my hands wet on the wheel: "Then there was the head cook."

"At Central Unit?"

"What we called Imperial State Prison Farm or Sugar Land for short, but yes. Shortly after I'd locked myself away—and you can see how obvious *that* is—he attacked me. He attacked me a few times really."

"What!"

"He nearly took my honor in the most dishonorable way."

Mrs. Tanya May Rogerton twisted herself in her seat so she fully faced me. "Oh my dear, I am so sorry. What happened? If you want to tell."

I cleared my throat. "He came at me with his member out—and this was after he'd showed me himself a few times before, only now he wanted to really use what he had made into a weapon. So I cut him."

She gasped. "You cut him—*there?*"

"I aimed there, but I caught his hand instead."

"Ha! Well, don't mess with you!"

"This relates to Rhodie. He'd gotten ahold of some letters she wrote to me and made them out to be nasty. Before that moment—and even some times after—this part of me agreed. I'd said it by the way I acted back then, all sheepish and distant, that it was OK to not care about me. That I was getting the distance I deserved for being . . . for being a pervert." My body filled with my own strength, the power of telling my story. "But that night when I cut him, I started to find this strength—

meager though it was then. And over the years, that strength grew and grew. So, in the end, his attacks were really blessings."

Mrs. Tanya May Rogerton reached over and ran her hand along the side of my head, like you do with a child. "Aw, hon."

"It was a long road after that to where I am now, but I found myself a good friend in Beauregard and a soul mate in my friend Huddie and a great man in the Warden, and then I got me some fabulous kids by proxy."

"Yes, you did."

I drove along for a minute, maybe going too slow for the freeway, feeling my emotions lining up and my life making sense. I saw how this kind of talking could give type of reality to feelings—make them *tangible*.

Mrs. Tanya May Rogerton waited, not saying anything. The lights on the sides of the road zipped by over my windshield.

"So that's it, really." I breathed out. "That's my story."

"I love your story. You are one strong woman, Nana Dara." She shifted in her seat again. "Now, about your friend Rhodie, you ever consider doing that again?"

I swerved just a little. "You mean . . . the Oscar Wilde way?"

She smiled with those flawless teeth. "Yes, ma'am, the Oscar Wilde way."

"Oh, not often."

"What does 'not often' look like to you?"

I laughed. "Maybe twenty or thirty times a year."

"Ha! Well, you ever think about The Oscar Wilde way *lately?*"

"I'm practically an old woman!"

She sucked her teeth. "Women in my family live until their nineties. That's twenty-five years of life left."

"My family doesn't live as long."

"Your family didn't turn a new side to a life of exercise and strong food."

I thought of Daddy when I set him up at that hospital for folks after their minds had gone, with his belly so big it hung several inches over his belt buckle. "True."

"You need to answer my question then, *young lady.*"

I didn't know what to say. Mrs. Tanya May Rogerton was about the prettiest woman in the town, but I didn't want to lose her as a friend.

"You first," I said, keeping an eye on the road since her headlights were about as helpful as cataracts. "You think of it lately?"

"Coward."

What they teach you in sales, Bo—the used-car salesman—once told me, is never to be the one to say the last word. Ask a question and leave it hanging. The one who answers first loses the deal. With the prowess of a used-car salesman, Mrs. Tanya May Rogerton waited, watching me.

"OK," I finally said, "yes, yes I have considered kissing a woman lately."

She smiled, popped another fig in her mouth, and rolled up her window. I rolled mine up to stop the whistle again.

"Me too," she said, a proud edge to her voice.

I almost couldn't take any more. I didn't want to know if it was me—I mean, I *did* want to know, of course—but I was one breath from exploding, and what if it wasn't me? So instead I just turned on the radio and told her to change the topic until I could have a proper amount of bourbon.

"Bourbon?"

"Yes," I said. "In one hour we are going to Maria's Roundabout."

"No—" she smiled—"what's say we go to the Opry instead."

I gulped and nodded.

× × ×

I hadn't been expecting company, much less Mrs. Tanya May Rogerton, so my bathroom was a little ripe. "Let me run to the bathroom," I said, hoping to clean up a bit.

"All right."

The cats came up to say hello or, rather, to make sure they approved. I introduced her to them: Pillowcase, Licorice, and Mr. Honky Tonk. "There's more cats—and some pugs somewhere around here—so watch your step," I warned. "Meanwhile, help yourself to a libation— there's some ice in the icebox."

I left her with the brood and headed to the bathroom. Kneeling down to clean my toilet with the door shut behind me was about as feasible as squeezing a parrot through a keyhole, so I stood up and did the best I could to stab at the brown ring around the inside.

"Oh hell," I said, deciding instead to bite off a piece of soap and spit it in there in the hopes of covering up everything with some bubbles and scent.

The trouble with biting soap is that you can't really rinse it out without stimulating more soap. *Great*, I thought, *now I'm foaming at the mouth.*

I stepped a hard foot into my white metal trashcan to compress all the tissues in there, folded the hand towel in three parts, and pulled the bath curtain—all wild circles in blue and green—as tight as I could against the wall. That looked better.

When I walked out of the bathroom, Mrs. Tanya May Rogerton held out a glass of bourbon on ice for me. She had one for herself, too.

"I found these nice glasses in your cabinet, along with a shocking number of tuna cans."

"Low in calories," I explained, adding, "I view my need to eat that much tuna as an atonement of sorts."

"I can see how you would, bless your heart."

The pugs shuffled in, chasing each other, their legs like tree branches tapping across the floor. One of them ran into the wall where it narrowed before the hallway.

"Not the smartest beasts," I said.

She smiled and sat down on the couch, leaving room for me.

I was so nervous that I guzzled my bourbon and suggested we go out for a cigarette.

"Sounds modern," she said.

"What else should we do after *The Trials of Oscar Wilde* but be modern?"

Once we were outside on the back deck, with me in my easy chair and her on the red vinyl chair I'd pulled out for her from the kitchen, she lit her cigarette off mine, looking at me over the burning embers, with me not sure what the hell was going on. We put our glasses on the white plastic bucket that served as my side table. I followed the line of old Christmas lights that wound around the edges of the porch. The crickets gossiped.

"Those blue eyes," Mrs. Tanya May Rogerton said, drawing in a deep lungful.

"I didn't know you smoked."

"Honey, we *all* smoke."

I smiled and hoped I wasn't sweating too much.

"I've always had a lot of respect for women who don't wear lipstick," she said, looking at the pale orange smudge on her cigarette filter. "Though I prefer the way I look with it on."

Then I did something I hadn't planned out. I leaned in and said, "Mrs. Tanya May Rogerton, may I kiss you?"

She pulled in a short breath and said, "I could never resist good manners."

And it was that easy. After thirty-five years, it was that God damn easy.

She held her cigarette out to the side. I bent in and I kissed her.

She set the pace, kissing me slowly. The way we kissed was a form of asking each other if it was OK to get a little more intense. I moved my hand up to the back of her head, gently, and she leaned into me. We kissed like there was nothing else anywhere, like we were floating together in space.

Just as the emotions started getting a little overwhelming, Mrs. Tanya May Rogerton pulled back. "Whew." She took a drag. "I vowed if the chance ever came up again, I'd do it. I am so glad I did."

"Well I guess you have completed your dare," I said, feeling like I was just a challenge she'd given herself.

She smiled. "Oh, you are *sensitive*, bless your heart." Then she leaned in and kissed me again, putting her free hand on the side of my face. Her mouth was soft and confident. I liked the taste of bourbon and cigarettes, and the smell of her tea rose perfume.

"This is as good as a perfect lemon meringue pie."

"Well, good," she said. "Now kiss me again because I can never get enough pie."

× × ×

We spent the next half hour kissing before she said it was time she got home. She was flushed and I could tell she was trying to pace this out.

"I hoped you were the kind I could kiss," I said.

She smiled. "I figured you might be."

I blushed. "Lemme drive you home."

"Then you'll have to walk back."

"I like walking."

She kissed my cheek, and we walked out to her car. And during the entire ride to town, the beautiful Mrs. Tanya May Rogerton's hand burned a mark on my thigh the same way holy water marks the possessed—deep, hot, and permanent.

HOW LONG?

Whenever I babysat for little dark-eyed PD, we'd click on the news. After a particularly informative program, PD later told her mama and her third-grade class that the people who did sit-ins for Civil Rights were "he-roic." In turn, Miss Debbie called me and told me that the news was now banned in her house. I considered asking Miss Tanya May Rogerton if she knew someone who could make PD a little black-baby doll, but came to my senses.

Then the Freedom Riders came through the South in 1961—these brave folks, both colored and white, who vowed to break racial lines everywhere they went. But the deeper they went, the harder it got for the group, who were mostly Yankees. When they hit Burlington, Alabama, the Public Safety Commissioner there gave the KKK a full fifteen minutes to beat them before the police moved in. And when they did, they mostly arrested the Freedom Riders, many who had their faces broken before being thrown in jail, where they were tormented by the officers.

The Riders moved on to Montgomery, Alabama, where five more had to be hospitalized after two hours of rioting. Dozens of people were injured. There were little colored children walking around fearful they'd be spit on and hit on the back with ropes.

Children.

I couldn't help but think of Huddie. How Huddie had managed to keep something as sweet and gentle as a dove safe inside his ribcage, despite the mental, emotional, physical, and, most certainly, spiritual beatings he took.

On the night the Riders made the news, rather than keep my odd, smoky pain to myself, I called Mrs. Tanya May Rogerton and asked her to come over. She didn't ask me why; she just said she needed a minute to fluff her hair.

When she reached my screen door, her eyes concerned, she asked, "You all right?"

"Come sit with me," I said.

She followed me to the couch. We sat, then I leaned over and moved the needle of my phonograph to start up an old record from the 1940s featuring "American Folk & Blues Singer Lead Belly." I held up the album cover so she could read it.

"This man singing here is that old friend of mine named Huddie, who folks call Lead Belly. I'm playing him on this night, when those people are out there trying to change a world filled with so much hate—a world that hurts children for doing nothing more than being born and hurts adults for crossing imaginary lines. I'm playing it in memory of Huddie, and I wanted to share it with you."

She leaned back. "Thank you."

I closed my eyes and listened to Huddie's voice pushing out from that tiny place he kept safe. I thought about him as a baby being rocked by his mother, and how a mother would feel knowing she'd brought a colored child into a world of such hate. Typically, folks feel joy at the news of a pregnancy, but did she?

With my eyes closed, sitting there in the moonlight coming in across my quiet home, I got lost in his music. I forgot that Mrs. Tanya May Rogerton had joined me, and I started crying. I cried for Huddie and for those people whose houses were being burned and churches blown up, and who rocked their dying babies as they were being ignored at the doors of hospitals. I cried for the Freedom Riders, some who might never make it back home to their safe places.

I cried for Eddie, and worried about her out dressed like a man. I prayed that she would never be arrested. I wondered if people had ever spit on her, and I was glad then that she *could* hide if she needed to—that she could pull her bobbed hair forward and slip on a skirt if she ever had to.

Under it all was the eternal question: *why couldn't folks just let people be who they are, with all the fairness entitled?* I mean, God dammit.

Meanwhile, Mrs. Tanya May Rogerton scooted closer to me. She put her arms around me, and I let her hold me while I quietly cried and Huddie sang on. Her touch helped the hurt find its way out a little faster. Allowing this connection to someone I loved balanced the scales against hate, and I had a revelation that this small act—this love realized—would, in its very tiny way, make the world a better place.

MAMA WHO?

We all met up at Miss Debbie's for her annual New Year's Eve party, ready to welcome in 1962: me and Mrs. Tanya May Rogerton, Eddie, Miss Debbie, Bo, and PD, who was ten—all bones and moods.

Nearly adolescent, PD managed somehow to be simultaneously sullen and serene. She settled on the armrest of Miss Debbie's rose-and-white floral couch, right next to her Aunt Eddie. For the festivities, she'd chosen her orange cowboy boots and even French braided her hair.

While PD drank lemonade from a glass covered with pictures of mushrooms, we all took cocktail-glass swigs of some stiff beverage dreamt up by Miss Debbie, something she called A Danger Ranger. The Ranger part is on account of the sprig of rosemary she put in every glass. The Danger part, she explained, is the rest of the drink.

Eddie took a generous gulp of her drink, moving the rosemary out of the way with her thumb. She looked up at PD, and I wondered what it must have felt like to hold your newborn baby, to breastfeed your newborn baby for only one hour, then pass her along—whether Eddie felt emptiness or relief or shame or anger or nothing at all. Not that it's any of my business—*mostly*.

"I like your braiding," Eddie said.

PD nodded and spun her finger around the ice cubes in her lemonade. "Mama taught me."

"I saw your mama's jack-o'-lantern do from last Halloween. Miss Debbie sure can do hair. Pity about the rain, though." She smiled. "Nothing sadder really than a sunken, melting pumpkin running orange rivers down the side of someone's face. Not a good look. Not at all."

"I can hear you, Eddie," Miss Debbie yelled from the kitchen. "I can hear you clear as a bell in a metal room!"

Bo smiled, shaking his head. "Your mama just dreams big," he told PD. "She's a romantic."

"It's true," Eddie agreed. "Miss Debbie *is* a romantic. Why, during her short life, she has fallen in love twenty-six times—Bo here was number twelve *and* number twenty-six."

Bo tipped his invisible hat without moving away from the doorjamb, a cup for chewing-tobacco juice in his right hand.

"You know what they say," Miss Debbie said while she walked over to give Bo a flirty peck on the ear, "save the best for last."

"And twelfth," PD added, smiling with those crowded teeth of hers.

Mrs. Tanya May Rogerton slapped her leg and laughed, and I couldn't have been prouder than I was right there, sitting with my ragtag family, sharing Danger Rangers and jabs.

Eddie adjusted her hat. During our private talks, she refers to herself as the "third sex," meaning she doesn't feel like she's a man or a woman. I can't quite follow all that, but I respect it. I figure, who am I to be telling people who *they* are, when they seem to know perfectly well.

"You with us?" Mrs. Tanya May Rogerton whispered.

I leaned up. "Oh yes, sorry—just lost in thought. What's the conversation?"

"Miss Debbie was just saying how she spent three months in clown school years ago."

"No surprise there."

Mrs. Tanya May Rogerton leaned back on the armrest of the velour chair that I was being sucked into while Miss Debbie refilled our drinks from a fancy glass pitcher. Catching the time, she set the pitcher down and ran off to grab the noisemakers that we were going to need in two minutes. "The countdown!" she shouted. "Get ready, folks! The countdown has begun!" Then: "Five-four-three-two-one!"

Midnight hit, and we all yelled and tooted our horns. Bo and Miss Debbie kissed, while Mrs. Tanya May Rogerton gave me a wink. Eddie gave PD a big kiss on the head.

From across the room, Miss Debbie said, "It's nice having you join the adults this year, PD!"

"Thanks, Miss Debbie," PD said, looking sleepier than a kitten wrapped in a yarn ball.

Then Mrs. Tanya May Rogerton, innocent of what she was doing, asked, "How'd you get the name PD?"

Eddie smiled. "Oh, I named her that."

"*You* named her?"

Miss Debbie hiccupped and blurted out, "Well, Eddie there is part aunt, part mama."

I blanched. PD stepped back and furrowed her forehead up in question. Bo, moving quicker than he had ever moved, clapped his hands and asked if anyone wanted to take some cookies home. Eddie cleared her throat over and over.

Miss Debbie, two sheets to the wind, did her best to cover by saying, "Just since Eddie's around all the time! She's like a second mother to PD here. Right, PD?"

PD didn't answer, and her mother seemed not to notice. Instead Miss Debbie started handing us cookies for the road, busying herself to get away from that moment as quickly as she could.

Eddie stood up. "Midnight has come and gone. Guess it's time to head out now."

Bo held the door open and nodded goodbye to Eddie, his eyes meeting hers to let her know that he'd do his best to stop this conversation from going any further.

Miss Debbie, Mrs. Tanya May Rogerton, and I had a post-party martini, concocted by Miss Debbie before I had had the chance to refuse. And that's when it happened, when PD asked Miss Debbie about her comment about Eddie—just when we thought we'd gotten away with it.

PD looked up from the floral couch. "So what did you mean to-night? Is Eddie my aunt or my mother?" This thing was not uncom-mon in Sugar Land.

Miss Debbie headed into the kitchen with a stack of dirty cups. "PD, there is no need to start looking for mysteries—you do, and I'm going to ban those books you've been reading."

PD stood up in her cowboy boots and walked past the overflowing ashtrays to the kitchen. Still in the velour chair, I leaned myself over as far as I could to get a view of them in front of the crazy brown-and-orange striped wallpaper Miss Debbie had installed herself a while back. Mrs. Tanya May Rogerton tapped me on the shoulder, and I raised my finger to tell her to hold on—I needed to pay attention to the conversation about to unfold.

Even looking at the back of Miss Debbie, you could see how ner-vous she was. She shifted on her cork heels while PD stood at the opening of the kitchen area and crossed her skinny arms.

PD said to her mother's back, "Something is in the air, and I need to know."

"There's nothing!" Miss Debbie yelled, a little too loud, before helping herself to some Danger Ranger residue in the bottom of one of the glasses.

PD, having been raised by the best, yelled back, "You need to tell me!"

Whether it was just too hard to keep the secret any longer or whether Miss Debbie was in the middle of another blackout, who knows. But whatever the reason, she turned to face PD and she told the truth. "Eddie is both your aunt *and* your mother," she said with a fast, intoxicated exhale.

PD's arms dropped. "I don't understand."

Miss Debbie looked stunned, like she couldn't believe she had just said that. "I'm drinking again, sugar. Let's talk in the morning. I am not making sense!" Her face flushed. Her hair unraveled. "Besides, I need to take some Flexeril for my cramps."

"Mama, you only get your period once a month," PD said.

"No, honey," she said, "I bleed *every day.*"

Miss Debbie, walking as sternly as she could, retreated to her bed-room where we all heard the loud click of her door lock. Maybe she forgot I was there, but PD didn't ask me anything. She just ran down the hallway and yelled outside Miss Debbie's door, "We are not done!"

"We better get going," I whispered to Mrs. Tanya May Rogerton.

She nodded and we tiptoed out. On the way home in the car, I ex-plained everything. The pregnancy and the transfer of the baby and how I found out and kept the secret.

"Well, this was bound to come out."

I ran my hands along the leather seats in her car, hoping to com-fort myself somehow. "I'm worried that Eddie will wander off again. That she'll just up and leave to avoid what is bound to be an awful situation."

"Well," Mrs. Tanya May Rogerton said, her voice as soft as pulled cotton, "people do what they need to."

"I don't want her to go. We got a routine going now. She helps me with my birdhouses every Saturday. We talk on the phone. We have tea."

Mrs. Tanya May Rogerton reached over and rubbed my knee, causing the car to veer onto the bumpy side of the road. "I know, hon. But she always comes back."

"So far," I sulked.

I worried I might lose Eddie permanently—that she might not make it through this revelation. There is probably a shame that some women carry who give up their children, especially when, for all intents and purposes, they could have cared for them. In this case, it would have meant living a lie, but to most folks, that would be a small price to pay for being with your child. Of course, most folks don't understand what toll *those* kind of lies take, how you blacken out pieces of who you are until you are nothing but an empty space of sad.

There was no real right or wrong here. There is only what was: Eddie would die if she lived any other way but truthfully—to keep PD would have meant death for her. And this way, having Miss Debbie and Bo raise her, at least she got to be PD's aunt—though, it seems, maybe only for a short decade.

× × ×

Mrs. Tanya May Rogerton came and got me the following morning to take me to Miss Debbie's to help clean up—as I'd said I would. She left me at the door and went down to her shop, where she had a meeting planned with a nervous bride. When I walked in, PD was wiping down the Formica.

"She's not up yet," she said, her eyes all bloodshot.

While I dumped out the ashtrays into a paper bag, PD loudly clanked all the glassware she was washing until Miss Debbie finally stumbled into the kitchen, shielding her eyes.

"You put brighter lightbulbs in here to teach me a lesson, PD?"

PD groaned. "Why do hangovers always *surprise* you, Mama?"

"Good morning!" I waved cheerfully from the living room.

Miss Debbie reached into the pocket of her pink robe and pulled out her pack of cigarettes.

PD stood her ground. "Our conversation from the night before is *not finished.*"

"Shush," Miss Debbie said.

"Miss Debbie, tell me the truth. What is going on?" PD crossed her arms, looking much older than she was—maybe from her stubborn streak or maybe from the way her hair refused to have any wave whatsoever.

Miss Debbie took a drag and cleared her tar-coated throat. "I am not getting into this," she announced.

PD took a step toward her mother, her *Nutter Butter* T-shirt so thin around the waist that it was nearly see-through. "Then I'm going to Aunt Eddie to get to the bottom of all this."

"You most certainly are not," Miss Debbie screeched, stubbing her cigarette so hard that it broke in half before it went out.

"I am old enough—"

"You better move your butt right back to your bedroom—"

"You'll just have to take care of cleaning up the place yourself, Miss Debbie. I am going."

The Look washed over Miss Debbie, who could go toe to toe with Joan Crawford any day—that is, if Hollywood wasn't the Devil's playground. But then she softened. "Please, PD," she said.

My jaw dropped open. PD stopped short. Miss Debbie had said *please*. For a minute no one knew what to say. I could tell by the way PD looked that she was struggling between what she needed to find out about her aunt and giving in on account of such a monumental thing that her mother had just done.

Finally PD said, "I'm sorry, but I have to find out what's going on."

Miss Debbie slammed down her Daffy Duck glass after swallowing the last bit of last night's cocktail, deftly avoiding the rosemary. She turned to face PD and me, just as I was shimmying one butt cheek at a time onto a stool at the kitchen bar. "Would you *want* her to be your mother?"

"Is this why you are always jealous that Aunt Eddie and I like each other?"

Miss Debbie huffed. "I'm not jealous. I just sometimes think you love her more than you love me."

PD rolled her eyes. "Mama—"

"I am telling you—no, honey, I am *asking* you to stay here with me and let this drop." Miss Debbie walked back over, her heavily lined eyes taking on that watery-drunk look.

PD lowered her head, guilty, but still reached for the book bag that was sitting beside me on a stool.

Miss Debbie's voice jumped an octave. She turned to face PD with that crazy look in her eyes. "I was the one who stayed up with you when you cried all night—you don't remember it, but you used to have nightmares. Fierce nightmares, PD, and it was *me* staying up with you, running my fingers through your hair. Me cleaning up this entire house when you had that stomach flu, not your aunt."

"Miss Debbie," PD sighed. "I'm not running away—"

"You might as well!" To emphasize her point, Miss Debbie took another dramatic gulp from her glass. "This is about loyalties! If you go to her, you might as well stay there."

"What?"

Miss Debbie set her drink down in a hurry and walked slowly into the kitchen area, right across from where I was sitting at the bar. "No! No! I don't mean that. Just please, stay."

"I'm sorry," PD said quietly, not making eye contact with her mother. "I have to go."

"Fine!"

"Miss Debbie—" PD said.

"And I am not Miss Debbie, *I am your mama!*" she yelled, then walked over and grabbed a new cup—Minnie Mouse—from the cabinet. She dumped in a glistening stream of gin from an open bottle on the counter, skipping the ice and the limes and the tonic. "I am your mama," she repeated, a little sadly, as she took a sip.

"I know," PD said.

Miss Debbie sighed. "OK. OK. Pass me them corn nuts behind you, PD, and sit your ass down next to Nana Dara so I can explain."

PD hooked her book bag over one shoulder, passed her mama the corn nuts, and sat down. Miss Debbie tore the bag open with her coffee-stained teeth and poured a few corn nuts into her mouth. She never ate them, she just sucked the salt from them, then spit them out, claiming she'd wreck her fillings if she were to go any further.

"I didn't give birth to you, honey."

"What?"

"Your Aunt Eddie met a man heading into basic training. She had relations with him."

"Oh," was all PD managed.

"Yes. And then she had you, but she felt she couldn't raise you."

"She could have done it . . ."

"This was ten years ago. Hell, PD, even now a woman raising a child alone—it's just not done."

PD was quiet for a moment. Then she said, "But I look like you—"

"Yeah, you do. You look like me, and you look a lot like Eddie when she was your age. Funny how raisin' someone gives them your mannerisms so even though you might look more like one person, you act more like another and the acting overrides the looking—"

"Didn't she love me?"

"Of course she did."

PD let her book bag quietly slide off her shoulder and fall to the floor between us. Miss Debbie crinkled the empty bag of nuts. I could see her trying to look casual, like this was all a perfectly natural part of life—and I could also see behind *that* that she was scared to death.

She forced a sigh. "Now go run to the store and get me some more corn nuts. The barbecue kind."

Miss Debbie's face looked suddenly pale and dried up. Her neck had that flush I recognized as the beginning of a crying spell, so I squeezed PD's shoulder and told her I'd take her to the store now, if we could borrow her mama's car.

"You and I can talk some more on the way, if you want to," I said.

Miss Debbie waved that the keys were still in the ignition. We said goodbye but she only nodded, her face turned away from us.

PD and I slid into her pink Buick, both a bit shell-shocked, and drove to the Quickie Mart a few miles past where the road got paved. PD didn't say anything for a very long time. We just sat there in that silence, listening to the car bump and complain.

"My whole insides are filling up," she finally said, looking out the window. "Did you know too, Nana Dara?"

"I knew and I'm so sorry. You don't deserve this, baby. I'm sorry."

I drove on. We pulled into the store lot. There's some redneck code that says if you own a huge truck with big tires and a gigantic payload—like the two in the Quickie Mart parking lot—you have earned the right to take up multiple parking spots, so I had to park clear around back. PD made no move to get out after I parked.

"How could you lie to me, Nana Dara?"

"I *omitted*, which is really a white lie. But yes, still a lie." I felt like an idiot for splitting hairs just then. "Peanut, I lied because I didn't want *you* to have to lie. You couldn't have told anyone who your mother was, if your mother was your aunt."

"That would have been *my* choice though. You gave me *no choice.*" PD ran a long pale finger along the edge of the silver radio. She had the kind of fingers sensitive people have. "I just wonder now who I can trust."

"This may not come off right," I said, "but you know this was all done out of love."

"I'm not ready to hear all that just yet." PD shifted toward the door with its bold silver door handle. "You need anything?"

"No, I'm all right," I said.

PD slammed the door, the way you had to in order to get it latched. I watched her walk around the gray concrete back of the store, hoping Miss Debbie was all right.

A while later PD, walked back across the sunny blacktop with her head down. Her cowboy boots crunched the ground, getting louder the closer she got until she creaked open the door and sat down.

"They didn't have any," she said—and I wondered if they had some corn nuts but PD just didn't want to get her mama any right now.

"Let's go to the Opry," I said. "Take some time to relax. Eat some grapes."

We drove on in silence until PD asked if she could turn on the radio, and we listened to some Conway Twitty. Forty-five minutes later, we turned off the road and onto the dusty gravel—or "unadopted roadway" as the city planning folks called it—leading down to the Opry. Driving up I realized that my powder blue prefab looked like it had been dropped from the top of a mountain and settled crooked. Thing had seen better days. *I best keep selling those birdhouses and picnic tables if I was ever going to fix her up.*

We parked and walked in. I sat on my mustard-colored couch while PD pulled over the kitchen chair. Like her mama, she didn't care to sit in the wobbly chair either.

"Tell me the story," she said.

So, there with the late-day sun streaming low in the front window, I let the whole story pour out. I told PD how I'd lost touch with my girls until the day Edna showed up as Eddie, carrying PD as a little baby. How I knew right off there was something special about PD— or something about her and me. I told her about the note and my conversation with Miss Debbie to keep things secret.

I went on to tell her how I had a secret that I'd swallowed when I married the Warden—the grandfather who'd died before she was born—and how I felt often like I'd been living a lie, a necessary one, but a lie all the same. How that secret affected things. How Eddie— as Edna—opened up to me on prom night, but I hadn't been brave enough to confide my lie and change the direction of our family away from shame.

"But if you had, then maybe I'd never be," she said.

I leaned back into the couch, stunned. "That's true."

The sun slipped down a bit. I could already tell it was going to be one of those nice, cool Texas nights, when the air comes in smelling like honeysuckle instead of dust.

A few mobiles over, someone put on some Mexican music.

"OK," PD said, leaning into the red vinyl chair back. "That all?"

My guts actually quivered, I was so nervous. I closed my eyes and I said it: "I am a lesbian."

"What do you mean by that?"

I opened my eyes and looked at her. "I mean I like women the way most women like men."

"Oh. Mama's not going to like that."

"She doesn't."

"She knows?"

"Yes."

PD paused for a minute. She dropped her head then looked up with her dark brown bangs in her eyes. "Is Aunt Eddie one too? Is that really why she didn't keep me?"

"Yes."

I hoped that PD would come hug me maybe, or tell me it's OK and that she still loved me—then I chastised myself for being so selfish at a moment like this.

"What the hell kind of family is this?" she asked.

"Your language has sure gotten colorful."

"Sorry, Nana Dara." She looked blankly across all the art on my walls. "I know it would be hard and all, but why couldn't Aunt Eddie just *try* to raise me?" she asked, her voice sounding like a little girl's, with me having to remind myself that she *was* a little girl. "Wait. Did Miss Debbie force her to hand me over?" Her face hardened. "Seems like something Mama might do."

"No, honey. Your mama did nothing of the sort. Your Aunt Eddie called out to her. Eddie did the best she could. It was a lot for her to just wake up in the mornings back then. The pregnancy was so difficult for her. But she got through—in a big part *because* of your mama. Eddie loved you enough to keep you in this family and close by—"

"But not raise."

"That wasn't about love."

PD looked down at my feet. I was still wearing slippers.

"Even during emotional crisis, a person should be comfortable," I said.

She smiled, and my heart stopped racing. Maybe we were going to be OK.

"Take me to Aunt Eddie, please."

× × ×

Eddie rented a room with a small kitchen behind a grand old house that looked like it was carved out of butter, situated just off the center of town. We walked up the driveway, climbed the white, rain-damaged stairs leading up and over the garage, and knocked on the door to Eddie's room. Eddie called out for us to come in, as if she was expecting us.

The green curtains were open, and there were fresh flowers on the nightstand. A cigarette twirled its tail from a clean ashtray on the arm of Eddie's rocker.

PD looked her aunt dead in the eye. "*I know.*"

"She knows," I said. "*Knows* knows."

"And I know," Eddie said. "Miss Debbie called."

"How is she?"

"As panicked as a fire alarm in a volcano."

Eddie leaned forward in her threadbare rocker. "PD, I am so very, very sorry if I hurt you. I want you to know—I need you to know—that I wanted you. You were such a gorgeous baby—but I couldn't, honey. I was in a state. It was so hard to give you up, but I knew how much Miss Debbie loved you. She loved you even before you were born. She used to sing to my belly—and it made it all worth it. You are so worth it . . . I love you."

PD was a tough kid, so I was shocked when her dark eyes welled up a bit. "I love you too, Aunt Eddie."

PD walked over, across the worn white carpet, and hugged Eddie, who started to cry in that way someone cries who has wanted to cry for a long time.

"I love you more than anything, honey," Eddie whispered. The light played on the fraying bits of PD's unraveling French braids. Eddie smoothed them down and smiled with so much love in her eyes I thought they might melt.

PD jerked her head toward me. "Oh, and she's a lesbian."

"I knew that."

PD stepped back. "You knew!"

Eddie ran a hand up and down her tailored pinstriped men's pants and suspenders as if to say: *Of course I knew—look at me!*

PD nodded. "Yeah." She shook her head and took in a deep breath.

I leaned down and nudged her. "You're doing great."

"I'm afraid I might still be in *shock*," PD said, very seriously. "I read about it in a magazine."

"Sweet tea?" Eddie asked. "We can drink it outside on that picnic table I got from you, Nana Dara."

The tea sat waiting on Eddie's tiny counter, a fresh coat of humidity on the outside and a dozen thin slices of lemon floating inside. Three cups with gold rings painted around the middle had already been set out. Clearly, Eddie had been waiting.

The day was cool, the way it can get in January, with the threat of thunderstorms making the air staticky and causing the droopy trees to sway back and forth like tassels on a child's bike handles. When I made Eddie that picnic table, she'd requested that it be painted green and blue to liven up the butter house's boring backyard. And it did.

We all sat down, me and PD wearing sweaters and Eddie wearing a black raincoat that she got in Boston, where she said it looks like a funeral whenever it rains. The three of us talked about all of it: Rhodie, Eddie's love of baby PD—and how she always secretly looked for the ways that they were similar, the things that live under their skin—how Eddie endured living here in a small town just so she could be near PD, even Mrs. Tanya May Rogerton.

"You have a girlfriend!" PD gasped. "Is that what you call her?"

"What else would she be? Though we are a little old."

"Scoundrel," Eddie said.

An hour or so in, we knew the rains would be coming and Miss Debbie was probably out of her mind with worry.

I said to PD, "We need to get going."

Eddie wrapped her strong hands around her cup of cold tea. She cleared her throat. "I want to say again how sorry I am for not telling you. It's cheap maybe to say that it was complicated . . ."

PD smiled at us from across the picnic table. "You know what I feel like?" she said. "I feel like a girl who is so loved that everyone did crazy things to keep on loving her."

I looked over at PD. *How did we deserve to be forgiven and accepted so quickly and unconditionally?* It was another miracle in my life that I never even asked for. I don't know who watched over me, but surely someone. My life was blessed—or maybe everyone's life is blessed, only some just can't see the miracles for the weeds.

Eddie wiped away a tear. "I love you, PD."

"I love you too, Aunt Eddie."

"Well," I sighed, relief warming my skin, "no one can accuse our family of being dull."

Eddie shook her head. "No, they cannot."

PD smiled with all her big crooked teeth. "Nana Dara, on the way home let's stop at the Quickie Mart so I can get Mama some barbecue corn nuts. They probably restocked by now."

THE DRAMA OF IT ALL

Mrs. Tanya May Rogerton chugged up to the Opry in her exhaust-heavy Volkswagen fastback, which she had recently painted powder blue with a bright yellow trim to go with her white-and-yellow leather seats. I told her it looked like she was driving in the clouds, and she said, "*That's* why we are together, you and me." Then she leaned over and kissed me on the cheek as I got in. My guess is that she was well aware that her breasts ran the length of my forearm in the process. That lady was a sneaky one.

She smiled. "Your summer pants look perfectly tailored. Whoever does your clothes?"

We took off with a bang and a burp of smoke.

My hunter-green pants sat low on my hips, with a thick fabric belt that was stretchy so I could tie it around my waist to give myself some dimension. The honey-yellow shirt she'd made me was drapey everywhere except the end of the three-quarter sleeves, which wrapped around my forearms to make the whole shirt look, according to Mrs. Tanya May Rogerton, *billowy.* She said that kept the eye to the upper portion of the outfit—"and those blue eyes of yours."

I grabbed her hand down low. "Wouldn't it be nice if we could go out dancing together somewhere tonight?"

"Dancing? That would destroy our culture."

My heart sank. "Really?"

"Yes, ma'am," she said, nearly slowing for a stop sign. "The needs of the few shouldn't ruin the foundations for the many."

I took my hand away. "How's that?"

"They let us dance, then where does it *end*? You want us let into church? We gonna let in robbers and molesters, too?"

My stomach dropped and my head spun. "You think we are like them?"

"Well, we all break the rules of God."

"Molesters, though?"

Mrs. Tanya May Rogerton made one of her famous hard rights, nearly clipping a telephone pole. I held onto the door handle.

"You think one sin means more than another?" she asked.

I couldn't believe this was happening. "Yes! That's why there's the Ten Commandments. Those are the big ones."

"So they let us in church, then what? We gonna kiss in front of children?"

She skidded through the gravel on the side of the finished road heading into town.

I said, "Honestly, I don't know anymore if I think that this is a sin. I can't seem to see who it is hurting. And I won't sit here and be likened to a murderer by the person who—who—"

"Who what?" She grabbed for her sunglasses in the glove compartment, moving more than a few times into the oncoming lane.

"Who I love!" I said. "There."

"Oh, you are *too easy*, Nana Dara. Here, hon." She pulled a pair of tickets from her bra. They were to some place called Kitty's in Dallas. "We are driving to Dallas. I got us a hotel room. These are tickets to a *lesbian* dance. We are going dancing." She leaned over and kissed me again, smelling like lemon. "And I'm glad that you love me."

"I don't understand. Do you think we're evil?"

She let out a heavy breath then laughed. "Oh, honey. I am kidding you!"

"You are meaner than a mongoose in a stocking."

"You know I just like drama." She squeezed my thigh. "And be warned, we are not *cuddling* in this hotel room. We are not *snuggling*, hon. My meaning clear?"

"Crystal," I said, rereading the tickets. We were going to make love. *Oh my.*

"You and I are leaving an hour after church. I will drive you home and wait while you pack." She touched my thigh again. "Prepare yourself."

"Yes, ma'am." I sat back, feeling anxious.

Mrs. Tanya May Rogerton smiled over at me like I was a kid on the special bus. She kissed my cheek and said, "For the record, I do not think we are sinners. We were just born too soon for the rest of the world to realize that."

× × ×

Service went fast with me worried nearly sick about my upcoming encounter with Mrs. Tanya May Rogerton. I watched her from the choir loft, singing her heart out like any other day, while I was up there perspiring and breathing deeply, so as not to trigger a heart attack. *What if our lovemaking is a disaster? What if I unveiled myself and she's not attracted to me? What about my feet, for God's sake?*

Then the world came to a halt. I realized she hadn't said she loved me back. I said I loved her in the car, and she hadn't said it back. Forget all the rest.

I barely got through the last two songs, missing cues and leaving my choir brethren in the lurch several times. After the service was over, Mrs. Tanya May Rogerton met me at the bottom of the choir loft stairs with a smile. My neck was sweaty and I had some kind of rash on the backs of my hands.

I said, "Let's skip breakfast."

She smiled, took her arm and wrapped it in mine, and walked me out past the precise white lines of Seventeenth Street Baptist's parking lot. All the while I'm wondering if she's just being polite somehow, like she feels badly for me being in love with her when she was just having fun.

"I have another surprise for you," she said.

"I don't think I can take it."

"Shush now." She looked hard at me. "I bought you that skin surgery we talked about. I know you are low in funds due to all the hospital bills and such, so I called a Dallas skin specialist and it's my treat."

I stopped short. "What?"

"You are going there right now—don't worry, I will feed your cats and the pugs. I'm driving you to the doctor in Dallas, but I'll come back and tend to things here. Keep walking or people will stare." She waved to a big-headed woman who always brought vanilla fudge with pecans to Christmas events. "The doctors need to see you for a day before you go in, then you need to recover for a few days. That'll be about a week. Just in time for us to use these tickets for Kitty's, the way I add it up—and I got all As in mathematics."

"I can't believe it," I said. "You got me the surgery? You're amazing. I just can't believe it."

"It's a *selfish* plan really." She winked. "You need to get comfortable in that body of yours. Oh," she said, snuggling in close to me, "and to intensify the drama of this moment: I love you too."

THE CATS AT KITTY'S

In Dallas I met several very nice doctors and grew indifferent to opening my hospital gown before total strangers. The healing process from my skin removal involved pressure bandages and drainage systems no doubt left over from the Inquisition. I will spare you the details.

Mrs. Tanya May Rogerton came by the hospital every day to lotion my hands and legs—I kept my socks on for obvious reasons—and change out my flowers. I was in reader's heaven, with the *Dallas News* delivered each morning, and a lady with a limp who wheeled a book cart up and down the hallways twice daily for me to pick and choose new material. In the evening, Mrs. Tanya May Rogerton brought me popcorn and we watched *The Ed Sullivan Show*, once laughing so loud that I started bleeding through my bandages and the nurse gave me a stern wag of her finger when she changed my dressing.

On that last day of my hospital stay, true to her word, Mrs. Tanya May Rogerton picked me up and drove me to the Dallas Hilton, where she'd booked us a room with a view and two double beds—"one for our clothes," she said, even though I knew that it was a way to maintain discretion. The room had this beautiful brown striped carpet and real leather chairs. They even set out a pair of coffee cups for us, with a selection of five teas, which Mrs. Tanya May Rogerton quickly shoved in her purse saying, "We paid for them!"

After we'd dressed—her in a blue dress with a sequined sweater and me in my favorite blouse and a new, skinnier pair of black pants—I waited for her to do her makeup before we headed out into the elevator to meet the cab that she'd called. The sun had already

gone down, but it was still hot. When the nice Hilton men in their
brown suits closed the glass doors to the hotel for us, the heat fell
down like invisible clouds.

She sighed. "Whew."

"Good thing you called a cab, rather than us walking," I said.

"Oh hon, I can't walk in these shoes."

The cab pulled up. It had been recently washed and had a sticker
of the star of Texas on the side window, beside a gold cross. We slid
in the back onto the hot seats. It smelled like pipe smoke and sweat,
but it was spotless.

Rather than say the name of the club, Mrs. Tanya May Rogerton
gave the cab driver the address. He sat still in his cowboy hat and
didn't turn around, which I took to mean that he knew where we
were going. For a moment I wondered if something awful was going
to happen to us, then I chastised myself for letting my old way of
thinking creep in again.

She leaned over and whispered, "You nervous?"

"The dances might be so different now."

"Well I'm sure they'll play some country—and that mostly stays
the same."

I relaxed. "Now ain't that the truth."

The city—with its tall buildings made more of glass than brick—
passed us by. Mrs. Tanya May Rogerton tickled the side of my leg as
we watched the scenes out the window, which I kept closed so her
hair would stay put.

Fifteen minutes later, the cab pulled over. From the outside, Kitty's looked downright dangerous, all flat-black paint with the only
mention of the name being the word Kitty's in white cursive on the
wood door. The door sat off to the side, not in front like regular doors.
And there were no windows at all.

The cab driver, still hidden under his black cowboy hat, didn't
turn around, so I dropped money on the passenger seat for him and
we got out. Outside the door to Kitty's, we each straightened our

clothes and got our resolve together. Walking through those doors took more nerve than I'd needed in quite some time, but we did it.

And inside was a glittery fairyland of lights and music and men in shirts that were unbuttoned to show some chest hair. Most of the women couples were set up so that one was the masculine one and the other was the feminine one. A few looked so similar to Eddie that I had to do a double take.

I leaned in to Mrs. Tanya May Rogerton. "Which type am I?"

She kissed my cheek. "Oh, bless your heart."

Dance music kicked on with a loud slam and everyone took to the floor like a gaggle of geese lifting off a pond, only in gold lamé. It was as if the Fourth of July was housed inside Kitty's.

Mrs. Tanya May Rogerton beamed at the excitement and shouted to me over the music, "Let's drink first!"

"I'll get them. You go sit down—someplace a little quieter."

She nodded and walked off to one of the tall white cocktail tables along the back wall. Each table had a purple carnation in a white vase on it and a little cup filled with wooden matches.

After I got us two drinks, the house special that night—something with a purple liquor in it—Mrs. Tanya May Rogerton confessed, "I've been watching *American Bandstand*."

I leaned close to her, careful not to tip over in my tall white chair. "What now?"

"*American Bandstand*! I've been *studying*. Most of these city dances are similar to country dances, only you move your upper body more. In short, I am prepared." She sipped her drink through a thin black straw and nodded, like she was making total sense. "That's also how I got the idea to do up my eyes like this." She shut her eyelids, showing me how carefully she'd drawn a wavy line from the lids out.

"Impressive."

She kissed my cheek, all flush with how open we could be. "What fun!"

A new song clicked on, something that sounded almost like a children's song, and she nearly squealed. "I know this one! Come on!"

"My drink—"

"Leave it on the table. Come on now!"

I held the black straw off to the side of my cup and gulped my beverage down in one mighty swig. She pulled on my other hand and towed us out to the dance floor to take our place in a long line of people, most considerably younger than us.

The music played, and I did my best to catch the groove and keep up, with her laughing and grabbing my hands across the line to tug me along with the music. The song thankfully gave you instructions how to do "The Loco-Motion," which looked like playing choo-choo train with your arms while doing criss-crosses with your feet.

It was hopeless. I waved her off and stepped out of the line, breathless and damp under the arms. She grabbed me and we walked to the table, laughing loud. "Good thing we stopped," she said. "This next one is 'the Twist'!"

Was she ever right. If I had stayed out there to do the Twist, it might well have been the last thing I ever did. Made me think of Beauregard—I bet he did a great Twist.

The next song was a slow one. I held out my hand and asked Mrs. Tanya May Rogerton to join me. Her face pulsed pink from the drinks and the heat of the place. Smiling her coy smile, she dabbed her napkin in a glass of water we'd been sharing, touched her throat, and stood up dramatically.

"Any time," she said. "I will dance with you now and any time hereafter."

I held her close and we moved so easily around the floor, doing a version of a waltz or something—I don't know. The younger folks smiled at us, the people they might be some day, and made room when we passed by under the glittery disco balls hanging from the ceiling.

The floor was icy gray, and that's what it felt like dancing with her, like we were on ice—so smooth and laid-back. When I looked into her eyes, I finally understood that it didn't matter who led the dance, just that there was one.

She leaned in, pressing tight against me, and whispered, "I love you."

"I love you too, Mrs. Tanya May Rogerton."

One hour and two more purple drinks later, we took a cab back to the hotel—one we caught a block away, on the recommendation of the bartender. The men in their brown suits tipped their hats and opened the doors for us again. We kissed in the elevator, pulling back just before the door opened, and nearly ran to our room, holding hands and making a ruckus.

I'd never felt freer, like I was a lion on the range roaming and running where there were no walls to be had for miles and miles and miles.

That night, us two middle-aged widows threw one hell of a private party there at the Hilton. Some of our lovemaking took a bit of maneuvering, given the few pressure bandages I still had in place, but we worked it out. We Southerners are a stubborn and resourceful breed, after all.

LIVING & DYING:
LESSONS FROM HUDDIE

1968—the year when the whole world wanted to blow out of their prisons. Mrs. Tanya May Rogerton and I had been together seven years, with us going on walks every day around the gravel roads near the Opry, where she lived with me. Folks thought we made the cutest old maids, especially when we walked those damn pugs, who I was convinced would outlive us all. We even brought those dogs with us to bingo on Sunday nights at the church hall, with all the other widows.

On our first Christmas, I framed the drawing Rhodie made for me back in 1923—the one with the two black circles and the white space they made when they intercepted. A Venn diagram, as it turns out. I'd kept it in my delicates drawer all those years.

Mrs. Tanya May Rogerton, always heavy on flair, hung it above our bed—where it took on a new, proud meaning. That picture was a prophecy fulfilled, she said, not some shameful part of myself to be avoided.

Eddie talked about moving into the spare room at the Opry, but she never did, which is just as well since Miss Tanya May Rogerton made that her secondary sewing space. Every Christmas Miss Tanya May Rogerton made Eddie two custom-tailored shirts, since it was difficult to find men's shirts that could fit over her breasts. Miss Debbie tsked every time Eddie unwrapped her gift, but she otherwise held her tongue.

PD stomped on her way to the beginnings of young womanhood, though from behind she still looked like a boy, especially given her continued embrace of the pixie haircut. I wasn't shocked when the boy she'd asked to her Sadie Hawkins dance had longer hair and softer hands than she did. That's what modern times do, they flip things 180 degrees and shake them until the old rusty things fall out.

Everyone came to the Opry for my sixty-fifth birthday. What would have made it perfect would've been to have the Fiddler there, too, but I suppose he was just a hard lesson I needed to learn. In losing him, though, I gained everyone else by opening up and not repeating the mistakes that had cost me my best friend. Everyone is here at the right time and everything has a reason, or so it seems.

Eddie showed up late to the afternoon party, having gone out to Kitty's on our suggestion the night before. She looked tired but happy. Miss Debbie was even later, though I have no idea why.

"Nana Dara!" Miss Debbie shouted, throwing open my screen door and sending two of the cats running for their lives. "Birthday girl?"

PD walked in behind her. She was growing so tall—tall enough to have stretch marks on her hipbones, Miss Debbie told me, after long nights of growing pains.

I yelled, "Come on in!"

I couldn't get the door on account of Mrs. Tanya May Rogerton insisting that I stay seated on the couch so I could be waited on during my birthday.

Everyone milled about while I moved my feet around inside my cushy socks, appreciating the results of a weekly pedicure—my Saturday outing with Mrs. Tanya May Rogerton before we get Mexican food downtown. Bo nodded to me, then walked into the kitchen where he popped open two beers—one for him and one for Mrs. Tanya May Rogerton who, to my constant surprise, loves beer. She followed him in and I could see them whispering about something.

"What are you two cahooting about in there?" I called out.

"Birthday surprises!" she said.

Eddie rubbed her eyes. "Can you pour me some black coffee, strong?"

Miss Debbie raised her eyebrows but couldn't say anything, seeing as her mouth was full of gin-soaked ice cubes.

"Coffee?" Mrs. Tanya May Rogerton shouted back. "Sure thing, hon. PD, you want some?"

PD, who was trying on a few bits of adulthood, answered, "Coffee? Yes, please."

Bo came out of the kitchen carrying a homemade birthday cake. I worried that the ashes from the cigarette in his teeth might fall in the cake, but realized that nearly everything in my life had gotten ashes in it at one point or another, so who cares. He looked so handsome with more of his hair now turning white and those deep hazel eyes of his that looked like stones you would find on the beach and keep forever.

Mrs. Tanya May Rogerton started the singing—"*Happy Birthday to you!*"—while she lit the blue-and-green candles before placing the cake before me on my gold-trimmed TV tray. The cake was a God damn mess. While Mrs. Tanya May Rogerton could make a wedding gown from an apron, she could hardly blanch greens without catching something on fire. On the top on the sunken disaster she'd written: "Happy sixty-fifth, Mrs. Dara!"

I looked up from the edge of my mustard yellow couch. "*Mrs.?*"

"*Mrs.* Dara in the way that I am *Mrs.* Tanya May Rogerton. We will be Mrs. together, even if we can't be Mrs. together!"

Miss Debbie clicked her tongue. The others all clapped and hooted.

From that day forward, everyone in my family except Miss Debbie called me Mrs. Dara. She never called me Mrs. Dara or sat Mrs. Tanya May Rogerton next to me at her New Year's party dinners— claiming the cycle of boy-girl-boy-girl that is present at any *decent* table would then be ruined—but all that said, Miss Debbie bought the lion's share of her outfits from Mrs. Tanya May Rogerton and gave her genuine hugs when they saw each other, which was more than I'd ever dared to dream.

And truly, it didn't matter if someone sat between us during Miss Debbie's New Year's dinners when I looked out over the table at all those people filling the spaces I didn't know needed filling forty-five years ago. That's what life is about—what you choose to fill yourself with. If you choose to fill yourself with heavy, dark secrets—and almost all of them are heavy and dark—there's not enough room left for much of anything else.

When Huddie died, I knew how I wanted to live. I wanted to find the *thing* I loved and be open to it and let it carry me past myself—past my own death, even. For him it was his music; for me, it turned out to be my family.

Now, when I die or the aliens come for me—as I believe they surely might—I will live on in the memories of people who knew me—*really* knew me—and loved me. It seems like this big-boned girl, who started out with two strikes against her, finally figured out what this living thing is all about.

Sugar Land Star Newspaper
June 22, 1981

This past week we lost a big figure here in the Sugar Land community. She was known to most as Mrs. Dara, even though she'd been widowed for some thirty years.

Mrs. Dara was born in Midland, Texas, on October 29, 1903. She graduated from Midland High School with the Class of 1922 before working for ten years in the kitchen at the Imperial State Prison Farm—now called Central Unit—where she met and married Warden Daniel Jones. She leaves behind her family and her friend, Mrs. Tanya May Rogerton, who will stay in Mrs. Dara's mobile home down off RR23.

The funeral will be held at 17th Street Baptist Church, where Mrs. Dara sang in the choir, this Sunday at 2 p.m.. A wake will follow in the hall, which is filled with—as most of you know—picnic tables made and painted by Mrs. Dara herself.

The wake will be hosted by Mrs. Tanya May Rogerton and Mrs. Dara's children. They request everyone dress colorfully—no black. There will be plenty of food, but you can always bring a dish—and everybody's welcome.

NOTES ON THE STORY

As with many fictional pieces, I took liberties to craft this book. Much of Huddie Ledbetter's story is true, to the best of my research. For fact-geeks, I'd like to point out a few places where I opted to shift history in favor of my re-telling:

Huddie was nicknamed "Lead Belly" at Huntsville Prison, prior to his transfer to the Imperial State Prison Farm. There, officials knew him as Walter Boyd because that was the fake name he gave when he was arrested. To streamline, I have the authorities know him as Huddie Ledbetter, his real name.

Lead Belly did sing publicly to the prisoners, the guards and their families, but he sang for his pardon during a private concert with the Warden, Governor Pat Neff, and his wife on the Warden's porch, which was located on the prison grounds (I situated my fictional Warden's house outside the prison land). While he sang for folks and was a favorite of the Warden and the guards due to his work ability (it was said he could pick 1,000 pounds of cotton a day), being African American probably kept him out of the "easy" kitchen work.

Also, though nearly one million women worked in agriculture on farms and almost two million women worked in manufacturing in 1920, it is unlikely that a woman would have been allowed to work in a men's prison, no matter how progressive the Warden.

The Warden of the Imperial State Prison Farm (which I nicknamed "Sugar Land" since most people prior to the 1950s were talking about the prison when they referenced Sugar Land) from 1919–1949 was R.J. "Buck" Flanagan. I created my own Warden, who loosely reflects several articles I read about Flanagan, but in no way is meant to represent him.

Additionally, the Warden at Imperial State Prison/Sugar Land was known as "Big Captain" and his assistant as "Little Captain"; I simplified by not adding an assistant and using the title "the Warden."

I use the spelling Lead Belly, as opposed to Leadbelly, since that is the way it is spelled on his headstone, by ethnomusicologist Alan Lomax in his 1935 book, by Smithsonian Folkways, and by the Lead Belly Foundation, started by his niece. That said, it's often spelled Leadbelly, and it's commonly accepted that either way will do.

SPECIAL THANKS

Thank you to my dedicated publisher, *Red Hen Press*, especially *Kate Gale*, whose devotion to art is an inspiration.

Thank you to my writing group, *the Guttery*, especially Melanie Alldritt, Mo Daviau, Lara Messersmith-Glavin, Michael Keefe, Tracy Manaster, A. Molotkov, Margaret Pinard, and Jamie Yourdon . . . to the positively golden energy of *Laura Stanfill* . . . to the Tin House Writers' Workshop and Antioch University, notably my mentors *Susan Taylor Chehak* and *Leonard Chang*, and to *Kate Carroll de Gutes* and *Gigi Little*.

To *Jillian Lauren*—you've always been there when I am in a panic about one thing or another. To *Steve Almond*, who first suggested I turn some short stories into this book. To *Caroline Leavitt*, my supportive freelance editor. To *Joseph Chinook*, my combat buddy who never says no to my asks. And to all my lovely friends, especially music wonder *Sadie Contini* and *Andrea Maxwell*, who read the manuscript in an early form. Andrea, my film project comrade and truly *superriffic* friend, also did my amazing book trailer. To my beloved ASSes, *the Tobey sister-poets*, "nothing compares to u."

Special researcher thanks to *Carol Beauchamp* from the Genealogy Department at George Memorial Library in Richmond, Texas; *Brett J. Derbes*, the managing editor of *The Handbook of Texas*; and *Jim Willett* with the Texas Prison Museum, who took the time to answer emails from me—a stranger.

There were also many books I dog-eared during my research, notably Tyehimba Jess's books *Olio* and *Lead Belly*, and *The Midnight Special* by Edmond G. Addeo and Richard M. Garvin.

Thanks to *Linda Epstein*, whose notes strengthened this book immensely, along with *Jeff Kleinman*, *Erin Harris*, and *Allison Devereux*—for being so instrumental and gracious when you didn't have to.

Thanks, finally, to my family, especially the Twesmes, the Hibsmans, and the Kennans. To my beautiful, patient lady-friend, *Karena Stoner*, our three children—*Oliver, Rosie*, and *Cedar*—and *Beth German*, the best ex (and co-mom of Oliver) in the world.

SUGAR LAND
Reading Group Questions and Discussion Topics

1. In the opening pages, Dara gives her first impressions of Imperial State Prison Farm. She says that its white walls are like "the walls of heaven—if heaven were an institution to house murderers and thieves, which it may be since we are all murderers and thieves in our own way." What did she mean by this? Do you agree?

2. Which character do you most relate to: Rhodie, Miss Dara, Beauregard, the Warden, Miss Debbie, Eddie, Nana Dara, Bo, Miss Tanya May Rogerton? Why?

3. As Dara sits in the Sheriff's station, listening to them talk about assaulting several women the night before, she says: "We all knew that there were different rules for the police, especially when it came to Negroes, but now I knew those different rules applied to me, too." Do you believe there is still a second set of rules for people in authority today? If so, what groups of people are often the targets? If not, what do you think turned the tide?

4. In real life, Huddie "Lead Belly" Ledbetter sang for a pardon from Governor Neff and was given one in 1924, on the Governor's *last day* in office. What does this say about Huddie? And about the Governor? Do you think this would ever happen today?

5. It wasn't until June 26, 2003, in the case Lawrence v. Texas, that the Texas Supreme Court struck down all laws making sex between consenting gay adults illegal. From a brief filed in that case, lawyers wrote that: "Discrimination against gay people peaked from the 1930s to the 1960s. Gay men and women were labeled 'deviants,' 'degenerates,' and 'sex criminals' by the medical profession, government officials, and the mass media. The federal government banned the employment of homosexuals and insisted that its private contractors ferret out and dismiss their gay employees, many state governments prohibited gay people from being served in bars and restaurants, Hollywood prohibited the discussion of gay issues or the appearance of gay or lesbian characters in its films, and many municipalities launched police campaigns to suppress gay life."

Growing up against that backdrop, how/why do you think Dara allowed herself to fall in love again? What events (both positive and negative) may have contributed to her being willing to try to love again?

6. Could Dara's life story serve also as the story of the evolution of American cultural and political beliefs? If so, how?

7. Lead Belly was one of the strongest prisoners. He was often given the role of watching over the other black prisoners working the fields, which included being allowed to whip them if he felt it was necessary. What does this position say about the prison guards and the Warden—were they confident, cruel, fool-hearted, lazy? And how do you think this affected the black inmates?

8. Discuss what you theorize may have driven the rebellious Miss Debbie back to "find the Lord" who was, as she said, " . . . never lost. I was."

9. In *Sugar Land*, what does each character's individual "prison" look like? What is yours? Beyond prison, the metaphor of prison walls is a theme in the novel, with Dara working throughout her life to "shrink" and "push back" those walls. Do you think this is what life is really about?

10. Do you consider *Sugar Land* to be a piece of literary fiction or historical fiction? Why?

BIOGRAPHICAL NOTE

tammy lynne stoner's work has been selected for more than a dozen anthologies and literary journals. Stemming from what her grandmother calls her "gypsy blood," tammy has lived in fifteen cities, working as a biscuit maker, a medical experimentee, a forklift operator, a gas station attendant, and a college instructor—among other odd jobs. She is also the creator of *Dottie's Magic Pockets*, and the publisher of *Gertrude* literary journal, and wrangler of the GERTIE book club, based in Portland, OR, where she lives with her lady-friend, Karena, and their three kids. She is online at tammylynnestoner.com.